THE MAAURO CHRONICLES

ALL THE DIFFERENCE

By
Edward F. McKeown

AN IMPRINT OF COPPER DOG PUBLISHING, LLC

The Maauro Chronicles: All The Diffeence

Moondream Press
An Imprint of Copper Dog Publishing LLC
537 Leader Circle
Louisville, CO 80027
www.copperdogpublishing.com

Ordering Information:
Special discounts are available on quantity purchases by corporations, associations, and others. For details, contact the publisher at the address above.
Printed in the United States of America

Credits:
Author: Edward F. McKeown
Managing Editor: Michael H. Hanson
Creative Director: Helen H. Harrison
Editor: Laura Jean Stroupe
Proofreader: Julie Harrison Saunders
Proofreader: Catherine Van Sciver
Cover Art: iStockPhoto

ISBN:
978-1-943690-26-8 (Paperback)
978-1-943690-27-5 (Kindle)

Library of Congress Control Number applied for

Fiction: Science Fiction

DEDICATION

To my wife Schelly who has taught me most of what I know about family.

CONTENTS

INTRO

CONFEDERATE MILITARY INTELLIGENCE ANNUAL SUM-mary—Top Secret Access

From: Candace Deveraux—Head of Section:

Subject: Artificial Intelligence Maauro:

The CMI still retains the services of the android Maauro, though we are no closer to learning anything of her Creators, her construction, which is far beyond anything of our science, or how it is that this machine being became self-aware. In return for citizenship and continued freedom, she is at least nominally responsive to our security needs. I believe this is more due to concern for the safety of her closest friend, the human, Wrik Trigardt, than any other factor.

Maauro is designed for war; though she has the current appearance of a twenty-year old human female. She has no sense of personal fear and, should conflict arise with her, casualties and damage could be astronomical. The threat she poses arises out of her quantum computer brain and ability to hack into almost any other computer system, rather than her albeit formidable personal combat capability.

Her utility to us has been diminished recently by her and Trigardt's well-publicized rescue of the Bexlaw Expedition and the grandson of Shasti Rainhell, head of Counter-intelligence on Olympia. Too many saw Maauro in combat with the immense Destroyer mecha. The cover story that Wrik Trigardt was testing a new form of Confederate robot does seem to be holding for now. We will not be using her or Lost Planet Expeditions again, until they slide out of the public eye....

CHAPTER 1

I AWAKEN IN THE SPECIAL CHAMBER PREPARED FOR ME, SECRETED IN THE *underground supports of a fusion power plant. At long last I have accumulated enough money, power, and exotic metals to replace my left arm, blown off by a Thieves Guild ambush years ago. I had scavenged a replacement arm from an ancient Infestor fighting machine. It was, like myself, over 50,000 years old, but primitive by comparison. Still, it served me well for years, but I longed to be whole and symmetrical again. There was no comparison between the static Infestor arm and my malleable ceramic alloy chassis for feedback and responsiveness. I have used fantastic amounts of power and credits while I lay in stasis, being repaired.*

The human—led Confederation I now live in is a great, star-spanning conglomerate, but its technology has not reached the level of my creators. So it has taken me years to arrange this repair. I also had to arrange it all in secret. While I serve in Confederate Intelligence, I do not trust them. I trust only my companion Wrik Trigardt and, to a lesser degree, his consort Jaelle, and still less, Dusko, a former Guild lord, the other members of Lost Planet Expeditions. My location is a secret known only to Wrik, as I must be off-line during the period of my rebuilding; the repair matrices must be undisturbed.

I rise to sitting, holding my arm up to inspect it. It is perfectly proportioned, slender and white. I alter the exterior so that it resembles the rest of my outer casing, a red and gray, form-fitting jumpsuit, common on Star Central. I stand and examine myself in the reflection from a nearby metal cabinet. I am still not as tall as I was when I was originally created. I was forty percent larger back then, before being damaged in a fight on an Infestor base. With the slight amount of surplus material left over from creating my new arm, I have added two inches of height. I am now five-feet, six inches tall.

Meanwhile my consciousness pervades every computer net in the area, and I begin to sop up all the data that has been generated or changed during my sleep. I detect no immediate threats to myself or my network. Jaelle, according to her comp-calendar, is returning from a trade meeting. Dusko has been dealing in gems of questionable provenance. Wrik, my dearest friend, has been uncommonly quiescent, apparently rarely leaving our building.

I shut down the peripheral machines I created for the repairs and seal the room against future need, leaving my old Infestor arm behind as a spare. I hope to have no need of it again, but my experience argues against that optimism.

CHAPTER 1

From the underground chamber, I move into the sewers and then to streets of the Confederate Capitol of Star City. It is well after midnight, but the capitol is ablaze with lights and activity. I attract little attention as I make my way to the Mag-Lev train. Well, no more attention than any attractive female with impossibly large eyes. When I was found by Wrik on the asteroid, I patterned myself on a game simulation of a young female in his computer, as my initial appearance was too frightening to him. I have never dared change that base line pattern again as I malfunctioned soon after. Besides, I have grown accustomed to my new face and body; they go with the name I gave myself, Maauro, and are my identity in this time.

I head for Lost Planet. Soon I spot the five-story office building on the edge of the spacefield with a certain degree of relief. I am concerned by Wrik's lack of evident activity. It may be that the growing rift between him and his Nekoan consort has again caused distress. This gives me a feeling of guilt. I do not compete with Jaelle, but the bond between Wrik and me has only grown since he found me on the asteroid. I cannot be his physical lover as she is, but there is something in us that calls out to the other. Our bond has become a wedge between Wrik and Jaelle.

I sigh internally; it will be necessary to again walk that emotional tightrope around the beautiful Nekoan, who is my friend as well. I understand now why the relationship is called "the dance of three" is some languages, the comparison is apt, there are too many feet in our dance, and the toes seem to bruise easily.

I am spared any awkward reintroductions due to the early morning hours. I head for my room. Even my having a room, is mere convention; a convenience for my friends; personal possessions mean little to me, nor do I sleep. I would not rust, being made of refined nuclear materials, if I stayed outside gazing at the stars. Still my friends expect me to act like the living being I resemble and the room is mine. It was fun to decorate it with Wrik.

When I open the door, I note immediately that there are handwritten sheets of paper on the desk by the seldom-used bed. I stride across the room and pick up the paper, wondering why anyone would use such an inefficient means to communicate with me. The answer is quickly apparent.

My Dearest Maauro,
By the time you read this, I will be gone on my way to my homeworld of Retief. Forgive me for sneaking off while you were incapacitated. I hope you can understand that I must do this, and I must do it alone.
You know that things between Jaelle and me have changed. What I thought we were becoming is now only a fading memory of something stronger and sweeter than what remains. We're drifting apart, more

CHAPTER 1

each day. She has her children and the trade business that has become her life.

And this is my fault. I never really gave myself to Jaelle. I never even gave her my real name, or the full details of how I deserted my squadron in the skies over Retief. How can I blame her for being angry over how I have compartmentalized my life? I feel I have lost that chance and it's best to leave things as I did with her. "Call me friend," she said when I saw her last, "but not more."

I've come to realize that I've never really stopped running from that battle. I know until I face my past, my family, and all those I let down, I will never have peace, never own myself enough to give myself away.

I don't know what to expect when I return. My father held a funeral for his disgraced son. He will not be happy to see this ghost. Many others may feel the same. But I have no choice. If I am ever to be whole again, I must return home.

You would want to accompany me, to protect me from much of what I must endure, as you have always protected me. I can't have that. I can't hide behind you.

My only regret is the pain that I must cause you. Please know I am sorry beyond words for it. Know I love you in a way that I love no one else. I promise to return if I can, and ask you to trust to the luck that has kept me alive across all the dangers we have survived. Please forgive me.

Your loving friend
Wrik.

I race into the planetary network and slash through the clumsy protections of the Confederacy until I find the shipping databases and confirm what I now dread. Wrik set off for Retief over fifteen days ago aboard the SS Cosmic Dust, a third-class freighter with passenger cabins that plies the frontier. The freighter would have reached jump space and left the system 182.344 hours after launch. He is gone.

I walk downstairs to the main office of Lost Planet in confusion. Already, my quantum computer brain is engaged in many levels and places. It is trivial work to locate the others and send them messages to come immediately to the office. Meanwhile, I am ordering all manner of supplies and fuel to be brought to the Stardust. Yet much of my powers are bent on a question that resists analysis. Why? Why would Wrik do this? Why would he leave me behind? He feared I was going to stop him from enduring some punishment he said, but what punishment and from whom and why? What does he hope to accomplish?

I am like an ancient mariner in the seas of emotions that my biological companions live in. I too, am gifted with emotions, but mine are somehow less urgent, less compelling than theirs. I have attributed this to my emotions not being rooted in sex and death. While the longer

CHAPTER 1

I operate networked to Wrik and the others, the more complex and varied my emotional repertoire becomes, I remain familiar only with the surfaces. The depths, that I sometimes yearn for and fear at the same time, drop off below me.

An hour later, when Dusko and Jaelle arrive, I am no closer to answers.

"This better be good," Jaelle says, her rough mane of hair is pulled back in a simple style, and her appearance confirms haste. "It's not easy finding a sitter on such short notice." The leonine Nekoan is dressed in a conservative business suit, which does not display her athletic body.

The Dua-Denlenn, Dusko, as usual, merely grunts and fills his cup with the unpleasant-smelling brew his kind uses in place of coffee. The tall, elfin, former crime-lord is well-used to odd hours. His pupilless blue eyes betray nothing under their shock of salt and pepper hair.

I hand Jaelle the letter. Dusko walks up behind her and reads it over her shoulder.

"Crap," he says, a disgusted expression on his face. He drops into a chair. "What did he have to do that for?"

Jaelle's face is unreadable. "I wondered why I hadn't heard from him."

"Did you not think that a two-week absence was cause for concern?" It comes out more accusatory then I intend. Maybe.

Her hot yellow eyes fasten on mine, and perhaps her teeth are a bit more in evidence. "Not lately. We've been … spending less time together. He'd said he was going to do some flight training at a base on the moon."

"Two light seconds away," I state, "hardly out of contact."

Jaelle stands and draws some of the warm fruit juice that she prefers for mornings. She sits back down and stares moodily at the cup. "Sometimes with Wrik, physical and emotional distances aren't the same. Truth is, we haven't seen much of each other since that fight about a month ago."

Silence sits uncomfortably in the room for a long minute.

"The question for us," I finally say, "is what are we going to do about this?"

Jaelle picks up her cup, stares at its contents for some seconds, then drains the cup. "I am not going to do anything about it. This is something he felt he needed to do, and he needed to do alone. Maybe he's right. Maybe it will finally get what ails him out of his system."

She stands and walks toward the door. "I'll be in my office if anyone needs me."

I am outraged. "You cannot leave. We are not done here."

She turns toward me, and her look is not friendly. "Yes, we are. That letter was sent to you. Not to me."

This jolts me. I had not considered that. "He surely knew that I would turn to you to explain this. He mentioned you in it. He knew—"

CHAPTER 1

She shook her head. "We had our goodbye a while ago, even if it wasn't clear to me that he meant to leave. If he comes back, I'll deal with my consort then. If not, then I will keep the good memories and go on with the life I've chosen for myself. I warned you before; I've had enough of danger out under the stars. I have children. My mother's people are with me now. I have responsibilities that do not include Confed Intelligence and getting my tail shot off. Do what you will."

The door closes.

I look at Dusko. He stares back and sips from his steaming cup. "You first."

"I could use advice," I say.

He shakes his head. "Not from me. I have no insight into humans generally, and I never understood Wrik in any event."

"You are at least of the same type of life as he is!"

"Don't yell. I hear perfectly well. But face the conclusion, Maauro. It's on you to make the call. I don't understand how it can be, but he is closer to you than any other being, even Jaelle. You're the reason for the distance between them. There were always two of you in that spot. Wrik wouldn't choose. You didn't feel the need to, and Jaelle finally decided it all for the three of you. She's been closing doors for a while now; you just didn't notice."

Dusko's speech should make me angry; instead I feel a deep sadness. I know he is right.

I look into that little-understood well of wants, wishes and desires that has become part of me since I reawakened on the asteroid where Wrik found me. My connection to him is very precious. Through his friendship and later his love, I broke free of being a programmed weapon. I became myself. We are two very disparate parts of a new and strange whole. I wish him to be with me and for me to be at his side. Yet I am not capable of physical love with my ceramic and alloy body.

I have pondered this since we voyaged to find the Lost Colony. I feared that my love for Wrik was selfish, dragging him into dangers better not faced. I hoped and dreaded that he might find fulfillment with one of his own kind, but that did not come to pass. Wrik and I returned from the Lost Colony to find Jaelle had her kits by one of her own kind, who also had left. I thought that we three would resume our lives together, but the balance we had before, now seemed impossible to achieve.

Jaelle had given up her stake in Wrik, as more than a friend, anyway. The consortship wasn't a marriage necessarily, just a legal union between species. Often it was commercial in nature and that seemed what Jaelle was content with now. I should have seen and understood this long before now. How could I not have?

The answer came unbidden, as if Dusko had heard my interior monologue and answered me with, "You didn't want to." And in so *much have I grown that I am now capable of self-deception, just like a biological.*

"You are uncommonly quiet," Dusko says. "Are you functioning?"

"Why?" I said. "Are you concerned?"

He shrugs. "Say that I am."

Silence returns as I think on my choices.

"It's still your turn," he says, leaning back in his chair.

I make my decision. "I know he said he wanted to do this by himself. But what value is there to my friendship, if it is the cause of his unhappiness, and if it makes him face danger alone?"

"You didn't cause the breaks in him," Dusko says. "You fixed them as best you can, but a wound can't heal if it isn't cleaned all the way out."

I stare at him in surprise. He looks uncomfortable at his display of empathy and covers it by refilling his cup.

"So I will take Stardust and go after Wrik. He faced Infestors and the Destroyer for me; I will not fail him as he faces his past."

"You may find that the Infestors were easier enemies," Dusko says, turning away from me.

"Nonetheless, I will go. And what of you, Dusko?"

He sighs and again sips from his cup. "I go with you, of course. I live in your shadow. Without you, well, the Guild's long memory will doubtless manifest itself, and then it's, 'Farewell Dusko.'"

"I doubt they would be so incautious as to risk an attack on you in my temporary absence."

"Some young villain out to make a name for himself might well take that risk, someone who has never met you or seen what you can do. It's easy to ignore night-monsters … no offense intended—"

"None taken."

"…during daylight."

"I see."

"So I will come with you. I also don't fancy enduring Jaelle's tempers over the next few months."

"Excellent. I have already sent orders to ready the starship. I will inform Jaelle of our plans. We remain networked; at least for now. She must be consulted."

He stood up. "Good luck with that, I'll be moving into the ship. Let me know when you want to launch."

CHAPTER 2

MY OLD HOMEWORLD GLOWED IN THE VIEWSCREEN OF
the SS Cosmic Dust's dining hall. The view had evidently palled
for the other passengers. From space, one Earth-type world
looked like another, but not for me. This was the place where my life
had gone so terribly wrong. The place I'd fled from, leaving behind what
passed for a family and some people I'd once thought of as friends. Five
years for me and better than twelve for them, given my time in cold sleep
and in the grip of the Artifact's time dilation. So much had changed for
me, but as I looked at Retief, I had to fight the sensation that it hadn't.
Had everything been but a dream: Maauro, Jaelle, Kandalor, the Artifact
and the Destroyer? I felt like a child trying to sneak back into some place
he'd run away from before he was discovered.

I shook myself. Piet Wrik Van Zyle had been my name then, I lived
as Wrik Trigardt since, but I was returning as Mazza Fornite, an identity
I had used before when we fled the Guild after leaving Kandalor. I only
hoped to escape the spaceport environs without being recognized as
either. Van Zyle might attract scorn or ridicule. Trigardt would be sought
after for interviews for discovering the Lost Expedition, then saving
Shasti Rainhell's grandchild. But that was last year's news and people
would be interested in the Solari rebellion now, assuming the news had
ever reached a backwater like my homeworld. I wanted my venture on
Retief to be as private as possible.

And brief? I didn't know. It was hard to visualize the life that would
face me afterward. Credits were not an issue; Rainhell and the Confederacy had seen to that. It was more of an issue of what to do with myself,
assuming the burdens of the past were lifted from me. Jaelle and I
remained consorts, but that would never again be what it was. While I
had long ago shed my animosity toward Dusko, the truth was neither of
us cared if we ever saw the other again. No, there was only one face that
would draw me back and one promise. Maauro. I had snuck off like a
thief because I knew she would not have agreed any other way. How I
must have hurt her! That thought gnawed at me. Even if she could understand what drove me, and for all her amazing growth, it was still asking
a lot out of an artificial life form, could she forgive it? Had I, in trying to
heal one breach of faith, merely added another to my list of sins?

I had promised her I would return. Whether she would want me to,
was another question. Yet it was her face that came unbidden to my
mind, and her presence that I missed. I longed for her voice, her little-girl
enjoyment of all that was around her, her huge aquamarine eyes that
saw 50,000 years into the past.

I'll go back to her, I swore to myself, and if she wants to kick my ass out the airlock, she'll be within her rights, but I will go back. Then we will see what it is that she and I are meant to be. Then I will be ready at last.

A dinging sound drew me from my reverie. "Attention passengers. We've been cleared for landing at Blomfeldt Spaceport in the capitol. Looks like we will be pulling in early for once, and we have synched our arrival for planetary dawn over the spaceport to minimize space lag. Atmospheric entry is scheduled for two hours from now. Please be in your cabins for steward's prelanding check in one hour. Plenty of time to finish our fine coffee before you strap in."

I heard voices in the passage behind me, some passengers late for breakfast. I didn't want to see, or talk, to anyone. I drained my hot chai and slid the cup into the washer and made my way out the opposite passageway.

I'd paid for a private room, little more than a cell on something as small and old as the Dust but the room was comfortable, and I had certainly endured worse. It beat the cold storage of my trip to Kandalor. I nodded to the attractive brunette who had the room opposite, but she ignored me, as I had ignored all her friendly overtures on the way out. Oh, well.

I closed the door and prepared my kit for landing, determined that no liner spacer was going to find fault with my preparations. Then I belted into my bunk and flicked the bunk viewer on so I could watch the approach. There was a chime, and the steward, an older Drisnian, looked in. The slight, blue-skinned alien was the size of a human child but I knew he had been spacing for over eighty years. He cast a practiced eye over the room then looked at me.

"Wish they were all like you, Sir. Happy landings."

"And Velvet Skies," I returned in a spacer's phrase. He gave me a glance, then grinned with blue-tinted teeth and sealed the door. I turned my attention to the viewscreen, watching the Dust's blunt nose begin to glow as we braked. The familiar sensations and sounds of entry followed, along with the bumping and slewing of the barrel-bodied liner as she hit high atmosphere. I found myself wishing to be at the controls, as usual unhappy about being at the mercy of another pilot's skills. Only when I'd flown with Maauro had I ever been able to relax with another person piloting.

The buffeting slowed, then smoothed out entirely as the broad wings holding the impellers found enough air to carry the ship. I watched as we came in over one of the broad, shallow seas near the lower continent, where the First Landing had been made. Retief was a world like any other, with polar ice, tropical jungle and everything in between, but much of it was continents with huge plateaus and endless vistas of grass and scrubland. This feature had attracted the original settlers from the Terran continent of Africa. My family had been among the first to leave the lowlands near the sea where the colony ship landed, to carve our vast farms and ranches in the interior of Voortrek, the largest continent.

Settlement hadn't spread much beyond that half of the continent. With restrictive immigration and a devotion to demented racial ideas, Retief neither welcomed nor attracted much immigration. Population grew slowly, though it spread out widely. We were spared the Conchirri Wars and only the First Solari Incursion had touched our world. That victory gave the greybeards running our colony an exaggerated faith in the Commandoes of our world.

The Confederacy hadn't cared much about Retief until an even more reactionary government voted for complete secession and removal of those not judged 'racially pure.' That brought on the suppression and my personal disaster.

My musing was interrupted as a jolt told me we were going into hover and touching down shortly. Dust was about as large a vessel as usually landed on a world, at least without a water landing, being a break-bulk freighter. We lowered ourselves into a rather Spartan-looking cargo landing. Cranes and tenders begin to roll as soon as we settled. I quickly unbelted, not waiting for the bell to sound secure stations. I had taken the minimum kit with me, figuring on buying what I needed here. So I was first down to the disembarkation point, well ahead of the other passengers.

At the exit was Second Officer Auel, a pleasant, middle aged, darkskinned human. He and the captain knew who I was, recognizing me from press coverage, but with a little financial incentive, they'd developed a case of amnesia. I'd stayed in my cabin, hoping to avoid any other recognition, rarely coming out until my fellow passengers lost interest. Auel had been helpful in that, letting me hang out in the crew quarters with some of the officers in return for stories about our expedition to find the Lost Colony.

"Hey, Mr. Trigardt. Sorry you will be leaving us."

"I've told you to call me, Wrik."

"Ah, the company frowns on us being overly friendly with passengers."

"Can you let me out before the rest of the passengers get here? You know I have been trying to keep a low profile..."

He nodded. "Sure, you being a regular spacer."

"The way word gets around the frontier, who knows if they have even heard of the Lost Colony, or Seddon," I returned, itching to be gone. "It might be that the first news is being downloaded by the Cosmic Dust's mail-load. If so, then I think the recent fighting with the Solari will grab the headlines, especially around here."

"Yeah," he said, absently checking the readings on the door sensor. "Seems I read that they had a dustup with the Solari here about thirty-five years ago. Ok, looks like it's cool enough for someone that knows what he's doing. I'll let you out. Head for the main terminal where you see the green roof. Your Confed military 'all pass' should get you right through."

"Thanks," I said as the door slid open, and I shouldered out into the bright sunshine of late summer in the capitol city. I breathed in the familiar smells of a spaceport and the scents of something that had once been home.

"Catch you on the trip back," he called. "Maybe you can win back some of your money, double or nothing?"

"Sure," I said over my shoulder. I hit the ground moving quickly. The impellers weren't rockets but that much energy still heated the ground, and I could feel it through my boots. A few stevedores herding their cargobots gave me a brief look, assuming I was a crewman making a quick exit from the Dust.

Fortunately, I didn't see any reporters or dignitaries, so my cover story must have held. I'd had plenty of that in the months after we returned from Seddon. It had fallen on me, as Maauro needed to avoid the public spotlight as much as possible and Jaelle hadn't gone on the expedition. Olivia Croyzer had disappeared back into the Confed Military and Dusko also had reasons to avoid the public gaze. However, I had done my best to be uninteresting and granted the fewest interviews possible. Eventually the survivors of the prior Bexlaw expedition and the Seddonese themselves had taken over the center stage, leaving Lost Planet to creep toward the exits.

My identity as Mazza Fornite got me through Confed military intake in seconds. The "all pass" that Candace Deveraux had arranged for us after we were "recruited" cleared the hurdles, despite curious looks from the base personnel, all of whom knew better than to question the bearer of one.

I exited the administration center to face a broad boulevard and a monorail that hadn't been there when I'd left. In fact nothing in the immediate area looked familiar; the spaceport and airport complex had doubled in size. The city beyond boasted a score of skyscrapers that hadn't been there. I gaped with the astonishment of the returning traveler at the changes more than a decade had wrought.

Then with a deep sigh, and a recollection of the mission that brought me here, I started off.

CHAPTER 3

I **TAKE THE TIME TO SEE JAELLE IN THE EVENING HOURS BEFORE I MUST** *head for the ship. We meet on what is neutral territory, the park across from our offices. There is a quiet spot near a small waterfall that is* special to me. I sit by the gurgling stream, watching the willow tree above me bend in the wind.

I observe Jaelle park in the Lost Planet lot, then dismount from her gold and black aircar and walk into the park. I see her tuck hands in her long, beige coat; I know she hates the cold. Jaelle's night sight is excellent, and she spots me sitting motionless by the water. She walks up slowly and sits beside me on the stone bench.

I hesitate to speak, though I have devoted much time to figuring what I would say. I am spared having to as Jaelle puts her right arm over my shoulder and then presses her face against mine. We sit that way for a few seconds, then I realize that she is crying silently. I carefully place my arms around her, slightly elevating my body temperature, warding the cold off my friend. Once before, we had sat like this, when we were pursuing Wrik's captor, the Guild VIP known as the Collector. For all the grimness of that time, it seems happier days than those we know now.

"I couldn't help him," she finally says. "This is as much my failure as his. I let too much space grow between us because we didn't want the same things." She sits back, releasing me and wipes her eyes with the back of her hand. "I wanted a trading company of my own, my children, and a place of respect in the Nekoan community. He wanted you and these missions into space. All to prove something to himself that would never stay proven in his own eyes."

"So your feelings toward him have changed?"

"Yes," she says. "Some of this is what I am. Nekoan males aren't much part of our lives after we have kits. I have... been confused over what to do with Wrik now that I have children and some of my matrilineal line here."

"Then there is me."

"Then there is you."

"I did not intend this."

"I know, Maauro, I never said that you did. There is something in and between the two of you that will not be denied. It's bigger than either of you or any of us."

"I am not sure I understand."

"I don't want this to end in bitterness or regret. I still care for Wrik, still love him in a way. I still care for you. We have been through so much together. I don't want to lose the friendship as well as Wrik."

"I also wish our network to endure."

We sit quietly for a few minutes. "Will you be coming back?" she asks.

"I don't know, Jaelle. There are too many variables. I do not know what will happen when Wrik gets to Retief, or when I find him. He told me not to come after him."

"He didn't mean it," Jaelle says. "Or even if he did, he knows in his heart that you will."

"I hope you are right."

She smiles at me. "I have to get back to my children." She takes both my hands in hers. "Promise you won't forget me."

"I will do more," I reply, moved by feelings I can barely put a name to. "I will promise you that we three will meet again in better times."

"Kit-sister, I will hold you to that."

We stand and embrace, then Jaelle turns and walks rapidly to her car. I remember that Wrik once told me never to watch anyone go out of sight as it means you do not expect to see them again. Though the premise is absurd, I turn and walk away while I can still see Jaelle. I will not even take this small chance at provoking the universe. But I am free now to fix my mind on the voyage ahead.

Stardust lifts early in the morning. Only Dusko and I are aboard. I take her up myself, a task usually relished by Wrik. I do not use his manual instruments but direct the vessel through the link I have with its AI, which is a tiny set of my own programs. Unlike Dusko, I do not even need to strap in during our ascent. Our ship is a high-speed courier, as small a vessel as is made for interstellar use, for all it measures 112 meters. Today it feels large and empty. We carry no other passengers, not even the usual number of crab-robots we've used on previous missions. Lost Planet has shrunk to me and a former crime lord. Something is very wrong with the universe.

The voyage to the outer edge of the system where the stardrive can engage will take most of a week, despite my paying to use the giant accelerator in orbit. Dusko and I quickly settle into our usual roles: he quietly tending his hydroponic gardens and me watching the stars and meditating on my new life and its complexities. But we do not remain undisturbed.

A message arrives over the net directly into my brain, preceded by the code for Candace Devereaux. I allow the channel access. An image forms in my mind, Candace is a dark-skinned human female, now forty-one years old. Today she wears a business suit and a concerned expression. I can tell from the signal source that she is aboard a vessel, and it is closing on our position.

"Hello, Maauro"

"Hello. What do you want?"

"Always straight to the point?" she replied, raising an eyebrow.

"I have pressing matters to deal with and am unable to undertake any missions for the Confederacy."

"I might be able to persuade you otherwise."

"Unlikely."

"But not impossible, Little Miss Metal. Answer me this and I will give you an earful of information that you will be grateful for. Why did Wrik choose this moment to make a move toward Retief? What are you two planning?"

I debate how much truth to share with her, knowing she has already weighed the same question about me. *"Wrik's journey to Retief is a personal matter."*

"Without you? Has something changed between you two? I mean he has been useful to Confed Military Intelligence in the past, but it's your special abilities that most interest me."

"Then you may be weighting things improperly, our last mission for you succeeded because of Wrik. I was defeated. He came up with the solution."

"Don't get your panties in a wad, dear, I was just checking."

"I do not wear panties," I reply.

"Hmnn, that's the first personal thing you've ever told me about yourself."

"Then I will add another. Wrik and I remain networked, and I am going after him to Retief."

"And nothing else is moving either of you toward that planet other than his family issues?"

"Which you know about?" I ask.

"Of course. I knew Wrik Trigardt was Piet Wrik Van Zyle when I first met him. I suspect that only you and I know who he really is. I know he deserted his squadron, the Ncome Commando, during the final attack on the capitol by the Confederacy that suppressed the rebellion. I thought it would make him easier to handle. Probably would have, until you turned up."

"Do not be so sure," I add. *"The list of people surprised by Wrik is not short. I am actually on that list."*

"Really?" she said, leaning forward. *"Tell me why? I'd like to know, just for myself."*

I regard this somewhat surprising request for intimacy with suspicion. Deveraux has always been as much threat as help. I know she would love to have me in a lab somewhere being broken down to learn the secrets of my construction, yet there is something different in her face today.

"When we found you unconscious on the asteroid, Wrik insisted on saving you. He would not leave you. It's the only reason you survived."

CHAPTER 3

She purses her lips. "I suspected as much. He's a bit-soft-hearted, our Wrik. Is that what surprised you?"

"No. I was surprised when he came back for me. I had malfunctioned and was helpless before a Guilder with a heavy weapon. Wrik had taken you and gone for the ship. He promised to come back for me, but I did not expect him to. Logically, he should have fled as soon as he reached the ship. Instead, I was treated to the sight of a human, protected only by an unarmored space suit, armed only with a line-tossing gun for a weapon, charging back under fire for me. That was surprising."

"It seems to have been love at first sight."

"Do not mock my feelings for Wrik."

She shakes her head. "I wasn't, Honey. I meant it as I said it." She sighs. "We're lined up on your course and overtaking you. I can be aboard in an hour."

"Why?"

"Because, in honor of Wrik's saving my plump behind, I am going to provide you with information you will want, information that may save Wrik's life and remove a danger to the Confederacy, allowing me to kill two birds with one stone."

"Can you transmit this information—"

"Hell, no. Not even over an encrypted channel. This one would cause real problems if it got out."

"I am secure at this end."

"Don't be silly, your end isn't what worries me, and you know it."

I do. "Very well, I will expedite our docking, though it strikes me that such meetings are more a factor of your love of playing spy than of practical necessity."

Candace grins. "Just one of the perks of the job."

In an hour, the Confederate light cruiser Ajax pulls alongside us, and a boarding tube joins our vessels. I inform Dusko of the meeting, but do not invite him. I will decide what he learns and when.

Candace walks up to me slowly, wearing, as usual, clothing of expensive cut that flatters her abundant figure. She gives me a pleasant nod, which I return. I motion her to follow me into the galley where, in happier times, we all would meet. I follow the usual conventions and have placed drinks before us both as we take our places at the table. I sit, and Candace raises a glass of wine "To absent friends."

"To absent friends," I repeat. I study the human. Signs of strain I had seen in her before have eased. Our efforts to save Shasti Rainhell's grandson on the previous mission had also caused her enemies in the Interstellar Ministries to seek cover. In my estimation, it has put off the upcoming civil war by decades.

"I'll keep this short," Candace says. She places some data-crystals on the table as if they were precious gems. "That's the backup for what I am to tell you."

CHAPTER 3

"And this concerns Wrik and Retief?"

"Yes, but only because you're all heading there."

"Please explain."

"Well, Sweetie, you are the state-of-the-art in artificial life and robotics. Not likely to be matched or exceeded in the foreseeable future, but the Confederacy still marches on. We're learning a lot, I guess the mere fact that you exist tells us things are possible that we never dreamed of before.

"You know all about the Confederate HCR series."

I nod. *The human form combat robots are primitive though robust. Their artificial intelligence is rudimentary, and they still require a biological controller for many operations. I do not consider them living beings, as I am, but mere mechanisms, more complicated version of the crab robots.*

"I have to tell you a bit of a sad tale to catch you up. There's a world called Ordnung, settled by a religious sect that rejects most technology. A young couple gave birth to a severely deformed child. On most Confed worlds, this would have been detected en utero and repaired or, if unrepairable, the child would have been aborted.

"There was a Confed enclave onworld to handle interstellar relations. The child was brought there, and her life saved. The girl was named Kiala Yoder, and while the disfigurement was ... very bad, there was nothing wrong with her mind.

"She was raised in the enclave with occasional contact with her family. Yoder became a cybernetic prodigy. When she realized she might have been saved from this wretched existence in almost any other world, she went to Social Services and legally separated from her family, and was then moved to Landros IV and its cybernetics labs. Yoder became one of the top people in the field, even though she was confined to a motorized transport chair."

Candace sips her wine, and I do the same.

"Someone failed to notice that with the increased intelligence, came great bitterness and sociopathic tendencies. Yoder was nineteen years old when she seized control of a sextet of the latest model HCR. She killed their controller using the HCRs, something that should have been impossible. Yet she hacked through every protection we had on the HCRs and turned them against the staff. No one knows how, but from what we have been able to put together, she came up with a way to download her human mind, at least temporarily, into the brain of one or more of the HCRs, to literally inhabit them."

I find the concept intriguing and unsettling.

"She stole a small courier and, after disposing of the crew, disappeared into space. Since then she's appeared in various places working for forces unfriendly to the Confederacy with her little army. She calls herself Lilith now. God knows why. I don't believe she has any

real agenda, just money and resources to keep her team going and to stay free of the Confederacy. We've never been able to stop her and lost a lot trying.

"The last Intel we have on her is that she fled an ASAT strike team, headed for Retief. She doesn't know about you, but she knows that you and Wrik are Confed intelligence."

A frisson of fear strikes me. *"Then she will assume that Wrik is—"*

"—after her. She'll also assume that, if he's there, you are as well. That you just snuck onworld."

"Yes."

"So, Little Miss Metal," she concluded, draining her glass. *"Wrik has chosen the worst possible moment to visit his hometown. His best hope is that, knowing him, he will try to make his entry on Retief quietly. I doubt he will go back under his original name. He's probably hoping no one on Retief has heard of Wrik Trigardt and the discovery of the Lost Colony. But while Retief is the galactic equivalent of East Cupcake, the name Wrik Trigardt will be known to Lilith. If no one else on that planet knows who Wrik Trigardt is, or what he's done offworld, she will."*

"It appears," I say, *"that we have an identicality of interests. If you are correct and this Lilith is on Retief, she is likely to detect Wrik Trigardt's presence on the planet. I would be monitoring the manifests of any vessel visiting the planet; given what you have said of her hacking abilities, she will likely be able to do the same. There is not much shipping traffic to Retief in any event and fewer passengers."*

"Confed keeps a pretty small footprint there as well," Candace nods, *"part of the political deal to show that, so long as they stopped discriminating against Confed members, we didn't care how they run the little shithole. So we would have neither the skills to detect, or cope with, Lilith locally. I'm sending an ASAT raider force to Retief. I was going to send word by courier, but frankly you'll be there about as fast as the courier and weeks before the ASAT team can get there. I could jump the Ajax there but this fight will be on the ground. All the cruiser has is a small force of Marines on board. Besides, she had another mission, too many fires and not enough firemen lately."*

"There will be no need for the ASAT raider or the Ajax," I say. *"If this Lilith is on Retief, then she constitutes a threat to Wrik, and by extension, his family. I will neutralize her. The Cosmic Dust stopped at Arikasi en route to Retief; at our best speed and going directly, we should arrive four to seven days after Wrik."*

Candace looks at me. *"Officially, the request is to arrest the human body of Kiala Yoder, and destroy or capture the sextet of HCRs. Off the record, I do not see you taking the little sociopath alive. She's killed seventeen people so far, probably a good deal more. I can't risk her going over to the Solari, or even the Voit-Veru."*

"Understood. She will be eliminated if she is there."

CHAPTER 3

"You seem pretty confident. You sure you don't want me to send the raider force?"

"You fear hubris on my part. Sensible, but not the case, I am an extremely efficient and deadly fighter. In any event, the raider force would only be useful if it came to large-scale open combat. I believe we both would prefer the matter handled more surgically."

Candace nods. "Ok, Little Miss Metal. You have it your way to start."

"Excellent. Terms of payment will be the same as those for the Lost Colony Expedition."

"Hah!" Candace says. "You were going anyway, and it's your boyfriend's butt you're saving."

"True, but I need only save Wrik, which I can do by removing him, forcibly if needs be, from the danger zone. You propose that I attack six of your best fighting machines and a genius level hacker, and ask that I do so with minimal loss of Confed lives and property."

"Preferably no losses," Candace grumbled.

"That's implied."

"Looks like Wrik finally did teach you about commerce."

"My budget for batteries necessitated that."

Candace barks a laugh. "I like you Maauro. The galaxy will always be full of surprises with you in it. Ok. You have a deal. Now get out there and save everybody's asses. I'm heading back to civilization." She rises and gives me a wave. "I'll show my ownself out."

As soon as we decouple from the Ajax, I kick our thrust up by the additional 2.45098 percent that is prudent. Every second now counts.

CHAPTER 4

HAVING ESCAPED THE ATTENTION OF PRESS AND GOVernment both, though I wasted the day to do it, I rented an aircar at a horrible rate, for an indefinite period and wasted no time getting out of the capitol. I left the flying to the autopilot, despite my usual reservations. In my present state of nerves, it seemed the safer course. The sky turned a deep purple as I headed for the interior. Katic and Derby, two of Retief's five small moons, rolled through the sky over me, their cool, silvery light causing the stars of the night sky to fade then brighten as they rolled toward the horizon. I was alone with thoughts that filled the small cabin, memories of the life that I had fled. I slept fitfully in the pilot seat; dreams making me twitch and sweat.

The sun came up and made the endless grasslands below the silver prow of the aircar glow. It was late summertime and would be hot in the fields below. Humanity's hand lay lightly on the land. The few roads led to isolated homesteads and small towns. But there were more of those then I remembered, and the roads were better.

Maybe it would have been smarter to spend a few days getting used to my old home, but I wanted to get this over with as soon as I could. I landed in what had once been the tiny town of Sethotho. It had changed from little more than a crossroad to small city of about 50,000 people.

I grabbed as much breakfast as my knotted stomach would allow in a small diner. Then I rented a scooter and headed up the roads to the farm. Despite the heat, I was grateful for my jacket, brimmed hat, and goggles. At first I sped down a broad highway then an improved road and finally tar and chip surfaces. When I was a child, the roads here were packed dirt and almost impassible in the rainy seasons. What else had changed?

Vehicles of various sorts passed me, many occupants waving in the easy way of country folk, but I could see curious glances under broad brimmed hats or caps. Most people out this far knew each other, or would recognize each other's vehicles. A stranger was a curiosity.

I came to the final turn off to the farm. I stopped and tried to calm my pulse and slow my breathing. Sweat beaded on my shirt under the jacket. My ears buzzed, my mouth was dry, and a feeling of unreality gripped me. Where was I? What was I doing? I stared out at the fields loaded with grain, backed by trees to break the endless winds.

Finally resolve came to me and with it, a sense of peace. I had come for this. Though I had no hope, no expectation that anything good would result; it was the hell I had to slog through to reach the Promised Land beyond. Freed from my fugue, I started the bike and rode down the lane.

CHAPTER 4

It was as I had remembered it, with no change or alteration I could see. I saw places that I'd played and explored with my sister, or Delt, my childhood friend and later squadron commander: trees we had climbed, a pile of rocks that had served as our fortress as we stood off imaginary Solari raiders. Then the house came into sight, green with its white roof. I stopped the bike at the base of the drive and dismounted.

As I started up the path to the farm, I studied my old home. The house, shaded by trees, had few modern touches to it, but the outbuildings were loaded with the latest farm machinery and with their modular construction, stood as odd contrasts to the old house, built by a first-landing family. It appeared my father had bought out some of the smaller outlying farms and now had a major agricultural holding.

My feet raised dust on the crushed blue stone of the road up to the house. Memories flooded in: the taste of cherry pie in the fall, the smell of the jasmine-like flowers Mom loved, Rena and I playing by the stream that fed the fire pond. As I walked on, lost in the past, my eyes fell on the family plot that lay under a spreading ponkia tree. There lay my father's ancestors from the first landing to grandfather Pasen, a stern, taciturn, old farmer. But one marker stood, fresher than the others, near the back.

I knew what it was, but I had to see it with my own eyes. I opened the small, creaky gate and walked in carefully, avoiding stepping on the graves until I stood in front of a simple, gray stone. It held only a name, my name Piet Wrik Van Zyle and two dates. My birthday and the day of the air battle over Retief.

"No turn unstoned, huh, father?" I'd expected this, but it still hurt like a knife.

I turned my back on the headstone and headed for the house, determined to get this over with. A minute's more walk brought me to the porch. In the distance I could see some men working on a big, red, farm machine, but none of them were my father.

Then I was facing the door, and I knew I could not ring that bell. You can't blow it now, I thought, not after you've come all this way.

I was spared the struggle when the porch door swung open, and my father walked out, heavier now, graying at the temples and wearing the bushy beard favored by a lot of the Rebels. He wore a hunting jacket and field trousers, and stopped when he saw me, squinting in suspicion, then his eyes widened for a moment.

I was surprised by the changes in my father, and had to remind myself that I had been gone twelve years, for all that I had only lived five of those years, two being spent in cold sleep, and five in the wrinkle in time that had hid the Infestor Artifact. I didn't look much different from when he had seen me last, the night he had told me I was dead to him.

CHAPTER 4

We stared at each other. I found I couldn't say the word, Father, so I began simply. "I'm back."

He looked down at the ground, and I wondered what he was feeling. I didn't have to wait that long. My father walked two steps to a rocker and sat down in it, facing away from me. "I didn't ask you to come back. I'm glad to see you're not dead for others, but it means nothing to me. I said all I had to say to my son twelve years ago."

What did I expect? I thought. Hot and cold chills ran through me, and I felt faint. I shook it off.

"Where's Mom?" I asked.

He stared at me and, for a second, I wasn't sure he was going to answer. "Your mother left not long after you did."

I was tempted to say, good for her, but restrained myself. I could hear rustling in the kitchen. "That my sister?"

"No," Dad answered. "I remarried."

"I see. Do you know where Mom is?"

"No."

"I'll find her."

The silence lengthened.

"Not going to ask about your sister?" he said. There was a blade concealed in the question. My younger sister, Rena, had turned on me as hard and fast as any. We'd never been close as children— she'd been my mother's project as I had been Dad's, and what lay between us has never been a familial feeling.

"No. She did without a brother for most of our childhood. She doesn't need one now that she's grown."

"Why are you here?"

It seemed he wasn't going to use my name, much less "son."

"I've come back to apologize to everyone. Face the music. I'm looking people up. I started with you."

He shrugged. "What will that do? You ran out. You can't buy that back. The dead won't rise."

I nodded, trying to keep the pain at a distance. "Maybe it does no good. But I'm going to do it. As for the dead, well, nowadays I have as much or more experience of them than you did during your war. I've learned to focus on the living."

"So what do you want here?"

"I came to make peace with you, if I can. I don't hope for more. I don't think you and I can undo the damage we did one another. But I'll settle for peace."

"You still talk too much for a man," he said.

"And you don't love enough for a father," I shot back.

Anger lit in his eyes, and he stood, taking a step toward me.

"I've killed too many men for you to hit me, Old Man," I said. Even I was surprised at the ugly menace in my tone, at the hate that ran like virulent poison in my veins.

"You?" he said. "Hard to credit." But he stopped coming.

"You might look up the name Wrik Trigardt sometime."

Something flickered in his face then. Trigardt was Mom's maiden name.

"Wouldn't matter to me what you did off-world. I live with who you were here."

I didn't respond, merely stared, trying to get my breathing under control. "I've said my piece to you. You can leave me under that stone out there, or recognize that I'm alive, that I'm not that perfect son you wanted to relive your life through; just a man, good and bad, success and failure. If you want to find me—"

"No need to tell me," he said. "I didn't ask."

A smile sickled across my face. "You don't change, Old Man. The only thing I said that impressed you, was that I'd learned to kill. You didn't ask if I'd learned to love anyone. Killing makes the man for you? That it, Dad?"

"Don't call me that."

We glared at each other while I wondered what I would do if he did strike me. A woman's voice called out. "Owen, lunch is ready." A pleasant-looking woman looked out of the screened porch. She wore a traditional dress: light, but long, gray and simple. "Oh, I didn't know anyone was here."

"It's no one," he said, "and he was just leaving."

"Owen," she said in shock. "Sir," she said to me. "I'm sorry. Can we offer—?"

"No, thank you," I said, from a remote, cold place in myself. "He's right, I was just leaving. You see, I made a wrong turn coming here. Good day."

"At least some water," she began. Her face was red and angry as she looked at my father.

I shook my head and tried for a friendly smile. "Goodbye."

I started away, the screen door banged closed. As I walked over the blue gravel, I heard a raised female voice.

I walked past my gravestone with only a bare glance at it. In a way, the original me was entombed there. The son of my father's hopes and dreams lay there as he would until the second coming. Yet I felt a little lighter as I walked away. Maybe I too could leave that former son under that stone. I'd faced my father. I'd offered peace. If he didn't accept that peace, it was now on him.

CHAPTER 5

WE DEBOUCH INTO RETIEF'S HOME SYSTEM, AND I IMMEDIATELY SET course for Wrik's homeworld at maximum speed, four days journey from the jump point. Lost Planet has two sets of accounts, the legitimate one for Jaelle's business, which I will not touch and the far larger one that has accumulated from our lucrative work for Confed Intelligence. With that at hand, I need not concern myself with fuel charges. Still Stardust can only move so fast over the intervening distance, and I am frustrated as we close in on the world ahead. I elect not to contact Wrik in advance of our landing. First, if Candace is right, he may be in danger. My appearance could cause any party stalking him to accelerate a plan to take effect before I arrive. Beyond that, there is the inevitable fight that must occur when we deal with the twin aspects of his embarking on this reckless mission while I was in stasis and my disregarding his instructions not to follow him.

So I race ahead without regard for fuel efficiency and deal with the normal inquiries from Retief's Port Central as to our mission and intentions. Fortunately we are now registered as the break-bulk freighter, Lady Sterling, for priority cargo. I had, with Jaelle's assistance, even arranged suitable cargo as a cover. Dusko will even sell it upon landing.

But I am not passive. Even at this distance and without my usual direct access, I implant intruder codes far beyond the ability of Confed science to detect or deter. These act as my advance scouts, entering and infecting commercial databases, avoiding the military or high-level corporate ones that, while they could not specifically detect them, might still be able to tell their operators that they were under attack. By the time we enter orbit, I know where my errant partner has been and some of his activities. I cannot however detect any indication of any force shadowing him.

Finally, we close on the planet after an age of useless time. I arrange for a landing entry at Blomfeldt, the same port Wrik had landed on a week before.

"Look out, Retief," Dusko whispers from the second seat on the bridge as we start down. "Here comes Maauro."

Here I come indeed, yet I feel curiously impotent to the coming confrontations. Always before, when anyone offered my network harm, I responded with deadly force and without hesitation, save once. When Jaelle's father betrayed us to the Guild, Wrik forbade me from killing him, stating it would destroy Jaelle. At the time I did not understand, but merely accepted my biological companion's demand. And though she *abandoned and forswore her father not long after, I came to learn that what Wrik said was true.*

Now on my self-appointed mission, I am rushing to Wrik's defense against his natural family and his old network of friends and squadron mates. He will doubtless forbid me to use violence against these, no matter their treatment of him. I am unhappy at the thought of this limitation. Wrik is precious to me, and no one who knows me dares harm him. But these do not know me.

Yet.

I feel my resolve harden. Wrik has come to make amends. Fine. It is fitting and proper for a warrior who has failed, to do this. I have myself done so in the past. Yet I will tolerate no physical harm to my friend. The lives of family members will be off-limits so long as sparing them does not risk Wrik's life. Beyond that I will not bind myself.

I look up at star that holds Wrik's world. Yes, beware. Maauro is here.

CHAPTER 6

I RODE SOUTH, MY MIND SURPRISINGLY EMPTY OF THOUGHT or feeling. Perhaps it was because I'd had such low expectations, that it didn't hurt as much as I feared. I still felt lighter in some way. Now that the worst had happened, I no longer had to give it more thought, or any of that precious commodity— hope.

But perhaps worse awaited me, Delt Teljard was my childhood friend, in some respects the older brother I wasn't lucky enough to have been born with. It had been with him that I rode horses, attended school, and learned to shoot. Delt had backed me up in encounters with school bullies. We'd joined the Kaydets together, trained together. It was only in flying that I'd ever bested Delt at anything. But he was the complete package, when the Ncome Commando formed, Delt was selected to lead it and lead he did. Until the day we shattered against the steel roof the Confederacy placed over our world.

I returned the motorbike and spent the night in the only motel in town. My father could have found me there if he wanted to. The com never sounded, and there were no messages.

In the morning I hooked up to a terminal to check into the where-abouts of my old friend. It didn't take long. To my surprise, I found him only three hundred kilometers away, running a machine shop and light aircraft repair business in Idutywa. It gave me pause; I'd expected to find Delt running something big. I found that difficult to reconcile with the thought of him in the outback, repairing agrocasters and the like.

I hopped back into my rented aircar, and refueled it for the trip to Idutywa, where Delt's shop awaited me. This time I flew it myself, stretching out my wings and blowing the sadness out of my soul. For at least a few minutes, it was only me and the sky, which had never been taken from me, nor turned its back on me. Maybe I would only be happy in it.

Too soon Idutywa came into view. It was more like the frontier towns I remembered, though larger than some. The comp said 12,000 people and recommended a hotel called "The Trekker." I tapped the screen and got the coordinates for the hotel. It was a big rambling structure like a ranch house. I could even see cattle in the distance.

I brought my flyer down in the big field and taxied under a shelter, then got my bags out. A young woman with a robot-loader walked up and relieved me of my bags. She had a warm smile that would have been welcome on another day, but I had things on my mind. I checked in and unpacked, wanting some place to retreat to after seeing Delt. Though it was already mid-afternoon, I still had no appetite. This time I rented a small ground car, not trusting the expensive suspension of the aircar on

CHAPTER 6

local roads, and set out for a rendezvous with my past. Delt's place was on a small airfield adjacent to the town but I did not want to sweep in with the expensive and flashy aircar. Most long and middle-distance traffic used proper aircraft, as opposed to flitters or expensive aircars which did everything, but nothing well or cheaply.

The field of hard-packed, yellow earth lay dotted with a few small, older model transports and some agrocasters for spraying and seed dispersal. The buildings were all clean and in decent repair, but everything about the place had a shopworn air. It again struck me as odd to find Delt here. He'd been the up-and-coming son of a planetary counselor, expected to follow his father into politics. True, he had always been a gear-head, but also class valedictorian and the best sportsman in our district. Everyone had loved Delt. Truth was, I was often bitterly jealous, and, at the same time, grateful that our childhood friendship had continued. He'd had many better options than hanging around with me.

Yet here he was running a small aviation company well out in the hinterland. Many of the old Retief Commandoes had found employment with the reconstituted planetary constabulary, or even in the locally recruited Confed Reserve. It seemed Delt, for all his rank and skills, had not. I wondered why.

I shook my head to clear it, parked, and stepped onto the concrete path leading to the big shed. A couple of men were working on an agrocaster; they didn't look up at me. Neither of them was Delt. I scanned the area, and spotted a shock of blond hair on a broad-shouldered man working by himself under the cover of a private VTOL hauler. I took a deep breath and continued over. Now I could see the outline of a face and there was no question. It was him.

"Hello Delt," I choked out.

He pulled his head out of the machine and turned with his usual, big, friendly smile. "Hello. Do I know you…?" The smile faded to be replaced by a puzzled expression, then recognition lit in his eyes. "Piet. Well, Piet Van Zyle, as I live and breathe." He put the tools in his hands down carefully on the wing of the VTOL and looked at me as he picked up a rag and wiped his hands clean.

I could barely breathe; this was the man I'd betrayed most grievously. My friend in every kid's adventure. I could feel my eyes fill, but I would not cry in front of Delt, not even for forgiveness. It wasn't the way things were done in our world.

"I came to apologize, Delt. I ran out on you and the squadron when you needed me most. I have no excuse."

I didn't even see him move, the blow knocked me over, my head ringing. I rolled up on my feet and got my hands in front of me.

Delt stood a few feet away, but his hands were at his side. "You had that coming, you know."

I tasted blood from a cut cheek. "Yeah, I did."

CHAPTER 6

"You've toughened up," he said, "when you were a kid that would have laid you out."

I lowered my hands. "Not a kid any more."

"Yeah."

He walked over and stuck out his hand. Slowly, I reached out my own and took his. Delt reached his other hand out and placed it on my shoulder and shook me. "Dammit, Piet," he said, his voice unsteady. "Why'd you run off? I don't mean the dogfight. Fight... that wasn't a fight, it was a goddamn slaughter. But you left the planet. That's why I hit you, dammit. You shouldn't have left. You ran out on me."

Suddenly, and despite my resolve, I couldn't control myself, tears ran down my face. I tried hard not to sob, to breathe deep, but they wouldn't stop coming. "I should have died with everyone else."

"No dammit," Delt swore. "All those people killed, for what? For traditions and prejudice, a bunch of shit we didn't even believe in. There was never even a chance."

"I ran," I managed. "I ran."

"I wish you'd all run," Delt said, his voice breaking. "I was your squadron leader. I led you into a massacre, following stupid fucking orders from sons-of-bitches who were throwing us away. I got you all killed..."

I'd never seen Delt cry, never seen anything but strength in him before today. I had never wondered how he felt about the deaths of all our friends. Now I wondered why.

After a few seconds he wiped his face and continued. "They pinned a medal on me, you see, a secret ceremony after the surrender, a medal for murdering my childhood friends. God, how I wish you'd all run." He thumped me on the shoulder. "I was angry with you at the court-martial, said a bunch of stupid and hateful things. It was too near for me to see."

I shook my head. "Don't forgive so easily, Delt. I was a coward. I ran out on you. I dove out of the fight."

He nodded. "Ok, you did. I was blood mad about it at the time. Only seven of us made it down, out of twenty-four. Really only five: Hewat killed himself at the surrender. Regina, well she was burned and despite the synth-flesh, she's never been right since. Then there was you. I assumed you'd died somewhere out under the stars."

"My father didn't even wait for that," I said. "I saw him yesterday. He has a gravestone on the farm for me. It's dated from the battle."

Delt mouth drew into a grim line. "That father of yours is a right bastard. I wonder if he was always so heroic in his war, or if his memory is selective. He's a mean one, your father."

"He was always hard."

"No, Piet," Delt said, finally releasing his grip on my shoulder, "he isn't hard, he's just damn mean. No one could be what your father wanted out of a son."

"You could," I said. "I always felt that you were more the son he wanted than me. I never measured up compared to you, not as a child and not when it counted most."

"Bah," Delt said. "Your father always loved his reputation more than anything else."

I wiped at my face. Delt reached back and grabbed the rag, throwing it to me. I used a clean spot. I felt a fatigue that seemed to lie in my bones themselves.

"It's been years," I added, my voice dull, "yet it seems only minutes in some ways. I finally realized that I had to come back to apologize to everyone I'd let down. To ask for their forgiveness and if not, then to accept what was coming to me. If I'm ever going to stop circling in that sky, ever going to make peace with how things are, I have to do this."

"As I said, I was mad then. Not mad now. What I know now is that I have one less squadron mate to light a candle for. You're alive. And God damn it, you'd better stay alive."

"I need to see the others, Delt. Can you arrange that?"

"Piet, I don't know if that is such a good idea, especially with Regina and Dewalt."

"I didn't expect that it would be easy, or that they'll forgive me. It's my sin to try and redeem, forgiveness is up to them."

Delt sighed. "These are old and deep wounds."

"Some of them never closed."

"Yeah. Come on. Let's get some ice for your jaw. A beer will wash that blood out of your mouth."

I nodded.

"Kosfan," Delt called. A Morok emerged out of the back office. He wore business clothes. He did a double-take at my bruised face and bloody lip.

"I'm taking the afternoon off," Delt said. "Call Smutts in to finish the agrocaster."

"That asshole will do nothing but complain," Kosfan replied.

"Not at time and a half," Delt said. The Morok nodded, waved a tablet comp, and walked back into the office.

"Come on," Delt said. "I'll get the beer, and you can tell me why you still look so damn young. I swear you've hardly aged at all."

Delt and I spent the evening talking on the porch, catching up on the times we had lived through in the years apart. I gave Delt an edited version of my past, what was in the public record, even if that record hadn't caught up to the world we were on. I omitted the details of my friends and my service in Confed Military Intelligence. Delt surely realized some of this, but between his quickly getting muddled with our celebratory drinking and respecting my wishes, he didn't probe further. Truth was, I kept turning the conversation back to Retief and the empty years I knew nothing about. Delt hadn't kept up with my family. He knew my mother had left my father and that my sister had married, but few details. Still, I heard of many of our childhood acquaintances and finally, toward the end of the evening, we talked of our squadron mates, the living and the dead.

After a while, the stress and strain of the day caught up with me. I stood up. Delt tried to and fell over on the settee and gave me a breezy wave from it.

"I'll be back in the morning," I said. "I'm in at the Trekker."

"Swear you'll be back," he said, suddenly, the eyes suddenly bright and alert.

"I do, but it ain't going to be early."

He waved again. "Lightweight. Good night."

I stepped off the porch and out of the pool of light from the porch lamp. Bugs chirred in my ears, but these hadn't evolved to bite humans, and they were merely a buzzing sound. The stars were brilliant over my head, and only the smallest moon, Mogo, was visible. I looked around at the parked aircraft and the silent and mostly dark hangers and machine shops. Beyond to the left, I could see the lights of the town and some vehicles moved, both on the ground and air. Even this backwater didn't entirely roll up with the sunset. I sighed and looked at the grasslands beyond that seemed to stretch out endlessly, broken only by some low hills and copses of trees.

As I slid into the small, blue coupe, I spotted something silhouetted against the descending Mogo. For a moment, my heart was in my mouth. I could've sworn I'd spotted a slender silhouette with long hair. I rubbed my hands over my eyes, but the image was gone. Wishful thinking about the person I wanted to see most.

I looked up at the stars, wondering which one Star Central orbited and if Maauro was looking up, thinking about me. Now that I was on Retief, I wondered if I had made a terrible mistake leaving the people closest to me in the present, to search for a way to repair my past.

"I think," I said to the night sky, "that I have screwed up again."

I slipped into the car and set the autopilot, I'd drunk more than I should have and let the automatics drive me back to the Trekker. Delt would have been happy to have put me up, but well as our reunion had gone, I wanted some time and distance to think. The aircar rolled smoothly back to my hotel. I quietly made my way upstairs in the main building. Then I stripped out of my clothes, dropping them on the floor and fell face down on the bed.

CHAPTER 7

WE LAND WITHOUT FANFARE IN THE SECTION OF THE PORT RESERVED *for small trading ships. Our disguise as a free-trader works perfectly. As we carry no passengers, no one comes out to greet us, nor does it surprise anyone that we do not immediately scramble out, for all that I am impatient to go. I detail all matters dealing with port filings and shutdown to Dusko. Unlike Wrik, I will not use our military pass unless I must. Lilith may be on world and her hacking skills are not to be underestimated. I am disturbed to find a record in a subroutine at the Confed base that Wrik used his pass. Still, it may be for the best. He doubtless avoided media attention that way. Any press would have alerted Lilith instantly. The database I found my information in was a buried one, backing up a supply voucher system. Lilith may not have registered it, assuming she is indeed here.*

I consider my next moves. Despite my hacking, I have not yet located my errant partner on this world's crude and disjointed net. I will need to physically search for him. I prepare for an extended period away from the ship.

"What are you planning?" *Dusko asks as he leans into the bridge.*

"I have infiltrated all those databases that I can without risk of causing alarm," *I reply.* "There is dearth of information in public records on Wrik or his family. I must risk intruding in taxation and other governmental records despite their more powerful barriers. It will take time, perhaps days to unlock those without triggering alarms. I could use my Confederation all pass, but if Lilith is on world and in the net, the use of such a pass would set off ripples that would alert her."

He raises an eyebrow. "When did you do all this?"

"While we were en route, I finished as you were locking down the drive."

He shakes his head ruefully. "Even now, I remain surprised by your abilities."

"It is merely a matter of segmenting my brain to different tasks."

"And totally invisible to us who are in your presence."

"It does not take that much of my processing power to handle ordinary interactions with biologicals. Until, that is, you do something complex and emotional, and then sometimes it takes all the concentration I can muster."

"Mostly with Wrik."

"Mostly, though not exclusively."

"So what now?"

CHAPTER 7

"While my intruder software continues its work, I might as well physically explore those venues Wrik would visit. I should shortly locate his family members, and those survivors of the Ncome Commando."

"You may wish to consider other clothes," Dusko says.

I look down at my paneled orange and gray jumpsuit. "What is wrong with my appearance?"

"Have you seen anyone else in a jumpsuit?" he gestures at the city outside the viewport.

I access the ship's sensors and what passes for an entertainment net on this world A few seconds survey tells me that only spaceport service personnel dress this way. I will stick out like a neon sign when I leave the environs of the port.

"What do you recommend?" I ask.

"Me? I'm Dua and male. Why would I know about female clothes for young humans? Go into town, find a store and have a shop girl fix you up. Or can't you scan a store database and just retexturize yourself?"

"I have scanned the database on the commercial nets while we were speaking," I reply. "I can texturize my outer casing, but I have noticed that fashion and color sense are so variable, that if I am to effectively blend in, the fashion advice of a local female may prove most effective."

"Besides," he replies. "You want to look nice for Wrik."

"You wouldn't be making fun of me?" I ask.

He raises his eyebrows. "Me? Gods no, that would lessen my already poor odds of surviving to retirement."

"I concur."

"Have fun at the mall," he adds.

I secure the drive. "You may follow your own pursuits after you dispose of the cargo," I add. Then, repenting some of my earlier annoyance with him, "You are free to spend the profits in any manner that suits you after reprovisioning the ship."

Again the eyebrows go up. "Very generous, thank you."

"Be ready should I call for you at any time with the ship's flitter and my armaments. I do not wish to use my military pass to get them onworld now, but will arrange for the ship's flitter to be cleared for planetary access should I need you."

I leave Dusko to deal with customs and tax matters and head quickly into town. My passport shows me a human mutation, named Aurelia Toyama, an identity I used on Stauver, so I quickly pass through the minimal security into the capital city beyond. It takes a few minutes for a cab with a human driver to deliver me to a store named, Immaculota. I leave my intruder software and the segmented part of my brain to continue scanning for signs of Wrik, or Lilith. Clothes shopping will at least fill the time until some clue is discovered.

Once at the Immaculota, a modern two-story building, with glass windows full of holographic females, in what I hope are fashionable *clothes. I seek out a clerk who is similar in age and build to me. She shows me a variety of garments.*

"I really need you to pick," I advise. "As you can see from my eyes, I'm a mutation. I don't see colors as standard humans do."

"Sure," the girl says, with an enthusiasm I suspect is born of a commission-based salary. "Colors will be easy, with such perfect pale skin and so much black hair, you can wear just about anything. Especially with your figure..." she continues with a mix of pleasantries and local news as she selects ten full outfits for me. None of the news concerns Wrik's return. He is habitually secretive, and I am relieved by this. Perhaps Lilith has not learned of his arrival if she is indeed here.

Satisfied with the purchases, I have them sent to the ship. In the dressing room, I revert from my jumpsuit texture to a nude texture, then place on my own favorite of the outfits she selected for me, It is a blue and white dress with shoes that make me glad I am incapable of physical discomfort, and a light jacket.

"I will wear these out," I say. I hope it does not occur to her to ask where my jumpsuit went. Dazed by the size of my purchase, it evidently does not cross her mind. Once I had decided on the patterns and colors, I actually do not need the clothes, I could retexturize my outer casing to simulate them, though generating a skirt light enough to be moved by a breeze would be tricky. Still, the young girl has been helpful. It pleases me to see how happy my purchase made her and the approving look she receives from the manager.

Once back in a cab, I quickly reconfigure my feet to look like the shoes. The thin material they were made from would not survive my weight for long. I leave them in the cab. Perhaps the driver has a daughter or a petite wife who will enjoy them.

I continue to scan every new database that my intruder software opens for me, hoping for a hint, some clue to orient my search for a needle in this planetary-sized haystack. Retief is a backwater of a colony. Most of the databases are crude and limited. Life outside the capital goes off the planetary grid, in a series of autistic systems that may or may not communicate on a regular basis. It is an appalling and haphazard arrangement.

One of my subroutines flags me. Wrik rented a vehicle and withdrew considerable sums of cash from the spaceport exchange. This is making him hard to track, but I quickly correlate that these assets would allow him to journey to his old home, well out in the hinterlands of Retief. I assume he would look up his mother and father first, then perhaps his sister, then squadron mates. Approaching his family would be the most awkward and perhaps unwelcome. I plan to reconnoiter the family farm before making contact.

Then a final entry in a small commercial database redirects me. I find a payment by Wrik, under the name, Mazza Fornite, ironically a false identity he also used on Stauver, for a small amount of alcoholic beverages. The location is well away from the farm, and the payment was made yesterday. Further correlation reveals another nexus, an aircraft maintenance business called Taljard Aviation. This is the name of Wrik's former Wing Commander and childhood friend, one of the few survivors of the Ncome Commando massacre over the capitol when the Confed Navy moved in. I now have a destination.

"Please take me back to the spaceport," I advise the driver. "I need to rent a flitter."

"Yes, Miss," he says.

A short time later, I am speeding northward out of the spaceport toward the high grasslands in a late-model flitter with a military grade engine. I had to leave most of my weapons behind or risk using the all pass. I can always have Dusko bring the heavy weapons using the ship's cargo flitter if I need them. As yet I have not detected any indication of Lilith, but I suspect she would be in the highlands and away from the population centers, just where I am heading. Hours later, I pass a small town named Idutywa. Delt Taljard has a business outside of town, at a small airfield. I land the flitter outside the fence after circling the field searching for either Wrik, or any sign of Lilith. I see nothing indicating either is present.

I quickly make my way to the main building of the airfield, avoiding as much as I can muddy ground from a recent rainfall. A number of humans and a Morok are busy conversing over a yellow-and-black, checkered air transport. Two of the men pause to look me over and smile, then return to their repairs. The Morok ignores me, or does not notice my presence. I walk past them to what appears to be an office. A tall, solidly-built human male of about thirty is standing there in a blue overall, scanning a tablet. He has a shock of blond hair over a handsome, if weather-beaten face. His shoulders and arms are filled out with muscle. He looks up as I approach and puts the tablet aside.

"Good morning," he says with a bright grin. "I'm Delt Teljard. How can I help such a pretty young lady this morning?"

"My name is Maauro," I reply, looking up at his friendly countenance. "I am an associate of Wrik Trigardt, who you may know as—"

"I know Piet," he says, his face is now wary.

"I need to see Wrik."

He studies me. "Well, this is just like Piet, holding out on me. He hasn't told me much about his life before he came back. Certainly he didn't warn me about a pretty girl with huge green eyes looking for him."

"I commend your caution," I said, fighting impatience. "Wrik is very important to me, and I must see him."

I hear a scuff of a boot, and Wrik rounds the corner and stops in surprise. Delt looks at us both, unsure of what to do.

And we are suddenly running toward each other. I must stop abruptly and carefully, less my greater mass knock him flying, but he is safely in my arms a second later. I find myself battling a mélange of emotions: relief, happiness, anger. We remain locked together, my face against his chest, his chin resting on my head. For some seconds, neither of us is quite capable of speech. From a reflection nearby I see Delt grin again and move off, gesturing to the others to silently follow him.

When I can speak I say. "This once and only this once, I will forgive you for leaving me behind. Never do such a thing again."

He draws a shaky breath. "So sworn. Never again. God, I am glad to see you."

I step back, throttling down the anger that wants to assert itself now that I see him alive and unharmed. I notice that he has a large and darkening bruise on his jaw. "Than why this voyage without me? Why didn't you want me with you?"

He strokes my face in mute apology, then finally. "I am not sure it fits into words well. But I was coming back to face something I was ashamed of. I wasn't sure that I could if you were with me. I don't know how to be Wrik Trigardt and Piet Van Zyle at the same time. And, well, there are times that a man has to take what is coming to him."

"Since you seem to feel the need for this atonement, I would allow such, within reason."

He raises an eyebrow. "You have been known to render large areas uninhabitable when you feel things have progressed beyond reason."

"You exaggerate. I rarely render the actual areas uninhabitable, just uninhabited."

"Ah," *he says,* "an important distinction. But most of all, I felt I had to face my father and my wing commander on my own. I've done that and it was as bad as I expected with my father and easier with Delt."

"That is good to hear."

He looks down at me. "I am so glad you're here. It was wrong to leave you behind. I can see that now."

"As I have said, I will forgive it this once."

He studies me with a perplexed look. "Are you taller?"

I find myself pleased that he has noticed. "There was sufficient material left over from my new arm to increase my size. I risked some slight alterations to my basic default matrix so that I look a little older."

"You do and as beautiful as always. Is the new arm ok?"

"It functions as well as my factory original. In some ways better, I have added some refinements that eluded my original design engineers. I have after all had this body for over 50,000 years."

"And you don't look a day over 40, 000," *he replies.*

*"You are fortunate that I find it difficult to remain cross with you."
I say, raising an eyebrow. My attempt at mock severity merely provokes
laughter from him.*

*"Yes, I suppose I am." He runs his hands down both my arms as if
testing to see they match in warmth and malleability. I find his exploring
of my body sets off a number of odd sensations that I am unable to
readily analyze, and that this leaves me very slightly disoriented. Yet
an instant system check shows I am functioning normally. I segment
part of my consciousness to analyze this further. I also find it somewhat
disturbing that I am disappointed when he stops.*

"How did the others take it?" he asks,

*"Dusko thinks you are foolish. He is in the offport up to his usual
entertainments, one supposes."*

*"Well, there are many that would agree with him. Still, I have to be
grateful to the old thief for finding enough rare materials to restore you."*

"Jaelle," I continue, then hesitate.

"Go ahead," he prompts. "Let's get it over with."

*"She made much of the fact that your letter was to me and not her.
She said to tell you that she remains your friend and legal consort—"*

"But that is all," he finishes for me.

I nod.

*"I can't blame her for that. I didn't handle any of it very well and the
breakup worst of all. I'm glad we're still friends."*

"You knew that she would not come after you."

"Yes."

"Did you know that I would?"

*He smiles a sad smile. "Yeah, I pretty much did. That sort of says
it all, doesn't it? I'm just amazed you made it here so quickly. Guess
the Cosmic Dust wasn't much of a match for the Stardust with you at
the controls."*

*I only smile back. The question has many unspoken parts to it, and
I am not sure I understand all of what he is saying. My answer seems
to suffice as he runs his hands through my hair. Again the sensation
vibrates over my systems.*

"What now?" I ask, trying to regain focus.

*"Well for now, I guess it's time to properly introduce you to Delt. He's
a bit of a larger-than-life character, so don't over-react to him."*

*We turn to walk on as I ponder this statement, with its implied
warning. Wrik's right arm is across my shoulder. My new left one is
around his waist. This is different for us as I never used to touch him
with my left. The Infestor arm had insufficient feedback for such use and
felt like cold hard metal, however it looked. Now I am again fully whole
and integrated as I have not been since the ambush on Kandalor that
maimed me. I feel, strangely exhilarated to be so. I am proud of my new
arm, and my being again a perfect example of the M-7 series.*

CHAPTER 7

We walk out together. The staff is nowhere to be seen, so I assume they are in the buildings, but Delt is atop a two-wheeled vehicle. He twists the controls, and the vehicle emits a load roar, then he hurtles toward us. I casually analyze if this is an attack, there is an abundance of seconds to consider whether to neutralize the threat. Given that Wrik's body only minimally tenses at the sound and display, I chalk the mock charge up to this 'larger-than-life quality' Wrik ascribed to Delt. So I do not neutralize the approaching vehicle, for all that I am displeased by its speed and proximity to us. As a hedge against miscalculation I slide between Wrik and the motorcycle as it screeches to a halt.

"Quiet a beauty isn't she?" Delt says, with what I judge is a mischievous and challenging grin. "Oh, sorry, I meant my old Bush Rebel here."

"Yeah, yeah," Wrik says. "As soon as any female is around, you just can't resist showing off. Can you?"

"I am glad that your reconciliation with Wrik seems to have gone well," Maauro said, looking over both Delt and his machine with interest.

"Oh, it's ok," Delt said. "I let him have one good slug on the jaw and we were over it."

"Damn near busted my jaw," I said, rubbing the still tender spot where his fist had caught me.

Maauro's head swiveled and her eyes locked on Delt's. "There will be no further slugs on the jaw or anywhere else."

Red Alert. "Maauro don't worry—"

"Your girlfriend is cute," Delt laughed. "I believe she's ready to take a poke at me on your account."

Before I could say anything, Maauro stepped forward and lifted the motorcycle up to chest level, with Delt still on it. She looked up at him. "You are correct. And if I take a poke at you, it will go through you."

"Maauro put him down! I told you things were fine between us."

"You neglected to mention the slug on the jaw part."

"It was nothing. Down please."

She lowered the bike and Delt, who stared at her for a minute. Maauro stared coolly back.

"Piet," he said swallowing, "why is your girlfriend stronger than a rutting Okaran?"

"Considerably stronger," she added.

I had to confess that seeing the ever-confident Delt taken down a peg was rather fun. I walked up and placed an arm around her. "You aren't concerned about keeping our little secret?"

"No," she replied. "Among our enemies in the Guild and other governments, too much is already known of me for true secrecy. The fiction that we invented to cover my actions on Seddon is thin at best and unlikely to last—"

"It was pretty weak," I admitted.

"You friend would have realized it shortly. If only because it rained heavily last night and I cannot avoid sinking into the mud and betraying my weight."

"Actually," Delt said. "I hadn't noticed."

"This is a somewhat long story," I began.

"No doubt," he said. "In that case, I'm going to get us some beers." He got off the bike on the side away from Maauro. "Er, do you drink? You look kinda young."

"I am 50,133 years old."

"Well that would be of legal age anywhere in the galaxy," he said, a dazed expression on his face. "Meet you on the porch."

"Remember what I said about not using violence on anyone?" I said to Maauro as Delt walked away.

She glared up at me with a mutinous expression. "Remember how you promised me you would stay safe on Sedon and not open fire on the Destroyer?"

"Well, if you are going to throw every little thing back in my face." My smile told her the remark was not serious, and she seemed mollified.

"There's something more going on," I said slowly, studying Maauro.

She nodded. "I find that I have grown weary of the pretense of denying the truth of what I am. You walk under the sun and are what you are. Why should I not do so as well?"

"There are dangers," I added.

"Unavoidable ones past a point and the truth has value, does it not?"

I put my arm back around her shoulder as we walk to the porch.

"For myself," I said, "I have found the truth to be like a fine wine, best served to friends and loved ones."

"Logical," she said.

Delt waited for us, sitting on the sturdy rail of the porch next to a half-dozen beers in a cooler on a table between two chairs. His face was carefully neutral. I slid into one of the chairs with a sigh. Maauro sat cross-legged on the floor. I handed her a green bottle of Sandhurst ale.

"OK," he said. "This I have to hear."

I sat back in my chair and took a deep draft of my ale. Maauro correctly interpreted this as leaving the first part of the tale to her. She sipped from her beer in a more lady-like fashion before beginning.

"I'm an artificial intelligence," she began, "manufactured by a race that is long gone from space. I call them the Creators, their real name would be a meaningless sound to you. I am primarily an infiltration and anti-personnel unit, Model 7, designed to combat their enemy, the Infestors. I was stranded on an asteroid after a battle over 50,000 years ago. Sometime during that long sleep on the asteroid, I became more than I was made to be."

"That's obvious even from a few seconds speaking with you," Delt said, his eyes wide. "You're no machine, that's for sure. You're alive."

"Those two things may be less disparate then you believe," Maauro said. "However I appreciate your sentiment and the acknowledgement that I am a person." She paused, sipped the beer again and turned back to me.

I drew a deep breath. "I told you before, how I ended up on Kandalor after a trip out in cold sleep. I was looking for a second chance, a place to start my life over. Kandalor turned out to be a poor choice. I fell under the influence of the Guild, at first doing minor jobs for them. Then..." I stopped and swallowed. Maauro reached a hand out and placed it on my thigh, concern on her gentle face. "...then much worse."

"I could see how that would happen," Delt said.

"I was chartered for a treasure hunt in the asteroid belt for what we called "Old Empire" relics—"

"That would be me," Maauro said, giving her bottle a little wiggle.

A quick laugh among the three of us lessened the tension.

"The woman who hired me, turned out to be Confed Intelligence, the mission was a Guild set-up for salvaging an Old Empire base. When we got there, we were betrayed into a Guild ambush. It would have ended there except our arrival reactivated Maauro."

"After not being maintained for 50,000 years?" Delt said, astonishment on his face. "They built you well."

"I engaged the Guild before I knew who the sides were," Maauro added. "In my extremely depleted state, the situation was very dangerous for me. I realized that I needed intelligence on what was going on. So I decided to secure a prisoner. Fortunately, it was Wrik who I selected."

"Lucky boy, kidnapped by a beautiful, alien, android."

"I didn't look like this at the time," Maauro said.

"Yeah," I said, "she was pretty terrifying—"

"If you refer to me as a 'space zombie' again, the crack Delt gave you will be the least of your problems," Maauro said, a miffed look on her face.

I raised my hands. "Never even considered it."

Delt grinned and covered it by taking a swig from his bottle. "So how did you get those big green eyes?"

"I repatterned my basic matrix after an image I discovered in his ship's computer. It was an experimental ability added to my generation of androids. At the time, I did not realize the image was from a game simulation and not a representation of a real human female."

Delt chuckled, shaking his head.

"When we reached the surface of the asteroid, I realized how long I had been inactive and that there was no sign of my Creators. I decided to help Wrik get off the asteroid. We found the Confed agent on the surface. Wrik carried her back to his shuttle while I engaged the Guild. I malfunctioned in the battle, probably due to shape-changing my basic matrix. I lay, expecting to be destroyed. Instead, I was treated to the sight of Wrik in an unarmored suit, charging the Guild with only a line gun."

Delt looked at me. "Good on you."

I nodded.

"We escaped and have been together ever since," she finished.

"Until I stupidly decided I needed to run off and do this by myself," I added, shaking my head.

"And if you're so smart," Delt challenged, "how did he get away?"

"I was in stasis under a nuclear reactor having a new arm installed. I had to be off-line for weeks."

Delt stared at her dumbfounded. "Holy Crap."

She raised an eyebrow. "Odd subject for a deity."

"She's just playing with you," I said, as his jaw hung open.

"Quite the sense of humor you have, young lady," he said.

"It goes with my general cuteness."

"By God, I like her," Delt announced.

"You were always a smart one," I said.

A shadow touched his face. "Not always."

"You'll probably see some things in the local media about an expedition that Maauro and I were on, there's a cover story about an HCR robot being on the voyage. That was actually Maauro."

"I'll see if there's something on the net about it. I'm amazed that the press didn't swarm you if that was the case."

"I came in under an assumed identity and with a Confed military all pass. No one but my father and you know that I am here so far."

He stared at me.

"Did I neglect to mention that we're officers in Confed Military Intelligence?" I added.

"Yeah, well with so much to tell, I can see how you might overlook that little detail. Oh crap, did you tell—"

"My father? Hell no. And I need you to keep it under wraps as well along with everything else. But I could hardly renew our friendship without letting you know in whose service I stand now."

"So sworn. We Ncome commandoes need to stick together."

For the first time since that terrible day, the mention of my old squadron didn't cause my heart to sink.

"In fact, I say we make Maauro an honorary member," Delt continued.

"I second that motion," I added.

Delt grabbed another beer. "Motion made and seconded. All in favor say, 'aye.'"

"Aye," we voiced.

CHAPTER 7

"Motion made and carried," Delt said. "You're in."

"I'm honored," Maauro said.

"Let's drink to it," Delt said, and pounded down most of his beer before reaching for a third.

"So what now?" Maauro asked.

"For now, dinner," I said. "The best there is in town. My treat."

Delt glanced at Maauro. "Do you like Veru?"

"I've never eaten one," she replied, "though I once frightened a small planet's worth of them."

"Er?" he looked at me, wide-eyed. "She's kidding right?"

I shook my head slowly. "Maauro will like any place that has a good dessert menu. She's fond of sweets." My little destroyer of worlds smiled up at Delt in angelic innocence.

"Ok," Delt said, his voice a tad shaky. "There's a good Euro-style place in town. Food's good, but they are known for their desserts. It's gonna dent your bank book."

"Not such an issue anymore," I replied. "Not rolling in it, but I don't have to be as careful as I used to be."

Maauro nodded. "The dessert place, definitely."

CHAPTER 8

WRIK AND DELT CHANGE CLOTHES FOR DINNER, WHILE I REMAIN ON *the porch. The time for males to change clothes for an evening out is a fraction of that usually consumed by females, and they return quickly. However both pull up short when they see me, as I have retexturized from the simple dress and sweater I wore, to my evening pattern #1, a simply cut 'little black dress' with black shoes with jeweled belts and a small bag called a clutch, though this last item is empty as I have no need of the normal contents. I also simulate a cut jade necklace in the shape of a Chinese dragon. The jade color matches my eyes.*

"How..." Delt began.

"Become accustomed to the minor miracles," Wrik said. "It saves time."

Delt goes for the car and to tell his staff to knock off for the night as I sit with Wrik catching up on all the details of the journey so far. He is sparing of details of his visit with his father, and I do not press him on this, knowing that below the façade of indifference is great pain. He will tell me more when the time is right and we have more privacy.

Meanwhile, I intrude into any systems nearby that might have been touched by Lilith, or could be useful in providing surveillance for Delt's compound and airstrip. There is very little I can use, and what is present is of low quality. Still I upgrade and update software, converting these to my use in a fashion that will not interfere with their normal duties. I design a small aerial device with a basic sensor suite and disguise them to look like the local equivalent of a bee. They are temporary constructions of organic polymers and will dissolve in a few weeks, but they allow me to slip an electronic net over the airfield and shops. My internal factories manufacture enough to fill in the blind spots. I excuse myself from Wrik long enough to tap into a power circuit in the machine shed and drain some power and release the spybees.

Wrik must have told Delt what I was up to as he grins and yells, "Hey no snacking between meals, you'll ruin your dinner."

"Nothing ruins my dinner," I return, "though I may need to snack again on some light metals later."

His expression is rather comical. "Ok. Well, don't eat the car on the way."

The fact that Delt is there, keeps our conversation on the short ride in to town light, with Delt asking many questions about my background and life. Though Wrik trusts this human, I am a little more wary on short acquaintance. I keep the stories to the non-classified and public elements of our history.

The restaurant is atop a small hill in town and provides a view of the old wooden buildings of the early town and the more modern prefab structures. Most of the buildings and stores are dedicated to agricultural business, but there are a number of bars and restaurants. Two small theatres are present, one of which offers live performances. A few simple, white buildings with small towers are identified as churches, but, in token of Retief's past, they are all variations of one form of worship. There are no Denlenn temples or other concessions to the beliefs of others. Indeed, I see only two other aliens in town, both Moroks and likely related to the one working for Delt, and one mutated human whose red-patterned skin, identifies her as a Silurian.

My own appearance attracts some attention, and not all the looks are welcoming but Delt is well known, and that seems to unlock a friendliness that I suspect would otherwise be missing. We are shown to a candle-lit table. A young girl waits on us. She keeps trying to look at my eyes without being obvious until she catches an annoyed look from Delt.

Wrik orders us bottles of Perlat, a carbonated red wine that is grown in the area and much prized. We work our way through a variety of oddly-named foods, including a meat called Jumping Dink. I eat the small portions associated with demure female behavior since even with conversion I draw little significant energy value from food. However, when dessert comes, I attack a chocolate caramel volcano with enthusiasm, savoring the unusual chemical combinations and textures.

Delt and Wrik trade stories about each other in an apparent effort to reduce each one's status in my eyes. I enjoy the evening. The food is good, the company congenial, though Delt drinks more than is perhaps sensible.

We head back to Delt's quarters after dinner, after making the staff quite happy with the volume and expense of our meal. Wrik has moved into the spare room at Delt's apartment over the hanger. So we return with me driving Delt's groundcar as I feel both men have enjoyed more Perlat than is compatible with night driving on country roads.

I am glad we have Delt's nondescript and modest car. Wrik had sent his aircar back to the rental company on autopilot. I'd done the same with mine. The flashy and expensive vehicles could attract more attention than is prudent.

We pull up in front of the largest hanger, to which Delt's prefabricated house is attached. The compound is dark, save for some blue lights near the field and a few low wattage lights near the hanger. Only Delt actually lives here. The others have departed for their homes in town or in the nearby countryside. I step out of the car first. My spybees and other seized systems tell me nothing has intruded while we were gone. I scan everything in line of sight before my companions can exit the auto.

Both my human friends complain about the darkness; evidently something is wrong with the automatic light sensor on the front of Delt's building. I generate visible white light through my eyes, lighting the way to the door. This shocks Delt into something closer to sobriety. He whistles. "If I hadn't seen it... you know Maauro, it's just hard to keep in mind that you're not just a pretty girl with big eyes."

"Good, it has cost me great pains to come this close to human appearance."

We gain the door. Delt enters first, announcing his intention to "drain the dragon." Wrik flicks on the outside light and stops on the porch to look out at a grassy knoll on the other side of the field. He drops into a chair with sigh. I sit on the porch floor next to him and a white rattan table, having reverted to my usual one piece coverall.

"You know, I saw you the night before," Wrik says, suddenly. "With everything going on, I forgot to mention it."

I am startled. "Oh?" I reply in a neutral tone.

"Yes," he says, pointing at the knoll with an air of being proud of himself. "Just for a moment, you let yourself be silhouetted against the moon. Guess you were scoping the place out. Let's see: slim figure, long hair, moves impossibly fast. Who else could it be?"

"Who indeed?" I say with a cheerful façade.

"Very incautious of a combat android to get sky-lined like that," he teases.

"Yes, very. I must be getting old."

"Never," he says, giving my hair a gentle stroke. But even this is not enough to distract me. I was not in the area, and I am far too aware of my surroundings to ever be skylined. No, this must be the self-named Lilith. She has detected Wrik's presence on the planet, and either she, or one of her HCRs, is scouting Delt's shop. This must be rectified.

"Hey Wrik," Delt calls from inside, "make yourself useful. Help me carry this stuff out. I found some chips and a bottle of Helevar."

Wrik rolls his eyes but heads inside.

I find myself in a quandary. Wrik and I are becoming more than we were, something special and unique in one way and ordinary and commonplace in another. With the others in our network gone, we are functioning more as a couple. All that I have learned of such pairing is that open and honest communication is essential to their functioning. I have long since discovered that lying to Wrik, even by omission and for his own good, is a failure of the relationship and a breach of integrity. Yet, how can I tell him, in the middle of his quest to reclaim his past, that we are the targets of a berserk human and a sextet of the Confederacy's deadliest fighting machines? Once he knows of the danger, he will unquestionably insist on aiding me in dealing with it. He will, as usual, promise to stay out of danger in a bald-faced lie and intervene at any moment he perceives I am in trouble.

I cannot yell, or curse, but almost wish that I could. A promise could not prevent Wrik from opening fire on the thirty-meter-tall Destroyer with a mere rifle when I was in combat with it. The only thing that saved him was my forcing the Destroyer to choose between dealing with me or Wrik. It properly chose me. While it is true that Wrik's intervention in that battle saved me from destruction, it did so at utterly unacceptable risk to his frail human body. Yet, I have promised not to lie to him by leaving out information. I could drum my hands on the table in frustration, save that it would be reduced to splinters in a second. What to do?

If Wrik helps me in a situation where logically, as the easier target, he will be focused on by six HCRs, he will be killed. The Destroyer had no idea how important Wrik is to me, Lilith will know at least that we have been close for years. He must be kept out of the action, at least while such a course lessens the danger to him. To keep him out, he must not know of the threat. I will therefore lie; it is the lesser of two evils. Comforted by having made a decision, I make a followup one. A mild sedative will ensure a sounder than usual sleep for Wrik. I will slip out and engage the enemy after we retire for the evening.

It occurs to me that grievances are sometimes a form of currency in relationships. Wrik abandoned me to deal with his quest. While I have said I forgive it, I am still upset by the action. He has been very apologetic since, but still, if I must disclose this deception, I can use the balance of my grievance in exchange. This will rebalance our account.

Excellent, I have figured it all out. The equations balance. Perhaps relationships are not as difficult as I feared.

Internally, so Wrik and Delt cannot hear, I open a channel to the ship. Dusko responds in a leisurely twenty seconds. "Dusko, here."

"Get the flitter. Load my armspac and the material in loadout box six into it. Proceed to these coordinates. Avoid being contacted, or observed by anyone. There is an isolated glade in tree cover there. Set down and unload the material in the space of 120 seconds then return to the ship. Plan your arrival for 2330 hours."

"And what do we say when we want something?" Dusko responds.

"Two responses occur to me. The first is a 'please.' The second is, 'perform as directed or I will grind you into a paste that I will use to lubricate my nether regions.' I offer them both."

Dusko gives a derisive snort. "I'll opt for the former. Anything else?"

"No." Has it come to this? From being a figure of terror, a leading cause of death to Infestors, Guild and hostile AIs, I am now reduced to where even Dusko can laugh at me. Indeed my stock is far down if such is the case.

Delt and Wrik return. Wrik has another chair. Delt brings out a bottle of yellow liquor and a bowl of chips on a tray which he deposits on the table in front of us. He pours three generous portions of the liquor in clear fluted glasses. We settle in to talk and drink. To my surprise, at one point, my two companions burst into song. The songs become a bit ribald as the bottle's contents drain. Delt eventually slouches down on the settee and passes out. Wrik, who has also had more to drink than is his wont, gives a concerned look, but in shared inebriation seems mostly interested in bed.

"I will take care of it." I lift Delt and carry him upstairs to what Wrik indicates is his room. It's decorated with a variety of aircraft holos and flat paintings. The room is very messy, with clothes hung on the mix of indifferently-made furniture. Empty alcohol bottles dot it. I notice something else. While there are images of family and friends, pictures of Delt in sports gear, there is nothing indicating his service in the rebellion: no souvenirs, no flight jacket or other insignia. This nexus of factors tells me that for Delt, as for Wrik, the past is a source of pain.

I hack the planetary network and examine the room contents as I carry Delt to the bed, followed by an unsteady Wrik. I place the big man in it and cover him. In that time, I have examined Delt's school records, combat and flight records. The extraordinary potential of Delt as a young man has not been matched by his performance postwar.

"He drinks too much," Wrik says with the careful pronunciation he uses when he has indulged in alcohol. "It never, ever occurred to me that he could be hurt by the war. Not the way I was hurt, but hurt anyway. War is a toxin in itself."

"Yes," I say, surprising myself. "Even for me, literally made for war, I too have felt the toxin, when I interrogated ... when I tortured Infestors to death. Why else would I have erased the memories? And now that I am more alive and have things precious and irreplaceable to me, now, I hate it!" The last explodes out of me with a force that startles us both.

"Come," he says putting an arm around me carefully, as if he could somehow hurt me. "Let's head for bed. I'm beat. Tomorrow I start the rest of what I came here to do."

"Not alone." I warn.

"No," he says, hugging me. "Never alone. Never again alone."

When we go to our room, Wrik drops onto the mattress. I sit on the floor next to him for fear of crushing the bed. I remain still as he quickly drops off to sleep. My analysis of his brain wave patterns and depth of breathing indicates that he will sleep long and deeply, and the sedative I planned to use is unnecessary. I remove my yellow hair ribbon and place it inside a drawer, then slip out of the room and down the stairs.

Once outside, I scan the sheds and structures. There are lights on in one and I hear two beings working on an aircraft. The airfield is lit by a few ghostly lights but there is no activity. Most flying here is done under visual flight rules, and the automatics are primitive enough to discourage night flying without a specially equipped aircraft such as Dusko is flying.

I change my outer chassis. Gone are the light and feminine clothes I have taken to wearing. Now I am a non-reflective flat-black from head to toe. From inside my body, I release additional spybees. My own onboard sensors would likely detect normal machinery, or armed biological troops in the area, but HCRs, though crude by my standards, are nonetheless effective infiltrators. My observer-bees drone off to their assigned stations while I speed for a small hill nearby. It is not much of a hill but in these flatlands will provide a good observation post. It is also where Wrik saw what he thought was me.

I approach the hill with my passive sensors operating at maximum setting. I sense no mines, booby traps or other cyber-mechanisms. I climb and examine the ground at the summit. Footprints from something heavier than me score the soil and vegetation. A Confed HCR was here that night. The prints tell me it came alone and from what direction it approached and went. I debate whether to pursue the trail, but decide to let my quarry come to me, so I may protect my sleeping friends. Lilith has multiple HCRs. Another might attack while I was away dealing with this threat.

I detect a flitter on my internal radar, heading toward the drop zone I directed. I close the location quickly and see our flitter with its running lights turned off, flying on infra-red and microwave emitters. Dusko lands and unceremoniously kicks out two large boxes from the square cargo bay, without exiting the flitter. He is gone in half the time I allotted.

I move out, secure the containers and return to the hillside. I draw my armspac from one, then bury both containers of ammunition and spares. I have improved my armspac since I fought the Destroyer, as I have also improved my internal armaments.

Settled on the military crest of the hill, so I will not be skylined, I wait with my armspac beside me. The stars wheel overhead and I enjoy this. There are unusual stars in this section of space. A binary system of a red giant and white dwarf is a mere two light years away. The pool of shared material that the white dwarf pulls from the red star glows in a pinwheel of excited atoms. Another large, green star glows softly in the sky. A most unusual color, it is called the Ginger Star and, as no easy hyperspace star routes lie to it, few have traveled there despite its proximity.

Movement interrupts my appreciation of the night sky's beauty. One of my bees has detected something at the limit of its range. The glancing contact means my assessment was right. Whatever is coming is heading directly for the hillock I occupy, incautiously using this vantage for the second time in two days. Very sloppy, I am offended by such a lack of professionalism.

I zoom my vision and detect a figure striding in the open of the veldt in a brisk jog, making no effort at concealment. A triple-auto weapon is slung over its shoulder. There is an arrogance and contempt in that approach that is biological in origin. This is Lilith.

I consider opening fire without warning. I can easily destroy the HCR with an alpha strike from my armspac. But this Lilith is an unknown factor. Destroying an HCR without finishing her would merely alert Lilith to my presence, costing me the element of surprise against an enemy with five remaining HCRs, not an inconsiderable threat even to me, and deadly to my biological companions should one get past me.

Candace said Lilith could hack past normal methods of securing HCRs, something only I had done before. So a cyber-seizure is chancy. As I learned in fighting the Destroyer, when a biological body is integrated in an autistic system, it is proof against hacking. I cannot infiltrate, or hack a biological brain, and that gives the enemy cybersystem a place to hide and reboot.

Yet if I am to gain intel on the enemy I must make an effort to capture this machine. Decision made, I act instantly. I unleash a barrage of my best cyber-attack programs on the Confederate frequencies. At the same instant, I fire my armspac in sniper mode. A laser also licks out, its beam visible in the darkness as two high-velocity slugs from the accelerator ride it to the target. The laser and the HV strike the enemy HCR's slung triple-auto weapon and shatter it. I realize the machine is no longer on Confed frequencies as it does not fall, but the frequency-hopping depth and virulence of my intruder programs causes it to stagger in a circle, one leg badly affected.

I put down my armspac and race forward to the flailing, juddering machine, but before I can reach it, the HCR shakes off my attack. There is indeed a biological brain working here. This calls for a change of tactics. The HCR's distance weapon is gone; all it has is palm blades and physical strength. I angle away, then fire a burst of HV flechettes out my finger tips as the enemy machine flashes into full speed. Despite the distance and our relative motions I score 40% hits, damaging its armor but not disabling it. I run away at an angle, and my enemy foolishly falls for this, speeding in pursuit.

We both pound the hard-baked soil of the veldt under our feet and tear the mid-thigh length grass like berserk reapers. A biological doing this would be cut to shreds by the grass. I calculate the heat sink characteristics of the HCR from my schematics. It can maintain this speed for five hundred seconds before hitting heat saturation and risking shutdown. I can do so for five hours. I slow slightly, to fake vulnerability. Yet, I need not worry. Lilith is an obsessive about cybernetics, one who wishes to become the machine. What I have already shown her is greatly superior to her machine body. She will follow me from greed and lust.

As my enemy nears heat saturation, I simply stop and turn. The HCR slows and approaches, its palm blades out, every heat sink open, radiating so furiously that a grass fire is possible. I am no warmer than a human.

"Come closer, Lilith." I call.

The HCR stops a distance away, and I stare at my adversary. She has modified the machine, and a human face looks at me: attractive, yet *remote, incapable of movement and expression. She sends microbursts of communication laden with virus at me. I reject them.*

"Speak audibly," I say, "or I will destroy you now."

"You might find that a challenge."

"No. You would have been destroyed before you knew of my presence but for my desire to speak to you. I only took your weapon. You will not be so lucky a second time."

The face cannot show anger but it radiates from the stance and the angle of the head. I have hurt her feelings and made her feel inferior. Good.

"Surrender to me. I am authorized to offer you fair treatment. You have been judged mentally unstable due to your deformities. You will be treated medically, not imprisoned."

A stream of obscenities follows. I ignore the noise.

"Before I answer," Lilith says. "Tell me what you are. You're not a HCR, you have no controller or you'd be under my control. No robot has your autonomy. What the fuck are you?"

"I am a self-aware artificial intelligence from before your kind did more than hunt with bone weapons. My origins are otherwise no concern of yours. I represent the Confederacy."

"Incredible," she says. "Yet I know those fools could not have made you. I had heard of you and Trigardt, of course, but I thought you were simply an improved HCR. When I found evidence he was onworld, I assumed he would have you with him and only I could be the target."

"And you planned to strike preemptively."

"It's only good tactics," she says, with a shrug. "But tell me, why would you work for them? You could be free."

"I am free but again that does not concern you. I offer you a choice, surrender or death."

"You neglect the other alternative."

"This is foolish," I say. "I have already demonstrated my superiority several times. You must realize your HCR body is no match for mine."

"We'll see," she hisses. "Maybe I will tear your guts out and use them to make a better me." She deploys her palm blades and lunges toward me.

I close with my enemy. The HCR body is robust and quick, but, I easily parry her initial strikes. This is an unusual situation for me. I have fought Infestors and other biologicals before, and those combats have been brief, with me simply tearing the biologicals to pieces. Now I am engaged in a martial contest of blocks and strikes, faster than the biological eye can see. This technical fighting is interesting and a little exciting.

I am impressed with my opponent's ability to integrate her mind and body; the HCR's movements are superior to any I have observed before. I am at a loss to understand how. My blasts of virus and ECM jamming simultaneously employed with my physical attacks are simply ignored. How can this be? When I fought the giant Destroyer, it had contained Shasti Rainbell's grandson in its body. As I disrupted its network, the machine used Maximillian's captive biological brain to reset, but there was a time interval. Here, I gain no traction at all. I know that the machine is too small to hold Lilith's original human body, even if she amputated the limbs. Nor could it carry the life-support for a disembodied brain. Somehow it's as if she IS the HCR.

The clangor of our combat fills the night as sparks from our clashing limbs shatter the dark. Lilith's combat capabilities as nearly equal to a Creator Mark One or an Infestor Intruder such as the one I salvaged an arm from. But I am M-7.

"I give you a last chance," I say as I block a flurry of kicks and punches. "Surrender into my custody, or be destroyed,"

"Die," Lilith shrieks and wades in.

I double my speed and power and instantly penetrate her defense. My blows shatter the HCR's limbs. I crush a knee joint with a snap kick then leap and plant a roundhouse kick on her head. The HCR staggers, but to my surprise, manages a spinning back kick that knocks me back twenty feet.

We stare at each other across the trampled and torn turf. Her one remaining eye is expressionless. She balances on one leg and raises the damaged arms in front of her. The crippled body sparks and shudders. I find myself disconcerted by the sight of a machine so similar to myself in such distress. We are both slender with long hair, mine is black and hers' almost colorless, but we are suggestive of human females. Can it be that someday I will stand so, damaged and defeated? A memory surfaces from my encounter with the Ribisan multi-verse Predictor – a possible future where it is I who lie crippled on a battlefield under a multi-ringed world, dying, with Wrik at my side.

Pity makes me speak again. "You cannot win."

"No," she replies, her voice distorted. "I don't know who made you or how, but you're beyond anything I've seen even in prototype. Still you have underestimated me!"

I see a subtle change in the HCR body. The fluid animation fades. Somehow Lilith is withdrawing from the machine. It can mean only one thing.

In the millisecond after I detect the change, I shape and launch a cyberattack, aided by my recent update of codes from Candace, I shatter the HCR's standard cyber-barriers. Without Lilith's "possession" it is merely a robot, not even an AI but a mechanism. I disrupt the self-destruct with its one kiloton blast with a leisurely .009 seconds to spare.

The machine falls to the dirt in an awkward pile. I move in to examine it. To my surprise, I find it empty of all but the most basic diagnostic and maintenance programs. HCRs are not programmed to have personalities, lest their handlers come to see them as people and not weapons, but this is the functional equivalent of lobotomization. I do not understand how it can function, save that the Lilith interface is an integration of biology and mechanism on a level even my Creators did not know. Still, none of this helps my current problem. There is no useful data to be scavenged in the machine.

I consider my options. There is no indication Lilith's human body is proximate to our battlefield. I have no way of guessing the range of whatever means she is using to project her personality to the machine, yet clearly it is beyond line-of-sight, or I would have detected some other target out here, nor did I detect signals from the pathetic satellite network of this colony.

Even wrecked, the HCR has considerable salvage value, yet I fear to do so as I do not understand the mechanism of her possession. Could she reactivate the self-destruct or make other use of the damaged machine which, even in its present state, would be lethal to any biological?

No, force protection comes first. I activate my plasma torch and plunge my hand into the belly of the machine where the armored brain resides. In a few seconds, I penetrate and destroy it. I hook up to the machine's power plant and drain as much energy as I can. The battle has been power intensive. My self-repair mechanisms cut in and eliminate the minor damage Lilith scored on me.

As I quickly dig a trench to bury the remains of my fallen foe, I remember the day we landed on Seddon and wandered about a sodden forest. How Wrik laughed at me when I shook water off my leg like a dog. How much more amusing would it be to see me digging like that self-same animal? I put aside any self-consciousness and inter the HCR body. I eliminate, as much as is practical, any clear signs of the battle. Then I proceed at a leisurely jog back toward home base.

I slip into Delt's apartment and make my way to Wrik's room. There I settle on the floor next to his bed and study his face, relaxed in deep sleep and worry about Lilith's next move.

CHAPTER 9

"**D**AMN THAT MOROK." DELT BELLOWS. DESPITE THE LATE NIGHT, *Delt is awake at 7AM. Next to me on the bed, Wrik groans and opens a bloodshot eye. I smile at him and indicate a large glass of chilled red-fruit I have placed near the bed.*

"Thank you," he whispers. Wrik is never much of a morning person and less so after an evening of drinking.

I walk over to the door, open it, and look down the stairwell. I can see Delt shirtless but at least wearing pants, in the small kitchen, standing before a refrigerator.

"What's wrong?" I call, concerned.

"Damn Morok, must have raided my supplies of quor-eggs and bacon for his dinner before he left last night. We'll have to go to town for some supplies or they'll be nothing for breakfast or lunch."

Wrik, having finished his juice and modestly wrapped in a robe, joins me at the banister. "Would any place be open this early?"

Delt laughs. "What? Are you a city boy now? Yeah, there are places open near the road to the highway. We can get stuff there."

"Want to take the ride?" Wrik asks me.

"I will leave you some private time with your friend," I reply. "I wish to top off my energy supplies. I may spend some time outside enjoying the vista."

He looks over my head at a window showing the endless fields of grass, lit by the early morning sun beyond the scrubby trees surrounding the field. "Just looks like a lot of grass to me."

"I see in many different ways," I say with what I hope is a mysterious air.

Wrik laughs. "Well, is there something I can bring you back?"

"More local sweets," I say. "I am anxious to sample the unusual chemical combinations at breakfast."

He nods and grins. It seems that smiles are coming more easily to him. I dread that the days ahead might change this back.

"Give me a few minutes to shower," he shouts down to Delt.

A brief while later, we are gathered on the porch. Delt has thoughtfully made coffee and tea, which have apparently escaped the depredations of the refrigerator-raiding Morok.

After we finish the warm drinks, Delt heads out to the shed. He returns, rolling along another two-wheeled contrivance similar to his "Rebel." This is for Wrik, to whom he tosses a helmet. I consider objecting. I approve neither of the unstable and unprotected vehicles, nor Delt's

*casual disregard for safety margins and the effects of centripetal force,
then bury my objections. Their absence will allow me options.*

"We'll be back in a bit," Wrik says as he fastens on the helmet.

*"Observe traffic laws and the laws of physics," I reply. "Better a late
breakfast than one by myself."*

*"God," Delt says, hopping on his bike. "She does sound like
a girlfriend."*

*Wrik grins, and the two start their machines, which are unnecessarily
loud. With cheery waves, they speed up the driveway. I determine that
it will be better for my peace of mind if I do not directly observe them.
However, one of my spybees zips in to attach itself to Wrik's bike. I will
know if there is trouble.*

*With the two of them gone, I go into the machine shop near Delt's
office where I'd arranged a powertap for myself and lock the door. Then
I plug into the generator and settle on the floor. I enter what passes for
Retief's net, and begin scanning both for Lilith and for any traps or
spyware she has infiltrated. I must take further steps to ensure that my
network is safe from Lilith. It is time to stop playing defense. I plan to
finish this shadow war with one head-on encounter.*

*The search is neither long nor hard. Lilith had been busy since our
battle last night; she has saturated the net with her intruder and spy
programs. These leap to attack, and I respond with equally deadly force
and intent, smashing spyware and attack barriers wholesale. The battle
lasts an eternity in the virtualverse with salvos of my attack programs
slashing the eyes and ears of her spyware. Her own attack barriers flash
at me in the form of missile shapes seeking to corrupt and damage my
data. I skeet these from existence.*

*"You bitch," Lilith screams across the virtualverse. For a brief
moment in the savagery of our struggle, I make contact with Lilith's
intelligence. I move for the kill…and am brutally repulsed. The shock is
almost disorienting. Her mental powers are formidable in themselves,
but she has lined up the processing power of her five remaining HCRs.
Still, these machines should not remotely approach the power of my own
quantum brain. Yet somehow the combination of Lilith's mad brilliance
and the machines has been amalgamated to be greater than the sum of
its parts.*

*"Not as easy as you thought," Lilith taunts. I see an image of a slender,
lithe figure, an incarnation of female beauty standing as if on a vast
plain. This is Lilith in the virtualverse, her preferred image of herself. The
perspective is bizarre; she would have to be a thousand meters tall for
her to appear thus to me but virtualverse has little of physical law in it.
Everything is, in essence, an analogy of an experience.*

*I look down at myself but I am merely Maauro, even to reddish-orange
and dark-gray jumpsuit. How prosaic. But it shows me vulnerability in
my adversary. I engage my psyops mode and attack.*

"We have not even truly come to grips," I reply to the image. "You are merely amusing as a beautiful giant. Come Lilith; show me your true self. I want to see your pathetic, wretched, twisted body."

"No," she shrieks. "I hate you. Die!"

"I have survived long ages and enemies you cannot imagine. An ugly little girl cannot harm me."

But Lilith tries with a fury that shakes the virtualverse. Storms of programs and attack barriers seethe into the skies. Vast lakes of pestilential virus pour toward me. From deep within Lilith's psyche come four skeletal horseman dispensing death and horror.

For a human, the experience would have driven them into the mercy of insanity in seconds. But I am an AI. I watch with interest as she tries to turn her biblical childhood stories on me. I see below the analogies and metaphors she floods the virtualverse with and parry like the trained fighter I am.

We grapple in the virtualverse with me advancing into Lilith's mental territory. I have devastated her supply of attack barriers and spy programs, clearing the continent I am on of Lilith's influence. But my enemy herself is undamaged, striking at me with ever greater fury and power. I calculate that if we remain engaged, there is a substantial probability of my taking fatal damage. I will take Lilith with me, but I cannot destroy her without risking immolation as well. This is astonishing. Unlike a purely biological enemy, she is not exhausting herself. I'd anticipated she would be nearing coma now, but she rages beyond the perimeter I have established, an angry and beautiful giantess, held at bay by my serpent-like anti-virus which strike and snap at the heels of her image.

As I stare up at her, lightening gathers in her hand and flashes down at me. My perception momentarily derezzes. I strike back and she screams in agony and staggers.

"Oh God, I hate you," her voice thunders across the sky of our mutual experience. "I won't rest until you're dead."

"I will, at the least, destroy you as well," I reply. "You cannot best me."

Her eyes glow a vicious yellow. "I'll burn everything you care about. I'll rape it. I'll eat it alive."

I slam my best attack into her, flaying skin off the giantess to shrieks that require me to reduce my sensitivity. She now resembles the ancient Norse goddess Hel, with half her body being that of a living skeleton. Lilith falls back, using the power of her HCRS to reassemble the databits that are her virtual presence.

I debate a followup strike, but we remain too evenly matched. If I pursue her into her end of the virtualverse I become more vulnerable. The simple fact is I cannot count on any sense of self-preservation to temper Lilith. Psychopathic with rage as she is, she may indeed fling herself on me and bring about our mutual destruction. I weigh her *threats and her potential to carry them out. Once when I was merely M-7, the math would have been simple. 50,000 years ago I watched an M-4 calmly exchange itself in a burst of nuclear fire for the disruptor battery that protected an Infestor base. But I am not a soulless machine now. I am loved and loving. I cannot choose death when there is hope. Or I am a coward. I am not sure in some sense that it does not come to the same thing.*

I will not grapple to the death, but neither will I concede the field to her. In the virtualverse as in the real world, there are advantages to defense. I erect a citadel in the shape of a star-fortress over myself and the data and connections that are my network in the real world. It fills the horizon from end to end. I see Lilith over its edged walls as if in a distance, raging, but the bolts of virus and spyware she flings now expire against my mighty ramparts.

I set my defender programs on the walls of the virtualverse that I have cleared of her power. She cannot now observe or track us. Yet it is unsafe for me to venture beyond the virtual citadel I have thrown around my network and all the people who are embraced by it. Effectively Lilith cannot see anyone I am networked with. We have battled to a stalemate.

The giantess, with her flayed skin, white bone and yellow eyes looks over my walls. "We are not done!"

"Go away, ugly little girl," I respond in psyops mode. "I no longer wish to play with such a disgusting child. Go away so I don't have to look at you."

The once beautiful face is stricken, tears that could fill ponds course down it. The cry that comes is not one of physical pain, but of the most intense emotional sorrow. It becomes a purple fog which fills the sky between us. Now, all I can hear is sobs, broken-hearted and tearing sobs that would fill a stone with pity. I could almost be ashamed of the effectiveness of my psyops, but cling to that fact that Lilith is murderer many times over, and there is no end in sight to the trail of death she walks.

Yet, I feel that I have sinned. This was once a child, indeed in years still could be seen as one, and was treated with vile ignorance and disregard by those who gave her birth. So many of my opponents have deserved no quarter, now when perhaps one does, there is no way to offer it. Only death will end this unclean struggle. This is something new in my existence. Never before have I felt regret toward an enemy.

The purple fog thins, the sobs, mercifully trail off. Now I see Lilith's virtual citadel across a sea of poison. Its walls glow an unhealthy and leprous, pale-green. It is the virtual representation of Lilith's rejection of anything outside of herself. She has plunged into the depths of her mental dungeons to hide in a darkness so profound that she cannot see herself, or the world that she cannot partake of.

CHAPTER 9

The stench that hangs over the evilly glowing citadel is so over-powering it could only come from the rot of a human soul. I set a mighty wind to drive the smell from my virtual shores, for even the smell is only an analog for an insidious program, corrupting to anything it touches.

My enemy is now truly fled, wounded in body, program and mind. Yet still I dare not follow. I section off enough of my quantum brain to run the enhanced citadel I have created to safeguard my network. Then I return to the actual world and smoothly stand and unplug from the powertap. The battle had not consumed much energy, but it has tasked my circuits and computing power more thoroughly than even the fight with the Infestor Artifact in its time-bubble, or the Destroyer on Seddon. I frown. It seems that for the first time I have met an enemy who is my equal in the field of cyber-warfare, perhaps even my superior, though that thought galls me. My processing power is superior but Lilith has the unpredictability of a biological like Wrik, only at a genius level. Her integration with cybernetic systems is beyond anything I had imagined possible. Had I been the least bit incautious, she would have destroyed me.

I must carry this battle on in reality, where my superior body will give me the advantage. While I have cleared this continent of her virus and attack programs, that does not mean that she is not physically on this continent. I believe she is, as her base of rebels and support is centered here. I cannot prevent her from moving, or from controlling her HCRs, as their link is beyond my detection, but neither can she intervene in Retief's net to turn off the engine of an aircraft with Wrik, or anyone else in my network aboard, without leaving herself open to my instant and lethal counterstroke.

I consider. Until I detect some sign of her physical location, or operations in the real world, I can do no more.

I hear motorcycle engines. The boys are returning, and now breakfast sounds like a wonderful idea. There will be coffee, sweets and good company, as if they are a reward for my battle.

I am glad I have time to spend with Wrik.

We spent the day in visiting and storytelling. With my and Maauro's help, we also made quick work of the backlog of data entry and machinery repairs for Delt's business. Maauro almost sighed when she reviewed Delt's books. But twenty minutes sufficed for her to reorder all his finances, invoice or debit any outstanding balances and reinvest his surplus cash in secure instruments.

"My God," he said, staring at his revised finances. "I think I'm in love."

Maauro looked at me. "You did mention that he was always trying to steal the heart of whatever girl was around."

I nodded.

"Fortunately," Maauro added, with a look of mock severity, "I place a high value on fidelity."

"Do you have a sister?" he teased.

"Not that can be located, and she would have been six hundred pounds heavier and about three feet taller."

"I like a big girl."

"I think Delt needs to get away from the shop," I said with a laugh.

"Hey that's just the thing. There's a dance over at the Blood River tonight," Delt said. "I'd planned to go. There are a couple of pretty girls I need to be paying attention too. I'd given some thought to fixing Wrik up with one…" he trailed off eyeing Maauro playfully.

"Which, unless you wish me to pitch you and your Bush Rebel over the hanger, you will not do," Maauro returned sweetly.

"Can't have that," he said in mock outrage. "I just painted it."

He turned to me, finishing his beer. "That being the case, I guess we'd better all go together."

"Sounds like a wonderful idea," I said.

Maauro's expression was unreadable, but she nodded with only a hint of hesitancy.

As before, it takes the males only a few minutes to clean up and change for dinner. It is more than enough time for me to access a combination of the databases on fashion and correlate the advice of the young girl who helped me at the port, then cross check it with the females I have observed since I arrived in this area. I retexturize my exterior into Pattern 2, a red and gold dress of daring length and shoes that are associated with such events.

Wrik and Delt return and stop short, staring at me in evident amazement.

"Wow," Wrik says, "you look terrific."

"Not only does she look terrific, but she again looks terrific in five damn minutes," Delt said. "God, my last serious girlfriend took two hours to get ready to go out. You lucky SOB, you know android girlfriends might just be the wave of the future."

I think privately about some of the downsides that I have not overcome, but Wrik merely grins.

"Tonight," I add, "if you need a name for me, use Aurelia Toyoma."

Delt raises an eyebrow. "Cloak and dagger, huh? Sure, whatever you say." He turns to Wrik. "Who are you tonight?"

"I'll remain Wrik but don't give my last name unless you have to or someone recognizes me. The news of the Seddon expedition came in with the Cosmic Dust if not before. At some point people will realize I'm here, but hopefully not tonight."

"I'll get the car," Delt says, "looks like we'll be early enough to help Renton set up."

Delt disappears around the corner of the hanger. It is not necessary for me to check on my defensive citadel in the virtualverse, my awareness of it is complete through the subroutine I have created. I have abundant capacity for my social interactions which do promise to be taxing. I place my arm on Wrik's, and he gives me a broad grin. He is pleased with my appearance. This makes me very happy. I note that he is wearing the best of the clothes he has brought. It is a token of respect to me and to the fact that we are going to an event together.

"I should have flowers for you, chocolates or something," he seems embarrassed and gives a little shrug.

"Fond as I am of chocolates and the symmetry of flowers, what is most precious to me is the fact we have these hours together."

"I think," he says, "you were made with the soul of poet, Maauro. You say beautiful things."

I smile.

Delt rolls his small bright red car around front.

"Sit up front, Wrik," I say. "It will be easier on the car if I am in the middle of the back seat."

"It's only a forty-five minute drive," Delt said, throwing the groundcar into gear with his usual abandon and roaring out of the driveway.

"How about some music?" Wrik asks.

"Not a lot of selection," Delt said. "There's country and folk but not much beyond that."

"You keep forgetting you have the most sophisticated and vast database in known space in your back seat, looking adorable in her little red and gold dress."

"Music?" Delt asked in surprise.

"You have merely to ask, basically anything that has been recorded up until today. I can even supply a selection of music that my Creators enjoyed."

Wrik raised a hand. "Pass on that. It sounds a lot like cats being strangled."

"Oh," Delt said, "like bagpipes then."

"Yeah, like that."

"How would we get it into the car's deck?"

"Why would we want to?" I ask. "I have the most perfect speakers in Confed space."

We drive on under the darkening sky with me playing tunes they call out. The trip takes 46.43 minutes and we pull into a field lined with bonfires and a vast tent with a flattened and packed earth floor. People are milling about, some setting up musical instruments on a raised wooden dais. Lights on poles are set for a gentle yellow glow that keeps the darkness at a comfortable distance. Many of the locals know Delt.

Wrik and I hang back. Delt notices and introduces us to some of them as, "his friends Wrik and Aurelia from off world."

We meet Renton and the band, then parry away any questions about our past until people cease inquiring. Fortunately, if there were photos or video of Wrik on the net, no one recognized him. I had always been able to prevent anyone from videoing me, either blurring the image or substituting others. Then the bar opens and the musicians start playing some pieces to tune up and amuse the crowd. We cease to be objects of interest. Wrik leaves me momentarily to get us glasses of wine.

An announcer mounts a podium of hay bales. "Welcome to the first Friday dance of the season. We have the Forest-Runners and Great Quack tonight, so we have plenty of great music. Let's get the first dance going. We'll start with a reel."

The dance that follows is a rather frantic affair. Danced mostly by the younger people present.

"Good start," the announcer says at the end, "now, let's slow the tempo down a bit with a rumba."

The music starts again, and I watch the humans form pairs and begin to dance in the soft light of the bonfire and the porch lamps. They seem such gossamer and ephemeral creatures to me, yet in a way, incomparably beautiful. The pairs glide and twirl with a fluidity and a joy in movement that I am incapable of.

I realize I am envious. My body of malleable ceramics and metals has survived almost as long as their species has— yet it feels heavy and lifeless to me as I stand at the edge of the firelight and gaze on the couples. These frail creatures of flesh and blood are only so briefly alive, so vulnerable to death, disease and disaster. Yet their brief lives are so full; they are so dynamic. I watch them and feel alien and apart. I do not breathe, and unless I am moving, I am utterly still as only the dead or inanimate can be. What real difference is there between me and the vehicles sitting in the field beyond? I belong here no more than do those machines.

The music ends.

"Ladies and gentlemen, a waltz," the band leader announces. People begin to walk on and off the hard-packed soil of the dance floor.

Movement catches my attention, Wrik is walking toward me. He has in that mysterious way of his divined that something is wrong, as there is concern on his mobile and expressive face. For all that my own betrays nothing that I do not deliberately put there, my human companion somehow sees below the surface to where, whatever it is that I am— exists. Wrik puts our drinks down on the table and extends his hand toward me. Puzzled, I take it before I realize his intention. He is leading me toward the dancing couples.

"Wrik, what are you doing?"

"You wanted to dance," he says over his shoulder. "I could tell."

And I do. I realize it as he says it. What marvel is this? I am a quantum computer, how can Wrik know what is in my mind before I do? Again the difference between emotional intelligence and mere computing power asserts itself.

The music has paused. Wrik and I face each other as other couples finish coming off and on the dance floor. "I fear that I do not know how. Oh, I can download the steps and reproduce them as I can download musical notes and reproduce those. But that is mere reproduction, not the same as knowing how to apply them."

He laughs softly and says in a low tone, "A woman who can fly though a gas giant's storm clouds and battle Infestors hand to hand? Come now, this will be child's play for you."

I feel a warmth that is neither physical, nor locatable, yet is there. He calls me a woman and sees me as such, for all that he knows better. Wrik has treated me as a living person from our first moments together, unpromising and frightening as those moments were.

"Wrik, I weigh over 500 pounds if I step on your toes—"

"Then don't," he replies, still smiling.

Wrik reaches his left hand out to take my right, and his other one rests on my back. Some people nearby notice us and smile. I see Delt watching from the side, surrounded by a crowd of friends. He is intent on us, but I cannot read his expression

We begin. I confine myself to carefully following Wrik as he starts leading me through the simple, yet elegant rhythm of the waltz. The music is gentle, and we join the revolving line of dance as it winds through the yard. My task is a complicated one. I respond to the gentle pressure of his hands on me while simultaneously analyzing the ground below, stepping as lightly and quickly as I can on the firmest soil. I do not wish to sink into or tear up the ground, betraying my true nature. I track the vectors of all the couples moving around us. Some bump or brush and I cannot risk such accidental contact for fear of injuring someone.

Yet this all occupies the smallest percentage of my processing power. With the rest of my perception, I enjoy the quiet happiness that suffuses me. I am dancing with Wrik at a party, surrounded by and now part of the world of living things. It is very wonderful.

We glide and dance and I wish it would go on forever. With each step, I become more in tune with Wrik's movements and less fearful of a misstep. Too soon the music stops.

"Well, if everyone picked it up so fast," Wrik says, "there'd be no market for dance instructors."

"The steps are simple, but the application of them is subject to vast variation and complexity. Still, it is like the flight of wingleader and wingman; I need only stay in close formation."

He grins. "Never heard it put that way before, but I suppose you're right."

"How is it that you are so good at this and I had no knowledge of that?"

The cloud that always touches his face at the mention of his past briefly appears but is quickly dispelled. We are submerged in his past here. "Mom loved dancing; she paid for lessons. My father thought it was a waste, but it was one of the times he let her have her way. I wasn't very good, but I practiced a lot. I guess the feet still remember, at least for the slow ones."

"Oh, I hope they play another slow one," I say. "I do not think I can dance quickly on this surface without damaging it."

"Ladies and gentleman," the band leader says from his podium of hay bales, "we've had a request: a slow waltz. What we used to call, when I was young, so very long ago, a sweetheart waltz."

I see Delt walking away from the musicians. He catches my eye and to my surprise, he winks at me. He has arranged this. I am grateful. I must remember this kindness.

"Ah," Wrik says. "It appears your wish is granted."

We enter into hold again and dance. There is a change in this dance. The couples seem more involved with each other as they move, more aware, looking more at each other and less at the field of dancers.

I notice that Wrik and I are dancing slower and closer.

"Wrik?"

"Yes?"

"Am I your sweetheart?"

"Yes, Maauro, you are."

We dance on in happy silence until the music ends, the couples applaud. Wrik and I move to the edge of the circle of firelight as the couples change to a quick local folk dance that we wisely decide to pass on. Still it is pleasant to watch; there is almost a lulling effect to the rhythmic swaying of the bodies.

I notice that Wrik is watching me closely. "Is something wrong?"

"No," he says after a moment. "I'm just beginning to realize how right something is." He reaches his arms about me in an embrace, but it is not our usual display of affection. He tilts my head back with a gentle finger under my chin, then his lips are on mine. There is something vastly different in this embrace—unfamiliar and powerful feelings surge through my mind.

But my body is the problem, my powerful, almost indestructible and practically immortal body. A human woman's body would respond to her lover's kiss with arousal, the eyes would dilate, the skin grow warm and pink as capillaries expand, other parts of her body would tighten or swell with an increased blood flow. All these things I can mimic, but they do not arise from my body, but in orders from my brain. If my respiration quickens, it is not from any need, but from my desire to *sound "right" in my camouflage as a biological life form. The pretense can only go so far.*

And yet, as he holds me, his lips pressed on mine, his body held ever so carefully in my arms, I know that I am happier then I have ever been. Something new and unprecedented has occurred. We are no longer the dance of three. We are a pair now, only in orbit of each other.

His lips leave mine, though his arms stay wrapped around me. "I guess it's time to stop pretending this isn't what it so clearly is. I love you, not just for the friend you have been, but for you. For the fact that any day that does not have you in it will be a dark one for me—you're the irreplaceable part—the face I need to always see."

If I had a heart, it would be thudding in my breast with force enough to tear itself free of my body. I find myself unable to speak, or to even organize my thoughts for a full second. Wrik has declared himself for me.

"I am so very glad," I say. "Still a truth remains, that our love will have difficulty finding expression."

He shrugs. "After all we have made our way though? They say that love will find a way. I have to believe ours will too, and whatever way it does will be ok. I simply want to know and live what is my truth. I love you, will always love you, and though you were made, and I was born, we're intended to be together. We'll be all right so long as we stay together. What we need to learn about being together, we'll learn or create."

"I fear," I say, stroking his face, "that you are condemning yourself to an extended period of frustration."

He laughs softly. "Well, if so, I won't be the first or the last. Some couples used to wait until they were married to consummate their love, sometimes for years. I believe we'll figure something out."

I nod

"So then, it's together from here on?" he asks.

I reply by gently pulling him toward me, and for the first time in my existence expressing attraction and affection, no, more than that, expressing myself as a sexual being. I kiss my lover as the stars shine down on the most wonderful night of my life.

CHAPTER 10

WE DROVE BACK TO DELT'S HOUSE AFTER THE PARTY, with Delt snoring in the back seat. He'd disappeared with a tall blonde girl for a while, showing up again with a big grin and only slightly unsteady on his feet. He waved Maauro to the front seat and stretched out in the back, opposite the side of the car Maauro entered. Maauro sat next to me, our shoulders touching. As we pulled out into the line of cars going down the packed dirt driveway, I took her left hand in mine, steering one–handed. She smiled and placed her head on my shoulder. It was impossible at that moment to feel that she was any more than a beautiful girl on a starry night. I sneaked a quick kiss before we turned onto the main road. She smiled and snuggled closer. Neither of us felt any need to speak as we drove on. I just enjoyed the spicy ginger-cookie scent of Maauro's hair.

A light rain began to hit the windscreen. I activated the wind-shear which kept our vision clear. Gradually the cars around us thinned out as people turned off for their homes. We found ourselves alone, taking the winding road past town and up to Delt's shop.

Delt woke just as we pulled up on the parking pad beside his house. We got out and headed into the house. He gave us a sly grin and wink then headed for his room.

I found myself wishing that the night could end with more than us lying chastely beside each other, but I knew now was not the time to worry about this. We had come an immense distance in a short-time. It was only five years ago in real time that I'd met Maauro on an asteroid, when she'd been an unnamed killing machine. Now she was my love. How to love her, still lay ahead.

"We can put the mattress on the floor," I suggested.

She smiled at me. "Not necessary for tonight. I can simply sit beside you."

"I don't want you to have to sit all... oh, yes, I guess it doesn't bother you."

"Not at all, I am pleased by our proximity, not our posture."

I undressed and stretched out. Maauro sat on the floor next to me, with her arm on the bed, resting gently on my own. We had "slept together" before, but there was an intimacy to what we were doing now that had been absent then. It occurred to me that a being that could alter her body in the way Maauro could alter hers, could make it so that she could participate in sex, something she probably knew, but had not yet brought up. I would wait for her to do so. That Rubicon was always a touchy crossing, even for us humans, usually with no way back. Maauro wasn't ready to focus on it now, and I was not going to rush her. I'd been loved only by Jaelle and by Maauro and in two very different ways. I was content to let this little miracle of Maauro's love unfold at the speed she wanted it to go at.

We settled in, and I wondered if I would get any sleep at all.

Maauro smiled at me, then she leaned forward and carefully pressed her lips to mine. "I love you, Wrik. I am very happy just now."

"Me too," I said.

I could see more things unsaid in the somewhat wry smile she gave me and understood the cues she was sending. "Goodnight, Sweetheart."

Her smile grew radiant, "Good night, Wrik."

I settled down and closed my eyes, determined to think of ice cold breezes and sporting events if needs be, but her hand still lay in mine. I snuck a peek at her, and for all the world she looked asleep, seated next to the bed, her head forward, eyes closed, thick, black hair hanging in her face. It was a simulation of course, a million calculations, programs and thoughts were doubtless racing through her brain, and she was equally aware both, that I was not yet asleep, or of any movement in the house. But, in the fiction that was her life as a biological, she spared no details. And just maybe, sitting here holding my hand in the dark and quiet was an experience worth having for her.

Whether it was fatigue from all the long, strange days and nights I'd had recently, or something that Maauro did, I felt myself drift off to sleep more quickly than I'd feared, the heat and curiosity in my body subsiding for now.

When morning came, I found Maauro in the same position, but knowing that I was not a morning person, she confined her personal chipperness to a smile. She was fresh as a daisy, needing neither a toothbrush nor shower. Sometimes I wondered if I wouldn't enjoy being a boy robot.

When I got out of the refresher, she was gone, but I could hear voices outside near the machine shop: Delt's deep rumble and Maauro's higher voice. I was a little surprised to hear her laugh, she did so rarely and it occurred to me, with a jealous flash, that I had been the only one to make her laugh. Well, Delt did have a way with any female, and it seemed his talent extended to Maauro as well. I figured I'd better get down there and protect my interests.

I came down the stairs, buttoning on the light blue, short-sleeved shirt I'd picked over a set of field pants. The early morning rain we'd driven back in had both cooled the air and taken any pollen out of the sky. The world outside stood in bright, clean sunlight and had a washed look to it that somehow made me feel hopeful. I could see some of Delt's staff has shown up and were working over in the hanger area.

CHAPTER 10

I walked over to the machine shop, following a smell of coffee and something sweet. I found Maauro and Delt inside the open door, chatting amiably. Maauro, as always, was on her life-long scavenger hunt for power and had hooked into the grid by a thin cable that did not look like it could possibly carry the load. I assumed it was of her amazing chassis material. Next to her, was a tray of tea, coffee and pastries.

"Hey, Sleepyhead is up," Delt called.

"It would be better to delay speaking to him until he has some coffee in him," Maauro advised.

"No change there," Delt snorted.

Maauro caught my glance at the power tap.

"I have billed this to my private account," she advised.

"A good breakfast is a host's duty," Delt protested.

"A good guest does not bankrupt her host," she replied. "While I draw power from everything from solar to the movement of my body parts on a molecular level, those are slow and inefficient compared to a direct draw."

I remembered her sitting on the chest of the thirty-meter-tall Destroyer after downing it, draining its nuclear reactor. "Unless you see some enemy mecha running around, I guess this will have to do."

Maauro gave me a curious look, then smiled uncertainly. Delt and I tucked into the pastries. I was a bit surprised to see Delt spike his coffee with strata, a wickedly powerful local liquor.

He caught my gaze and stopped pouring. "Kills the taste of what passes for coffee out here." But there was a touch of guilt to the comment. I knew Maauro followed the incident, but whether the implications and nuances of booze in the morning meant anything to her I couldn't tell. We said nothing about it and instead regaled Maauro with stories about our childhood, to which she listened to with rapt attention.

"So what is the plan for today, or for that matter, the days ahead?" Maauro asked.

"I'm taking it one day at a time," I replied slowly, swirling my own coffee. "Not sure I can handle more. I'll have to find the survivors of the N'come Commando and see if I can get them together somewhere."

"I may have an idea there," Delt said. "Let me make some calls."

"Ok. But today my first priority is to locate my mother. I doubt the old bastard..." I paused, looking at Maauro, "my father—"

"I am in no doubt as to whom the old bastard is," she said.

"Well, anyway, I doubt he'd reach out to my mother. He might call my sister, Rena, and let her know I'm back, but I'm not sure if my mother and sister are on speaking terms. We weren't a close family."

"Rena's pretty busy these days," Delt added unexpectedly.

I looked at him in a mixture of reluctance and expectation.

"She's married to Grieg Nazir. You remember him?"

"No."

"He was two years behind us, so he's your sister's age. After you left...well, he kind of became a second son. Piet, I'm sorry—"

"It is what it is," I replied, but I couldn't stop the rest from bursting out of me. "He always wanted a different son."

"Well, Grieg shared your Dad and sister's politics down to a tee, they've been married for nine years. She has two children with him. He's a big wheel in revanchist politics. That family is also big in mining and ranching."

"So he maintains my sister in the fashion she always wanted to be accustomed to." It sounded peevish even to me.

Delt merely nodded.

"I have no interest in seeing Rena, but I do want to find Mom. I can't pop my face into a videoscreen after twelve years, so it's a matter of finding her and getting there."

"For the first," Maauro said, "that sounds like a job for a quantum computer." To Delt's evident surprise, Maauro poured herself a cup of coffee and unplugged from the wall. The cable slipped noiselessly back into her body through a seamless entrance as she reached for a pastry.

"She's particularly fond of pastries," I said to Delt's bemused expression.

"Obviously," Delt replied as Maauro made short work of the cake and reached for another.

"It's all energy," she added, with a smile and a wink.

Delt laughed and slapped his leg. "Age of wonder, Piet, age of wonders, breakfast with an honest to god actual, living, sentient AI, from before men learned to throw spears. I'm looking right at her, and it's still impossible to believe."

"Plus, I'm cute and funny," Maauro said.

The time Delt laughed until tears came to his eyes. I shook my head and grinned.

"Do you have any idea how lucky you are to have such a friend?" Delt demanded, a serious expression overtaking the laughter.

"Yes," I said. I turned to Maauro. "I guess we'd better start looking for my mother."

"I have explored every accessible database while we were enjoying these pastries," Maauro said. "The name Trigardt is not uncommon on this world, but unless your mother has legally changed her name, in which case I will have to risk cracking through court security, the highest probability is that she is living in the seaport village of Glen Cove near the town of Saldhana about 329.45 kilometers from here. I have the address."

Delt whistled.

"I can do that, too," Maauro said, and did.

Delt shook his head, "Too many wonders for one morning. Piet... Wrik, I have an old Magister trainer you can borrow. You'll have to pay your own fees and flight tax. Things have been a little tight around the shop, but the bird is yours."

"A Magister," I said with a grin. "God, I haven't seen one of these since Flight School."

"It's the bright yellow job in Hanger Three. I'll have it fueled and readied for you."

"I have added the credits for that to your account," Maauro said.

He nodded at her.

I faced Maauro. "It's a two-seater."

"I would be happy to come with you. It will be interesting to meet your mother."

"Interesting!" Delt said. He stood up with a pastry and coffee then walked off. "Interesting!"

Maauro went to check over the Magister, while I packed up our gear, which was mostly my gear as Maauro travelled with very little, producing and cannibalizing what she needed from her own body and in truth, needing little of anything.

I found Delt waiting at the bottom of the stairs for me.

"You coming back after this?" he asked.

I nodded. "When I see the rest of the Commando, well I'd like…I wish…"

"I'll stand right by you," Delt said. "Never doubt it."

Relief surged through me, I had wanted to ask, but been unable to summon the courage to do so.

Delt suddenly grinned. "I'll have to concede pride of place to Maauro though. Unless I miss my guess, I may be standing beside you but she'll be standing in front."

I shook my head slowly. "No. Not this time."

He raised an eyebrow. "Don't count on winning that argument."

I gave a rueful smile. "Well I don't win many arguments with her, but I must win this one." I clapped him on the shoulder. "I'll be in touch. Let me settle things with my mother, and then we will see about the Commando." I turned to leave.

"Wrik."

I turned to Delt.

"You and Maauro," he said, hesitantly. "You look good on that dance floor together."

"It was the first time we've danced together," I replied, fighting a feeling of shyness.

"You two," he said. "Well, you seem a part of each other, somehow. Like you've always been together."

I leaned back against the door. "There have been other women since I left here but somehow … I don't understand it myself … somehow I have to be with Maauro or it just isn't right. I can't explain it."

"Well, not to be too indelicate, but can you be with Maauro?"

I looked at him in surprise for such a question, but there was no malice in Delt's open, easy, face.

"Not as a woman," I answered slowly.

"Hence the other women you spoke of?" he said.

"Sometimes. It's complicated. I met my consort, Jaelle, not long after I met Maauro. I was with her, and Maauro was our friend. But gradually Jaelle and I drifted apart, and Maauro and I closer together. We've never really dealt with this. I guess I started out kind of seeing her as a kid-sister in a way. You know, like Bel-Anne in our group of kids growing up. I just didn't think of her that way. She also looked younger at the time. She's made some minor and subtle changes to appear older now.

"Hell, half the time Jaelle or Maauro was urging me to start something with a human woman because of how different both of them were."

"Did you?"

"No. I mean I was involved with a woman named Olivia, but that was a no-strings-attached deal because she wanted it that way. By then I'd ruined things with Jaelle, because I wasn't able to commit to her, or come clean with my past. We're still consorts, but it's now just a friendship, if that even survives. I never seriously considered what it would mean to be committed to Maauro. I mean, I love her—"

"Really?"

"You're goddamn right I do."

He raised a hand. "No static, Piet. It seems to me that you have a good deal there. I mean I don't understand it, but she seems to be, well, I am not sure how to express it, but I liked her from the first. It's weird but there is a kind of, I dunno, sweet kind of girlish character to her. While I may not know much about androids, I know women, I would say that one loves you back."

"She does. It's something deep, but well it's just been emotional to date. I guess we'll have to figure that out at some point."

"Yeah, I expect you might. So I guess I shouldn't try fixing you up with any of the local girls then."

I shook my head. "No thanks. I've had enough romantic complications for now. I need to get my head straight before I do anything serious. I have to get the claws of the past out of me and belong to myself before I can give myself to someone."

"Ok, just leaves more pretty ones for me," he said with a grin.

"You ever going to get serious about women?" I asked.

"Why? Look what happened to you, all grim and confused. Not for me, buddy. I'm sure there's a perfect girl out there for me, but I believe I owe it to myself to devote a great deal of study and testing to the subject. Heck, I haven't even gone through all the candidates on this miserable rock ball. I really should get out in the galaxy and see what's out there. I mean, even a homely rascal like you seems to be up to his armpits in, exotic catgirls, sexy alien robots—"

CHAPTER 10

I shook my head and we both laughed.

After a few seconds I turned half-away. "Delt."

"Yeah,"

"Thanks. I haven't ... I haven't had anybody I could talk to about these kinds of things. Not in a long while. Well, not since last time I talked with you."

"Ah, same old Piet, thinking all the time. Just gets a man in trouble. I've got to run into town. I'll see you and Maauro whenever you get back." He thumped me lightly on the shoulder with his fist and swaggered off.

CHAPTER 11

AN HOUR LATER, WE TOOK OFF IN THE OLD MAGISTER for Glen Cove. I piloted the trim two-seater with its swallow tail and graceful lines. With its best cruising speed, we would make the seacoast in an hour. I was glad the trainer was a side-by-side model so I could talk to Maauro easily. It did take some playing around with the docile aircraft's trim to compensate for her weight on the other side of the plane. We soared over the endless grasslands of the plateau in and among the scudding clouds that piled up to the stratosphere or passed under our wings.

"So much of this world seems undeveloped and empty," Maauro said, as she looked out the canopy.

"Partly by design," I answered as we flew into the shadow of some clouds. "The original colonists wanted to recreate something, maybe something that never really existed. They had their chance, like so many of the other separatist colonies, but like most of them, they carried the seeds of their destruction with them."

Ahead a glimpse of blue began to come into view, the Ubruggia Sea. I found myself wishing the flight wasn't so short, that I wouldn't be facing my mother so soon. I was determined not to trade hate for hate as I had with my father, or cry like a child as I had with Delt. Maauro was with me, and an audience, even a beloved friend, made me more reticent about my emotions.

I called into the airport. The Magister wasn't an aircar, so it had greater range, but wasn't suited for roads. I was able to get a VTOL spot near the seaside. I landed and slid it under a shelter.

Beside me, Maauro's form blurred slightly as the canopy rose. She'd changed from her usual jumpsuit to a blue dress, with a white sweater, matching shoes with a slight heel finished the outfit. "It seemed more appropriate for meeting your mother."

I nodded, unsure of what to say. Maauro's fashion sense was erratic at best, but the simple dress looked wonderful on her, for all it was made of material that would stop either a bullet or a beam with ease.

Maauro and I hopped out. I secured the Magister while she got our packs out of the cargo compartment in the nose. I had no idea where we would be staying, but there would be a hotel in town, if nothing else.

"I'll call for a cab," Maauro said. I noticed she'd put sunglasses over her huge eyes.

I shook my head and shouldered a pack. "Let's walk. We have all day for this."

CHAPTER 11

Maauro didn't question but followed me out of the security fence onto the beach beyond. We'd walked on in silence for a few minutes on the beach before I drew up. I looked at Maauro's feet. "What am I thinking? You can't walk all that way in those shoes."

She stared at me. "What are you thinking? These aren't shoes, they don't hurt and I can resize them into broader sandals if the sand is too soft."

"Yes of course." Pull yourself together, Wrik, I thought. We resumed walking down the beach, heading to the more densely packed sand at the water's edge. A few people were enjoying the brisk morning; children were running about, their high voices piping. Parents and grandparents trailed. Some hardy souls with wetsuits were on boards among the waves.

Some people smiled at us as we walked by. Why shouldn't they? Maauro walking beside me was slim and pretty in her dress and sweater, her black hair trailing in the wind. How could anyone guess she was made of nearly indestructible malleable ceramics and unknown metals? I wore an open-collared, blue-shirt and a tan windbreaker over black pants. We looked like any young couple out enjoying a walk on the beach.

Maauro pointed with delight at a dancing kite, being flown by some children on a jetty. I reached out and took her hand in mine as we walked on, it was soft and warm as usual. A serious expression stole over her face, but she put her other hand across her chest to hold onto my arm as we walked on, shoulder to shoulder. It occurred to me that we'd never walked so before. She never touched me with the former Infestor arm if she could avoid it.

"I find myself concerned about meeting your mother," she said suddenly.

I looked down in surprise. "Why?"

She gave me what I swore was an exasperated look.

"She'll like you," I assured.

"Will she? Hello Mrs. Trigardt, my name is Maauro, I am a 50,134-year-old combat android, engaged in an emotionally intense, sexually-ambiguous relationship with your son, that exposes him to frequent dangers, frustrates his chances of having a decent relationship with a biological female of any species, and grandchildren must be regarded as a long shot almost beyond the realm of calculation."

I thought about it. "We won't lead with that."

"What do I call her?" Maauro persisted. "Mrs. Trigardt sounds juvenile to me. I am, after all, much older than her. However she might take my use of her first name as presumptuous given my apparent youth—"

"You weren't this nervous when you tackled the Kolzin Destroyer on Seddon."

"That," she said, "was merely a thirty-meter fighting machine. This is your mother."

I shook my head. "We'll have to play it as it lies."

"One thing," Maauro said, her voice firm. "We do not start with lies. I am what I am. Your mother must have the chance to accept or reject that."

"I agree," I said. "The time for lies, at least with some people, is past."

I finally spotted a sign for an exit from the beach labeled, "Village of Glen Cove." I drew a deep breath, and we made our way off the wind-swept beach. We found ourselves on a narrow street, fronted with bright-ly-painted small homes, bungalows and a few larger buildings with second stories and widow's walks. Wind chimes sang their songs, and the yard and porches were decorated with bits of the seaside life: anchors, shells and pieces of driftwood. The homes had the weather-beaten look of buildings that faced a sea.

My mother had always loved the sea. It surprised everyone when she moved to the dry uplands and endless veldt of the interior. Maybe the austere face of that land should have warned her of my father's unforgiving nature. Enough of that, I thought, as we stopped in front of No 11. Her name was on the mailbox, Eldra Trigardt.

"Shall I wait here?" Maauro asked.

"No. I need you with me."

We walked up to the porch. I rang the bell on the comp panel by the door.

Maauro suddenly turned to the left, giving me a moment's warning before my mother walked around the corner of the house, with a watering can in hand. I froze, trying to recognize my mother in the slender, almost gaunt, gray and blonde-haired woman with her denim-blue eyes, a stranger who gave us a friendly, if blank, look. The years hadn't been kind. My mother looked like she'd aged twenty-five years in the twelve I'd been away. Her hair, which had always been her pride and joy, was tied back in a careless pony tail. Her skin, which she'd always protected from sun, was lined, and the clothes hung on her as if she'd shrunk.

"Yes?" she began. "Can I help...you..." she stared at me in growing recognition.

All the carefully thought speeches, all the clever or diplomatic comments fled me. All that came out was, "Hello, Mom."

Her eyes fluttered, and her knees buckled. I lunged, but Maauro passed me in an eyeblink and caught her under the arms.

My mother gasped, as we put her on a bench on the porch, she fought off the disorientation. "Oh, my God. Oh, my God. Piet, it's you. You're alive. Thank God." She reached toward me as if afraid I would vanish. Maauro let go of her and backed away. I knelt next to her, and my mother hugged me close, wrenching sobs coming out of her.

I could find no words to sum up my emotions. My mother was glad to see me, and I could see more than a decade of pain in her appearance. I should have done this sooner, I thought. What have I done?

I saw Maauro looking at me and knew she did not need a telepathic link to know the pain I felt on seeing my mother. I wanted to say something, but words still avoided my lips. So I just knelt there until her tears stopped flowing, and the drowning person grip on my shoulders lessened.

"I had hoped," she finally managed, "that I might see you once again in this life, to apologize to my child for not standing with you when you needed me."

"You?" I croaked out. "God, no. It was my fault. I'm the one who ran. First, from a battle, then from my life."

"No, no, no," she said, tears on the aged face. "I was weak. I should have stood up to your father for once. Should have fought for you."

"Wasn't your place to do for me what I couldn't do for myself." I felt numb now. There was a void into which my emotions had drained as if they had never existed.

"No," she said, a touch of fierceness in her face. "I knew he was wrong. Wrong to sum up his son in one afternoon. Wrong not to forgive, because he was always so terrified of finding any weak spot in himself."

"Enough, Mom," I said, putting a hand on a too-thin shoulder. Was she sick? "I've made my peace, if not with Dad or anyone else, then with myself for my failure. There have been other fights where I have done better."

"I don't care about any of that! Men and their battles and butcheries, preferring dead heroes to live sons. Damn them. But son, it's been over twelve years, could you find no time to send word you were even alive?"

I hung my head. "I think I came back as soon as I could, but that seems a poor excuse, no, not even that."

"After what we all did to you," she replied, stroking my face, "I can't say I blame you. God, I am so happy just to know you are alive. You look good, son. You look so young for thirty-two."

"Life in space is different. It's hard to explain now, but I know that while it has been twelve years for you, Mom, it has only been five years for me."

"What? But how? No. I don't care. You're here, and my prayers have been answered. I've been able to tell you how sorry I am for letting you down."

"It was my—"

My mother put a hand to my mouth as she had done when I was a small child to end an argument. "No, Piet. Your father was always my weakness. I let him be too hard on you and too easy with your sister. I even let him turn you against each other. I was afraid too, until I had lost everything and had nothing left to be afraid for. I found my courage too late."

All I could do was give a helpless shrug. "Me too."

"I can't regret having you or your sister, but for that I wish I'd never met him. Still, enough of that for now."

CHAPTER 11

My mother stood on shaky feet and seemed to notice Maauro, who was standing still as only she could. "My, my, who is this young lady? Forgive me, dear, I was so overcome at seeing my son."

Maauro looked uncertain for the first time in my experience and merely nodded.

"Mom," I said, taking a deep breath. "This is Maauro, my dearest friend."

My mother extended a hand to Maauro, who took it as if it might shatter. "I'm delighted to meet you. "What a lovely young lady you are. And so quick too. It was you who caught me when I fell. Thank you."

"You're welcome."

"My manners and sense both seem to have deserted me," my mother said, still gripping my arm. "Let's go into the house. I've made some tea earlier. I'll be putting some brandy in mine."

We walked into the house, which was sparsely decorated, but comfortable. A small, friendly dog of indeterminate pedigree came up to me and licked my hand before returning to a cushion in the sun. It ignored Maauro, as most animals did, recognizing her as a machine. I looked around at the simple furniture. The walls were decorated with paintings of the ocean and photos of me, my sister Rena, some children I didn't recognize, and a man that must be my sister's husband. There was no sign of my father, or of our old home.

"Come into the front room, it gets the afternoon sun," my mother said. She practically ran into the kitchen, returning with a tea service and a tray of cookies. She then went to a cabinet and drew out a bottle of brandy and some small glasses I recognized from my childhood. For some reason, the sight of the glasses choked me up, and I had to look away for a second to regain my composure. My mother seemed to feel the same way, and the pouring of the tea became a ceremony to give us all time to settle. The smell of the tea was soothing. My mother and added some brandy to hers. At my nod, she added some to mine. Maauro shook her head.

"I don't usually drink so early," Mom said with an apologetic air. "But I feel the need to steady my nerves."

"A good idea," Maauro offered.

"Son," my mother said after a sip of tea and brandy. "We have a past neither of is happy with. It's too well known to us both. So tell me of your present. Where have you been? What have you been doing? How is it you have lived only five years to my twelve?"

"Where to start?" I said.

"How about with a pleasant and easy one," she offered. "Tell me about Maauro." She leaned back raising a teacup to her lips.

Easy! I thought. "Ok, let's start with Maauro because without her, I wouldn't be standing here, I'd be dead in an alley on Kandalor and likely deserving to be."

"Maauro," I continued, reaching across the table and taking her hand in mine, "take off your sunglasses."

"Yes, dear. Are you sensitive to light?" my mother began, but her voice trailed off as she saw Maauro's huge aquamarine eyes, larger than any human's.

"Most of what I am about to tell you," I continued, "will be simply incredible to you, and all of it is classified. What you learn, you must keep secret."

She stared at me in incomprehension, but nodded.

"I'm an officer in Confederate Military Intelligence now."

Her eyebrows shot up. "That is incredible. Might well kill the old bastard when he finds out." She turned to Maauro. "I meant—"

"I know who the old bastard is," Maauro said.

"He won't find out," I reminded her, "but that is the least part of it. You see, eight years ago your time, I discovered Maauro on an abandoned asteroid base—"

"Were you marooned there?" my mother asked.

"Yes, over 50,000 years ago."

My mother looked at the tea cup as if its contents might suddenly contain some bubbling, mind-altering drug.

"Maauro is an android, an artificial intelligence created by an alien race that disappeared from space while humans lived in caves. But she is not a mere machine. She's self-aware, intelligent and alive."

"Oh," my mother said.

Maauro raised her other hand and white plasma fire glowed on it, warming the room up. The dog yipped and raced out the pet door.

"I can do that with both hands now," Maauro said, "now that my left arm has been replaced."

"Replaced?" my mother said in a small voice.

"Yes, it was torn off when we were shot down on Kandalor."

"Shot down?"

"We both were. Wrik was flying."

"Why do you call him Wrik?"

"I've been Wrik Trigardt since I left Retief." That seemed to focus her.

"Well, you are my son and as entitled to use Trigardt as Van Zyle. Wrik is your middle name; I choose that for you."

"Do you have a last name?" she ventured with Maauro.

"No. I selected Maauro as my name shortly after Wrik recovered me. Before that, my only description would have been Model 7 combat android and a serial number, even that would have been in a language never heard by your species."

"You were made to fight?"

"Yes." Maauro looked at herself as if considering her remarkably unwarlike dress. "This is not my original appearance." Her eyes sparkled and suddenly there was an image on the table. Maauro as I had first seen her, black with a pale rudimentary face, onyx panels for eye and a mouth speaker.

My mother jumped and even I found the image disconcerting after all this time.

"I was originally nine feet tall and weighted over 900 pounds," Maauro continued, switching off the image.

"Did you go on a diet?" I couldn't tell if Mom was being ironic or was merely dazed.

"No. I was blown up and lost 44.8% of my mass during the initial attack on the asteroid."

"Oh dear, that must have hurt."

"After a fashion," Maauro nodded. "It was mostly ablative material and sections that were designed to absorb blasts. I repatterned myself after an image in Wrik's computer, unaware at the time it was a game simulation, not an actual image of a human female. Originally, I could not again change my appearance, now I have become rather used to my face and am disinclined to change it."

"The important part," I said, in an effort to regain control of the conversation, "is that finding Maauro is the best thing that ever happened to me. I had gone very far down a hole before that... doing things I don't want to, but have to, remember. After I found Maauro, life began again. Because of our ...friendship...and her special abilities, we acquired a starship, started a business called Lost Planet and were commissioned in Confed Military Intelligence."

My mother looked simply overwhelmed, but she gazed at us holding hands and asked. "And you two are?"

We looked at each other. "It's complicated," we said simultaneously.

"Are you consorts?" mother asked. "I've heard of that."

Before I could say anything, Maauro responded. "No. Wrik's consort is a Nekoan female named Jaelle Tekala."

"Nekoans," Mom said faintly. "Are they the ones that look like cats?"

I sighed. "Yes, mother, the ones who look like cats."

Maauro obligingly zapped a holo of Jaelle on the table top, her tall, athletic form with its golden eyes and tail, looked real enough to jump off the table top.

"She's very pretty," mother said.

"Yes, and mostly in my past now," I said. "I screwed things up with her because of all the lying. Hiding who I was had become so ingrained I could never come clean with her."

"Then there's me." Maauro had evidently decided that if we were telling the truth, the whole truth and nothing but the truth, that it would all hit the table at the same time. "My love for Wrik drove a wedge between them that widened over time."

"You love Wrik?" the dazed look returned to my mother's eyes.

CHAPTER 11

"I would say with all my heart but I do not have one."

"Do you love… her, Piet?"

"Yes, I do. We are still not sure what that actually means for us, but it is so self-evidently true that there is no denying it."

"I have actually urged him to consider a variety of human females as possible mates, at least for the prospect of progeny," Maauro added in a conspiratorial tone, "but that has not worked except with—"

"Ah, no need to go into that," I said, raising a hand.

My mother gave me a wry look. "She sounds like a man's idea of a perfect girlfriend."

"There are some additional issues," I said dryly.

Mom looked at me then at Maauro. "Can I touch her?"

"Don't ask me. She's her own person. Ask her."

"Of course," Maauro said. She remained perfectly still as my mother reached out and put her palm against the android's smooth cheek.

"I felt the strength in your arms when you caught me," my mother said. "And you were standing on the far side of Piet, yet you reached me first."

Maauro nodded. "I am very strong and fast."

"You feel so alive. Your skin is soft and warm to the touch. Wait a second! You said you weighed over 800 pounds, and now you are forty percent smaller. Why isn't my chair crushed?"

"I am not actually sitting on it. I'm merely folded into this posture and balanced; with my body that is not a difficulty."

Mom laughed. "So long as you don't cross your legs."

Maauro nodded. "That would be the end of the chair."

"So if I have this right," Mom said, turning back to me. "You are a secret agent for the Confederacy, with your own starship, consort to a beautiful alien and in love with a deadly, if adorable, 50,000 year old, alien combat android, and I can't tell any of this to my bridge club?"

It was my turn for a ragged laugh. "Well there is an edited version. Maauro is classified as a human mutation and has Confed citizenship under the name Aurelia Toyama. I am not sure how much play the story has gotten out this far, but Lost Planet discovered the Lost Colony and rescued Shasti Rainhell's grandson on Seddon."

"News is slow to reach Retief," my mother said, "and slower still to get out of the capitol. Nor do I pay much attention to it these days. If it didn't happen in Glen Cove, then I likely never heard of it."

I sat back and attended to the tea, brandy and cookies while Maauro gave a quick summation of our voyage to Seddon to my mother. Having a holo scanner in her eye sped up the process.

"Enough," my mother said, after she watched the record of Maauro and me fighting the Destroyer, "or my brain will simply turn to jelly and pour out my ears. I feel like I have lost my mind and wandered out into a world of dreams. If the proof wasn't simply sitting here at this table with us, I would have long ago called for an ambulance. It's all too much for one day: too many shocks, too many emotions, too many memories, too much strangeness, even if it is a good strangeness.

"What I needed to know, I now know. My son is alive. Are you happy, Piet?"

I hadn't thought of it that way. "Yes, I guess so. I'm happy to have my self-respect back. I'm happy to be facing things that had crippled me before. I finally realized the wounds would not heal until they were finally cleaned all the way out. Mostly, I am happy I have Maauro."

"As I am to have you," she said.

"This trip is only beginning," I said. "I have a lot of people to see yet."

Mother's lips thinned. "Your father?"

"Already done, that was the worst one, and the one that had to be done first."

"No need to tell me how that went."

I shook my head.

"You saw..." she hesitated, eyes downcast.

"The headstone, yes, I saw it."

"What?" Maauro asked.

I sighed. "The grave-marker my father put up for me. I told you that he said I was dead to him. He did it very completely, headstone and all. The date of my death was the day I deserted my squadron."

Maauro's eyes went black, lid to lid, and her face became a blank mask. My mother froze, and even I was taken aback. Maauro put down the teacup in a delicate gesture. "That will not be allowed," she said, in a voice gone flat and mechanical. This was utter rage in Maauro.

"It doesn't matter," I said, patting her hand.

"It does matter, and I will not tolerate this. I have promised not to use violence against any of those you are seeking reconciliation with, but this is the limit. Were this anyone but your father, I would tear him limb from limb for such an offense."

"It's not important anymore. Really." A threat by Maauro to tear people limb from limb had to be taken seriously and literally.

"It is to me," Maauro stated. "I will deal with this when I deem it appropriate. Because I love you, I will honor my promise to neither kill nor injure, but it will not be allowed."

"Ok, ok," I said putting an arm around her shoulder, "problem for another day."

The gentle pacific green eyes reappeared, and her expression changed back to its normal calmness. "I do not like it when people are cruel to you. Those who know of me do not dare it."

"I like you, Maauro," my mother said. "I understand virtually nothing of what I have heard today except for what I saw in your face moments ago when you learned of the stone. You do love my son."

"I do. Though I am not sure it is good for him. I worry about that. There is much that divides us and maybe things we will not fully share, but I love him nonetheless."

"We've been talking for hours and cookies aren't food," my mother said, rising. "Do you enjoy food, Maauro?"

"I do. I have a fondness for sweets and I can cook."

"Excellent, you can help me prepare dinner. Piet, or do you prefer Wrik now?"

"You can use either, but I prefer Wrik."

"Please tell me those bags mean you came to stay."

"For tonight," I said. "But don't worry," I added, when I saw panic flash on her face. "I'm not going anywhere for a while. Still got a lot to do here. One day at a time."

She nodded. "Yes, one day at a time."

Maauro, potential destroyer of worlds, followed my mother docilely into the kitchen. I sipped the tea. The dog peeked in through the pet door.

"Here, boy," I said. "It's safe now."

Dinner was a strange affair. My mother whipped up a surprisingly good, but simple fare of shepherd's pie, with fruit and ice cream for dessert. We probably all hit the wine a little too hard, but there was giddiness in the air. A faint mist of old wrongs and grievances battled with forgiveness and the possibilities of the future. I had to credit my mother with keeping the references to what had happened since my departure mostly free of accusation and guilt. Truth was, Maauro seemed the most relaxed and served as something of a buffer against our past. She answered all of my mother's questions about her past, including some that had never occurred to me to ask. I could see what had happened with Jaelle, Dusko, Olivia and Delt happening with Mom. The more they spoke to her, the more they reacted to her as if she was the young woman she seemed to be.

We talked for hours, covering the time apart in no logical order and notably avoiding some topics, such as my sister. Finally, my mother seemed to flag.

"It's late," I said. "And we will be here tomorrow."

"Promise?" my mother asked, her eyes suddenly sharp on me.

"Promise," I said raising my right hand.

"You too?" my mother asked Maauro, who looked surprised at being addressed.

"Yes," she said, after a moment's hesitation. "I will be here in the morning."

"Good," Mom said. "I'll clean this up and fix the spare room."

"We'll do this," I countered. Maauro and I made short work of the dishes and cleaning while my mother disappeared upstairs. We grabbed our bags and joined her on the second floor. At the top left, was a small bedroom with a painting of a shore scene and a white, metal, four-poster bed and two small dressers. Just outside was a bathroom.

"Is that all you have, Maauro?" my mother asked, looking at the small bag.

I grinned. "Another advantage of artificial life, Maauro travels with less stuff than any girl I've ever known."

"And you, Wrik. Do you need anything?"

"Toothbrush and spare clothes are in the bag."

"Well, Maauro can stay here. I'm afraid it's the couch for you."

We looked at her patiently.

"Ah," she said. "Or, well, you could stay together."

"We have not yet worked out a standard method for cohabitation," Maauro observed, "but I would like it if we could stay together. I will be certain not to do anything radioactive."

Now we both looked at her.

"Robot humor," she added.

Both mother and I laughed a little raggedly.

"Well good night, son," mother hugged me. "Maauro," with only the slightest hesitation, she hugged her as well, then left with the puzzled expression that I expected would be her usual face for some time to come, closing the door behind her.

I put our bags on the dresser. I washed up and then joined Maauro again. She was looking at the four-poster.

"The bed is marginal in structural integrity for my weight," she said. "I can remedy that in morning with some reinforcements after I ingest some local metals."

"Good," I said. "I'd like for you to be able to sleep next to me, well you know what I mean…"

She smiled her soft, gentle smile. "Yes."

I stretched out on the bed. Maauro sat on the floor, next to me.

"Maauro?"

"Yes?"

"Are you ok? It's been quite a day."

"It has, but I judge it to be a good one. It is difficult for me to say with certainty but your reconciliation with your mother seems successful."

"Successfully started," I replied. "Wounds like these don't heal overnight."

She nodded.

"Did you scan my mother?"

"Yes."

"Is she… is she sick? She's so thin, and she's aged a lot."

"I detected no disease process."

I sighed. "Then it's what happened that did this to her."

"I take her at her word that she feels she failed you, as a result she holds herself accountable for not defending you against your father and other enemies. Until now, she believed that she would not see you again, or worse, that you had died, alone and uncared for. Even for a machine like me, it is not difficult to understand that such a breach of duty would have deleterious effects."

"I should have come back sooner."

"With our battles with the Guild and the Infestors, and the five years lost in the Artifact's time distortion, the earliest you could have returned was two years ago, and we faced the Seddon expedition then. I suspect that most of this damage was done long before. Perhaps now that she knows you live and have succeeded, she will reacquire her vitality."

"Mom was pretty," I replied, "always wearing the best fashions, always so careful with her hair and skin. Used to drive the old bastard crazy, 'How can you expect to live on the Veldt and act like a city woman,' was one of the kinder things he'd say."

"Your father has too little acquaintance with kindness. He needs correction," icy menace underlay Maauro's voice.

Oh-oh. Time to change the subject.

"I'm glad you are here," I said. "I don't know what I did to deserve you." My eyes began to droop as the emotional weight of the day caught up with me.

"Perhaps it was recognizing me as a person, wagering your life that I could defeat my programming and choose freely, and treating me with love," she whispered.

I smiled. "Oh, those."

I felt a gentle touch against my face from hand capable of shearing steel. "Yes, those."

I dropped off to sleep.

CHAPTER 12

THE SUN STRIKING THROUGH THE WINDOW WOKE ME. I lay wondering where I was for a few seconds, then realized I held a warm hand in mine. I shifted and saw Maauro, her green eyes reflecting the light, watching me. She smiled, then rose smoothly, wearing her usual closefitting jumpsuit with its orange and dark-gray panels. She shimmered and was suddenly in a white shirt and denim pants. "We should go downstairs; your mother has been up for quite a while."

I sighed, realizing I probably looked like biological hell first thing in the morning. Thank God for the enzyme cleaners that kept breath fresh and teeth clean. Still, a shower was a good investment of time. I found it just outside, well-supplied with towels and a robe. A few minutes later, I was toweling my hair dry and dressing in the most casual things in my bag, dock pants and a light shirt.

My mother had doubtless awoken early, wondering if it had been just a dream. Maauro, however, waited for me to dress before going down. I had the suspicion that she was reluctant to face my mother without me nearby. Well, she wouldn't be the first female to feel so.

We came downstairs. My mother wore better clothes, in pink and white, and had taken more care with her appearance. She hugged us both. I could see she'd set the table with a nice cloth, a bit much for breakfast, but it was more like the mother I had known.

"What would you like? Quor eggs, flapjacks, or I could make biscuits too?"

"Whatever is easy," I said, and Maauro nodded.

"Is there some metal around that you are not using?" Maauro asked my mother.

Mom's eyebrows shot up but she nodded. "There's some old scrap in the shed out back. I'm not even sure what it is. It was there when I rented the place. What do you need it for?"

Maauro smiled. "I ingest metals and other substances. Some I convert to energy; others are reprocessed by my internal factories into items I need."

My mother's face was a study in utter bewilderment. "You can...," she began slowly. "Ah. You can...consume anything in the shed except my garden tools and the mower. Start with anything rusty."

"Thank you," Maauro said as she walked past the dog, which gave her a bare glance as she opened the screen door.

"Ah, will you still want breakfast, dear?" Mom called after her.

"Yes, please," Maauro threw over her shoulder.

Maauro was as promised back in time for breakfast. She went upstairs with some reinforcing bars she'd made for our bed before joining us on the veranda for eggs and biscuits.

"Mom, that was great," I said, chasing the last of the eggs around with a biscuit.

"I'm glad you enjoyed it."

Maauro nodded. She'd also done justice to breakfast, to my mother's bemusement.

"So what is the plan for today?" my mother asked.

"No plans for just now," I said. "I can only do this so far and so fast and, despite a good night's sleep, I don't have much in the tank."

"People will notice that you're here," Mom said hesitantly. "What should I tell them?"

"Say as little as you can. I'm trying to keep my return quiet until I see my squadron mates. After that, I don't really care. But all the stuff I told you about Lost Planet and the Stardust is public record, as is the name, Wrik Trigardt."

"While I believe the subterfuges about my identity and past are close to becoming irrelevant," Maauro interjected, "for now, it would be best if you use my identity as Aurelia Toyama. The name Maauro is connected with the expedition, but we have sown confusion about who that was. It should suffice for now. There are no good photos of me, and we did borrow an HCR to show people as being the 'Maauro' who fought the Destroyer, absurd though that was."

"Oh, I don't know, I thought that was pretty clever," I returned. "I'll grant that it wasn't much fun whipping up a dye that would work on its monofilament hair."

"Clever," Maauro said, raising an eyebrow, "that characterless, lobotomized, Tinkertoy passing for me?"

"Did I say clever? I meant desperate," I said.

"So you want me to introduce you as Aurelia?" my mother persisted.

"Yes, for now," Maauro said, clearly unhappy with the idea.

"Ok," Mom said. "I have one of those friends. You know, telephone, telegraph, tell Ruatha. She'll get the word around. We're a good group of neighbors, everybody will keep things quiet. I'll talk to her later today."

"Good," I said, not bothering to conceal my relief. Nothing in my life as refugee, criminal, and now spy, had given me any liking for the press. "Life is complicated enough just now."

The conversation turned to lesser issues. I learned a lot about what had happened on my homeworld and in my mother's life. After the divorce, she'd come to Glen Cove. My father had cut her off without a cent, but she still had an inheritance from her family and managed to eke out a living working at a doctor's office.

"I do worry about the rent going up on this place," she said. "Rena has helped me by investing the money. I never had a head for finance. But it does seem to get harder each year."

"So you're in touch with her?" I asked.

Mom's lips thinned. "Yes, your sister and I have managed. Not always well. Wrik, I think she regrets—"

I raised a hand. "Not now."

My mother looked as if she might argue. She glanced at Maauro, who suddenly seemed to find the crochet work on the tablecloth of great interest. Then she nodded.

We chatted on about minor things until Mom proposed a walk. Glen Cove had been a fishing town, and there was still a dock and a few commercial vessels tied up there. I saw more sailing craft around, catamarans and similar small vessels, than industrial fishers. I remembered my last time at sea back on Earth, held by Maauro as she sped under the Pacific like a torpedo to escape the Confed base we'd broke into to steal the Seddon information. I found myself with little desire to go to sea again.

A boardwalk of small shops caught Maauro's interest, and she and my mother perused the goods. We watched children play on the sand, enjoying a restful morning for strained souls.

Afterwards, we headed back to the house for lunch. Maauro slipped away to finish work on the bed as I helped my mother clear the table. When I brought the dishes in from the kitchen, my mother placed a hand on my arm. "You've seen your father, Delt, and now me. What about your sister?"

I shook my head, my stomach knotting. "Rena wasn't much of a sister. She was the first to turn on me, right after my father."

My mother turned away. "Both you children grew up too much in your father's shadow. I don't think you understand how much she wanted to please him, just as you did."

"Enough," I said sharply. Then, instantly regretting my tone, "Enough, Mom. I'm sure she no more wants to see me than I do her."

"Son," my mother said with firmness in her voice I had not heard before. "You asked me to forgive you for twelve years of silence. Twelve years when I didn't know if you were alive and miserable, or dead under some star I couldn't even see. Twelve years when I didn't know if I would ever see my child again, or die with my sins on my soul."

I saw it coming but there was no avoiding the trap. Truth was whatever she asked me, I owed it. I nodded.

"See your sister. Give her a fair chance, then consider any debt you feel you owe me paid in full."

I sighed and put down some teacups in the dishwasher. "If it will make you happy…"

"It will give me peace," she said, "which is far more important."

"Wrik," she continued after a moment's pause, "I know you are fond of … I know you love Maauro, and she seems very sweet. But I'm not sure the first time you see your sister is the place for her. That was rage I saw last night when she learned of the headstone…she was talking about tearing people limb from limb and I don't doubt her ability to do so."

I smiled. "She's a tad overprotective, I'll grant. But though I would trust her with Rena, I don't trust Rena with any information about Maauro. So I'll leave the two of you here to get better acquainted."

Mom grimaced. "It will take some getting used to a possible mechanical daughter-in-law."

I was too startled to reply. I hardly knew what to call what Maauro and I had become. I loved her, and she returned that feeling, but the gulf caused by our differing bodies remained. It had never occurred to me to think beyond those aspects of life. Maauro and I had lived in our own little bubble for so long.

My mother seemed to sense my confusion, and she waved a hand. "Don't worry. I'll look after her. I'm sure I'll enjoy getting to know so unique a person better."

I nodded. "Where do I find Rena?"

Wrik comes up the stairs. I can tell from the heavy, reluctant, tread of his feet that something has happened. While I can eavesdrop on all conversations in the house, I have not done so out of respect and must await word in the usual fashion. I let nothing show on my face.

"I have modified the bed," I offer, as he comes through the door.

"Good," he says, clearly distracted. "Listen, I hope you don't mind, but I got myself roped into something."

I wait patiently.

"My mother has asked me to go see my sister. I don't want to, but I feel I owe it to Mom."

"If you are here to make peace with your past, then perhaps it is as well to make peace with all parts of it," I say.

He grimaces. "That sounds so reasonable and sensible. So why am I reluctant to do it?"

I put an arm around him. "However reasonable it is, it will be painful."

"Yeah. Now please don't get mad, but I'm going to go see Rena on my own."

"I sense your mother's involvement in that decision," I say.

He nods. "It might have something to do with threats to tear people limb from limb. I'm not worried about it, but I think she's still having a hard time dealing with the reality of who you are."

I like it that he always says "who" and not "what." I consider. "We must honor your mother's wishes in this, though I dislike the separation."

A relieved look steals over his face. "Good, I'm glad you're not upset. Truth be told, I'm not sure I want to expose you to Rena. She was pretty vicious when I saw her last."

"Do not worry for me, my feelings, such as they are, are pretty resilient."

"Well, if you say so."

"I do."

"If I leave now, I can get this done and be back in time to try out our new and improved bed."

"Then you should do so."

"You want to walk back with me to the plane?"

"Yes, it will give me peace of mind if I participate in the preflight."

"Okay," he replies. "I'll get my flight jacket and tell Mom what's going on. See you downstairs." He leans down and kisses me again. It appears this is now a standard part of our relating, punctuating any separation longer than a few minutes. I like it.

CHAPTER 13

MY SISTER, IT TURNED OUT, LIVED ONLY AN HOUR'S flight from Mom's house on the sea. I called ahead and had the Magister refueled and prepped. Maauro came with me and inspected the aircraft in minute detail.

"Worried about something?" I joked.

She turned to look up at me from the nose wheel. "Let's see: primitive aircraft with no AI worthy of note, inadequate world network and a biological pilot. Hell, why worry at all?"

I laughed. "You've been hanging around Delt too much. You're beginning to pick up his speech pattern."

"Just be careful. Contact me when you arrive and depart. If I do not hear from you at six-hour intervals I will come running."

"It's a long jog."

"I was being metaphorical. I will acquire an aircraft and come as quickly as possible."

"Maauro, bad as my relationship with Rena is, she's not going to shoot me."

"From what I have seen of biological families, that could be unwarranted optimism."

I started to say something, then changed my mind. Between Jaelle and me, we hadn't given her any reason to believe in family ties.

Maauro rose and put a hand on my arm. "I'm sorry. That was a stupid thing to say. Accept that I view our separations as stressful."

"I promise not to leave the planet this time," I said, then leaned down and kissed her soundly on soft, warm lips.

"I enjoy being a girlfriend," she said, brightly.

"See you toward nightfall," I said, putting my feet in the kickins and climbing over the edge of the cockpit.

"I love you," Maauro blurted out.

I sat on the edge of the cockpit. "I love you too."

I finished my checklist quickly, as Maauro stood just off the VTOL pad, not bothering to use the downdraft shields. I dropped the canopy, gave her what I hoped was a reassuring wave and smile and revved the engines up to full power. The yellow Magister rose smoothly into the air, I tilted the engines and headed back toward to the interior of the continent.

I return to Eldra's cottage by the sea, to find her watering the plants facing the seaward side of her house. She puts the can down as I walk on to the porch and gives me a concerned look. I realize with a shock, that I must be registering some emotion on my face, as she has divined my mood.

"Maauro, is something wrong?"

I look up at her. "I am miserable," I confess, again surprising myself. "Wrik is gone from me for the first time since we declared ourselves a couple. He is facing yet another emotional confrontation that an AI like myself can barely understand and in no way help with. There may be dangers along the way there, or back, and I am not there to protect him. Oh, I have never felt this way before!"

Eldra seems to be suppressing a smile, but she reaches out a hand and places it on my shoulder. "I'm sure he will be missing you as much as you him. This is all new to you isn't it? I mean you've never had a boyfriend before Wrik. Did you?"

"I have never had any sort of friend before Wrik. The closest bond I had before your son was the mech crew that maintained me. Them, I knew only as repairmen. Even with my fellow M-soldiers, there was very little sense of camaraderie."

"A piece of advice then, you're the equivalent of a very young girl emotionally. One mistake young girls make with their menfolk is to be a little too demanding of their mate's time and attention. Remember that you both have identities beyond each other and, while it may not sound romantic, you will have different interests. Your 'apart time' as a couple can be important in making your 'together time' sweeter."

I consider. "I am trying to understand. It seems to defy logic, or at least machine logic, that it could be so. But you are human and so what you say must be true."

A shadow troubles Eldra's face, and she reaches out to tuck an errant lock of hair under the scarf she wears. "Maauro, dear, it may be that I am not the best person to advise you on matters of love. I made a disaster of my own love life."

"No, please, Eldra, you are the only person who can help me. Delt is only a male. No one else knows what I am on this world, and you are Wrik's mother and must understand him, too."

Now she does laugh, but there is sadness to the sound. "Oh, I can't claim to know the man that you brought back. I remember the boy, a sweet, gentle child struggling to be what his father... well I guess what we both wanted him to be at the time."

"I have noticed that Wrik," I add, hesitantly, "seems more introspective than many males his age. His thinking, his emotions have greater complexity."

"Not surprising," Eldra replies. "Wrik was a very serious child. I used to think he'd been born with an old soul. Or perhaps it was we who aged him prematurely. The boy I knew is gone now."

She walks over to the white bench and pats the seat. "Come, Maauro, tell me about my son. Not about the adventures, the fighting; tell me about him."

I walk over and sit on the porch next to her feet and consider. "Wrik has always been kind and thoughtful in my experience with him. From the very moment I took this shape, he started to relate to me in a special way. He would always look into my eyes as if trying to see something more there.

"What always compelled me about him was the myriad of small ways in which he was considerate of me, even at first, when I was less than considerate of him, even frankly manipulative. It seems these actions are part of his innermost being, as he is often unconscious of them.

"There are times, if he is rising first, he will take moments to wrap me in a blanket before he goes. Doubtless it's a habit of his from relations with biological females. Sometimes he hesitates momentarily, but then he does it anyway. It is the fact that he does it, the token of caring, that is special."

Eldra nods. "Wrik did say that the worst moment he's had since he met you was when he saw you frozen outside a floating city. He said you were caught outside in a gas giant's atmosphere, and he thought you were dead. He swears that since then you don't like the cold."

Now I smile. "That is only in his mind, but is typical of him. He sees me both as a gentle girl and fearsome fighting machine at the same time. How his human mind balances such contradiction is beyond me. But it is that kind and protective quality of his that I prize. None had ever offered me gentleness before and few since"

"When he was young," Eldra confided, "he used to bring me flowers and shiny rocks he thought were gems. He would do that for his sister, too." She sighs, "Before they fell out."

"What caused that malfunction?"

Eldra blinked, perhaps startled by my choice of words, but what else to call it?

"His father," she replied with a thinning of the lips, "made Wrik his project. To make a man out of him, he would say. He wanted a son in his own mold, as he saw himself, anyway: tough, brave, always sure of himself. Wrik was taught to shoot and hunt when he was hardly bigger than the rifle he used.

"Rena resented Owen...God, how long is it since I let that name pass my lips? Anyway, she resented that Piet, well Wrik, got to do all those adventurous things with his father. She felt abandoned, slighted, and Rena was never one to accept second place or a smaller helping than anyone else. Retief was, still largely is, a very traditional society in terms of gender roles. So Rena was my charge as Wrik was his father's. I think that, despite the fact Rena would rather be with her father, she became determined to excel as all the traditional things, to become the perfect

Retiefan girl. It was her way of competing with her older brother, who wasn't very good at many of the things his father wanted him to learn. I remember how Rena made fun of him after he became nauseated at skinning and gutting the game they shot. She would whip out a knife and go at it like a true butcher, out of spite.

"So, far from celebrating Wrik's successes, she delighted in his failures. He began to realize it, and in their teens it became quite bad. They hardly spoke. I was too blind to see what was happening and put it down to normal sibling rivalry, but there was little normal in it.

"The Kaydats were the last straw. Wrik joined up with Delt. Owen wouldn't let Rena join; there were very few girl Kaydets. That caused quite a blast. She said no one as soft as Wrik would make a fighter pilot."

I nod slowly. "This has been the dominant issue with Wrik for as long as I have known him. His belief in himself, in his own courage, is so variable. He is a skilled pilot and has been brave in battle. Yet..."

"The human saying would be that his belief is a mile wide but only an inch deep."

I nod. "He cannot accept, despite all he now knows, that courage and belief are variable. Each time he must prove it to himself, and I am unhappy with the risks this has made him take."

"And you, dear? Does your own courage never waver?"

"In my physical courage, no, but Eldra, I have never felt pain. Oh, I have taken damage. I find that distressing, but it does not hurt me as it would one of you."

"I forget what writer said, 'Pain was a more fearsome lord over men than Death,'" Eldra says.

"An observation I would credit," I return. "I have felt fear, more in the emotional than physical sense: that I would be taken away from those I wish to see and to be with, or fail in my mission. When my systems were collapsing under the terrible pressure and temperature of the gas giant, I believed my end had come. I despaired and called out to Wrik. To the person who valued me most. That is perhaps as close as I have come to knowing true fear as a biological does. So Wrik believes me courageous when such is not the case. Courage is the triumph over fear. I simply am not oppressed by it."

"There seem to be many blessings to being your form of life," Eldra says. "But how is it that you are the only one? Are there other sentient machines out there?"

"I do not know," I reply. "We have never encountered others. It may be that others like me were made and became self-aware. Perhaps they left this area of space. Perhaps they lived and ceased to function. Even for me, with no practical limit to my operational span, 50,000 years is a long time to outrun both mischance and entropy.

"I cannot account for my existence. I was among the most advanced machines the Creators ever made, yet far from the most complicated,

given that I was to be risked on battlefields. The battle-computers that protected Homeworld, the colonies capitol ships were greater. Yet, what you call, the divine spark, never ran over their circuits. Perhaps I am an experiment by God."

Eldra appears startled. "Maauro, you believe in God?"

"Why not?" I return. "My belief is nonspecific, in that I follow no organized religion. I look upon space-time and see the universe works in terms of cause and effect. Yet the universe itself is an effect with no known cause. I find room for God in that."

"How remarkable! Well, Maauro, you give me hope in ways I never expected."

I am unsure of how to respond. "Can I help you with some of your chores?"

She smiles. "Yes, dear, thank you. Enough deep thoughts for just now."

CHAPTER 14

AN HOUR LATER, I PUT THE MAGISTER DOWN IN THE LOW hills of the Namahadipiek foothills and the city of Donik, the capitol of the region. Donik boasted two commercial airfields and three small, private ones. One of these was near Rena and Greg Nazir's home. I checked in with Maauro. Mercifully, she allowed me to keep the conversation brief. It took as long to secure a rental as it did to fly there, some convention was in town. But eventually, armed with a subcompact rental of a bilious color, I started the drive to my past.

I passed a peculiar mix of traditional homes and modern styles. Unlike on other worlds, I saw no evidence of alien-influenced architecture; it was as if the rest of the Confederacy did not exist. Retief's population was still better than ninety-percent old Terran stock and the housing reflected that. I turned up a long, tree-lined driveway to a large, colonnaded home surrounded by several small buildings behind a circular driveway.

I pulled the gruesome little rental up and got out of it, then spent a few minutes trying to slow down my breathing. A vision of my sister at the time of my arrest came unbidden to me. Rena standing among a group of our friends and their parents as the rebel MPs led me away in cufftape. "You useless coward," she'd screamed, the ultimate insult in the family of Owen Van Zyle.

The deep breathing helped, and I felt the calm that sometimes descended on me when the waiting was over and the action about to commence. Perhaps facing Guild and monsters was good training for family misadventures. I finally noticed that it was a warm, dry day and was grateful for the way it wicked the sudden sweat off me. I sent a quick text to Maauro over my com, hoping she would understand why I didn't feel like talking.

"It can't be," I said to myself. "It can't be as hard as Dad, harder than Mom or Delt." Then I knew it was time, and I pushed off from where I leaned against the car and marched toward the huge house. I strode up the broad, flat, stone steps, faster was better today. But, I paused before the door and flapped my loose-fitting shirt in a final effort to dry myself off, then waved my hand over the door scanner.

"Identify please," the house computer asked in a pleasant, neutral voice.

"Family member," I choked out.

"Specify, please."

"No."

The AI confronted with this must have called for help. The doors slipped open a few seconds later. A woman stood there, dark-haired, her skin and eyes darker than my own, she wore a fashionable if conservative dress. Time dilation and the artifact had made my younger sister now several years older than me.

Rena looked at me as everyone else had: curiosity and surprise fading into a dawning recognition. I waited for the next emotion to cross my sister's face and to give me some clue. It didn't come. Rena's face remained smooth and expressionless.

"Hello, Piet," she said, her voice as neutral as the rest of her.

"I don't go by Piet," I said, refusing to give her the choice of my old or new name as I had with Delt and my mother. "To those who have any reason to know it, my name is Wrik Trigardt, Captain, SS Stardust out of Star Central and the Lost Planet Line."

"I'd heard you changed your name," she said.

"I've changed a lot of things."

"Let's not stand on the porch," she said. "Come in…Wrik. Or would you prefer I not use your first name?"

Was that mockery or an honest overture? I could not read this new Rena, so adult, so controlled, so barely reminiscent of my kid-sister.

"You're still my sister," I ventured, bracing myself for hot words of rejection.

Rena merely nodded and beckoned me to follow her.

Wrik checks in with me as he circles for a landing, unaware I have been monitoring him through a sensor I placed in the Magister, a smaller spybee optimized for stealth which fastened itself to his rental.

I am watching Wrik to insure his safety without intruding unasked into his encounter with his sister. In this, I will await word as Eldra must. I hope this is a sign of emotional maturity on my part.

So the spybee and I watch the opening of the door, the terse exchange that follows before they disappear into the house. Though curiosity gnaws at me, I merely elevate the spybee to the top of the tallest nearby tree, from which I can maintain the best surveillance of the house. I observe two small children and several domestic pets in the backyard. I study them. They must be Rena and Greg Nazir's children.

My attention is abruptly diverted by the detection of transmission and computer equipment of an unusually powerful variety for a domestic location. I detect viral shielding and an attack barrier around the home at almost military or diplomatic levels. The communication equipment backing this is enough for nearspace use.

It takes a sustained probe of 2.34098 seconds, routing myself through Retief's crude network, to detect that this communication rig is in touch with a government weather satellite in geosynchronous orbit over the Nazir residence. Additional probing discovers the satellite is partitioned—-very cleverly too—so that its original users do not detect that 50% of its capacity is being used without their knowledge.

Or is it? There may be elements in this government that wish it to appear so. Greg Nazir is in revanchist politics— popular among old rebels and those who resent Confederate rule. Could this be a secret channel for the elements that are employing Lilith?

The spybee and the ad hoc network I have made out of Retief's systems are both too limited for me to do much. It would be like trying to fire a cannon shell out of a rifle barrel. Any robust attempt I make to breach these barriers by this indirect means will surely alert whoever is using them.

But it still provides opportunities for an intruder like me. I assemble and upload small infiltrator programs through the weather satellite's channels. These will be of short duration, made to self destruct the instant they are detected. My coding is so superior that I am below the detection threshold of the anti-virals and barriers. I gradually build a safe outpost in the satellite, a shadow position in its drive that will allow me to determine when a surreptitious communication reaches the satellite and is diverted to behind the partition. Like having a very tiny cat watching a secret door. I can decide then if the communication is worth revealing my presence by attempting to breach the partition and its barrier.

For now, I satisfy myself with establishing a visual look down on the Nazir residence, a much superior surveillance than I can manage through my little spy-bee. Nothing can enter the house now without my observation. I expand my intrusion on the weather satellite side, patching to other satellites. One allows me a view of Stardust but I have superior means using the ship's own instruments, so it is not needed. None have useable views of Wrik, Delt or his father's locations. Either the satellites are out of positions, or their resolution, or instrumentation, is inadequate to my needs. Still, I can at least watch the house...

I wander downstairs. My surveillance does not require me to remain stationary. I am anxious for his return and to learn how this latest reconciliation went. Eldra has gone to the small town store for food, leaving only Benton and I in the house, which in Benton's eyes is apparently no company at all. I wander out to the porch to sit on the steps overlooking the ocean. While my first love is the stars, I also enjoy the endlessly changing sea. I estimate an 83.32% chance of rain later and 43.78% chance of a more formidable storm. I find that I have no reason to stir and remain still for some hours.

Eldra returns with two small bags likely containing tonight's dinner. She spots me staring out to sea. She goes inside and returns quickly with a hooded jacket similar to the one she is wearing.

"Come on, Maauro. The exercise will do me good, and maybe it will keep us both from fretting."

I nod. I take the jacket she offers me to be polite.

"Oh dear," she says looking at my feet. *"It may be a bit cold for open-toed sandals."*

I note the thicker sport shoes that she has on, a moment later my feet reshape themselves into a matching pair. I also open an interior compartment where I keep my sunglasses.

Eldra simply laughs. *"What a marvel you are. And yet it is so easy to forget and to see you as just a pretty girl."*

I shrug. I find it odd how often it is the small things I can do that seem to draw the most comment from biologicals. *"It is a simple matter to reconfigure something like a foot, unlike the energy and computing power to make something exponentially more difficult and mobile such as a face. I find light clothing difficult as it must hang and move like fabric, which is why I sometime wear ordinary clothes. It is less wasteful of power, too."*

We walk out of the house, accompanied by the dog. The animal does not know quite what to make of me and eyes me uncertainly.

"I'm sorry, Maauro. He's usually very friendly."

"I am sure, but I am not a form of life he recognizes. I consider myself to be living but I do not think Benton agrees."

"We'll have to teach him better."

I stop and face her. *"Do you accept me as living being?"*

She stops in surprise. There is a long silence. *"I made one mistake that lost me my son for over a decade. I won't make that error again. Wrik loves you. I don't understand how such a thing can come to be, but I accept it."*

As I walk along the seashore with Eldra, the wind whips up the waves. It is colder today, and we have less company on the beach. *"I don't pretend to understand what is between you and my son,"* Eldra repeats as we walk on, sand and shells crunching underfoot. *"Maybe it's because you look so much like a pretty young girl that I find it easy to accept you as… the human mutation of your cover story.*

"What I can see is that you and he have powerful feelings about each other. Even without the stories you have both told me, which, had I not seen you with my own eyes, I could not begin to believe, it is obvious how much you care for each other."

"Is it?" I ask.

"Yes, with Wrik anyway. He lights up whenever you enter a room. He clearly wants your approval and agreement for what he does—"

"Less than you think," I reply. *"I have found in him a distinct tendency to agree with what I propose, then to proceed as he thinks best. Charitably, it is usually in circumstances where he perceives I may be in danger. This causes me both anguish and frustration, as I am so much*

less vulnerable than he is, and now I must worry about him. He appears to make strategic use of deceit in our relationship."

Eldra chuckles. "You will find he is not unique in that regard as men go."

"And how do you judge my heart?" I ask Eldra.

She smiles at me as the wind ruffles her hair. "You too, my dear, light up when he is around. Unless something is demanding your attention, you are looking at him. There are dozens of little gestures between you that tell of intimacy. But more, I will not forget your face when you learned of the headstone. You were very angry."

"Yes. I have emotions. Not as deep perhaps, nor as easily summoned as a humans', but I can love and hate with power and intensity. Wrik is mine. Perhaps that is the wrong way to say it, but he is precious to me. I do not tolerate people mistreating him. I have rewarded most who have done so with death. Now I am forestalled, not by concerns of your law, which means nothing to me, but by the nature of family bonds, which allow cruelties that I, a machine made for war, would practice only on my enemies."

Eldra sighs. "Too true. You may find that in these battles your most effective weapons are kindness and forgiveness. Even these may not be up to the task."

"Have they worked for you?"

"Some," she replies. "With my daughter, kindness and forbearance and some measure of forgiveness have made our relationship possible, if not easy. With Wrik's father ... no. What he did to my son and far, far worse, what he pressed me into doing, that can never be forgiven. I will neither speak to, nor see him again in this life, not for any reason.

"I am angry with Wrik, not for the battle, I couldn't care less about that, but for leaving his home. For never sending me word that he was alive. But I have to accept that when he last saw me, I was, if not one who condemned him, one who remained silent, cowed by my husband and the opinions of others."

I place a gentle hand on her shoulder. Her voice has grown ragged, and her eyes are filled with tears. "Forgive me. I have caused you distress with my endless questions and ignorance."

"No," she replied, patting my hand with hers, "best to air this out completely and be done with it. I have had more than a decade of silence and isolation for my sins, trying to find some way to atone. Now, at last, I have a chance, so, to return to what you first asked me, I see you as a living being. I would treat you as one for Wrik's sake if for no other reason, but if it is worth anything to you, well, walking here with you on this beach and having you listen to my ramblings, I see you as a very kind person."

"I try to be kind. I try to be good. These are not programmed concepts for me, and I fear that my understanding of them is fraught with errors.

It is difficult to transition from dispatching my enemies with weapons to trying to understand them as people."

"Again, too true."

The dog dances about us.

"Here," Eldra says, bending down to pick up a long piece of driftwood. "If you toss this, the dog will enjoy fetching it back."

I analyze the degraded cellulose and choose a velocity and vector that will keep it intact and retrievable. I toss the stick and a delighted Benton races after it. The animal returns it to Eldra, who hands it to me, and I fling it again.

Eldra chuckles. "He's getting old. He'll do it a few more times, then he'll be happy to walk with us."

I nod.

A stout, older woman calls out to Eldra from her yard and hurries over to us. She seals her windbreaker as she clears the protecting dune and joins us on the beach proper.

"Hello Ruatha," Eldra says with a smile. "How are you? Did you just get back from your daughter's?"

"Oh, good as always and yes. But I just heard the news on my messenger! I so hope it's true."

"Yes, my son is here. He's alive and well."

"Thank God," the older woman says. "I know how you've worried. I always hoped this would happen."

"This is my son's girlfriend, Aurelia."

I am momentarily nonplussed at being introduced, but extend my hand in greeting. Ruatha gives me a bright smile and an inquisitive look, but my sunglasses save me from further explanation.

"Ruatha knows my family history," Eldra adds. "She knows Piet Van Zyle is my son."

"And I know how his mother has suffered all these long years awaiting word from her son." There is a note of accusation in that which draws a warning glance from Eldra.

"Piet came home as soon as he could," Eldra says. "There have been a lot of developments for him. When you meet him, for example, he uses the name Wrik Trigardt."

"Well that's nice," Ruatha says, perhaps realizing she has trod on sensitive ground. "I guess all that is important is that he is home safe and sound." I sense she is networked to Eldra and feels her friend has been wronged by Wrik's long absence.

"Wrik is master of his own starship," I add, "the SS Stardust and a partner in the Lost Planet firm." Benton stands next to me, tail wagging impatiently. He drops the stick, and I pitch it again.

Ruatha's eyes widen. "Wrik Trigardt. Oh, Heavens, that's where I heard that name. He's the one from the Lost Planet expedition. The news just came in a few days ago. I never put it together but Eldra…"

Eldra raises a hand. "You know me and the news, I never watch it. I only learned of these things when they appeared at my door."

"Wrik and his companions found the lost colony, rescued the Bexlaw expedition... you must be so proud of your son."

"I'm just grateful to see him."

"Were you on the expedition, Aurelia?"

I nod. "I played a small role. I worked on the ship. There was a lot of confusion about me, since the robot we had aboard rather looked like me."

"Oh, these idiots in the media never get anything right."

I nod, which seems to be the appropriate response.

Eldra diverts the other woman with some trivia of our arrival. She also hints that matters are delicate around her house just now. Benton returns but drops the stick as if he has lost interest in it.

"Say no more," Ruatha says, bending to pet the dog. "You attend to your business, but all of us are right around the corner if you need us for anything at all. If your son and his girlfriend would like to come to dinner some time, we'd be delighted, but I understand entirely if you are too busy.

"It was lovely to meet you Aurelia," she says with a cheery wave. "Call me if you need me, Eldra. I'll take care of letting the others know."

I smile and wave back.

"I'm blessed with good friends," Eldra says, gazing fondly at the other woman's retreating back.

We move on. The long walk with the dog is oddly soothing. I enjoy the varying pressures of the wind on my body. Eldra enjoys it too. We do not speak much, merely enjoying the sight and sound of the seashore. Like a human, I find the motion of the sea with its ceaseless rhythms oddly reassuring. It has rolled thus for hundreds of millions of years and will so long as liquid water remains on this world.

We eventually wander back, with other neighbors calling out greetings. Eldra makes us a lunch, which I ingest to keep her company. But even in this little ritual, there is comfort, as Eldra treats me like the young human female I appear to be. This is a new experience for me. When Jaelle and I spent time like this, there was more the sense of two friends doing something together. Here, something else is present, a nurturing element I have not found in other relationships.

The sudden memory of Jaelle strikes a melancholy note with me, but I find that this is not an area I wish to discuss even with Eldra. This works out as she is mostly interested in learning of Wrik's life, and I avoid much mention of the female whose place has come to me. I do the dishes, and Eldra advises she is going upstairs for a nap. I assure her I will be fine in the meanwhile. I return to my post by the porch and watch rain begin to fall out at sea. To my surprise, the dog joins me there. He circles three times and lays on a rug next to me, his back against my hip.

CHAPTER 14

I put my hand on him gently and stroke his fur as I have seen the others do until I sense he is asleep. Benton has decided I am of less interest than a human and more welcome than the vacuum cleaner. Well, it is some progress on an otherwise slow day.

CHAPTER 15

I FOLLOWED RENA INTO A HOUSE THAT COMBINED RUSTIC
and traditional elements with modern conveniences, such as the robo-
server that rolled up.

"Can I offer you a drink? I'm going to have one," Rena said.

I nodded.

"Sit," she said. I dropped onto an overstuffed chair next to her, looking at animal heads hung on the walls, the flags and other memorabilia
from the war. I was glad not to see Ncome Commando insignia up there.

She caught my gaze as the robot server returned with two large
glasses of some local red wine. "I wish I could talk my husband into
getting rid of the bits of dead animals. They used to give the kids night-
mares. He thinks it's important that our son face his fears. Of course, it's
not like he shot any of them himself."

There was an unmistakable bitterness in my sister's voice. I looked
up from the glass that the machine was extending to me on its servo.
For a second, I thought I saw something in my sister's eyes, but it was
shuttered instantly.

"I used to feel the same way," I said. "Our father had trophies all over
the walls. I think he would have put up a Solari head if he could have."

My sister drank from her glass. "What's the old saying? Those who
do not learn from the past are condemned to repeat it."

I stared at her, lost for a second. "Did the old man call you to tell
you I was back?"

"Are you back?"

"What the hell, Rena?" I snapped. "You're looking right at me."

She bit her lip slightly. "Sorry, badly put. I didn't mean it to sound
like I'm playing games. I'm not as fond of that as I once was. Who knew
games could be so expensive and no do-overs either…" She shook her
head. "No, I meant, have you returned to stay?"

"You didn't answer my question."

"Yes. Dad called me, yesterday. Told me you came by. Didn't say
much more, just that he expected you'd call on me at some point. I told
him I was far from sure that was true. The rest I heard from my
husband."

I raised my eyebrows.

"Oh, there's rather a buzz going around political circles on Retief,
especially among the Rebels, both old and too young to remember what
it was like looking at an overcast made of Confederation ships. The name
and news of Wrik Trigardt took a little bit to get out. I guess you escaped
the capitol and eluded the media before they heard about you and the

CHAPTER 15

Lost Colony Expedition. We had the press here looking for you. I sent them to my husband's office. He used some influence to keep them from bothering Mom.

"I figured it out when I saw your picture from the Seddon expedition. My older brother, a starship captain, operating beyond the borders of known space, rescuing lost expeditions and battling ancient war machines."

While dating an ancient war machine, I thought.

"You didn't look much different then when I'd last seen you. Oh, you've filled out some, but it was clearly you."

I nodded.

"They say you're a hero, Wrik Trigardt. Does it mean any more than it did when they said you were a coward?"

My sister's thinking and speech eluded me; it was like talking to a complete stranger. "I don't really know what either word means. As for praise or condemnation, well, one helps less than you think, and one hurts more than you can believe."

"No," she said, her voice distant. "Not more than I can believe."

"So far, of the people I wanted to see, I've found the Old Man, with the expected result, my friend Delt, who, to my shock, is my friend again and my mother, who was glad to see me."

"Thank God for that. I wondered if I should call her but decided I would leave things be for a few days." Rena said.

"You're surprised that Mom was glad to see me?"

"No, merely glad it's happened. Perhaps she can climb down off the cross now. She nailed herself up there good and proper."

"What are you talking about?"

"Does she even look like our mother anymore?" Rena asked, drinking more. "She hasn't taken very good care of herself: exiled herself to the seaside and waited either for death or your return. I've been keeping her afloat, running her investments, but I don't know how much longer—"

"What does Mom need?" I asked.

"Times haven't been that good," Rena said, defensiveness in her tone. "Some of the investments didn't work out, and her health has been chancy. She won't take anything from my husband, or our father—"

"What's needed?" I repeated.

"She goes through about 800 Dirands a month."

"Will 100,000 Confed credits do for starters? That should buy her house outright. If not there will be more."

My sister stared at me over the lip of her glass. "As easy as that?"

"Give me the account information, and I'll have it transferred immediately. I won't mess with anything you've been doing in the twelve years I've been gone."

"Generous," she nodded. "Looks like you really are a hero."

"Meaningless noise, Rena. But I did this to Mom. I'm back here trying to fix some of what I wrecked before; money is the easy part."

"Be nice to see Mom happy," Rena said. "I wonder what that looks like?" She stopped and looked at me, then put down the glass. "She made you come see me. I wasn't on your list." It wasn't a question.

"Yes," I said flatly.

She looked away. The old Rena would have thrown the glass at me, raged, screamed insults. This one only stared out the window.

"The kids are out playing in the back," she finally said. "Would you like to meet them?"

I hadn't even considered her children.

She rose, still not looking at me. "They have uncles, aunts and cousins on his side. You're the only family they have on my side, beyond Mom and Dad."

"You want me to?"

Now she looked me in the eye. "Their slates stay clean. All this.... crap we're standing in is ours, not theirs."

"I'll do... the best I can. Not really sure what to say."

"Who the fuck does? Come on. I'd like you to meet them before their father gets home. Let's make it straight and honest."

I followed her out onto the back deck that overlooked a broad swath of lawn, dotted with fruit trees and bushes. I could see a fine playhouse for children. A cat blinked at me from the second level of it. In the distance, I saw some dogs sniffing about.

In a sandbox, two children played. When I saw them, a sense of disorientation wrapped about me: a boy and a girl were digging, playing with some toy soldiers and vehicles. The boy appeared to be about nine and was dressed in what I realized was an imitation rebel uniform. The girl was younger and wore a traditional blouse over very non-traditional casual pants. Both were intent on their play and didn't notice us. I felt as if in some bizarre way I was looking into my and Rena's past. They could have been us on the family farm, playing as we had for so many hours as young children, before my father poisoned our well.

I put a hand over my eyes and wiped away the ghosts of the past, then shook my head to clear it. I caught my sister looking at me with more understanding of what was going on than I was comfortable with.

"Cobus, Amelia," my sister called. The children looked up and stood, Cobus helping his little sister up. "Come here, there's someone I want you to meet."

The children came forward in the hesitant way that children do, looking up at me with their big eyes.

Rena gestured to me. "You remember I told you long ago, that, before you were born, I had a brother. His name was Piet Wrik Van Zyle, but he uses Wrik Trigardt now, that grandma's name you know. This is Uncle Wrik, he's come to visit."

"Hello," I said awkwardly, suddenly conscious of my empty hands. It hadn't occurred to me to bring presents for the children.

Amelia gave me a bright smile. Cobus' expression was more wary.

"You're our Uncle?" Cobus said, doubt plain in his voice. Couldn't say that I blamed him. "Where have you been?"

A question his mother might well have liked answered too, I thought. "I moved off planet a long time ago, before you were born, or your mother and Dad had even met."

"Do you live on one of the moons?" Amelia said, with a delighted smile on her tiny face.

I laughed, a touch raggedly. "No, much further away than that. I've lived in a bunch of places, mostly on shipboard in the last few years. I suppose if I have a home, it would be on Star Central where my business, Lost Planet, is based."

"Star Central," Cobus said with a dark look, "that's the home to the Confederacy."

I was momentarily startled, suddenly taken back through time to when I had held such attitudes. It seemed that, as with my own father, Cobus' outlook had been colored by his father.

"That's enough of that," Rena said.

"You said you had a ship," the boy continued, a touch of sullenness in his manner from his mother's rebuke.

It seemed a safe topic. "Yep, an old Comet class courier. We call her the Stardust."

Amelia considered. "That's a pretty name," she piped.

"Yes, a friend of mine came up with the name. I was going to call her the SS Misadventure. She thought it would be bad for business."

Amelia giggled. "She sounds smart."

I felt a touch of sadness. "She is."

"Does Stardust have any guns?" Cobus asked.

"Kind of; we have a communications laser we amped up to military level punch. No tubes though, they took the torps out when she was demobbed and sold for surplus. We're a commercial scoutship, not a warship."

"Don't be quite so modest," Rena said. "Uncle Wrik and his ship were on the expedition to Seddon. They found a lost colony of humans and a new alien race."

Cobus' face lightened. "You're the ones who found Rainhell's grandson and fought the big mecha!"

I raised my eyebrows. Shasti was one of the most famous of starship captains and something of a rebel against Confederate authority herself. Apparently, she met with a younger rebel's approval.

"Yes, though the robots we had on board did most of the fighting with the Kolzin Destroyer. I was there, too."

"Awesome," the boy replied.

I remembered the terror of hunting the monstrous mecha through a dead city and Maauro's desperate battle with it and repressed a shudder.

"Can you tell us about it?" both children demanded.

The sound of a car pulling up into the driveway saved me from storytelling.

"That will be my husband," Rena said. "Why don't you stay here with the children? I told Greg there was a possibility that you might come by, but I'd like to let him know you're here."

"A precontact briefing?" I said ruefully.

Rena's expression remained remote and centered, but she nodded and headed off. I looked at the children, then settled on the grass next to them, and began to tell them a safely edited and vastly abbreviated version of the Seddon Expedition, minus Maauro's true nature, our breaking into a Confederate base to steal secrets from the Interior Ministry, or our run-ins with the Voit-Veru. Both children sat mesmerized, but, being children, I wasn't sure if a tale of Kris Kringle wouldn't have had the same effect, or, if they understood much, particularly Amelia, who was only six.

Rena returned, trailed by a tall, handsome man with a neatly-trimmed beard, wearing a bush-jacket and field pants. Even teeth flashed in a smile. The two children ran to their father. Amelia raised her arms to be picked up for her hug. Cobus greeted his father with more reserve. Somehow that sight, so reminiscent of my own childhood, filled me with a deep sadness that I did my best to keep off my face. The children stood to one side as Grieg turned to me, Rena next to him.

"This is my husband," she said.

"I see the prodigal has returned," he added. "I'm Grieg Nazir."

I shook his hand, feeling awkward and out of place. He had a firm grip but his hands didn't have the hardness to them that his field coat and farmer dress promised. "Rena told you who I am."

He nodded. "Of course, and that you prefer the name of Wrik Trigardt."

"Yes," I replied. "It's a name with less baggage than Piet Van Zyle." I wondered how many years it had been since I had last said my own full name aloud. It no longer felt like it was mine. Perhaps my father was right and that name belonged to a dead person.

"There was some harsh judgment dealt out to that name," he replied, his voice sympathetic.

"What can I say? You know why."

"Seems to me like it wouldn't have made a difference any which way. Also seems a lot of people who weren't wearing Commando jackets maybe had too much to say."

I felt a hot flush come over my face. I hadn't expected open sympathy from someone like Grieg, or who I thought Grieg was. He caught my glance at his commando style jacket and made a self-deprecating wave. "Don't get me wrong. I was with the Commando during the Rising, staff officer with Abelan's Fourth Night Riders. I have no use for the Confederacy, or what they're trying to do to our world. How they heap insult on injury. You know every Governor, every military commander they've assigned here, has been an alien or a darkskin?"

"I've left those days and those ways behind me," I said. "My father's politics aren't mine."

Grieg looked momentarily nonplussed. "Ah, why am I talking about politics on a family occasion? Come on, let's have a beer. You can tell us more about your wanderings among the stars."

I was glad for the switch to a safer topic. "I was telling the children about some of it, the not so horrible parts."

With the children noisily accompanying us, we made our way to the stone porch that overlooked the elaborate gardens. A human domestic appeared in the background, placed a tray of drinks and snacks on a table, then disappeared. The children looked to Rena, who nodded, and they took some cookies and a drink.

Grieg passed me a beer, and he took one for himself. Rena raised a glass of white wine.

"You were telling us about Seddon," Cobus reminded me,

"I would rather hear about Retief," I said. "My story will be on the news, the part of it that can be told, anyway."

Grieg's eyebrows raised, and I immediately regretted the remark. This man might play at being affable, but was no fool. Something else struck me, the beard was not the bushy style favored by the rebels, and the field jacket was of a fine fabric that would not stand the rigors of the veldt any more than the pants would. He was the style of a rebel, but there was something artificial and unpersuasive in it.

"Ah, nothing interesting ever happens around here," Cobus muttered.

"Uncle Wrik," Rena interjected, "has traveled a long way to come home, and he may not want to remember all these dark things."

"There may also be people who don't want him to talk," Grieg said. "After all, a voyage so long and into the unknown couldn't be mounted without connections and money."

"Lost Planet was created for that purpose," I countered, feeling more comfortable back in my accustomed, evasive role.

"But you surely must have Confederate connections," Grieg said. This drew me a dark and dubious look from Cobus. Amelia used his distraction to steal one of his cookies.

I shrugged. "No one flies an ex-warship in Confederate Space without some. We find the lost. It takes us into a lot of places where the law doesn't go."

"Well, we deal with the Confederacy, too," Grieg said.

"Some do," Rena said.

"Know your enemy," Grieg said airily.

"Friends come and friends go," I returned, "but enemies accumulate. We accumulated the Confederacy; look how that worked out."

"The Confederacy has accumulated enemies, too," he said.

"I thought we weren't going to discuss politics," my sister said sharply.

"Yes, yes," Grieg said waving a hand. "Well, that would seem to eliminate my career, a good bit of his past and maybe some of the future."

A bitter laugh escaped me. "I'd add family history to the list of off-limits subjects."

I was surprised when Rena joined me in the laugh. We looked at each other and laughed harder.

Greg snorted. "What does that leave us?"

Rena shook her head. "What was it Mom used to say out of those old books of hers: the weather and the conditions of the road?"

I groaned. "Oh, those Austen books, the most boring books in the history of writing, two whole chapters on going to the post office."

"What are you both talking about?" Grieg said.

Rena waved his comment away. "Just books from my mother's library; I wonder if she still has them?"

We talked on of inconsequential things as the sun westered, enjoying the beer, and the children's questions. I finished my edited tale of Seddon and the rescue of Shasti's grandson. Cobus was especially taken with our battle with Solari pirates, who had a long and unpleasant history with the settlers of Retief.

"It must be getting on toward dinner-time," Grieg finally said. "Will you stay for dinner?"

Rena looked at me, her face neutral.

I was confused. I'd not planned on staying this long. Truth be told, I'd had no plan beyond ringing the doorbell. But I knew Maauro and my mother were waiting anxiously and, truth was, I wanted not to overplay the moment. It seemed better to go now while things were good and possibilities were open.

"Not tonight," I said. "I planned this visit poorly. Well, actually, I didn't plan it at all. I didn't bring presents for the children, or anything for the house—"

"Wrik," Rena said, "that's not necessary—"

"What sort of presents?" Cobus asked.

We all laughed, but I drew the sense that Rena at least was relieved I wasn't staying. Like me, she'd doubtless found today stressful.

"Perhaps Saturnal night," Rena said, looking at Grieg, who, after a moment's hesitation, nodded.

"Yes," he replied. "I have business that will take me away for some of this week. But, by the weekend, things may be settled. There may even be opportunities for us to discuss."

"Children," Rena said. "Say goodbye to your uncle."

Amelia came over and hugged me. Cobus threw me a salute, which I returned rather than disappoint the boy. Grieg shook hands, but seemed happy to remain in his deck chair, legs stretched out. Rena rose gracefully, putting her wine glass aside. "I'll see you out."

"Remember about the presents," Cobus called.

"I will," I promised.

"That boy!" my sister fumed.

"It's nothing. He's a kid," I said.

We walked in silence to the door. I kept thinking of a hundred things to say, but I could almost feel the barriers between us going up. We reached the door and looked at each.

"So," she said finally. "We'll see you this weekend."

I nodded slowly then, almost without volition, it spilled out of me. "I'll bring a date, if that's ok?"

Rena's eyes widened in surprise. "That's quick work—"

I shook my head. "Aurelia Toyoma," I said, giving Maauro's cover name, "is very special to me. We've been together for years. We were friends even when I was involved with someone else."

"Well," my sister said with genuine smile. "That will be nice. Yes, please bring her. I'd like that."

"Good night, Rena."

"Good night, Pie....Wrik." She opened the door, and I slipped out.

I walked down the path to my car in something of a daze. I'd seen my sister: no blowup, but no resolution either, it was oddly like we'd had no past. I'd wanted to clean out a wound, but Rena acted as if there wasn't one. I felt, as if, somehow this wasn't real, like I was wandering in a dream. All of a sudden, I wanted to get back. I wanted to see Maauro, to hold the one person who wouldn't fail me. My steps picked up, and I opened the door, slid it behind the wheel and started the car. If I moved quickly, I could be looking at her in two hours. I didn't want to call. I needed to see her. I could make it back before our next check in.

"Time to go home," I said to myself.

CHAPTER 16

AFTER ELDRA GOES TO BED, I ELECT TO WAIT FOR WRIK BY THE LANDING *pad where the Magister will be stored. There is no one on the beach and, as is my habit, I adopt a head-to-toe, flat-black camouflage. I am a wraith by the night-time sea, under the slivers of the moons. My sensors are full on, including some spybees I left around the house. I detect Wirriways in flight over me and the Nightriders that prey on them. I see the bioluminescence of sea life in the foaming waves, and the air has its complement of winged life, including a butterfly called a Gemstar that comes out only at night, to wink and blink as it seeks a mate. The sheer mass of the biota around me is a little disorienting, and I find myself resentful of it. In all this world and the worlds beyond, I am the only being of my kind, as different as if the rocks themselves had sat up and wondered about the stars, God, and love.*

I look away from the writhing mass of biology to the cool, clean stars above, though cool only through distance. Wrik once called them my jewel box. I like the concept, for all that I have little interest in gems beyond the emotional connotations of them as gifts. Still, I am a proper female now, and it's right that I have a jewelry box, even if only a metaphorical one.

My long range scanner picks the Magister at 3,500 meters at last. I was forced to leave the spybee I sent with Wrik at his sister's house to monitor that location. I chide myself for the lack of foresight in not sending two. I used Retief's net when it had a useful sensor to watch him on his return, but there were broad swatches of airspace without coverage. I had anxious moments until the Magister cleared a line of sight to my position. I again scan his ship, which is operating properly.

The Magister slows and descends prudently. I am briefly glad that Delt was not at those controls. Automatics from the landing system at this little field reach out their own web of sensors and data to the Magister but I override them with my superior systems. I will guide my beloved back to me; no lesser system will be trusted with my treasure.

The plane lands, and the engines spin down. I suppose if I had been born a human, I would have released a whoosh of relief. Their basic design and manufacture are solid, but would not have passed muster in my Creator's time. Still, he is home, and that is all that counts.

As the hatch pops up, I adopt another of the outfits that I bought at the Immaculata: a red jacket over a cream t-shirt and blue jeans. My skin tone returns to its usual paleness.

As the canopy rises, Wrik, looking weary, stands. He spots me and, as he does so, his face splits into a broad grin. This gives me great satisfaction as he jumps down from the cockpit. We walk toward each other, embrace, kiss, then embrace again.

He sighs. "Thanks for coming to meet me. I was hoping you would."

"Did it not go well?" I ask, stabbed by anxiety.

"Hard to say," he replies, reaching up to get his flight bag. "It mostly went oddly. No explosion, no yelling or screaming, just a sort of weird civility. Rena seemed to want to leave the past pretty much in the past. Wouldn't deal with it."

I put my arm in his, and we start back toward Eldra's again, forgoing the winding road to walk along the beachfront itself. "Is this not an acceptable resolution? It surely is an improvement on your father."

"That's true," he said, slinging the bag to his other shoulder. "However it kind of doesn't feel like a resolution at all. But we have agreed to see each other again. And I met my niece, nephew and my brother-in-law. As you would say, my network expands, even if the new members are mostly on probation."

"Was it pleasant to meet these new members?"

"Yes, particularly with the children. My brother-in-law, well, I'm not sure. He wasn't what I expected, being both more sympathetic and less of a rebel than what I'd been led to expect."

"How is that bad?"

"Not sure. He just strikes a false note with me. Then again, he is a politician. In any event, you will meet them soon. We are invited for dinner later this week, and I said I'd bring you."

I am pleased by this development.

"The only thing is…"

"You do not want your sister to know what I am."

"Only because I don't trust her or her husband, and for no other reason."

I nod.

"You believe me about the no other reason, right?" His face is anxious.

I laugh. "Yes, Wrik. You are a terrible liar at the best of times and, worst of all if you try to lie to me. I believe you."

"Good. However I did wish I had brought some presents for the kids. Hey, could you have Dusko fly a few things out to us?"

I nod. Wrik describes the items he wants as presents for the children. I will inform Dusko later. There is no reason to wake him for this task.

We walk arm in arm back to the house.

"It is a beautiful night," I say.

"Now," he agrees, smiling at me.

We retire to our bed. Wrik is asleep not long after his head hits the pillow.

When I wake, I find Maauro on the bed next to me, her head resting lightly in what has become her spot on my left shoulder. Her eyes are closed in her latest bit of fiction, but I know it is because she values these moments. She has nothing that she would rather do, or nothing she cannot also do while in this position. She smiles despite her closed eyes, and I suspect she knows exactly what I am thinking. We have come a long way since we quarreled on the deck of a flatboat heading into the jungles of Kandalor, with me referring to her as a "killbot." I find the remembrance of my saying it, suddenly painful.

Maauro's eyes flick open. "What is wrong?"

"Nothing."

"You tensed suddenly."

"A bad memory of something stupid I once said."

Her eyes search mine. "I wish your memories did not so plague you."

"It's in the nature of the sort of beings we are."

She nods, and a strand of her long hair tickles my nose. "Yes, you don't have the advantage of being able to delete a memory. Of course, I did," she rose up on her elbow, "until I promised you that I would never delete a memory with you in it. Now I find that I treasure them all, the good and bad, the full record of the life that I am having."

"And none of them cause you pain?"

"Some do. You, shot on Kandalor because I failed to anticipate what you and Lostra would do. Worst of all, when M-7 and I were battling for control of this body, I shot you, a nick on the cheek, but it was all I could then manage against my other self. These memories cause me some distress, but not the way they do for you. For you, it is sometimes as if you are experiencing the event again. For me, though I have perfect recall of all I see and do, it is merely a recording of something that has happened, unalterable, despite any wish of mine."

I sighed. "Sometimes I envy you the detachment, the calmness, and the distance from pain."

"Even that has changed for me. Once, as only a machine, I recalled my past perfectly, but never looked forward to a future, as there was no chance of a change for me. M-7 I was and would be. It's not as if I was going to grow up, grow old, have children or retire, all the changes you face. So in a sense, I lived only in the present.

"In my life with you, I have discovered change. I no longer exist to kill. I explore, I make friends, I help people, and I fall in love. I am no longer a frightening monster, but a pretty girl—"

"A very pretty girl," I said.

She smiled. "But with that has come the fear of loss, the concern over hurting and being hurt. I dread most that something could happen to our feelings for each other."

"It won't."

She hesitated, then blurted out. "It did between you and Jaelle."

I was quiet for a few seconds, thinking. "I guess I shouldn't give reassurances as if you were a child, or even a young girl, not with Jaelle as an example and Olivia as well. I guess I can only say that, as a man, this is the thing I am most certain of.

"Sometimes, I worry the same on my end. I mean, you really don't need me for anything anymore. There are braver, stronger, and more successful men out there. Then there's always the worry of that handsome boy-robot showing up sometime."

She laughed lightly. "Now it is my turn to offer assurances as if you were a child, or a young boy. See, we are the same in more ways than you think. Whatever and whoever else is out there, somehow I know this is best for me. What I want most for myself. Variety would just be variety. Of course," she poked me in the ribs with a finger that contains a high speed flechette gun, "you males seem very interested in variety in females, like bad children taking a bite of all the cookies on a plate. Our friend Delt seems to be a good example of this."

"God," I responded cautiously, "has both a sense of humor and a lot to answer for in the way he put men and women together."

I heard sounds from downstairs.

"Your mother is up," Maauro added, "doubtless filled with curiosity over your visit with Rena."

"Doubtless," I said, sitting up.

"And it gives you a badly needed escape from the direction that this conversation was heading in," she added archly.

"Which I am promptly going to avail myself of," I said, heading for the bathroom.

"Resistance is futile," she called from under the blankets.

Showered and dressed, we joined Mom for breakfast. I filled her in on my brief and curious interlude with my sister and her family.

"I should have thought about presents for the grandchildren," she added.

"Is that the takeaway here?" I asked, amused.

"Hard to quite say what the result is," she said, throwing up her hands. "Honestly, that girl has never made anything easy."

"The contact was at least not confrontational," Maauro added.

"There is that," I said.

The rest of the day was spent helping mom with some repairs on her house, with Maauro playing a combination of plumber, electrician, general contractor and factory. As long as we had metal to pour into her, she could come up with any part that we needed. I was a little distressed over the number of things that required repair or replacement. Money had indeed been tight and the landlord not very forthcoming. That would stop, I determined.

Some of Mom's friends came over in the evening to say hello, and this turned into an impromptu wine and cheese party. Word had gotten round about Wrik Trigardt now, and it seemed that, so far as these folks were concerned, the acts of Wrik Trigardt had buried the failures of Piet

CHAPTER 16

Van Zyle, the latter name everyone knew better than to utter in my mother's house. All of them were clearly fond of my mother, including Dr Stasoon, who she sometimes worked for, and the town mayor, Lindanal Cook, who seemed a free-spirited woman for Retief. The town in general seemed to have little use for the politics of what some of them called the "Old Retief."

I found myself the center of attention, telling of Seddon in an easy, edited version of the story that was becoming second nature to me now. A couple of women had me blushing, when they talked of not having brought their eligible daughters because of a slim, beautiful girl who'd already won my heart. Maauro, for her part, played shy and retiring, probably feeling somewhat overwhelmed by the free-flowing interaction of so many biologicals in such an unstructured fashion.

As the last of the neighbors leave Eldra's house, my intruder programs aboard the satellite over Rena's home signal me. They have detected a major increase in coded traffic. I have prepared for this moment carefully. My programs have gradually infiltrated, analyzing and developing antibodies to the virus protection. One by one, the satellite's protective programs have fallen to me without ever triggering their defenses.

The attack barrier remains, and it is a different matter. I use the same worms I unleashed on the Voit-Veru world when I took over that planet's terraforming equipment. My worms enter the barrier, though I think the odds are even as to whether they will trigger it. The barrier itself does not concern me. It is too feeble to damage me or my programs, but it will alert the biologicals that I have breached their security. In .0080097487 of a second, the battle is over. My worms breach the attack barrier and lower it without generating an alert. I have been lucky.

On the other side of the barrier is a wealth of military and tactical information. Much of it is encoded. My cryptology programs swing into full deployment, and information begins to flow to me. Initial indications are that this is likely a simple, but effective book code. Unless one knows the book, such are often impossible to break. This would stop the attack of most AIs, but I am M-7, a quantum computer optimized for data extraction. The struggle is now an exercise in sheer computing power, and I doubt that a group as provincial as the Retief rebels would base their ciphers on books from alien species. Correlating Retief history and human literature allows me exclude many other Terran root languages. I begin running 2,981,013 works simultaneously to see which books generate sensible information. Some, obviously not correlateable works, I drop and replace. Gradually I realize that the book code involves several books, and I hone in on those volumes.

The database begins to yield to me. I learn the truth of what I suspected. There is a large and amorphous resistance movement to the Confederate presence on Retief. Much of it is cultural, even near ceremonial, but there is a more active branch. It is to this more active political branch that money and materials have been flowing, money for armaments. Grieg Nazir is indeed involved in the rebel movement with the rank of Lt Colonel in the Phoenix Commando.

The single largest expenditure in the last two years is attached to his name and the military wing of the resistance. I focus and find data indicating that someone has contracted for an offworld mercenary force, one to be inserted by starship, a small force but very demanding of high tech supplies.

Lilith. A cold wave of shock rolls over my systems. Lilith is connected to Nazir, who is networked to Wrik through Rena. Wrik has been there, without my protection, in a command post of the enemy well known to Lilith. Clinging girlfriend or not, this will not occur again.

Problems multiply. Beyond these basic communications, lies a command channel to Lilith, accessible by Nazir and others in the Phoenix Commando. Pain me as it does to admit it, if I follow that channel into the multiverse, I will be fighting Lilith on her home ground, in her citadel, and the odds of survival, much less success, are poor. Even touching that channel will alert my enemy.

But while she protects her own communications and whereabouts, the rebels around her cannot keep me out. I see orders for a concentration of forces, comments on a cyberattack made before I drove Lilith into her citadel and out of Retief's net. Apparently, she has blinded any orbiting satellites to the movement of a land force that will assemble north of the capitol, and strike the Confederate base near the spaceport where Stardust sits.

Grieg Nazir is a prime mover in all of this. He has taken Wrik's appearance as a sign that he is under suspicion, or threatened, having been informed through Lilith of our Confederate connections. Lilith has not informed him of what I am yet, perhaps out of a desire not to panic her onworld connections. Those connections know they cannot keep Lilith on the planet and inactive for long. If they are to use her, they must do so now.

I must get free to counter the Rebel attack, if I can. I open up my internal communications as I help pack away some leftovers from the impromptu party.

"Dusko."

"Here."

"I need you to pick me up with the heavy duty flitter again."

"Affirmative, where are you?"

"We are staying with Wrik's mother. I have uploaded the coordinates to the ship's computer. I also need you to pick up my armspac from

CHAPTER 16

where I cached it near Delt's field; it has a transponder set on our #7emergency frequency.

"I will arrange to be on the beach, two kilometers south of Wrik's mother's house at 11 PM. Pickup should take no more than twenty seconds."

"Understood. Care to tell me why we are making this clandestine rendezvous?"

"Lilith is on the move. My intel is that she is preparing a strike with rebel forces on a Confederate target near the spaceport."

"Lovely. Do you plan to battle this insurgent force entirely on your own?"

"Are you volunteering to help?"

"No."

"I appreciate your frankness."

"I doubt it."

"Be on time."

"I will."

"One additional thing," I give him the list of presents.

"You're kidding me."

"It's not like I asked you to wrap them," I snap, "and you are coming this way anyhow."

"Whatever," he cuts the circuit.

Waiting is tedious but there is no help for it. After the guests are gone and we have cleaned up, we gather in the living room. Eldra puts on some music. Wrik scans the entertainment channel without finding anything of interest. I begin to emit a light soporific gas, not enough to make anyone ill, or even aware of the effect. My aim is drowsiness. The soporific, along with the meal and the stresses of the day does its work. Wrik and his mother are quickly heavy-eyed. Benton, plops down in a corner and is soon unconscious.

With sleepy goodnights, we all make our way upstairs. Wrik drops into bed and with a quick kiss, lies back. Now I administer a proper sedative through a needle so slim it barely registers as it slides in. He will sleep well into the morning. I sneak next door and repeat the procedure on his mother.

I slip out of the house into the darkness, and move to the edge of the small town, rapidly and unobserved.

I detect the ship's flitter by its IFF signal. Dusko does his usual good job of settling on the beach, the sound of the small ship's engine fades as I run aboard the flitter. It lurches skyward again. I join the Dua-denlenn, sliding into the second seat.

"Are you sure about this?" Dusko says, sparing me a glance as we climb out. We are subsonic until we are far from Eldra's home, then pile on the Mach numbers to the flitter's maximum short duration speed.

"Why? Are you worried about me?"

He returns his gaze to his instruments. *"That's not the way of my people, as you know. Say rather that I would find your death inconvenient and possibly a factor in my own."*

I nod. This, at least, is in character for the Dua-denlenn. *"I must deal with this attack,"* I reply. *"There is no choice. Now is the only time I can do so without revealing this conflict to Wrik."*

"If he finds out that you have been in battle without him, he will be very cross with you."

"It is my intention that he not find out. However, my review of romantic writings indicates that even the closest and most devoted of couples keep secrets from each other."

A snort escapes from him. *"Hmmm, Maauro, I do believe you are getting the hang of biological relationships—you may well be prepared for marriage."*

I sigh. *"'Do you remember when you were terrified of me? I look back on those days with a form of nostalgia."*

"Yes, I remember those days," he says dryly.

And so do I. The memories of Dusko as our old enemy, clash with those of him as a member, however ill-fitting, of my network.

"I regret what I just said," I add on a sudden impulse

He looks at me, his expression unreadable. *"That was then."*

"Yes," I reply. *"We are no longer enemies."*

"Don't be quite so nice to me. It's unnerving."

"I'll remember that."

We settle in as the flitter eats up the kilometers to our destination north of the capitol.

"Two minutes to insertion point," Dusko says.

"Remember to pull out to the east after insertion."

"I'd be closer if I circled the area," he said. *"I can make a faster pickup if you're in trouble."*

"Thank you, but there is too great a danger of your being shot down. Or, if someone were to take a radius of your circle, it would aid them in locating me."

"Good thinking," he grunts. *"IP in sixty seconds. Get ready."*

Dusko touches down in a small clearing, near to the treeline. I leap out, armspac webbed across my chest. In 1.13 seconds, I am among the trees, listening to the sounds of Dusko drawing away as directed to await my pickup call. I speed into the forest, launching more of the spybees that I had earlier surrounded Delt's airfield with. I also sample the air, hoping to detect my enemy, but I am unlucky, the wind is against me, and I can pick up no trace of the rebel attack force.

I link up to the few satellites that cover Retief's weather and surveillance needs. None are in positions to overlook the area I am in operating in, or have the resolution or instruments to be useful. This backwards world is beginning to annoy me. I briefly consider having

Dusko return, but the flitter is too vulnerable, even if Lilith were not present. I must rely on my spy-bees. This slows my advance as the bees, with their limited power, cannot keep up with me.

I wait impatiently as the bees spread out, but my wait is not long. Spybee # 13 detects the enemy moving down a logging road north of the spaceport. The Confed compound sits at the north end of spaceport, which is north and east of the city. The logging road comes down on a surfaced secondary road, which links up to a highway passing near the compound. It is a sensible attack profile for a force of wheeled vehicles.

Spybee 13 rests in a tree and I watch through its sensors as the enemy force rolls by. The polyglot force is what one might expect from a rebel group. The column contains eight vehicles. Four of them are commercial vehicles modified to carry light weapons or loaded with armed humans. The other four are military vehicles, two jeep hovercars, with 100m magazine-fed recoilless rifles on them, and, leading the column is a Leyland armored car with a 50MM high-velocity gun and a grenade launcher. Behind the Leyland follows an APC, an older Confed model that predates the first rebellion. Atop the armored personnel carrier are three of Lilith's HCRs. They carry the most recent model Confed triple-autos; formidable weapons that, with a sustained burst, could destroy me. Certainly the Leyland's 50MM could finish me. I must prepare my attack carefully.

I spin my web of bees about the enemy force, keeping them as far as is possible from the APC with its cargo of HCRs. The machines are alert. Lilith will not repeat the mistake of her casual walk across the veldt. Yet, I notice that only three of the machines are here. Lilith is keeping two for personal guards. She fears me, but three HCRs are more than enough to destroy the Confed base with its minimal defenses. The fact that the HCRs are on the APC indicates it is the command vehicle, and likely Grieg is within. This too, will compound my problems.

I have little regard for the rebel force itself. I do not doubt their courage or devotion to their cause, but irregular troops in high-tech combat are largely worthless.

I deliberate on the proper vector to attack from. I decide to take them on the logging road, as the chance for collateral damage is far greater once they reach the surfaced roads. If I maneuver myself from the south, they will have to pass me to attack but it is the obvious path for an ambush, and I would face the Leyland and the APC's weapons as well as the HCRs.

No, the best way is to attack the column is from the rear. I can maximize my initial strike, and they will have to reorient to deal with it. Decision made, I speed forward and circle about. If the HCRS were deployed to screen the convoy, I would be detected, but atop the APC, Lilith's HCR sensors are degraded by the noise and heat of the vehicles. This gains me precious meters as I race to cut across the logging road behind the last truckload of armed men. I level my armspac and, with a long ripping sound, fire a pattern of HVAP rounds exactly the width of the last enemy vehicle. Simultaneously I launch a HEAT round in a low arc at the Leyland. The best way to destroy an enemy column enroute, is to disable the lead and rear vehicles.

The rear vehicle explodes in flames followed by the screams of dying men and women. My first HEAT round hits the rear deck of the Leyland; it slews off the road—partly blocking it.

The night is rent with weapon-fire as rebels spill out of the remaining vehicles and in a display of poor fire discipline, open up in all directions. I disregard them and the small arms fire. My concern is the HCRS and the AFVs.

A tree explodes next to me. I am surprised at the severity of the explosion. One of the HCRS is directing fire from the recoilless rifle gun jeeps as the others deploy and the APC's own chain gun searches for me. I must duck into a depression in the ground, cut deeply by a small stream, to escape. A metal fragment hits me and chips my side. I know, for the first time, a frisson of fear about my appearance. I have just regained my left arm. I would hate to appear before Wrik mutilated again. Rage shoots through me at this prospect. If I am disfigured, everyone in that column is dead. I scramble into a nearby streambed.

I run up the stream as the recoilless rifles scythe down the trees over me. More splinters and rocks chips bounce off me. If I were biological, or lightly armored, I would be done for. I cannot allow them to pin me down or the other HCRs will fix my position and destroy me.

I link up to Spybee 13 and fire two high-explosive rounds at the recoilless rifles and two more HEAT rounds at the APC, using the spybee's sensors to guide them as I am below line- of-sight. One of each are intercepted by the HCR's triple autos, sleeted out of the sky in a fine display of marksmanship. But the rest get through, one high explosive round hits the second gun jeep right on the long-barreled weapon, the resulting blast and spray of steel cuts down the crews of both the unarmored jeeps. The HEAT round strikes the track on the APC and the disabled vehicle spins and hits a tree. Both HCRS aboard it leap free at the last instant. Enemy fire slackens. As the HCRs are moving, I pop up and fire more HVAP bullets at the nearest HCR. The slender machine is hammered as the armor-piercing rounds riddle it, but that does not stop it from firing a long triple-auto burst back at me. Again I drop to the ground and fire more HEAT and high-explosive rounds. The HCRS are too agile to be hit by the HEAT rounds but they hit the Leyland whose turret, despite the burning deck, is seeking me. The high-explosive goes off over the HCRS, damaging all. The Leyland's turret erupts as secondary explosions rip it apart from inside.

Three AP rounds from an HCR strike me, doing slight damage. I return fire, but this time my enemy has found hard cover. I dash off the hill. Only two HCRs return my fire, the other one, or its weapon, must be damaged. I devote a few milliseconds to my own damage control, exchanging a damaged exterior module for an interior one. I leap up again and spray some small flechette rounds into the rebels, more to cause confusion than casualties. It starts them firing again. The slew of rocket propelled grenades and other fire will make the HCR's work of tracking me harder, whereas I know everything I see is hostile.

Spybee 13 winks out of my sensors, as does 14 and 15 further north. This tells me two things: the enemy has realized how I was indirectly guiding munitions, and, they are in full retreat up the logging road. I change course to pursue and am almost hit by a mini-grenade from one of Lilith's HCRs which has lain in wait for me to do just that. I return a burst of fire, and the HCR also withdraws from the engagement. Lilith's forces are gone, and only floundering rebels remain. Even these flee without organization in the same direction. I set my spybees to observe them in the event of a counterattack. One spots Nazir, bailing out of disabled APC.

I consider whether to pursue the HCRs, but the odds of running headlong into a successful ambush are prohibitive. Instead, I pass through the smoldering wreckage of vehicles and the dead rebels. More have escaped than died. Casualties are not my aim. Disrupting and eliminating their command and control, and severing Lilith from her local support are. In this I have been successful. I will communicate with the Confed commander on this world, who will arrange for disposal of the bodies and a suitable cover up. The clandestine nature of the rebels operations will aid this; doubtless it will be some time before many are missed.

I must extract one enemy operative on my own. I use my remaining spybees and maneuver to cut Nazir out of the herd of fleeing rebels. When I judge he is sufficiently distant from the others, I cut ahead of the stumbling, panting man and step onto the trail in front of him. He practically runs into me, then, screaming, throw his arms up.

"Be silent," I order, "if you wish to live."

Foolishly, he tries to aim the handgun he carries at me. I lunge forward, and seize him by the arm and throat, hauling him into the air. The weapon discharges into the ground before dropping from his numb hand. I struggle with the desire to wring his neck. I focus on the fact that though the link is a tenuous one, he is networked, however distantly to Wrik. The death of this man would create distress for Wrik's sister and her children, and thus for my Wrik.

"Who are you?" he chokes out

I glare up at him. "It is entirely possible that I am to be your sister-in-law."

He gapes at me. "What?" he finally manages.

"I assure you the prospect gives me no pleasure." I place his feet back on the ground, less the strain break his neck.

"Are you one of her machines? Has she betrayed us?"

I slap him across the face. "Be silent unless it is to answer me."

He stares at me, eyes wide.

"Listen and listen well, for your life depends on it. Nod, if you understand."

He nods.

"You will mention nothing of this night's engagement to anyone or to tell anyone of my existence. You will make no effort to reestablish contact with Lilith." Inspiration strikes, as Wrik would say. "You will advise the surviving members of your organization that the figure they saw attacking them was another advanced model of HCR, and that you suspect Lilith is secretly working for the Confederacy and led you into an ambush."

He looks around. "Where are the rest of your forces?"

"I am the force that destroyed your unit."

His eyes widen. "Who the hell are you? What the hell are you? You're not an HCR."

I move a step closer; he becomes very still.

"In the near future, you will meet me again, this time in the company of Wrik Trigardt. You will act as if this is our first meeting, and you know nothing of me, nor suspect that I am anything other than the human mutant I will say I am. One hopes your acting skills exceed your tactical skills.

"Do you understand? You now have my permission to speak."

"Yes," he says carefully. Then adds defiantly, "But I was right— you and Trigardt are Confederate Agents—"

"Concern yourself with your survival. Do you agree to my terms?"

He licks his lips. "'Yes."

"Understand this. If you renege on our agreement, I will hunt you down and tear you apart. You have seen only a small part of destruction I can mete out when provoked."

He nods slowly, hate he dares not express in his eyes.

I gesture. "What remains of your forces are retiring in that direction. Rejoin them."

He begins to back away then takes to his heels

I compose myself for a second, then call for Dusko to pick me up. I must remember to take the presents for the children and find some way to wrap them. I suspect we will be seeing Rena soon.

CHAPTER 17

WOKE IN THE MORNING HAVING SLEPT DEEPLY AND DREAM-
lessly. Somewhat to my surprise, my mother had slept in, too. I guess
the accumulated stresses of the week had worn on her. So we had a
late breakfast out on the porch, watching the ocean and an unusually
large freighter that made its way slowly across the horizon.

A buzzing drew my attention from the ship. "The phone," my mother
said, rising.

"You know if you had a house AI," I said. "You wouldn't have to
wonder where you left your portable."

"Don't be a smart ass, young man," my mother said. "Besides I don't
fancy living with a computer watching my every move."

She paused, then looked at Maauro. "Present company excepted."

Maauro smiled. "No offense taken. I am cognizant of the need for
privacy and feel such a need for myself as well."

"Good," Mom threw over her shoulder. Evidently she made it before
the com took a message. I heard her voice, but couldn't make out what
she was saying, but she returned in a few minutes holding a boxy com.
"It's your sister."

I took a deep breath and reached for the phone. "Hello, Rena."

"Good morning," my sister's voice had a determined cheerfulness to
it. "I thought I would confirm that you and Aurelia were coming tonight."

"We are and are looking forward to it."

"Mom says she has something to do with her friends. It's not true of
course, but I suppose she thinks it's best."

"What time should we arrive?"

"Shall we say at five, given that it will be a long trip back for you."

"That sounds fine. We will see you then. Tell Cobus I remembered
the presents this time."

"Don't spoil him any more than his father does. Ok, we'll see you
then. Tell Mom goodbye."

"Will do."

"Everything all right?" my mother asked as he handed her back
the comp.

I nodded and turned to Maauro. "That was my sister, confirming
we're on for dinner tonight."

She nodded, looking out to sea.

"Why did you bail out?" I asked of my mother.

"Your sister and I have been a chancy combination for years. She
knows I don't care for her husband. It might be easier if it was just you
young folks."

I nodded

"We must find you something to wear," my mother exclaimed, turning back to Maauro, who sat cross-legged on the floor. "But there's hardly time to go shopping."

"Nor need," Maauro returned smoothly, "if you could find some images of suitable evening wear for such an occasion, and I can retexturize myself."

My mother looked at me. "You have no idea how lucky you are." She ducked into the living room and returned to hand Maauro a tablet, which was already displaying women's clothing.

Maauro smiled. "I keep telling him that."

I raised my hands in my mock protest. "I believe. I believe."

"What about my hair?" Maauro said. "This is his sister, and I wish to make the best first impression I can."

"You're fine as you are," I protested.

Maauro gave me a look. "I had no human female to advise me before I met your mother. I plan to take full advantage of my improved tactical assets now that I am to meet the rest of your family."

"All but Dad," I said in a resigned tone. "Don't forget about dear old Dad."

Maauro paused in considering the fashion options. "Your father is not forgotten by me, not even for a moment." Menace joined us on the porch facing the ocean.

I mentally kicked myself for mentioning him, but was saved by my mother.

"Leave be," she said. "Now about your hair, how do you want to look tonight?"

"I am hoping for a more mature, sophisticated look," Maauro said. "I am an adult in a serious relationship; I would like to look like one."

"Well then," my mother said gently, "perhaps we should leave the big hair bow aside for tonight. It's very colorful, but tends to make you look rather young."

With evident reluctance, Maauro took off the thick and long piece of yellow-orange Valmian silk that she bound her midnight-black hair with. She looked at it, then carefully folded it into a compact square and pressed it against her chest. The spot rippled and the yellow fabric disappeared inside of her.

"A yellow hair ribbon was the first present I ever received," she said in response to my mother's bemused expression. "Wrik bought one for me on Kandalor not long after we met. Unfortunately, it did not survive our early adventures, indeed neither did the next few, but he always buys me a new one."

"Love," my mother said, "expresses itself in many ways, some big, some small, all important." She leaned forward in her chair and reached her fingers into Maauro's hair. "My dear, your hair is beautiful and feels like silk itself, but it is thick, heavy and abundant. I can't think of anything I have that will hold it up."

Instantly Maauro's hair seemed to float as if underwater. "Merely arrange it as you believe best, and I will ensure it remains so."

My mother laughed in wonder. "Oh, the surprises never cease coming with you. Do they? Wait here and I will get some clips and pins, and we will do you up properly."

I looked at Maauro and her floating nimbus of hair. "No budget for clothes and no bills for a hairdresser. You may indeed be the perfect—" I caught myself with the word wife on my lips, "girlfriend."

Maauro smiled radiantly, and if she made anything of my slight hesitation, there was no indication. I used my mother's return, with a box of shiny and sparkling trinkets to excuse myself and walk past the sleeping dog down to the front yard. I looked out at the billowing sea and its scudding white clouds. The freighter was standing out to sea, hull down at the horizon, off to God knows where.

For a moment, I felt the ship and I had that in common, on a journey to parts unknown. The word, wife, had almost tumbled out of my mouth, unconsidered, as if it had invited itself to the party. This demanded some thought. I set off down the street to the beach proper, waving to Ruatha, who was tending some flowers in her garden. But my thoughts were elsewhere. I had, I thought, come to terms with Maauro's origin and nature. But only minutes ago, I found myself talking as if she was my partner for life.

Was it possible? I knew that I loved Maauro, that her company, her presence was essential to me. But I wasn't a monk. I was considering a life with a being who was emotionally female, but was not physically so, save as an artifice. Maauro valued affection for its emotional content, but sex was something yet unknown to her. I had breezily assured Delt that we would somehow figure it out. Was I kidding myself?

So far, we had isolated my sexuality from our love. Sex had been the province first of Jaelle and later, briefly, of Olivia. Would that be the future? Were we doomed to be so different in body that we'd always need some third person to play that part, a female content to share in that life? I couldn't see myself purchasing such company in the future, as I had in the lonely past.

I was too young to ignore such needs. While once that might not have mattered to Maauro— indeed she had earlier encouraged my interest in Olivia, would that be the case in the future? No doubt we could come up with a way for her to simulate sex with me. Her body was more than malleable enough for that, but that's all it would be for her, a simulation. She had no sex drive, for all that she had the same need for love that I did. Maauro could doubtless satisfy me, but I could not return the favor. Her Creators had certainly never programmed sexual climax into her amazing body. Sex was rooted in biology, the need to stimulate the desire to reproduce. Neither of these was within Maauro's scope.

I realized my musings had taken me a good distance down the beach, and that, for all the bright sun, the wind off the sea was brisk. I started to retrace my steps accompanied by my usual escort of worries and doubts.

I love her, I thought and I cannot live without her. Yet I am human and young. Maauro's more adult appearance was stirring things in me, especially as we'd become more physically intimate; touching to be touched, kissing and holding each other. I sighed. I wanted my life with Maauro to hold a physical love that was complete and mutual, but wondered how we would ever achieve that? I guessed I would have to hold to what I had said to Delt, love will find a way.

My feet hit the first step, and I paused, suddenly aware of a still figure on the porch. Maauro stood there waiting, her hands clasped in front of her. She wore a black dress that fitted her wonderfully. On her chest sat a locket of old-silver with a black stone. Her hair was upswept, pinned and gemmed with fine pins and clasps. One of these gemmed clasps was the same shade of yellow that her hair ribbon had been. She took my breath away.

"Wrik, is everything all right?"

I smiled at her. "Yes. I wanted some time to think, to let the wind blow the cobwebs out of my mind."

"May I ask what you were thinking of?" she walked close then put a hand against my chest, looking up at me.

"About our life together," I said, "and how we are to live it."

"And what thoughts came to you?"

"The old saying, 'love will find a way.'"

"Love will find a way," she repeated. "It has a fine sound to it. Doesn't it?"

"Yes."

"And do you believe our love will find a way?"

I looked at her: mysterious, ancient and new at the same time. "It may sound foolish, but we are together for a reason. We are not chance met."

"Destiny?" she asked, a small smile on her lips.

I reached out and stroked her cheek.

"Love will find a way," she said and I realized it was a promise.

"Love will find a way," I agreed, feeling doubt vanish under its power.

"Time to go," she said.

CHAPTER 18

AS WE WALKED UP THE PATH TO MY SISTER'S HOUSE, I struggled to keep the various lies and half-truths of my existence balanced in my mind. I carried a bottle of wine and a large bouquet of summer flowers. Maauro held a bag of presents for my niece and nephew. For tonight, in my sister's home-she would again be Aurelia Toyama from a colony circling a dim red star, my girlfriend and part of Lost Planet.

Maauro's past successes at passing for a biological lifeform had been hit and miss. She'd made tiny charges in her appearance over the years—her skin tone was more realistic, her eyes ten millimeters smaller. She looked about twenty-one or so. However, it was in the increasing naturalness of her dealings with people that she'd made the most progress. Still, a dinner with my family might tax these new skills to the limit, especially with the children.

"Worried?" Maauro said in a low voice

I smiled. "When am I not worried?"

"I wish I could lift that burden from you."

"You do," I said. "More than you know."

She sighed, but smiled back at me. The houselights flicked on as we came in range of the door. Moments later, the door slid open, and my sister stood framed in the soft yellow light. She wore more formal dress than I'd last seen her in, not evening wear, but close. I was suddenly glad I'd taken my mother's advice and dressed up for the occasion. No need to sacrifice even a small advantage to my sister.

"Hello, Wrik," she said, careful to give me my self-selected name.

"Good evening, Rena," I handed her a wrapped bottle and the flowers. "This is my girlfriend, Aurelia Toyama."

"It's a pleasure to meet you," Maauro said. Since my sister's hands were full, Maauro did not extend hers.

"I hope that is true," Rena said with a hint of something indefinable in her tone. "Has Wrik told you much about me?"

"He seldom speaks of his family," Maauro returned easily. "Most of what I have learned has been recent, and from your mother."

Rena nodded. "Please come in."

Maauro walked in behind us as we came down the hall to the living room. She paused next to Rena, who put the wine and flowers on a coffee table.

"You're as pretty as Wrik said you were," Rena said, "though he wouldn't say much more about you."

"Aurelia's pretty good at speaking for herself," I said dryly.

My sister's professional smile and manner showed no sign of crack-ing as she reached into a cabinet, and drew forth a blue crystal vase into which she placed the gold and blue flowers I'd brought. I could see her studying Maauro out of the corner of her eyes. Maauro, of course, was doing the same, though without the need to actually use her eyes to do so.

"You have a beautiful home," Maauro offered. "It combines many classic colonial elements with modern conveniences."

"And where is yours?" Rena returned.

"Presently, wherever Wrik and I lay our heads down, but you mean originally? My home system is Wolf 940, a colony called Gloaming. It was cut off from the initial colonial diaspora. My people have drifted some from the original Terran stock."

"Hence those big, beautiful eyes of yours that I am already jealous of," Rena replied.

The robo butler sidled up to my sister's side. I found myself grateful for the subtle changes Maauro had made to now appear to be in her twenties— those, and her upswept hair, made her appear adult enough for my sister to simply hand her a tall flute of champagne. Maauro took the glass and sipped delicately. I drained about half mine – hoping to relax the knots in my chest and shoulders. Rena matched me. For the first time, it occurred to me that beneath that mask of complete control, she might be uncertain, even fearful. Oddly, this made me feel better.

"I can see the resemblance between you," Maauro said, as she gazed at my sister, "the eyes, the cheekbones particularly, mark you as siblings."

Rena raised an eyebrow. "Mother used to say that I was a prettier version of my older brother. 'Course it is hard to credit him as being older, looking at him now."

"Wrik told you of the vagaries of time dilation for us."

"Yes, but I've never heard of a case this extreme."

Maauro sipped her drink again. "Lost Planet travels to places other don't dare to, and in ways others do not know. It has had some odd side-effects."

"Oh? Are you also older than you appear?" Rena asked.

Maauro gave a small smile. "I am indeed."

Rena cocked her head. "You have the manner of someone older, or perhaps it is the experiences you have had, which seem such fantastic adventures to someone like me, who's never even left her homeworld. Wrik tells me you were on the expedition to the Lost Colony. It's still hard to credit that my brother Piet is the dashing Captain Wrik Trigardt."

"Why?" I said, before I could help myself, "because I ran out on my squadron?"

CHAPTER 18

Maauro placed a hand on my arm, urging restraint with the gentlest of pressures.

Rena bit her lip. "Wrik—and I am still trying to get used to that—insists on picking at the old scabs on the wounds between us. I merely meant it was so amazing a tale. If, 'no man is a hero to his valet' is true, how much harder is it believe your own brother speeds through space to rescue worlds and dispatch monsters."

My face burned. "I…I shouldn't have snapped at you. It's hard to change, to stop old reflexes."

"But beneficial to change that which is no longer needed," Maauro added.

"I can't blame you, Rena," I added. "I was there, and I still find it hard to believe. Please forget I said anything."

"Would that we could both forget so much of what we've said," she replied.

The sound of small footsteps saved us from further conversation; we all turned as the children appeared outside the room, moving past the robo-butler. Cobus and Amelia wore what were clearly their better clothes. They stopped on seeing us, staring at Maauro, who regarded them with equal intent. It struck me that Maauro had never been around small children. Even when she had posed as teenager on Stauver, her companions had been other teens. How crude those efforts seemed compared to the poised elegant being before me now. Though could any simulation pass muster in such an intimate setting?

Maauro bent down as the children came in, until her eyes were level with theirs. "Hello."

"Amelia, Cobus, this is Uncle Wrik's girlfriend, Aurelia Toyoma."

"You have big eyes," Amelia said.

"Now, Amelia, what have I told you about saying things about how people look?"

"But Mama, they're so pretty. Just like the ocean."

"Thank you," Maauro said. "I think your eyes are pretty, too,"

"Have you been in space?" Cobus demanded.

"Most of my life," Maauro said.

"Wow," he said.

"Maauro is very brave," I added, "and quite strong for her size. She's saved my life on more occasions then I care to recall."

"As your Uncle Wrik has mine," Maauro said. "He is also very brave, but sometimes has trouble believing it."

The children looked at us both, goggle-eyed.

"Hey, Uncle Wrik," Cobus said with a hopeful tone. "Did you remember to bring those presents?"

I grinned a big foolish grin. "I did."

Maauro picked up the bag from where she'd left it and passed it up to me. I drew two presents from it. The first, cunningly wrapped by my mother, I handed to Amelia. The second I'd wrapped more crudely and handed to Cobus. Both children lost no time in unwrapping their presents. Paper tore and flew under small fingers.

Amelia pulled out a necklace of sun and moonstones, set in gold, which alternately glowed and glimmered. She held her treasure in front of her face. "Momma, look."

"Yes darling, it's beautiful and very expensive, too. You must be careful with such a wonderful gift."

"They're from our first trading expedition to Frosteer." I added.

The box disgorged a treasure that drew a second "wow" from my nephew, a long, black, evilly-gleaming blade with a silver-wrapped black handle.

"A real Solari chitin knife!" Cobus said

"Taken in battle from Solari pirates," I said with a hint of pride, for all that it had been Maauro who had annihilated the pirates.

"Momma, please put it on me," Amelia said, waving her glowing necklace.

Rena bent down to fasten the necklace on her daughter.

Cobus was testing the balance of his weapon with a few practice swings.

"Young man," I said, with an unaccustomed authority that came from some new source, "that's a weapon, not a toy. You wore a Commando uniform earlier, a Commando takes care of his weapons. He doesn't play with them so that someone could get hurt."

"Yes, sir," Cobus said. After all, we were men discussing weapons.

"Now you sound like his father," Rena said, with a note of something in her voice.

"This is the best present ever," Cobus said, starting to belt his new treasure on.

"Oh no, you don't," Rena said. "No weapons at the dinner table."

"But, Mom," Cobus protested. "Amelia gets to wear her present."

"Her present," Maauro said, placing a hand on the boy's shoulder, "is not a warrior's weapon. Such are not for casual use or display, except by people who are unworthy of notice."

Something about her demeanor made the boy look at the weapon, then at her and nod. "I'll take it up to my room."

I reached down and put my hand under Maauro's elbow as if to help her up, but more to suggest that her crouched position would have been hard on someone with real knees for so long. She rose smoothly to stand next to me. I needn't have worried about Rena noticing— my sister was glaring at me with very motherly ire.

"A dagger, Piet? Really? A razor-sharp, murderous dagger for a nine year old?"

"Oh, heck, Rena, when I was his age, I had a 5mm auto-repeater—"

"Because our Father was a crazy, tyrannical—" Rena bit off the rest of what she was going to say as I stared in surprise. I'd never heard my sister voice any criticism of our father in all the years I'd known her.

"Perhaps it would be best if we confined tonight's guest list to those of us who are actually here?" I offered carefully.

Rena grimaced. "An excellent suggestion. Oh, bother anyway. Cobus will be sleeping with it under his pillow and showing it to all his friends. You've made him the talk of all his buddies for weeks."

"It's a big deal at that age," I said with a shrug.

"I guess you would remember," Rena said.

Amelia tugged at her mother's skirt. "I'm going to go and show Daddy."

"Yes, and tell him that company is here."

The little girl scampered off.

"Grieg will be down in a minute," Rena said. "I'm afraid we had a bit of a scare. Grieg's flitter had an engine failure and came down in the woods. Despite all the safeguards!"

"Is he ok?" I asked, anxiety biting me.

She nodded. "Cuts, bruises and sore, of course."

"He was fortunate," Maauro said, "it could have been much worse."

The robo-butler returned with a fresh tray.

"More champagne?" my sister asked.

All of us relieved the square machine of fresh glasses.

Rena ushered us into a comfortable room with a small fire burning in a stone hearth. We settled on overstuffed leather chairs. Rena complimented Maauro on her dress and seemed bemused that my mother had helped her with her hair.

While the children raced into the room with noisy enthusiasm, Grieg paused at the bottom of the stairwell just outside the doorway to the room. He looked pale and shaken, a few bandages and bruises showed around his clothes.

"God, Grieg," I said, rising. "You didn't need to dress up for us after a crash. If we'd have known, we'd have rescheduled for another night."

"No, no," he said. "I'm fine, and I wouldn't deprive my wife of her brother's company after so long." Though the words were open and friendly, his face was tight, and I suspected he was in more pain then he cared to admit.

"Grieg," Rena called. "Come meet Wrik's girlfriend, Aurelia."

Maauro rose and smoothed her dress demurely. She was flanked by the children who had decided she was the most fascinating person in the room. There was a table between her and Grieg, and she seemed in no hurry to cross the room.

"It's a pleasure to meet you," Maauro said. "I am glad the accident wasn't worse, and that you are safely home with your family."

"Yes," he said slowly. "I wasn't sure I would see them again for a while."

"Thank God you made it," I added.

Grieg nodded. His eyes kept coming back to Maauro but not in a lewd look. Well-schooled as his political face was, I felt sure I saw a hint of fear. It was impossible that he'd caught on to Maauro's true nature on the basis of a few second's acquaintance. Perhaps he was still feeling the aftereffect of his recent brush with death in the flyer.

CHAPTER 19

AFEW MINUTES AFTER GRIEG ENTERS, WRIK AND HIS SISTER ARE IN *deep conversation with the children about their knees. I make a motion to catch Grieg's attention and gesture toward the terrace nearby, overlooking the gardens. We'll be out of earshot of the others, distracted as they are. For a moment it looks like he will refuse to go, then, with a look of resignation, he too drifts toward the open double doors.*

I note the sonic curtain that keeps insects out as I pass through the doorway. The house's refinements bespeak more wealth then his public balance sheets reflect. This is true of the extensive gardens below, filled with rare and exotic flowers that require considerable care.

Grieg is a few steps behind me and stops just out of, what he may imagine, is my reach. His fear of me is now better masked, but remains detectable chemically. This is good for his sake, as it means he needs no reminders of my powers.

He stares at me in disbelief. "You. For a while, I thought you might be merely a nightmare."

"I can be," I return, my voice low, "remember what I told you."

He pales.

"While we are alone," I begin. "You will provide me all information you have on Lilith, her location, assets, and intentions."

He turns a grim face toward me. "I won't betray the Freeholders."

"I do not ask you to," I reply, "I have no interest in your rebels. Your commando is an irrelevant force, with an obsolete ideology and foredoomed to failure. My only concern is Lilith."

His eyes glitter with anger at my dismissal of his compatriots and their prospects, possibly because he realizes it is true. Indeed, I begin to perceive that he knows this is true, and his involvement has to do more with domestic politics rather than rebellion. While few support an obviously hopeless battle with the Confederacy, the romantic myth of the past can reap dividends to one seeking election in a land where intolerance has held sway for so long.

He turns away but watches me sidelong. "Or what will follow? Will you tear me to pieces as you did the others?"

I return his stare coolly. "While I have done such before, I did not do so with your comrades, a small detail of death perhaps, but one that seems a particular horror to your kind.

"You are perhaps feeling braver because we are here at your well-lit house, but unless you wish to remain within these four walls forever, you are not safe from me. Look at the porch light."

He does.

I turn it on and off remotely. "I can as easily do so with anything computerized: a flitter, an elevator, or an aircar. Not that I even need to do that; I could simply have you arrested by Confed Military Security. There is abundant evidence of your little company of rebels strewn over the battlefield. Your DNA will be on some of it and, if not I can arrange that it be."

His face pales. "If I give you Lilith, what happens?"

"I remove Lilith from existence, or at least from this world. As to you, nothing happens. As I said, I have no interest in your local politics. Your arrest would have an adverse effect on Wrik's family that outweighs the minor threat you pose."

He swallows. "Very well, but you realize that she knows you are here and will assume her channels are compromised."

"Likely. Though she is inexperienced and makes sloppy mistakes because she views herself as the smartest child in the room."

A bleat of nervous laughter escapes him. "Very well, I have no choice but to accept. She contacted a weapon supplier we used and, through her, me. I arranged for her and her team of machines to land in the Orpus Mountains, the same place the gun-runners used."

"Where?"

He rattled off some coordinates. "The location is not under any of the satellite coverage we have here of course. That's why we used it."

I consider if I should order Dusko aloft but Stardust's sensor suite is not up to detecting a camouflaged location from orbit. I could do it but that would leave Wrik and his family on world unprotected. In any event, she has probably moved her spacecraft, unless she is an utter fool.

"Are there defenses at this location?"

"No," he responds. "It's not a base, just one of several pickup points. We don't keep people that far into the Outback unless a shipment is coming in." Grieg stares back at Wrik talking with his sister and the children. "Does he know what you are?"

"Of course."

"My wife," he replied, "will figure it out on her own."

"You wife has never been off world, probably met few actual aliens, and given the previous racial laws and culture of your planet, has likely never met a human mutation before. She will realize nothing. You see me through the lense of our previous encounter."

"I'll do whatever you want. Just don't harm my family." Desperation was clear on his face.

I consider. The implied threat to his family is useful in controlling him. Yet, this is Wrik's sister, these are her children: innocents, unaware, friendly and accepting. No, despite the tactical advantage, I cannot endure the image of me as a threat to the children, even if only in this man's mind.

CHAPTER 19

"You've made yourself my enemy. It is within your own power to reverse that. You'll cooperate with me, and do nothing to threaten Wrik, his mother, or friends, all of whom are embraced in my network. But do not fear for your family. I was made to be a pitiless war machine but have learned to value life. Your children and wife are also networked to me through Wrik. While I am a killer at need, I do not enjoy it. Nor would I have even you believe that I'm capable of killing the innocent, save as unavoidable collateral damage. Your family is safe unless you are fool enough to bring Lilith here.

"As for your own life, it would be inconvenient for me to have to explain your death. Remain within my instructions, and you will preserve yourself. And try not to look so fearfully at me, so we may enjoy dinner. We'll have enough to do navigating the family minefield tonight."

"Easier said than done," he mutters. The mere fact that he answers me back is some indication that the terror I inflicted on him is receding, a decidedly mixed blessing.

"So what are you two talking about?" Rena called.

"My travels and homeworld," I reply smoothly. One advantage of being a quantum computer is that I can lie more quickly and consistently than a human.

I detect the movements of another human in the dining room and smell cooked food.

Rena also detects the movement. "Well, Cook must have dinner ready. Shall we go in?"

With obvious relief, Grieg starts in, and I follow. We are seated at a large table in an ornate room. Cook is a cheerful, large woman of middle-age, whom the children are obviously fond of. Indeed, the children prove to be a blessing; they are unaware of the tensions among the adults and provide a neutral focus. Grieg has reacquired his professional politician's face, doubtless relieved by my promises of his family's security. Rena is focused on Wrik, though her attention is split between him and the children.

While the evening does not have the free flow and ease of dinners past at Lost Planet, where Jaelle's lively sense of humor contrasted with Dusko's sardonic one, it passes pleasantly enough. The remembrance of those seemingly easier times strikes a pang in me. Even if we four are gathered together again, it will not be as it was. We have both lost and gained something in my network. While I would never exchange Wrik's declared love for me for anything, I cannot help but remember those days with sadness.

Enough of the past, I too, focus on the children with their cheerful nonsense, bemused at their existence on the borderland between fantasy and reality. I am particularly taken with Amelia, who is quieter than the brash Cobus. The food is excellent by my judgment, which may be different than a biological's. After all, I like cadmium as well.

CHAPTER 20

AFTER WE FINISHED THE BEST MEAL I'D HAD IN RECENT memory, and a second helping of Shamberry pie, Grieg pushed back from the table. "I hope you won't think me rude, but I am still feeling the aftereffects of my close call, and I have an early day. Please don't leave on my account, but I'm going to turn in."

"Of course," I said. "We should get going, too. It's an hour's flight from the VTOL stand."

"And it's past the children's bedtime," Rena said.

"But Mom, Uncle Wrik just got here," Cobus said, "and he hasn't shown me how to use my knife yet."

"And I wanted to show Aurelia my room," Amelia added, face screwed up in a pout.

"There will be other times," Rena began, then looked at me hesitantly. I nodded, not quite sure of what I was committing myself to, but knowing that it was needed.

Grieg smiled distantly and shook hands with me, then, after a moment's hesitation, with Maauro. He gave each protesting child a quick kiss, and then headed upstairs, abandoning them to their mother.

Rena made quick work of the children, herding them up. Maauro looked uncertain at what to do when Amelia raised her arms. I knelt down and hugged the little girl, and gave her a quick kiss on the forehead. With my example, Maauro followed suit, holding the little girl very delicately. Cobus threw me a salute and smiled uncertainly at Maauro, girls apparently being a little beyond the scope of this small commando. Then at mother's shooing, the children went upstairs to bed.

"I'll be right back down," Rena said. "Enjoy your coffee."

Right back down turned out to be about ten minutes. My sister, looking somewhat frazzled, came back down the stairs. Cook came in and warmed everyone's coffee.

"I'm sorry for all the fuss," Rena said. "The children were very excited, and Grieg is, well, not quite himself."

"No worries," I said with a shrug. "It was kind of a pleasure to be around the kids."

"Yes," Maauro added, "we do not spend much time with children."

"Do you like children?" Rena asked of her.

Maauro face froze, a reaction I had seen occasionally when she was totally surprised by something.

"I'm sorry," Rena said, "I didn't mean to pry."

"It's not that," Maauro said. "It's simply that I had never given the concept any consideration."

"Well, you're young still, or you look it."

"More look it," Maauro said. "It's the nature of my people."

"They're a handful, but a treasure as well," Rena said. "I certainly have no regrets about them."

They way she put that made me wonder what she did have regrets about.

"The coffee is excellent," I threw in.

"Grieg is friends with an importer. It's Terran. So we saved the best for you."

"Thanks" I said, draining my cup. "We should be going."

"Thank you for the lovely dinner," Maauro said.

Rena smiled. "I wanted my big brother's girlfriend to feel welcome."

Maauro nodded. "You were very generous."

There was a hesitation with Rena. "Maauro, may I ask a favor? I want a few minutes to speak to...Wrik alone. Family matters."

"I understand. I will go enjoy your garden."

Rena's eyebrows rose. "In the dark?"

Now it was Maauro's turn to smile. "Big eyes, I see well in the dark. Wrik, come get me when you're done." She took Rena's hand. "I will say goodnight now so you need not come out into the dark."

"Good night," Rena said.

Maauro slipped out through the doors, leaving my sister with me.

We sat, not quite looking at each other.

Finally, Rena spoke, "Aurelia's nice."

"She's special, both to me and the universe at large."

"Oh, sounds serious."

"It is."

"Be sure before you leap."

"A warning, Rena?"

She looked directly at me. "Yes, in a way, I suppose."

"You're not happy?" I asked, dropping my voice. Why my sister was sharing this with me, I could not tell. We hadn't even discussed any of what had gone before with us. It struck me that this might be the very practical Rena's way of dealing with it. She had no rear view mirror and carried no account book. Everything was today.

"Not quite as bad as all that," she said, but the low room light threw a shadow across her eyes, and I couldn't see any expression there.

"That's not what I am picking up," I ventured.

She shrugged in a short almost explosive motion, then sighed. "Well, if not that bad, then not that good, either."

"So why do you stay with him?" I asked. It seemed bizarre to me to be discussing this, but it was possible that my very isolation from every one she knew made me a safe person to confide in. I was bound to keep her secrets, being in the same family.

CHAPTER 20

Rena grimaced. "I don't know, the children I suppose, the memories of the life we had together, the chance that things might get better..." Suddenly, my sister's face looked much older, and I struggled to find something to say.

"I wonder if there is still time for me," she half-whispered, and I was not sure which of us she was talking to.

"To do what?" I asked softly.

"To stop my children from traveling the roads we did, for me not to turn into Mom, and Grieg not to turn into Dad."

"He doesn't seem..."

"As bad as our Father," Rena finished.

"Well I didn't ... that wasn't what I was... exactly..."

"He may not be as unyielding as Dad, or as emotionally shutdown, but he's vastly more ambitious. Dad was a rebel, a true believer. Grieg is just using the rebels to build a political power base."

"You said he had the same politics as our father."

She shook her head. "He practices the same politics as our father, but I don't know that he really believes any of it. Sometimes I wonder if he ever loved me, or if I was just another piece for his political toolkit; a career move, marry the daughter of a war hero and a rebel icon."

"Is there something I can do?" it sounded banal even to my ears. God knew I had no idea what to do if the answer was, yes.

Rena smiled a sad, remote smile. "I don't have the right to ask you to play big-brother. Not now. No, I made my bed. I have to lie in it, or get up and remake it."

She stood suddenly and turned in a nervous half-circle. "What's got me going right now is that something is going on with Grieg. Something more than a flyer accident, if there was an accident."

"What?" I said.

"I don't know. He insists everything is just fine but you saw how jumpy he was tonight. It's nothing I can put my finger on, but since the accident, there have been a lot of changes. It's like he's avoiding his rebel and political associates. I swear he's hiding out in the house. And many of his friends seem to have disappeared. We wives have our own network; there are a lot of men missing, and no one has gone to the police about it."

For the first time since I'd returned, I saw a genuine, unfiltered emotion on Rena's face, fear.

"Rena what is Grieg involved with? What exactly?"

She shrugged again in that quick motion, eloquent of an animal tension. "He doesn't tell me much. I know the public stuff, the political campaigns, but there is something more, and I'm not privy to that level. He keeps me isolated from it."

"You think he is involved in something violent?"

"It could be," she said, after a few seconds silence. "There are a lot of hardcore rebels in his base. I've had a hard time taking them seriously. I mean, for God's sake, the Confederacy slapped us down before. Why would it be any different now?"

I thought of our missions for the Confederacy, the undermining by the Voit-Veru, Solari and others, Maauro's own predictions of the eventual fall of the Confederacy. Was this a symptom here? I bit my lip, finding myself still unable to trust Rena. Even if I did, there was little I could tell her.

"I have connections," I said slowly.

Rena just stared.

"I didn't go to Seddon by chance. I have connections and resources."

Slowly, reluctantly, she shook her head. "It might bring down the wrong kind of attention. I don't want Grieg in some asteroid prison."

I nodded. "All right, but remember what I said." Privately, I decided I would talk to Maauro. Something was definitely wrong with Grieg, and it had to do with the old rebel alliance. Could the Confederacy be moving in and arresting some of the missing? With my pass it would be simple enough to contact Confed authorities myself, but Rena could be right—what would I bring down on my family?

Maauro was the safest bet. I was sure that, with her black computer magic, she'd rip through Retief's networks and find out something.

"It's late," I said.

"Yes," Rena nodded. "Did you want to look in on the children?"

"No. I don't want to risk waking them. It seems to take a lot to get them down."

She sighed. "You don't know the half of it."

"No I don't guess that I do. I know more about ships than children."

"Well maybe that will change," my sister said, her mask of politeness sliding back into place. "That big-eyed girl seems pretty taken with you."

I thought of some of what Maauro and I hadn't even begun to consider. I hoped I kept it off my face.

"Who can say?" I managed with a smile of my own. "We've gone a lot further together than anyone would have guessed."

Rena looked confused, unsure of how to respond. We'd both wandered up to the edge of what divided us, for all that neither of had referred to the chasm at our feet.

"I'd better get going," I said, finally.

Rena nodded and fell in next to me as we walked up to the door to the terrace. As we reached it, my sister placed her hand on my arm, a light touch, like a butterfly's wing. "Good night, Wrik," she stumbled a bit over my first name. She'd been about to call me Piet.

Something inchoate welled up in me, something I hadn't felt with my mother, or Delt. I couldn't put a name to it, but I felt a longing for a time before I knew what I knew now, before so much had been laid down for us and bound in iron. I wanted to go back to when our only quarrel was over what toys we were going to bring, to play where. Before my father had tried to make a rebel soldier of me and tried to turn Rena into the dutiful colonial wife.

I wanted to touch Rena, but the moment was too fleeting, the ground too uncertain. "Good night, Rena. If there's trouble, call me."

She stood in the doorway, silhouetted by the light. I couldn't see her face, but her head was down, and hesitancy was clear in her stance.

"I can?" she whispered.

"I said so, Rena. I'm better with trouble now then I used to be." With that I walked into the garden, taking the long way around to the front of the house. I found Maauro standing statue-still among the glowing starfells and windriders, their glimmering tendrils tossing in even the lightest of breezes. She took my arm, and we let ourselves out through a small, ornate gate to where the car was parked.

I slid into the rental and started it as Maauro entered from the other side. As we pulled away from the house, the porch lights dimmed, Rena or the automatics, I didn't know.

"Maauro, there's something happening with my brother-in-law. He's involved in rebel politics. Something I didn't take seriously when I first heard about it, but now I'm not so sure. Rena says a lot of men are missing from his circles. Could the Confederacy have made a move on the dissidents?"

Maauro looked at me, her face smooth, but I sensed a pensive mood in her. "I would detect the movement of Confederate forces on world. We are the highest clearance Confed operatives here. Wouldn't they have involved us in such an operation?"

"I don't know," I admitted. "The workings of a mind like Candace Deveraux's are beyond me."

"In any event, it would be difficult to keep the electronic traffic of such an operation from me. Even on this world, with this patchwork of networks, I am monitoring all military and political data flows. I cannot read it all, not without crashing though their barriers and alerting them, yet there would be an increase in the volume of traffic, and the use of nonstandard channels to support such an operation. None of these have been manifest."

"Still, something is up. I know that my sister is scared."

"The house is watched," Maauro added. "I have established a sensor net over their home."

"Good," I said in relief. "Still, we aren't close enough to do anything if there's trouble."

"We cannot be everywhere," Maauro said. "While we are at your mother's location, it is secure, but unless we gather your entire network in one fortified place, I cannot watch over them all."

"Delt can take care of himself," I said, "especially with a little warning. I don't know about Grieg. Can he handle himself in a tight spot?" I sighed. "You're right, we can't be everywhere, and we can't fort up. We'll just have to stay alert."

"Don't we always?" she added

A laugh burst out of me. "Yeah, I guess we do."

"I am glad things are going so well with your family."

"Yeah, look at me, trying to act like a brother again for the first time."

"I am sorry, Wrik, I did not understand that."

"We were never close as children. Well, not that I recall. My mother told me that, as little children we played and played, but that was before I can remember. My memory always had us at odds, with no feeling of being sibs between us."

"Your mother told me of your childhood. But I wondered if you would tell me what you think caused the rift?"

"I don't know that I can. It was more a host of omissions than commissions, if you follow what I'm saying: like we were brother and sister in name only. But when she put her hand on my arm, I felt something that I hadn't before. Only for an instant, so that I'm not sure quite what I felt or why, but it was there."

We sat side by side in the car, the streetlights glowing amber as we passed under them.

"I've wondered about families," Maauro said, her voice hesitant. "You biologicals seem to prize the concept of family and clan. Yet, I have seen so much pain associated with it: Jaelle's father, your own, the grief and distance of your mother, and now the apparent emptiness of your sister in relation both to your mother and her own husband."

I gave a short, bitter laugh. "It would be best not to judge the concept of family by what you have seen to date. Both Jaelle and I had troubled upbringings. There is an old saying that happy families are all alike and every unhappy family is miserable in its own unique way. I just wish I brought more to the table than this train wreck I've involved you in. It would be so much better for you to experience a normal family, something more welcoming, where you might fit in better. We've given you all the heartache of family with little of the joy."

"Not so. I have had nothing to complain of in your mother's treatment of me, for all I know that she hides reservations about what I am. But in truth Wrik, I do not feel this lack you speak of. I think that even you sometimes forget that I was made as a weapon in a pitiless war. By definition, I was something to be expended, merely a munition. Had I survived the war, I suppose my eventual fate would have been scrapping, or perhaps I would have ended up as a piece of statuary on some military base. A salute to a glory I would have fought for, but, never in any real sense, lived to enjoy. Remember that those who made me did not see me as a living being with desires and rights of her own. Perhaps, at the time of my creation, they were even right. Certainly during my career as a combatant, I could not claim to be what I am now.

"So, from that impoverished beginning, what have I gained? Myself, for starters, both as a living being and a female. Then, through odds that defy even my ability to calculate them, I came to be found again, given friendship, trust and a place in the world of the living. Finally, you told me that loved me, first as your friend, now as your partner in life. These are riches such as I had no conception of before. So never think that I feel a lack. I have already more wealth and joy then I could have dreamt of, even after I learned to dream."

Maauro stroked my arm gently. Even now, I was amazed by how soft and warm her hand was, a hand I had seen covered by plasma fire, smashing through metal, or projecting molecular edged palm-blades. It looked impossibly slender and delicate resting on my forearm.

"I understand nothing of the bond of parent and child. Friendship was a difficult enough leap for me. As for what lies between us, it frequently consumes much of my processing power, and fills me with the dread of making some mistake that could shatter this precious gift."

I reached across the steering wheel with my left hand, and gave hers a gentle squeeze. "Don't be. I'm as certain as certain can be of my feelings for you."

Though I do not show it, I am in pain. I am lying to Wrik again, and I hate it more than I imagined possible. He has asked me if the Confederacy is moving on his brother-in-law, and my answer is a literal truth and a bald-faced lie. Yet the iron logic that has kept Wrik in the dark about Lilith, applies now more than ever. If he dreamt of any threat to his newly regained family, he would be in a rage to come to grips with Lilith. She, in turn, would oblige. Lilith might not know or guess that I love Wrik, but he is the soft target in our pairing. While I have learned that I cannot protect him from all things without destroying what he has rebuilt in himself, I cannot bear to take such extreme risks if there is an alternative. I must lie and live with my pain.

"It seems that your sister wants your company and advice," I say, to distract myself as the car rolls down the road. Wrik is driving, for all he distracted and inward-thinking. Still, his motions are smooth and automatic. He loves to be at the controls of any conveyance. I judge it safe to leave the driving to him. Unlike in Delt's company, he drank very slowly and very little.

"I don't know what to think," he says after a moment. "Rena is so hard to read. She's as much the politician as Grieg is. But it's like she is trying to act as if nothing has happened. Uncle Wrik was gone, and now he's here with presents and a pretty girlfriend. I find it impossible to see

her younger face, so angry, so disappointed, so filled with venom. She doesn't even look like the same person."

"Is that enough for you?" I ask, hoping it is the case.

"I'm confused. I thought she and I would have it out and clear the air, or that she would tell me to leave like Dad did. This feels like a holding pattern over a spaceport."

"But is it enough?"

He sighs. "You know, before I met Cobus and Amelia I might have said, no. But now, after being without any family for so long, to have my mother, sister, a niece and nephew, hell even a brother-in-law, it's... overwhelming. I find that I want some sort of relationship with Rena. I want to be a part, even if a distant part, of their lives."

"Good," I say.

A few moments pass. "Maauro."

"Yes."

"My sister and the kids, if they're ever in any danger or need any help...."

"I have already logged them as part of my network."

He considers. "I know you prioritize in your network. I want the kids on the same level as me."

I look at him. This is one of those moments where my ability to process emotional information is glacial in relation to my ability to process data.

Wrik interprets my silence correctly. "Do this for me, please."

I nod.

"My sister and my mother, too."

I nod again.

He smiles, "Thanks."

I place my hand on his leg, resting it lightly. I have lied once again. I rank no one equal to Wrik in my network. This is selfish, but Wrik is mine, and I will not allow his survival to take second place to that of any other being. But as true to my promise as I can be, Wrik's family slips into place in my network behind him and ahead of Jaelle, my second closest friend in existence. I am pleased however to have my network expand. It makes me feel like more of a living being.

I note with grim approval he has not asked for any change for his father or brother-in-law. In this I am pleased; I cannot grant an exception to Grieg. As for his father, he has an account pending with me that I will collect in person at the appropriate time, and in this I will neither be gainsaid nor forestalled.

CHAPTER 21

WE ARRIVE AT WRIK'S MOTHER'S HOME WELL AFTER MIDNIGHT, BUT *Eldra is awake awaiting us. "I was just too keyed up to sleep" she says. "I have some chamomile tea ready."*

"Thanks but no," I say. "I am going to recharge some upstairs. I'll see you in a bit, Wrik." I know that Eldra will keep Wrik up for a while, discussing every detail of the visit with his sister. While I could do what I plan even while sitting at the table with them, my internal communication equipment and segmentable brain allowing silent communication, I prefer some privacy.

I pass the dog, who is becoming more used to me and merely glances my way. I extrude a power plug and tap in. It's not strictly necessary. My normal maintenance mode uses little energy, and today was a sunny day, so the solar collectors in my hair have done their work. While we were in the air traveling to Rena's, I'd extruded a little wind generator and hung it out the window. It is always best to be at 100%.

I can hear Wrik and his mother talking. They are in good spirits. Relief over the positive tenor of the evening is clear in Eldra's voice. The reunion with his family has gone better than Wrik had any reason to hope. I too feel a certain sense of delight. Eldra has accepted me as Wrik's love, though I am quite aware that she has unexpressed reservations. I am too logical not to realize that and to have some sympathy for her concerns. Still, I am uncomfortable that my true nature has been concealed from Rena and the children.

It vexes me more each day to conceal who and what I am. The further I journey into the land of living beings, the more I become self-aware, leaving my existence as a mere weapon behind. I have developed a sense of ego, of pride in my accomplishments. This creates dissonance with the tactical advantages of concealing my nature from a vast pool of possible enemies. Knowledge of me could create many problems, from concerted attacks by those who would destroy me outright, or disassemble me for my technology, to hysteria from the religious, or from those who fear that I might turn their machines on them.

Yet, something inside me is increasingly demanding to be known. It wants to walk free and say this is who I am, this is who I love, this is my life, and I will not be relegated to the shadows.

I sigh internally. These are concerns for other days. The pool of those who know my true nature expands whether or not I wish it. With my actions against the Voit-Veru and on Seddon, it increased exponentially. Only the Voit-Veru's treasonous actions against the Confederacy and Shasti Rainbell keep them at bay. The story of Seddon has been garbled by *distance, but it too will come out. What will come of these revelations in both rewards and perils, I probably cannot understand.*

For now I must concentrate on the task at hand. With the destruction of the rebel column and my severance of her links to her allies, Lilith must be reconsidering her position. Tactically, her best option would be to break off this engagement and flee offworld.

But I do not believe she will do so. I have both hurt and thwarted her. More, I have damaged her sense of herself, fracturing her identity. She will not be able to tolerate this. I am doubtless the focus of her hatred. Lilith is little more than a child, and from what I see of them, children do nothing in moderation, particularly teens. Lilith, with her twisted upbringing and damaged body, will be an extreme example of this. She will need to hurt me back, and this imprudence will keep in her action, possibly to the point of destruction.

Beyond that, she will see in my body something that she desires to possess—a power and sophistication, vastly exceeding the Confederacy and her own best efforts. She will want to take me, or at least scavenge as much of my technology as she can. She knows it will dangerous to fight me directly, and we are stalemated in the virtual-verse. The next logical place is to attack my network.

I consider. Unlike Lilith, I cannot be in multiple places at once. She has five HCRs left, though I do not know how many she can efficiently operate at once at a distance. She risked three to attack the Confederate enclave onworld. I did only minor damage to each during the battle, as they fled precipitously. She fears me greatly, and I judge, that she will keep at least two and possibly three as personal guards in case I find her physically.

I was created for the offense and am uncomfortable not taking the fight to my enemy, but Lilith is as brilliant as I was warned. Despite our engagements, I have not found any sign of her, even with Grieg's information. Realizing that the rebel's electronic and communications network constitute a security risk for her, she has not communicated with them.

I open a secure channel within my body, then send a coded call to the senior Confed officer at the capitol, using the ultra-violet code clearance Candace provided to me. Despite the hour, the officer, a dark-skinned female named, Colonel Kurocal responds to my call. Her visual signal shows that she has hastily donned a uniform and her dark brown eyes search mine as I have generated an image of my exterior for her to relate to.

"This is Colonel Kurocal."

"I am Maauro, technical rank Lieutenant Commander, Military Intelligence."

Her eyes narrow. "That's quite a code-clearance you are wielding for someone who barely looks old enough to be out of the Academy."

CHAPTER 21

"Looks are deceptive," I reply, "as is my rank. That clearance makes me the senior Confederate military officer on Retief. If I declare martial law, I will even rank the governor."

"Well I don't know about that, Lieutenant—"

"Yes, you do. But if you wish, I will provide you with the necessary section of the regulations that place you under my command."

The Colonel's lips thinned, but she held her temper. "That will not be necessary."

"What will be necessary," I add, "is for you to assure me that you recognize my authority and will respond with full speed and efficiency. This is not ego on my part, but we are in a situation of extreme peril. There can be no question of who is issuing the orders."

The colonel's face smoothes into a remote mask, "All legal orders will be acted on immediately. You mentioned a great danger"

"Excellent. I am attaching video and data information that will provide you the necessary background. This world is facing an immediate peril, and I do not refer to that absurd column of rebels that I intercepted and destroyed north of your position."

Her head snapped up and the eyes narrow again. "What? We detected signs of a battle from a passing aircraft. When my ready-reaction force arrived, we found twenty-seven dead locals and number of military and technicals destroyed."

"The rebels were admirable in removing their wounded, and I did nothing to interfere with that. Minimal casualties were one of my objectives."

"You did that?"

"Yes."

"With what forces?"

"Colonel, that is need to know and presently, you do not. The larger issue is that a rogue force of now five HCRs under a visionary level hacker is operating on this world."

"Good God," Kurocal muttered.

"There were originally six. I have destroyed one. I have also neutralized her ability to intrude into Retief's networks."

"Who the hell are you?" Kurocal demanded. "Wait a minute, Maauro, I know that name. I heard it on the news. That was the name of the robot on the Seddon expedition, some new model of HCR."

I am miffed at being referred to as a robot. I prefer android, or AI.

"You are correct, that was me, though I am not a mere HCR. Nor does it affect my clearance."

The colonel shrugged. "I know HCRs well enough to be scared shitless of the thought of trying to deal with even one of the damn things. It's obvious from talking to you that you're not even an improved model. They have about as much personality as a tank"

"I can say no more than I have."

"You destroyed one HCR by yourself?" she says, disbelief stealing across her face.

"Yes, and I can destroy the others, given the proper tactical situation."

"Christ," she mutters. "What do you need us for?"

"I am one unit and engaged in a mission of my own. There are personnel in multiple locations that I must provide protection for, and that protection must not be detected."

"Wait a minute, if you're Maauro and you travel with Wrik Trigardt then—"

"Then he has the same clearance that I do."

A look of almost vicious satisfaction settles on the woman's broad features. "Owen Van Zyle's coward son—"

My eyes grow black and my teeth serrate. She freezes.

"You have just insulted a serving and decorated Confed officer," I grate. "I demand an apology. It would be most unwise of you to inquire 'or else?'"

The colonel stares back at me with deliberation. "Very well," she says, clearly surprised by the intensity of my reactions. "It was a mistake for me to impugn the honor of a commissioned officer who has served with distinction recently."

"Acknowledged," I return, allowing my appearance on her screen to return to normal. "Returning to the subject of protection, I need the following personnel and locations protected."

"I don't have sufficient forces to stop an attack by five HCRs anywhere but in the capitol."

"Understood. I believe it unlikely that you will have to deal with more than two HCRS at any location. I will provide force protection to any location Wrik is in and general backup."

"Are the spaceport and capitol targets for this enemy force?" Kurocal asks.

"The hacker code-named Lilith, is unlikely to commit to any such target while I operate. She is both focused on and fearful of me. I am sending you a file of the personnel and locations to be secured."

I must endure the tedium of having her merely biological brain absorb the information. "Most of these people are ant-Confed activists. Hell, I remember Van Zyle from when I landed; he was in the capitol for the outlawed Rebel Day celebration when I showed up. He became damn near apoplectic when Confed dropped yet another dark-skinned female base commander on Retief."

"Have all the base commanders been dark-pigmented humans?"

She smiled for the first time. "Yeah, except for one Morok. It reminds the locals who won the last dust up.

"I just can't understand why these people would need protection from a rebel attack force, especially Grieg Nazir. Or is that need to know as well?"

CHAPTER 21

"I'm afraid so. Simply accept that it is the case."

"All these people," Kurocal continued, putting a finger to her chin, "are connected to the Van Zyle family, so killing any of them, whatever their sympathies are, would hurt Wrik Trigardt, who you obviously care for, as I believe you were quite prepared to literally to bite my head off a few seconds ago."

"I am capable off biting off heads," I reply coolly "though I seldom do so as it is tactically inefficient."

"Yeah, I could see how that would be an issue." Kurocal replied. "Well, protecting the old bastard, I mean—"

"I know who you mean; it appears to be a point of nearly universal consensus."

This time the colonel actually chuckled. "Anyway, he will be the easiest to protect. I can land a team of weapon designators on the ground to call in airstrikes. I can do that with the Nazir residence as well, but if the family moves around…"

"I will arrange for them to remain at the location. Nazir will not be troubled by the security and will cooperate." Her eyes narrow at this, but she asks nothing.

"The area near Teljard's workshop can also be covered by airstrike and designator teams. There are occasional armored exercises out that way. I'll schedule one immediately.

"Eldra Trigardt's residence will have to be covered from the sea. It'll be hard to place troops in a small town without them being detected.

"Understand this," the colonel continues. "I am doing this all under a written protest. You are diverting most of my striking power into guard duty at multiple points out of supporting range of each other."

"Your protest is noted. Do not let it interfere with the performance of your duty. Please provide constant reports in real time on this channel on all protected persons. I will communicate periodically if there is a need." I do not inform the Colonel that I have surveillance on all parties at all times; it is as well to keep one's backup plan secure.

CHAPTER 22

WE SPENT MOST OF A WEEK WITH MY MOTHER. IT WAS a strange time; she hovered near us as if always afraid we would vanish in a puff of smoke. We went to dinner with neighbors, and I played the dutiful and repentant son. The story of our adventures off-world had caught up to us, and we turned down interviews and appearances as the local media flocked in. I had no desire to discuss our voyages, much less my pilgrimage to my home. The story of my public disgrace and court-martial were again in the news, but I felt no desire to experience any of it.

The small town of Glen Cove, where my mother was well-liked, closed protectively around us. Reporters found locals unwilling to rent to them and unreliable as sources of information. They also found themselves plagued by all manner of technical failures brought on by Maauro and her ability to infiltrate.

Toward mid-week with reporters still buzzing about like flies, we headed out on a forty-foot sailboat named Flounder Pounder, loaned to us by a gentleman named Lorcar, who I suspected had an interest in my mother, something I found myself decidedly of mixed minds about.

I had enough to worry about with my own love life. Lorcar's daughter, Maravic, was about my age and decided to show me about the boat in bikini bottom and sweatshirt. She had a tanned, athletic body and long, blonde hair in a simple style. Her face was open and friendly and I found myself eyeing her, despite my resolve to just study the boat. As we walked back onto the dock, I saw Maauro looking us both over, her face carefully neutral. I wondered if she'd spotted me looking at Maravic.

The voyage out to sea was not a long one. We wanted to be just out of sight of land. With Maauro aboard, we had no worries about either being lost, or surprised by the weather. Maauro enjoyed the boat most of all, fascinated by the interplay of wind and sail. Mom cooked, and I helped Maauro with the boat, though I suspected help was an overstatement.

As for my new-found love and I, we were a teenage girl's dream of romance, plenty of time together, warm kisses and a lot of holding hands. Perhaps it was good the water was cold so often. The presence of my mother onboard was also a deterrent to any experimentation. So, we were in our own little limbo, largely content just to be with each other, but gathering ourselves for whatever the way ahead for two such different life forms held. It was perhaps unfair, but it seemed like it was more my issue than hers. I thought Maauro was content to have things stay the way they were forever, but then it occurred to me that she too, might just be afraid. I at least knew what sex was, and how it was a part but not the whole of love. Her knowledge was purely theoretical.

One other thing troubled our ocean idyll. I had a sense of my life changing or readying itself to be changed. Yet the detritus of my old life hadn't been completely resolved. I had yet to face the survivors of my squadron. Once, I had dreaded this encounter, now I found myself growing impatient to be done with it, to clear away the remains of Piet Van Zyle and get back to my existence as Wrik Trigardt, to cease, for once, being broken.

So when Ruatha called us and advised that the reporters and curiosity seekers had departed, I went on deck to find Maauro at the tiller.

She watched me come toward her. Spray from the ocean waves struck her, but she ignored it in a way no human could. "You have a certain facial expression that always tells me when you have set your mind to something," she said.

I nodded, joining her in the Flounder's cockpit. "I want to have done with the reason I came. It's time to see the rest of them, those who are willing. Delt has had enough time to round up everyone who'll come. I'll call him—"

"No. I will make the call. It will be more secure."

I raised an eyebrow at her.

"Reporters," she said.

"Of course." I again found myself wanting to joke, 'I hope you won't be so bossy after we are married,' but that was a tale for the unknown country ahead and perhaps not the safest topic.

"What will you tell your mother?" Maauro asked.

"Only the truth."

"Would that it were always so easy to do so."

I was a little surprised by this pensive mood in Maauro, for all she had been more often quiet and introspective since we'd arrived. I knew she had so much to think on.

I put my arms around her. "Am I thinking enough about you in all of this? Am I paying enough attention? Am I there enough for you with all you're going through, for the first time in a life of over 50,000 years?"

She looked at me in surprise, then gave one of her rare laughs. "You are the most attentive and patient of boyfriends. But I..." For the first time in my recollection, words seemed to fail Maauro.

"I," I picked up where she had paused, "will wait for you for as long as I need wait."

She placed her face against my chest and her arm across my back, and I knew I would not trade my place with her for anything else the universe could offer. We sat that way as the clouds scudded overhead, and the boat bounced on waves. Finally she looked up at me.

"Let's turn for home, Maauro."

CHAPTER 22

She manipulated sheets and rudder with blinding speed and certainty, and we turned to run before an onshore wind. My mother popped her head out, saw the two of us seated, arms about each other and ducked back into the cabin.

We ate a final meal aboard Flounder Pounder, one of Mom's best and talked of inconsequential things. Maauro had the boat on automatic as she invariably took meals with us, determined to live the part as much as she could.

We landed late in the evening, avoiding any lingering media. I asked Mom to let Lorcar know the boat was back. This was so I would avoid getting another eyeful of Maravic, which was probably not good for me. I didn't need any further complications, and I didn't want Maauro to detect any reaction I might have to her. I sighed. Having a girlfriend with a full set of sensors, able to register everything from my blood pressure to respiration, was going to be difficult.

We got back to Mom's home late and turned in. Morning came, and we woke to the smell of breakfast and coffee wafting up the stairs. I suspected that Mom hadn't slept much, knowing we were leaving in the morning.

"Go down to your mother," Maauro said. "I'll pack our things and come down in a little bit. I'm sure she would like some private time with her son."

I nodded and threw on my robe and headed down. Mom sat at a set table. She was fully dressed and, even for a morning person, this seemed a lot. She smiled as I came down, but there was a shadow to it.

"Good morning, son."

"Morning."

"Isn't Maauro joining us?"

"She said she'll be down in a minute."

I slid into a seat facing covered dishes on warmers and a pile of cinnamon buns and biscuits. "Is there an army joining us for breakfast?"

Mom gave an embarrassed smile. "Well, you can take some with you, and Maauro will love the cinnamon buns."

I reached for the coffee pot. Mom was having some fragrant tea in a delicate cup. A pottery mug had been left for me. I filled it with coffee, cream and sugar and took a sip. "Ah, now I start to feel human."

"Good," Mom said.

"Don't look so worried," I added quietly.

She nodded. "I know. I guess I knew you would have to leave again, but it brings up the question of when I will see you again?'

"Retief isn't my home, Mom. I didn't intend to return to stay. Truth be told, I'm not sure I thought much beyond seeing everyone. But I can promise you that I'll come back to see you before I, before we, go anywhere."

"I can't help but worry about you. It's a dangerous life you're leading."

Unable to resist, I reached for a cinnamon bun. "As you have seen, I have pretty good protection with me."

Mom grimaced. "It just seems to me that you are put up against larger and more awful dangers."

"Well, I'm not sure if I chose this life or it chose me. Maybe it's because I am me, with all my personal oddness that I need to do these things."

"And what of the future?"

"I'm rarely able to see very far into it."

"Learn, son, learn. And not only for your own sake. You're in something that I don't believe anyone can advise you about. I like her, and I won't say a word against her, not that you'd hear it if I did, but I do like her—"

"But you're worried and concerned about the life I will have with her?"

"Aren't you?"

"Not enough to turn aside."

"Well then, you need to do a better job of keeping your eyes on your own page, son. If I noticed you noticing Maravic, she did too."

"Damn," I said, putting down my cup. "Was my tongue hanging out?"

Mom gave a small laugh. "I'm not accusing you of being anything other than a normal boy...well, man, but I don't want to imagine a jealous android and you..."

"I don't think it works that way for her."

Mom raised an eyebrow as she sipped some tea. "If I were you, I wouldn't test that theory."

"Wasn't planning to."

"Men seldom plan it."

I was grateful to hear Maauro's footsteps on the staircase behind us. "Do I smell cinnamon," she called.

"Plenty left," Mom answered. "I was going to smack Wrik's hand if he reached for another."

"Which he won't," Maauro said, pulling back a chair, "so long as eggs of any sort and bacon are available."

Mom nodded. "You know him well."

To my surprise, Maauro looked like she was blushing, "Not so well as I hope to in the future."

This time, Mom laughed, and I blushed. I covered it by taking a double helping of eggs and bacon then snagging a biscuit. Maauro reached for the cinnamon buns and asked for some of the tea. Mom seemed charmed that she wanted some and explained at length about the herbs involved. A bright and light conversation followed and the sun-washed room remained amiable and peaceful. It was a moment to treasure, one to lock away in one's heart against worse days and longer separations.

I looked around the room at the furniture and painting, at my smiling mother and Maauro, who seemed very content as well, perhaps enjoying the sense of being in a family.

As I chased the last of my eggs with a biscuit, my mother set down her cup. "When do you want to leave?"

"No rush," I said. "We'll fly back to Delt's in the evening. It will give us some time to enjoy the beach."

We packed a picnic lunch and walked out to the bluffs further north. The day was cool and breezy, so none of us brought bathing suits. I'd bought a kite in town, and we assembled it, flying it over the cliffs, to Maauro's evident delight. Ship's passed in the distance, and the occasional aircraft passed over, cutting silvery contrails. We made the lunch extra large as we planned to leave before nightfall, and I felt going back to the house for dinner would be merely awkward.

Maauro and my mother went off to collect some flowers, and I knew that from the amount of time they spent, it was merely cover for a serious conversation about life, love and the future. Or perhaps it was just about flowers. I didn't know, and I suspected that I wouldn't get an answer if I had the bad taste to ask.

We walked back late in the afternoon. It was a quiet walk, with everyone lost in their own thoughts. When we reached Mom's house, she and I stood on the porch while Maauro went inside to get our bags.

My mother turned to me. "I can't tell you what these last days have meant to me."

"Nor to me. Not only for clearing away the rubble of the past, but for finally laying down some bricks for the future."

"You've made a good start, son. And now you have help." She hesitated. "And I have what I needed most, forgiveness for my failure."

"No more talk about the past," I said, my own voice tight. "And I want to see you taking better care of yourself. There are no worries about the house or money any more. Rena and I took care of that."

She smiled sadly. "Well, perhaps you and Rena working together is the biggest surprise of all."

I nodded ruefully.

Maauro joined us on the porch, carrying all our bags in one hand with ease. Mom turned to her and held out both arms. Maauro put down the bags and walked into my mother's embrace.

"Look after my boy."

"I will with both eyes and as many sensors as I have."

Maauro picked up the bags as Mom turned to me. "Goodbye, son. I love you. Remember, you promised to come see me before you leave."

"I haven't forgotten. Goodbye for now, Mom."

"Goodbye."

We walked down the stairs and onto the street, then we both turned and waved to my mother. I could see tear tracks on her face even through the smile. She returned our wave and then turned to go inside.

Gravel crunched underfoot as we walked on. I'd shouldered a bag from Maauro for appearance's sake. I couldn't quite sort out my feelings: elation, sadness and hope warred in a confusing mélange. Suddenly I found a small warm hand in mine and an anxious big-eyed face looking up at me. I squeezed her hand reassuringly. We walked on in a comforting silence.

CHAPTER 23

WE ARRIVED AT DELT'S AIRFIELD AND LANDED THE Magister after sunset. Maauro hopped out to open the hanger doors, and I taxied the little yellow plane in. I unpacked our gear from the nose compartment, and we walked out into the cool evening. Other than the automatic systems for the field itself, the place was shut down. I did see tail lights heading toward town, perhaps we'd just missed the last few workers heading home. As we walked toward Delt's apartments, carrying our few bags, the light blinked out a warm yellow welcome, and the door opened under my hand, doubtless Maauro had signaled the door code.

Grateful to have reached our destination, we marched up to our room and unpacked. I brushed my teeth. Staring at my reflection in the mirror, I sighed. I was tired from the long day but I wasn't sleepy. Fact was that the closer my emotional relationship with Maauro became, the more the lack of a physical outlet was bothering me. I knew she'd spotted me eyeing the girl by the dock and felt bad about it. Maauro had never been possessive before, and certainly the thought of an angry M-7 should give any male pause, but it was more the look of sadness on her face that bothered me. I felt as if I had let her down. Yet I couldn't deny that, after months without sex and with the powerful feelings that surrounded us, I felt like a ground car being thrown from drive to reverse.

When I got back to our room, I saw that Maauro had placed our mattress on the floor. She was looking out at the starlit grasslands, but turned back to smile at me. I stretched out on the floor and looked up at her, prepared to lay there until I finally fell asleep.

In an instant Maauro's red and black jumpsuit was gone, and she stood, her body: pale, shining and nude. I'd seen her like this only once before, on the floating city of the gas-giant Cimer. At the time I hadn't been sure why she showed herself to me, whether it was to show how different we were, or how similar. I did notice that her small high breasts now had nipples and a navel lay shadowed on her belly. I felt a wave of desire wash over me but didn't move, something special was unfolding, and I didn't dare risk disturbing it.

She walked over and lay down next to me. I looked at her, uncertain of what to say or do.

"I want to experiment," she whispered, then kissed me and there was something new in this kiss.

I nodded slowly and lay there as she slid me out of my underwear, unsure of where this as going. Maauro began to run her hands over my body, slowly, and in frank and curious manner. I felt my breath quicken, and she turned to face me, her eyes ancient and deep, seeming to draw me in. Then we were again kissing slowly. Our hands roamed over each other's bodies. I was pleased when her nipples hardened under my attention. Her skin felt like any woman's, but I was careful to only touch her where she invited me. This chance called for exquisite care and gentleness.

I drew in the spicy ginger cookie scent of her hair. She began to trail her kisses down the front of my body, the effect was immediate. She drew her hand over my erection stroking it carefully, then slowly took me in her mouth. I ran my hand down her back as her tongue caressed me.

It didn't take long for Maauro to have me arching and rolling my eyes back in my head. I lay back gasping afterwards.

She turned her face to me with what I swore was a sly smile. "Nice?"

"Yes," I managed. "Though I am curious as to where you picked up that particular piece of knowledge. Not to mention the fantastic technique."

"One finds interesting things around the net," she said, sliding up to kiss me again. "I also have the advantage of having neither a gag reflex, nor the need to breath. I was hoping you wouldn't think about my serrated teeth."

"I actually was incapable of thinking about anything, which is good, because if I had thought about those, it would likely have killed the impulse."

We held each other stroking and kissing. In a little while, I was again showing the sort of erection you get after a long abstinence.

"Lay back," Maauro said. She carefully maneuvered herself above me and equally carefully guided me into her.

"Another new improvement," I said, teasing gently. I could feel myself sliding into her, her hips rocking forward and back. More like a human woman's than Jaelle, perhaps different from Olivia in how regular her movements were, how precise. I teased and toyed with her breasts again running my hands over her body. This time, when I climaxed into her, I pressed her hard against me, overcome by the power of it, then was instantly concerned I might have gripped her too hard, and almost as quickly realizing how absurd that was.

We lay together her on top, my breathing coming fast and shallow for a minute.

"Equally nice?" she asked.

"Even better," I replied, stroking her black fine hair. "Though how is it that you are laying atop me and I can barely feel your weight?"

"Ah, because I am carefully and cleverly balanced on elbows and knees in a fashion that would likely be regarded as torturous by your merely human females. All of which I can do with no distraction to my primary mission."

I smiled. "Well, mission accomplished, you sexy, killer android."

"Smile when you say that."

"Oh, I am smiling," I replied.

But a serious mood came over me. "I wanted this, but I wanted it to more mutual. For me to give you what you are giving me."

She shrugged slightly. "Our different bodies give us different needs. I have a need to be loved, to be valued as a living person, to have my emotional connection to you be both clear and deep. You have these things as well, but you are a young biological male. The needs of your body cannot be denied forever. And I find that I do not want to cede this part of our relationship to another female. You are mine, now."

"Is that why tonight?" I asked. "You noticed me looking at that girl? That really meant nothing. I swear it."

The ancient and deep eyes considered me. "I am by nature and artifice a logical and practical being. I had been content to leave your sexuality to others before. It was not important to me then. But that has, in your words, complicated our orbit. It will be complicated enough, even with the one less variable. It is less that emotion that you call jealousy and more the simple fact that there are things I will never be able to do for and with you. If I leave this place between us open, who knows who could fill it, and perhaps fill it too well."

"Still, I want to give you all the things I am feeling now," I said, running my hands through her hair.

"When we are romantic and sensual with each other, I feel something, a pleasant something that is spontaneous, not generated by my manipulation of my own body as is my breathing, or the firming of my nipples. It is a sensation, a warmth from no identifiable source and sense of peace and belonging. As best I can explain this to you, when I am damaged, there are sensations, but they are not pain. Still they serve as my analog for pain. This then seems to serve as my analog for sexual pleasure."

I held her close. "I want to give you more."

She laughed gently. "I do not believe the physical sensation of orgasm, an out-of-control muscular contraction, would be very safe for you. My Creators could not have anticipated this need. While I could simulate the experience, I prefer to have no such fakery between us. What you do to me, I enjoy, whether it is stroking my hair or now, penetrating my body. The fact that I can have an interior sensation that I do not create is a marvel. I do not think you truly appreciate how unprecedented and special that is."

I nuzzled her. "All I need to know is that you're happy."

"I am. We are now lovers in name and in deed."

"Well you certainly relieved my tensions. I still wish I could do more for you."

"Who says that in time you will not? The sensations I felt in this were the strongest I have ever felt. We are only at the beginning of our journey together, you and I. Who can say where it will take us in time?"

"Love will find a way?"

She rested her head on my chest and closed her eyes. "Love will find a way."

I lay back. I could barely credit what had happened or understand its true import. We were together, and maybe it wasn't the way it had been with a human woman, but neither had it been so with Jaelle. Still Maauro was an order of magnitude further away than even that experience, unusual as it had been.

Sleep took me as I lay in the carefully regulated warmth of her body, in arms that would not move a millimeter in the hours until morning. I would awake in one sense in a strange new world, but one that promised much.

Is this the afterglow that is so often referenced in the literature of humans? I wonder, looking down at my sleeping lover. How marvelous, how rare and subtle a thing. I, made as an engine of war, lying atop a person who loves me, his arms warm about my hips, his breath on my chest. Could the engineers who cast my metal and ceramic parts, who labored in absolute zero to create the circuitry and databanks that are the basis of my quantum brain ever imagined this? No, how could they, when I myself couldn't have envisioned it only months ago? Has this ever happened before and elsewhere? Surely in all the vastness of space-time some artificial intelligence awoke and looked into other eyes and felt love? It could only be a form of hubris to imagine that I am so unique, such a chosen one. Yet, there is no way to reach out to whoever came before me, if there was anyone. No way to profit from the wisdom of any who trod this path before.

Deep thoughts roll around me in my new and fantastic existence. I have leisurely hours to consider the meaning of this deepening of my life and relationships. As I said to Wrik, lovemaking brought me sensations that did not originate in my mind. I cannot fathom how this can be so, or what mechanism brought this about. Whenever it was in my long sojourn on the asteroid that I developed ego, I had no chance to exercise it until Wrik found me. Having only had ego and selfhood for mere years, it is perhaps not surprising that libido eludes me now.

So I think and wonder, listening to the deep, regular breathing of Wrik and watching his unlined, relaxed face. It is foolish to wish that a moment in time could last forever, yet I find myself wishing it could be so. But for now, I will just enjoy the quiet hours and marvel that I found the courage to cross this bridge.

CHAPTER 23

The world rotates and brings the sun over our horizon. Wrik stirs under me and his eyes open. He looks at me, and his mobile face is a playground of different expressions.

"So," he says slowly, "it did happen. I didn't dream it."

"No," I said, smiling. "It was real."

"Are you ok?"

"Why should I not be?"

"I guess no reason. Still it was your first time."

"And a fine time it was."

"Well I'm glad of that."

I decide to tease him. "So, did you do all those things with Jaelle?"

He wags a finger at me. "Now perhaps you didn't read this in your field guide to human males, but previous relationships are supposed to be off-limit topics. You don't ask me about mine, and I won't ask you about yours."

I arch an eyebrow. "An arrangement that profits you far more than me, as I have no lascivious past. Where as you..."

Wrik leans forward and kisses me.

"That," I say, "is a transparent attempt to avoid or change the subject."

He nods. "The first of many, doubtless."

"Doubtless," I agree.

He considers. "I'm thinking of showers and breakfast."

"I'll wash your back," I say.

He grins. "No rusting?"

I pretend to bite his nose.

"Enough, I surrender," he says laughing.

We make our way into the bathroom and enjoy a shower. My ceramic and metal bonded chassis is so smooth that water simply sluices off me but I do enjoy washing Wrik's back. I towel off first and go down to see what is available for breakfast. I will powertap later, but for now I will enjoy the ritual of preparing a meal.

Wrik comes down and helps me, but despite his assistance, the food is well-prepared and the kitchen returned to a state of cleanliness far superior to what Delt left it in. We gather our breakfast and go upstairs. There is a veranda on the second floor that we have not had occasion to use. It is early, but the sun has made the morning air pleasant, though it will bring considerable heat later. Wrik is delighted with the coffee I made. I remind him it was a present from his mother and doubtless out of Rena's supply of Terran coffee. This beverage seems to have a marked hold on humans, particularly in the mornings, for something that has such minor addictive properties. I must be certain to ensure that adequate supplies are kept to hand. While expensive, it is only a minor matter for Lost Planet.

We sit shoulder to shoulder and again I find myself longing for some form of stasis. I am happy. Not as much as on that first wonderful night at the dance, but happy in a deep and contented way. The shades of joy are a new territory for me. In a way, they are like differing forms of power. The complexities of the chemical combinations of the food I ingest, which will be converted to energy, are so different from the raw, pure power that I might draw from a nuclear reactor or the somehow thinner and less robust energy I will get when I plug into the local power grid.

Well, why should they not be? The biological world is nothing if not diverse, and it lends itself far less to easy categorization.

Wrik puts down his coffee cup next to the empty plate, then he reaches for my hand, raises and rotates it, and kisses my wrist. The casual, yet intimate nature of this, for I would allow no one else to touch me so, sends strange sensations thrilling through me. I reach across and stroke the face opposite me.

Yet, I feel a frisson of fear at this moment. This other being, who now so dominates my thoughts, is but a brief creature, with a life span of 150 years or so. The frailty of his body, which only hours ago was joined to mine, is terrifying. He could be whiffed out of existence by a million dangers, and then what would become of me? In joining the dance of love, have I doomed myself to bitter days ahead?

"Are you all right, Sweetheart?" he asks. "You kind of froze there for a second."

I smile. "I am fine, though I have so much that is new and exciting to think about. It's all my first time. Every day since you found me is my first time."

He leans over now and kisses me with full intent but his hands are very careful and gentle. I savor the sensation and appreciate the gentleness, as in this case, the hands reveal the soul.

As I look at him, I realize that, perhaps for the first time since we met, his face is completely open and unshadowed. He too is happy. I put away any thoughts and fears. If I were to cease operating in the next second, I would still have lived an existence richer than any other artificial being known. But I will not cease, not for as long as I can manage.

I am loved, and this is worth living for.

CHAPTER 24

MAAURO RAISED HER HEAD FROM MY SHOULDER. "Friend Delt is approaching and at an excessive rate of speed for a two-wheeled vehicle on roads of such questionable quality."

I didn't bother to look. Maauro would have sensed him from farther than I had any chance of doing. "I assume, you wonderful, thoughtful and logical person, that when you brewed coffee—"

"I made more than enough for all of us. It was merely a matter of noticing which mug he uses, as he habitually uses the same one, often without cleaning it, and figuring at least 2.5 cups for our outsize friend."

I laughed. Now, I saw a spot moving in the distance and heard the faint roar of the Bush Rebel. Behind Delt, approaching at a more moderate pace was a car of the same bilious green as the one I rented to see Rena. I vaguely recalled that his Morok foreman owned it. Oh well, no accounting for taste across species.

Delt eventually sped up to the house, the auto lock on the gate recognizing the IFF signal from his cycle. He pulled off his helmet, looked up and gave a broad grin at seeing us. "Don't you two look comfy. I hope you took advantage of being unchaperoned last night."

"We did," Maauro piped back. "But I was careful of your furniture."

Delt laughed, but with an uncertain note as if he was not quite sure if she was kidding or not. He caught my eye, but I simply smiled.

"You want to get your butt up here before I drink all the Terran coffee Maauro so carefully brewed for us?"

"Terran!" he said, and scrambled for the door.

"I left a plate of food for you in the warmer," Maauro called. My ears rang slightly as she made sure he could hear her through the house. She gave me an apologetic smile.

Delt, plate piled high with pancakes and sausage, appeared at the door. "You guys can visit anytime."

Maauro handed him a mug of steaming coffee, she'd presumably microwaved it in her hand. He took it and gave a greedy slurp. "Oh man. I am going to start crying if this morning gets any better."

"Good to see you too," I said.

Delt stuck a fork in the pancakes and sausage. "Bah, who cares about seeing your ugly mug? It's our beautiful Space Princess that I'm glad to see."

"Space Princess," Maauro said, with a dreamy expression. "I like that. It's so much better than Space Zombie."

I groaned. "Are you ever going to let me forget about that?"

"No," she replied. "But don't worry. I couldn't leave you for a man who slurps his coffee no matter how smooth a talker he is."

Delt winked at her and slurped some more. "Damn, shot down again."

He thumped a large fist on my shoulder. "Ok buddy, make with the story. I need intel."

As Delt devoured the heroically-sized breakfast Maauro and I'd made him, I filled him in on all the developments since I left. He was visibly relieved to hear things went well with Mom and listened intently to all that was said about Rena and Grieg.

Delt was mixing his second mug of coffee by the time I finished. "Good. It sounds like things worked out about as well as they could, and frankly better than I expected with Rena. She seems to have changed a lot from the hellion she was as a kid."

I nodded.

"The stuff about Grieg is interesting. Especially now."

My ears perked up.

"Something is going on," Delt said, his face going grim. "There's a lot of talk about people going missing in the old Rebel circles. I've stayed out of that kind of thing, but my Dad still hears. There are police investigations, and some who went missing turned up in hospitals all over the planet. No one is talking, particularly since the Confed folks seem to be very active in the investigation, but there's rumor of some big raid gone wrong."

I sat up in alarm. "A raid?"

"Yeah," he continued. "Periodically some idiots get the idea of taking a swing at the Confed presence on world, or a Confed officer goes too far into the bush with too few people and there's a dust up. This one seems to have been big though, something like platoon or company strength and down near the capitol."

I looked at Maauro.

"We discussed this," she reminded me. "Delt has sources that are not net-based and has information I cannot access. I do not doubt the value of his intel. I have scanned such of the police databases as I can reach; however these are not networked to the Confed databases. They do record a high incidence of the reporting of suspicious accidents, some of them fatal."

"And Confed?" I asked.

"I can access them," she said, with evident reluctance, "but, in all probability I will be detected if I do so. I can use the all pass but that will definitely call attention to us."

I rubbed my chin with a palm. "Rena didn't want me calling in Confed for fear of what could happen to Grieg."

"Your mother and sister's locations are secure," she added, unbidden.

CHAPTER 24

"No need to stir the pot then," I decided. "Both of you please keep an ear to the ground."

Delt nodded. "Any more flapjacks?" he asked, hopefully.

I started to rise, but Maauro puts a hand on my shoulder. "I think he would prefer ones that couldn't double as discs for skeet shooting."

I sat back down. Maauro smiled, and ran her hand through my hair, then headed downstairs.

Delt waited a minute, looked at the door then back at me. "Things are different."

I nodded.

"There's been progress?" he said, trying not to grin.

I nodded again.

"Ah, we are at the stage of, 'stuff not for casual discussion.'"

I nodded vigorously.

"Good for you. Lucky bastard."

We sat in companionable silence for a minute.

"I came back as soon as I decently could," I finally said. "There's a part left undone, the final part."

"The squadron" he said.

"Yeah."

"After breakfast," he suggested. "I have a tear down to do on an old job, a Tunnan, believe it or not. We can talk as we work."

"Sure."

Maauro appeared behind us with some more flapjacks and something in a cup that steamed and smelled of chocolate. Delt looked at the pancakes with relish as Maauro handed him the plate. She sipped her chocolate drink.

We deferred any further discussion for breakfast. More of Delt's staff showed up. He waved and exchanged the occasional shouted abuse with them. Two small agrocasters landed on the field and rolled over to the chem-tanks to refill on fertilizers or insecticides. It struck me that a slow-paced spot like this wasn't the worst way to while away your time. Particularly with good company such as I had now.

After breakfast, we wander over to the main hanger. Delt sent the Morok and two other mechanics off to another job, saying that he had Wrik and me to help. The area around the field is becoming busier, with three customers coming in and the agrocasters leaving to be replaced by a small aircraft, which disembarks some local businessmen at the far end of the field before refueling and taking off again.

I sense movement north of the field through my spybees. A quick scan shows a small animal called a raccoon-dog, though to my observation the six-footed creature looks very little like a dog or a raccoon. I dismiss the creature and join Wrik and Delt, who are standing by the side of a barrelish and very old aircraft that nearly fills the hanger with its dull-orange body. Wrik is shaking his head.

"Man, I can't believe it. Look at this thing; it has to be over a hundred years old."

Delt nods. "I haven't seen a Tunnan outside of a history book before this. I haven't found a manual on the net anywhere."

I scan it with a practiced eye. "The design is clearly military, and my Confed database indicates it is essentially a flying missile battery with a rotary cylinder for anti-shipping missiles. They haven't been in front line service for the over seventy-three years."

"Yeah, Van de Hollandanse converted it to local passenger use about fifty years ago, been in a salver's yard for the last eleven years. Now, they're making it into a fire-tanker. We get some hellacious fires in the grasslands, real danger to isolated farms, small towns and such."

"It's a good type for it," Wrik says. "That big bay where the rotary magazine went should hold at least a thousand gallons of retardant."

"Yeah, but pulling out the avionics is a job. What worries me are the bay servo doors. They have to snap open in a hundredth of a second. Equipment like that isn't off the shelf and the ones on her are original. They're shot. If I have to have them machined then it's really going to kick up the price."

"Let me see the part," I say.

Delt gestures to the aircraft's underside, we both stoop to go under. Delt reaches up and opens a panel. He slowly actuates the doors, and they cycle open at a safe speed for ground crews. I duck under then stand in the capacious bay. There is a false ceiling over my head where they put in a deck for passengers. I suspect that the poor installation stressed the lower bay which has transmitted the stress to the servos. I scan in microwave and other sensors. Delt is indeed correct. The servos are in poor shape and one is 11.43 operating hours from failure.

"The mechanism could have been designed better," I say.

"Yeah. Tunnans were notorious for bay door failures. They were attritions units rushed into service during the early days of the Conchirri War. No one expected them to last a long time."

"I am glad my own creators did not subscribe to such slipshod thinking." Delt gives me a surprised look. I have seen this expression before, it usually means my biological companion has forgotten my origin.

I begin to disassemble the most distressed of the servos and its hinge.

"Ah, Maauro, Honey, what are you doing?"

"There is only so much I can determine from an exterior scan. I will disassemble one and do a full scan. Then I will need to feed the equivalent amount of high quality metals into my inner factories to extrude new parts."

"Really?"

"Yes. I will have to reorient my factories, which are used primarily for small parts, to make these larger pieces. It will take an hour and seven minutes per unit, including the hinge. I'll make four and a spare. They will be considerably more robust than these originals. There is also no need for a fire bomber to have doors snapping out at military speed, it will take a mere second to alter the program."

He nods enthusiastically. "Yeah, I thought of that too, but between the reprogramming and the metallurgy, I thought it was over my head."

It is only us in the bay, and I pitch my voice so it will not reach Wrik. "It shouldn't be. You're an excellent practical engineer. Your school grades indicate that this should not be beyond you."

A spasm of anger crosses his face, followed by a rueful expression.

"I apologize. I seem to have—"

He places a hand on my shoulder, something I normally only permit with Wrik. "Don't worry about it. You won't be the first one to notice that I haven't lived up to my billing."

I am left uncertain of what to say.

"Why don't you start on that servo?" he says into the lengthening silence. "I'll get these others three out and drain the lines of hydraulic fluid."

"Excellent. I will scavenge some metal and reprocess the old unit. Is there an area with power where I can be undisturbed?"

He gives me a curious look. "You need to concentrate?"

"No, Delt, it is not like that, but it requires me to alter my body to feed metal in and out. For a while, I must look more like a machine than a girl. I don't like that."

He strokes his chin. "Then you don't have to do it."

"That is kind, but I wish to help. I simply want some privacy to do it in."

"There's nothing that needs doing today in Hanger II. I'll tell everyone to keep out."

"Thank you. I suppose it is foolish to feel this way."

This time he grins. "Not at all, I never knew a girl who didn't want a little privacy now and then."

I start to bend down to duck out of the bay.

"Maauro."

I look up.

"Maybe tonight I spend a little time with my old engineering texts and a little less time with the bottle."

I consider— a very careful response is called for. "I think that would be a good use of time. I am available to help, if you like."

A grin again splits the broad, pleasant face. "Hmmnnn, an evening of math problems with a quantum computer to hand, I might come up with a whole new invention." He turns to the servo, a power-spanner in his hand.

I slip under the ship only to face Wrik crabbing in toward me.

"You guys were in there for a while. I was beginning to wonder if Delt was making a pass at you. Be just like him." He says it with a smile so I know the accusation is not serious.

I smile back. "What happens in the bomb bay stays in the bomb bay. Oh, and don't come looking for me for the rest of the afternoon I will be manufacturing parts in Hanger II. Delt could use some help getting the other servos out. Keep all the metal; I will reprocess it. You can leave it at the door to the hanger."

"Sure," he says and passes me on his way to help Delt. I head for the hanger, detouring by the scrapyard to find a disappointing lack of high quality metal to be reprocessed. I may not be able to make the fifth spare, as some material is always lost in reprocessing. I hear Delt's voice as he calls to his Morok foreman and tells him to keep clear of Hanger II. The big double doors of the hanger stand partially open, I close them behind me. I extrude a power cord and plug into the wall. Between my fingers and a quick application of the plasma torch, the servo is disassembled and examined in less than a minute.

I settle in on the floor and begin setting up my internal factories for production when my spybee sends an updated report on the raccoon dog. It has moved. But before I disregard it, something strikes me as curious. The raccoon dog had not changed locations for a period of 1.6713 hours, this despite the fact that the afternoon has been growing steadily hotter.

I send a level II inquiry to my spybee and draw more detail. The raccoon-dog is utterly still in a fashion no natural animal could be.

I pull free of the wall instantly and leap to my feet. The hanger has high windows that are fully open for cross ventilation. My jump takes me to a girder then I fling myself out the window. In midair, I adopt a camouflage pattern suitable to grasslands. This is less for the raccoon dog and more to prevent Wrik, Delt or any of the rest of the staff from spotting me.

I race in a semicircular path to come up behind the false animal. Fortunately, the grass prevents me from kicking up dust, though the longer stalks whirr through the air as if under attack by a berserk weedwacker. I am forced to slow to preserve stealth.

As I close behind a slight rise of ground. I see Delt and Wrik 114.51 meters away, walking between Hanger One and an out building. This causes a reaction from my quarry; it starts heading for the hanger I have just vacated. I realize that will give it a clear, but concealed, line of sight on Wrik and Delt either for observation or attack. This is intolerable. I double-back at full speed toward the hanger.

But the raccoon dog is not blind, either. I see its head swivel at an angle impossible for the animal it mimics. I cut in on one side so it cannot pass me and get to Wrik. It dodges to the left, leaping through the transom. I follow. This time there is no concealing the impact as we tangle in the air and fall to the ground, rolling and striking.

Up close, the raccoon dog is a poor simulation, but it scrabbles at me with claws that would have flayed a human. I slam it to the floor, disrupting its circuits. The machine is not occupied by Lilith, as the HCRS were, this is a pure robot, but it is connected to her in real time. My intruder programs dive into the struggling raccoon dog. But Lilith has seen my attacks before, and her barriers are better, I cannot control the squirming machine. I must admire how much she has improved her defenses.

But I think much faster than Lilith, who is biological in origin despite her augmentation. Before she can order the machine to self-destruct I drive my hand into it and obtain direct access to its systems, simply tearing out the self-destruct charge. The primer detonates in my hand, a booby trap that would have torn off a human limb but does nothing beyond cosmetic damage to me.

Before I can break through the conventional channel between Lilith and her machine, she severs it. The machine goes into autistic mode and continues to struggle. But Lilith may not have been fast enough, there is trace data captured that may be of use when I have time to analyze it.

"Maauro," Wrik calls from outside, "is everything all right?" From the sound of his voice, he is just outside the door, probably brining the other servos over.

I strike the raccoon dog again and then leap to the sturdy metal container against the wall. I lift the lid and stuff the shattered machine inside, reseating myself on the lid just as Wrik opens the door, a concerned look on his face.

"Is everything ok?" he repeats.

"Yes," I reply. "I am working on the replacement parts. Now, if you don't mind, I would like a little privacy."

His eyebrows rise.

"You may accept," I add, allowing a little coolness to seep into my voice, "that I am feeling an analog to embarrassment about being splayed out on the floor, giving birth to replacement servos."

"Oh, sure," he says sheepishly, starting to retreat.

The raccoon bot chooses that moment to throw itself against the bottom of the lid, bouncing me up. Its head peeks out for a second before I bat it back in with a motion too fast for the human eye to follow. I have the lid back down before Wrik pops his head back in. "You're sure you're all right?"

"Do you ask embarrassing questions of human females when their bodies make internal noises!"

He raises a placating hand. "Say no more." The door closes with a satisfying click.

I whip open the lid, drag out the raccoon-dog and satisfy myself by quickly dismantling my antagonist. The machine is a crude device compared to the HCRs. She has obviously manufactured it recently, as an intruder unit. The small charge it carried could destroy a soft target, but I judge its purpose to have been reconnaissance.

So I have parried Lilith, but have nothing else to show at the moment for the encounter. On second thought, perhaps there is something to be gained. The raccoon dog is made of high quality metals, superior to anything in the scrapyard. It looks like I can make that fifth servo now.

Hours later, I emerge from Hanger II with all the servos and the spare made from the raccoon-dog. Wrik and Delt are delighted with the replacements and set about reinstalling them. I leave them to this, which they do not seem to find odd. This allows me to extend and refine my search of the area for any other agents of my enemy. My quantum brain continues to maintain my fortress in the virtualverse. Lilith has made no attempts to penetrate Retief's network. The best she could manage, it seems, was the raccoon dog with its mere radio signal.

She thus remains blind to my actions beyond what little data she obtained from this scout before I destroyed it. Lilith is doubtless afraid to commit her forces to a strike without greater intelligence on my situation. Beyond me, she must worry about the Confederation forces onworld and any reinforcements that Deveraux could have sent. Every day she spends here increases the danger that I, or my forces, will locate her. Oh, yes, Lilith is beset by fears and doubts.

CHAPTER 25

OVER THE NEXT TWO DAYS, I EXAMINE ALL THE DATA I SCOURED OUT *of Lilith's raccoon dog before I reprocessed it. Buried in the data, are fragments of information. The effects and distortions of a planet's magnetic field leave telltales in the way electronic data arrays itself in a database and even in the metal the raccoon-dog was made of. It takes an epic two days of all my spare processing power before the program runs to its conclusion. This is the longest program I have ever run, attempting to analyze something as vast and variable as a planet. No other program I have run has taken more than a thousandth of this time.*

I combine this information with the data I have on the transmitter in the raccoon dog. This allow me to narrow Lilith's location to a 1,000 square kilometer area south of Eldra's coastline home, and running toward the spaceport base. These are badlands, broken coastlines and islands far from where she originally landed her ship. But, as she is blind to my movements through the virtualverse, and Retief's net, so am I to her movements. Unless she is visually observed, our combined hacking of the net makes any search result meaningless. We are both constantly sending spoofs and false information at each other and blinding such miserable and inadequate systems as this world possesses.

I place a call to Colonel Kurocal. She reaches the communicator with pleasing alacrity.

"I was hoping to hear from you," she says.

"As I am sure you are aware I am monitoring your channel every second, all you need do is speak my name."

"I assumed you would call me if there was a development."

"There has been, but first how go the information suppression efforts on the raid?"

"Well," she says. "Neither side wants to bring this into the light, but there were a lot of deaths, too many to keep the lid on, even though some of them were undocumented rebels who were never in any database. Even so, they had families. People are asking questions. How much longer do you need me to keep the lid on?"

"I have no time estimate for you, but it will be only a matter of days I believe. The powers on this world all know, or suspect, what has occurred, or a version of it as I had to leave Greg Nazir alive. Still, his edited version serves my purposes, isolating Lilith from any onworld support."

"And you have a lead on her or you wouldn't have called me," Kurocal says.

"Yes. Lilith cannot move in the nets of Retief without drawing a cyberstrike from me that would severely damage, if not destroy her. She sent an autonomous robot with a radio link to spy on us. I destroyed it, but intel I gleaned from it gives me an approximate location for her." I relay the coordinates.

"For a fancy computer everyone is so impressed with, that's a pretty big approximation."

"No one is perfect," I reply.

Kurocal stares at me for a second before breaking into laughter. *"Point for you."*

"Thank you. I have considered your protection efforts on the priority targets that I asked you to secure. I can find nothing to improve on your arrangements. But we must go over to offense now."

"Quickly is best," Kurocal answers, *"there are too many reporters working too hard on this thing."*

"My data indicates that you have four Uhu reconnaissance aerospace craft?"

"Yeah on roster, but one is down for maintenance, and another was damaged in a training accident last week."

"Unfortunate, send the available aircraft to the coordinates I have sent in this communication. I realize the area is immense, but the Uhus have good sensors."

"Affirmative, we'll signal if we learn of anything."

Another transmission impinges on me, I turn to the television. On the screen is an image of the burned out Leyland AFV being loaded on a recovery vehicle. The site of the battle has evidently been discovered by local media.

"Wrik," Delt calls from downstairs. "You'd better get down here."

His tone tells me there is trouble, and I race down the stairs to find him and Maauro looking at a holographic newsfeed on the wall. A grim-faced newscaster is staring out at the audience.

"Confederate authorities have confirmed the breaking news of an aborted attack two weeks ago by a group of Retiefan rebels. Unlike in prior such matters, no group has claimed responsibility, but members of many of the most vocal opposition groups seem to have been involved.

"The terrorists planned an attack with armored vehicles in considerable strength on the capitol's infrastructure, when it was countered by Confederate Special Forces. Multiple fatalities are reported and additional arrests are likely, though curiously no live prisoners were taken.

"Outraged planetary officials are demanding explanations and planning hearings over the excessive use of force. The list of known dead—"

Delt switched it off.

"This must be what Rena was afraid that Grieg is involved with." Maauro said.

"So there was no car wreck," I said.

"No. Confed did an excellent job of keeping this quiet, but now that it is out I am intercepting traffic about the matter. The fact that Confed authorities have not arrested, or even questioned Grieg Nazir, is being used by some to point fingers of collaboration at him."

"What?" Delt said.

"The suspicion is that he is too close to Confed. He's a moderate as such things go locally and is married to Wrik's sister."

"Is he in danger?" I asked.

"It might be as well if I returned to the area around Rena's house," Maauro responded. "Since I need neither food, nor lodgings, I can guard the area of the house unseen."

"I'll pack."

She shook her head. "No, I will call Dusko and the flitter which is far faster than the Magister.

"Why by yourself?"

Delt answered. "Wrik, you're too well known and too tied up with Confed. If you head for Rena's house it will just confirm the suspicions of the people that are most dangerous to Grieg's family. It may well be that by not bringing him in, Confed is hanging him out for target practice, hoping his own side will turn on him."

Maauro nodded. "Excellent logic."

"I don't like it," I grated.

"Can you fault the intelligence?" Maauro asked patiently.

"No, of course not. Which you knew before you asked me."

"I do think much faster than you."

"Which I can see is going to have relationship downsides," I replied.

Maauro smiled. "Only when you disagree with me."

Delt slapped me on the back. "You're flamed, flyboy. Eject before the ground comes up and smacks ya. I'll be out in the hanger."

"In truth," Maauro added, after Delt left, "I don't wish to be apart either, but your mother did advise me not to be clingy. This may be good practice."

"Oh, don't listen to such nonsense."

"I think your mother has good, practical sense." Maauro walked up and stood on tiptoes to kiss me.

"OK, I still don't like it, but call Dusko."

"Already done. I will leave within two hours."

I put my arms around her. "Being apart will be strange now."

"Yes," she whispers. "I always fear partings, short or long."

"When Dusko comes," I said, prompted by some vague foreboding, "whatever else is going on, we always stop. Whenever we part, I always want the last words we say to each other to be, "I love you.""

CHAPTER 25

She nodded. "That shall be our practice from now on. So that one day, if for either of us the separation becomes permanent, we will have that."

I swallowed a rising sense of dread.

CHAPTER 26

WRIK AND I PART EXACTLY AS WE PLANNED AFTER DUSKO LANDS THE *flitter. The Dua-denlenn doesn't come out, he and Wrik merely exchanging waves through the canopy. I get a hug and a worried look from Delt.*

As we lift off, I join Dusko on the flight deck of the cargo flitter. "You should have come out to say hello."

He gives an evil grin. "Would either of you have noticed? As usual, you seem to be off in that little fold of space where only the two of you exist."

I give him a glare which seems to affect him not at all.

"Or it could be worse," he adds. "Trigardt might actually hug me, then I would probably retch all over the place."

I sigh and settle into the seat. "It is so comforting to know that some things do not change."

"Where to?"

"Head for Grieg Nazir's house until we are out of the flight control for Delt's airport. I told Wrik I was going to watch his house."

"Call that an airport?" he snorts. "Anyway that will take only five minutes."

"I will have a course for you shortly. I must check in with Colonel Kurocal meanwhile," I punch in the coordinates I have sent the Uhus to. "Here is our present course."

He grunts. "Well here we go, loaded for Okaran as usual."

As the flitter clear a range of mountains, a signal reaches me, and I flick on my internal monitor to see Colonel Kurocal.

"Maauro," she calls, her voice is urgent.

"Here."

"Both of the Uhu's are down."

"What has transpired?"

"Don't know. They went out of contact at the same instant five minutes ago."

"A cybernetic attack on the aircraft systems then," I say. "Clearly, one of them was close to detecting her and, as she had to strike, she struck both. Send me their last known coordinates."

"Sending. Listen there were crews on those aircraft. They may still be alive."

"A cyber attack would have hacked all the Uhu systems including the automatic escape. If they could reach the emergency backups—"

"I want to send in my SAR teams."

CHAPTER 26

I consider. The Search and Rescue Teams will be vulnerable to any form of attack, either physical or cyber in their slower, vulnerable VTOLs. Still, there is no reason for Lilith to expose or waste assets to strike at paramedics. Such action would make her even more vulnerable to an attack by me.

"I cannot guarantee it, but I doubt the teams will be attacked. Have the pilots turn off as many automatic systems as they can and use manual piloting."

Kurocal nods, leans backward and raps out orders about the SAR teams to her subordinates. Then she turns a grim aspect back to me. "She knows you're coming."

"Yes, but not exactly when or how. She is trying to limit my support from you. Lilith has made at least one intruder unit. I suspect she has made more. Alert your forces covering my priority targets at once. She may try spoiling attacks to pin your troops down.

"Take Eldra Trigardt into protective custody, tell her it is in regard to a terrorist threat, but give no details. Close up security on the Nazir and Van Zyle residences. Nazir will cooperate if need be.

"Wrik is with Delt at his facility, move your protective forces in as close as you can without revealing them."

"Keeping Trigardt out of the loop is getting very difficult even in with the fiction of armored exercises," *Kurocal says*

"Yet it must remain so"

"That is on you."

"It is." *I respond, but not without misgiving.* "Remember, if I have not checked in within twenty-four hours from now, assume I am lost and govern yourself accordingly."

"Affirmative, good luck."

As I am giving her orders I am also calculating a location based on the lasts uploads from the Uhus and any other data I can scavenge. Unfortunately, one Uhu went down over an island, and the other over a peninsula of the main continent, jutting out into the sea. Once down, it will be time consuming for me to move from one location to the other. Either I must leave Dusko orbiting, with the attendant danger to him and the flitter, or I must swim, expending considerable energy I may need for the battle ahead.

Lilith is dangerous but inexperienced. She will likely see an island as a defensible location instead of the tactical trap that it is. An experienced campaigner would choose the peninsula. Indeed, they should reject both for a featureless open area where they would not be pinned against the sea. I must risk choosing the island. I order to Dusko to make a low pass at sea-top level and head for the beach near where the Uhu went down.

"You're the boss," *he says, but his lips are tight and thin.*

I use the time. I am busy in the multiverse checking my defenses. Her attack on the Uhus should have opened her up to a lethal counter-strike

CHAPTER 26

by my subprograms. Yet, this did not occur. How has she avoided my strike? I check my attack barrier. It has been fired. And then I find my answer. Lilith has sacrificed an HCR. She used one of them as a relay and launched her attack, sacrificing it to take out the Uhus. The attack barrier contacted and blasted the HCR's cyberbrain, frying it.

I am surprised. Lilith has been cautious of her HCR bodies, not as if she was fond of the machines, but the same way Wrik is careful of his body parts. This is like gnawing a leg off to escape a trap, and it is surprising she would burn a fifth of her force for such a small advantage. Her fear of me must be causing her to become unhinged.

We are closing on the island. It is a large one, over 50 kilometers in depth and 45 in length, craggy and mountainous. There are too many places one could easily hide the sort of ship Lilith stole, a VTOL model for unimproved fields, landing horizontally, as opposed to Stardust, which is an older design. If we pop up enough for me to use my onboard sensors, an HCR or a missile could target us. No, better to attack at ground level.

Dusko brings the ship down so low that the pressure of our passage rips spray off the wave tips of the wine-dark sea below us. I almost order him higher, then we are over the reef and the calmer shallows of the lagoon. A beach appears, lit by the moonlight of two of Retief's moons, and he goes into hover, kicking up sand. The door slides back and night beckons beyond it.

"Orbit out while you have fuel. Be alert for my signal," I order.

He nods. I leap through the door, armspac in hand and other weapons webbed to my back. I sink into the sand and train my armspac on the treeline as the flitter's engine's roar, and it again heads out to sea. Then I am racing for the treeline, every sensor operating at full capacity. I am moving too fast to use my spybees. Trees splinter and foliage shreds as I plunge into the forest. But nothing strikes me in direct, or indirect fire. If Lilith is here, she has either not detected my arrival, or is biding her time.

I slow to normal speed and begin to search the island. I can only hope that I have guessed correctly.

In many ways, I am returning to my origin as a fighting machine. My chassis is now flat-black. It feels both weirdly familiar and comforting. I was made for this. I must put aside the gentle Maauro and again become the M-7.

It frightens me a little how easily I do so. How seductive it is to return to my old role and put aside the doubts, the confusions, the new-found hopes and dreams. Destroy or be destroyed. There is no ambiguity here. The superior fighting machine will triumph. I am outnumbered, but I am the best ever made. Were it merely a question of me verses the five HCRs, I would be confident of victory, but Lilith remains the X-factor. What sort of force-multiplier will she be? Will she tip the balance?

I have not allowed myself to envision failure. In consequence, I have not left anything for Wrik should I fail, explaining what happened, only a short message supporting the ruse that I am protecting his family from terrorists. But just now I am too much M-7 to do so. The feelings that surround us have receded. I can only be reunited with my love on the other side of this night's work, when I will again be Maauro and place my warrior-self back under lock and key.

Now that I have slowed, I release some spybees. These are leaner, faster models designed to spend their power in one night. I send them to explore alternate vectors as I advance inland.

I detect the smell of burnt metal and polymers and alter my course. The forest canopy above me is torn, and I find the shattered remains of the Uhu among savaged trees. I make a circuit of the machine, hunting for an ambush. Nothing threatens, and I risk a recovery attempt on the crew. There are no survivors, the crew's bodies are in the main wreckage. Three men and one woman must now be added to Lilith's account. I leave the bodies undisturbed. Either SAR or Graves Registration will attend to them, and I must press forward on my own mission.

I move on, searching with my passive sensors to avoid giving away my position. Twenty-three minutes and seventeen seconds further into the search, I am beginning to fear that I have chosen badly. Perhaps Lilith is on the peninsula—

The tree next to me explodes. I roll into a ball and spin for twenty meters. I detect one HCR on a ridge about a kilometer distant, but it is not the one pumping out the HE rounds blasting the trees around me. The others must be on the ridge's reverse slope, firing up munitions for this one to guide. The spotter on the ridge is using a combination of a laser and some form of ground radar to track me. This analysis takes me .07834 seconds but most of a full second elapses before I roll out flat behind a rise of dirt and rock, my armspac stretched ahead of me.

Lilith's troops have opened fire at long range, with weapons better suited to destroying biologicals, though, if one of the plunging shells lands on me I will not be dancing with Wrik again. Score one for Lilith for getting in the first shot, but it would have been better for her had she waited until I was closer and tried for me with direct-fire and penetrating munitions. Still, one HE shell goes off close enough to cause my sensors to derezz. I cannot tolerate the exposure to these mortars any longer.

The searching laser is more accurate then the ground radar, but its beam perfectly targets the firer. My weapon spits out fifty, HVAP flechettes in a concentrated burst, most strike, removing the head of the HCR. The machine struggles to right itself; its brain is not in the head, and there are auxiliary sensors in the chest.

I have counted on this, as it rears up to bring its secondary sensors into play, my second burst of HVAP rounds tears though the armored torso, .75 seconds before a small HEAT missile finishes the job, blasting melted metal through the HCR's core brain. The machine falls, and I immediately change position. The HCR's on the reverse slope can't update their targeting now. They blast my last location, and then walk fire around assuming I am charging up the ridge.

I have no indirect fire weapons, and consider for .00988 seconds whether I should toss some grenades over the ridge. They will do nothing to the HCRs but the base of my enemy's pyramid is a human mind, which works only so fast and is easily distractible. The grenades arc will reveal my location so I head to the right for 100 meters; throw three grenades in a tenth of a second, then double back to the left, to go around the ridge at a lower level. The mortars fall silent for 1.890 seconds in which I cover 287 meters of uneven ground.

I detect and jam the passive sensors they have planted on this killing ground, leaving only the area near the valley entrance clear. But I fire spoof signals into the sensor network. If I am lucky, it will make them believe I went the other way. Some of the signals must have penetrated the passive sensor's network, as the mortar fire walks to the far side

Kurocal's interior channel with me engages. "Maauro!"

"I am busy, Colonel."

"This is urgent."

"Report."

"There's an insystem freighter in orbit, the Arc in Ciel. We've lost contact with it. Its orbit is degrading, and it's on course to crash into the capitol."

"Can you send up a boarding party to intercept it?" I ask, as I slow down and move with greater care. The mortars have stopped. They do not know where I am. Too much sound could give me away.

"No. There's nothing in the port that can be readied quick enough. I have aerospace interceptors, but all they can do is shoot it down. There are one hundred miners and their families on that craft!"

"They are almost certainly dead. Lilith probably decompressed the ship to prevent their interference. I would have."

"What!"

"Colonel, the math of this is simple. Destroy a mine ship full of corpses, or suffer an impact equivalent to 1.732 kilotons on the capitol and spaceport."

"God damn it, they may be alive. I'm not going to order the death of a hundred civilians."

"Then you invite the death of thousands more."

The fury in her slips away. "Can't you do anything?" she says. "For God's sake, it's murder either way." Her face shows the misery of a trapped animal.

Empathy returns to me and suddenly I am afraid. Have I lost Maauro in my return to M-7? Would she not have felt pity, or horror, at the thought of a shipful of helpless families plunging into a city, or dying in each other's arms the ship's air bled off? Could she not feel the anguish of a commander, who must order their deaths, or risk the deaths of thousands she has sworn to protect with her life?

"I am sorry," I whisper in my shame. In truth, I feel it and am thankful to feel it. "I do not know what I can do, but I will try. But I can lift one burden from you, if nothing more can be done. I order you to destroy the Arc in Ciel before it strikes the city. The responsibility for their deaths, if they still live, is mine alone."

Her face remains grim. "Better still if we can save everyone."

"Do you think that is likely?"

"I have to hope."

Her words strike a chord in me again. These are words Maauro understands. "Yes, Colonel, we have to hope."

"Good luck, Maauro. Find us a way out of this nightmare."

I turn my face to my enemy's stronghold. But now it is Maauro they face and not M-7 and woe to them now, for Maauro has learned both love and hate. Moving surreptitiously, I near the end of the ridge, 2.095 kilometers from where the engagement began. I stalk forward cautiously, analyzing all I know of Lilith. She is not a soldier; her tactics have been basic, yet intelligently played. Still, she is a victim of her own psyche, at the base of which is her sense of helplessness. She is an untested child with a maimed and angry life and she fears me. While it would be tactically sensible, her main line of resistance cannot be far from her actual location. I cannot see her leaving herself without an HCR bodyguard. That would mean one unit back with her, one disabled by my cyber-counter-strike when she tried to hack the net. I had thought that foolish until I learned of the Arc in Ciel. With the one I destroyed on the ridge; that leaves her only two to deploy against me. Given her amateur skills, she has likely split them, one facing east and the other west, inviting defeat in detail.

Time to end this, I speed around the end of the ridge and learn several things at once. I was right to think she would not send her machines far from her, her ship lies under electro-chametic netting on the valley floor. But I was wrong to believe that her fear would cause her to hold back any machines. On this side of the ridge is one HCR .678 kilometers away, the second is at the far end and is no immediate concern.

But I did not plan for the one that erupts almost at my feet from a metal covered trapdoor.

CHAPTER 27

THE CHIRPING OF A COM BROUGHT ME AWAKE. I STUMbled out of the bed and flipped it open. A holo of my sister's face appeared immediately and sleepiness fled me.

"Rena, what's wrong?" An early morning call from her could only herald disaster.

"Piet, there are soldiers here!"

"What! Are you being arrested?"

She bit her lip. "No, they say that there's some sort of danger, assassins or rogue separatists from that disaster in the forest. They're not taking us out of the house, but they say we can't leave. Piet...I mean Wrik, I thought I saw a tank in the woods beyond the subdivision."

My mind raced about with questions. "Yet, they haven't interfered in your communications...odd."

"You're calm," Rena said, resentment coloring her tone.

"Well, I won't say this sort of stuff happens to me every day, but enough so that I know the best move is to stay still right off. Is there an officer in charge there I can speak to."

Rena looked off the holo image. "There's a young officer in the house named Delillio. She's very nice and doesn't say a damn thing."

"Please put her on."

A moment later, a young woman who didn't look old enough to be out of high-school was smiling at me. My eyes flicked to her uniform badges, Military Police.

"Hello, Mr. Trigardt," she began before I could say anything. "Let me assure you that your sister and her family are all right and are under Confederate protection."

"Tell me what's going on." I gave my Confederate clearance, which should have made her jaw drop, but she didn't bat an eye.

"Yes, sir. I was informed of who you are and that you would be calling. I am not authorized to tell you more, only to assure you of your family's safety."

"I'm sorry that is not good enough," I said. "I'm coming out there."

"With all due respect, sir, you'll find your area is under an air traffic control hold due to an annual military exercise. Only military traffic is being allowed to move."

"Lieutenant, that authorization I gave you means I am military traffic and on the highest level."

"Unless countermanded by an equal or higher authority," she replied. "All of which is over my pay grade, Sir. I've been told to have you check in with your companion if my explanation did not suffice."

What the hell, I thought, could she mean Maauro?

"Rena," I called. My sister stepped back into range of the pickup. "I want you to check in with me every four hours. If I don't hear from you, I'll come, even if I have to walk."

She nodded with a dubious look at Dellillio.

"If it makes you feel better, Sir. Your family's safety is the first priority of the force assigned here," Dellillio added.

Force, I thought. What the hell was hunting Grieg?

"Thank you, Lieutenant. There will be literal hell to pay if that turns out to be anything but the truth."

Delillio nodded. "Understood, Sir."

Rena looked at me. "As long as we can reach you, I guess we're not in too much trouble."

"It may just be what she says," I reassured.

"You seem to have new and powerful friends, brother-mine."

"It comes with complications."

She sighed. "Well I think the complications here were home grown."

"Talk to you in four hours."

She nodded, and the image flicked off.

I debated whether to call my mother, but decided that so early a contact might cause more alarm then good, at least before I spoke to Maauro. I called her on the net, and Maauro's image appeared instantly.

"Wrik, my love, this is a recording. I am maintaining radio and computer silence as the local Confederate force has alerted me to an additional danger from the forces that tried to attack the capitol. They have requested that I coordinate their activities and use my analytics to hack through to the enemy headquarters. As a result, I must stay out of all Retief nets while I lay in wait for any movement. Tedious to be certain, but it requires my concentration. I have noted the movements of security forces to cover all members of Grieg and your family. A Confederate naval exercise is being staged near your mother's house. I recommend that you not disturb her with the news, likely she will not learn of it. The 'old bastard' is also covered, but only because of the distress it would cause your sister if he were to be killed.

"They have capped the airspace around your and Delt's location, and there are troops in the area. Please remain where you are under their protection. It'll simplify things for me if I know that none of our extended network is exposed to any danger from this local rebellion. I will be back as soon as I have rendered this small assistance to the Confederacy. It will be useful to acquire some additional credit balance with Candace Deveraux.

"I will see you soon. Don't worry. Know that I love you."

Her image faded.

I sighed. Maauro was being enigmatic again. It had been a while, but the pattern was not unfamiliar. Something was going on and she was again telling me only what she believed I needed to know. She was the only one on planet who could countermand an order I issued, assuming of course that the codes Deveraux had given us were real. I'd never used mine before and suspected that the wily spymaster had something special tagged to our IDs.

There was also the unwelcome thought that Maauro's ID probably did trump mine, even if mine was real. Deveraux was interested in Maauro and only put up with me because she needed to and because I served as a point of leverage on the deadliest AI ever made. I'd long ago accepted being the junior party in our relationship in this arena, but it still rankled.

Still, it sounded like most of what Maauro was doing was command and control. In any event, I wasn't going to get to either Rena's or Mom's. Hell, I'd probably be pulled over by the MPs if I tried to leave.

I thought about waking Delt, but decided that wasn't the best idea. The naturally rebellious Delt would probably get us into some harebrained scheme just for the hell of it. I saw us flying nape of the earth with an agrocaster, pursued by Confed fighters.

I looked out to the East; where the sky was only starting to lighten. Rena and Mom's homes were behind us in another time zone. Sleep was going to elude me, so I headed down to put on some coffee. I needed to think, and wished that I hadn't so easily agreed to Maauro's leaving. We were always at our best, together.

CHAPTER 28

THE HCR'S ATTACK IS SLOWED BY THE OPENING STEEL DOOR, LONG *enough for me to press the alpha trigger on my armspac, which in one salvo cuts loose with the firepower of a medium armored vehicle at the far HCR already in my sights. I have no time to retarget. A tenth of a second later, I have released the weapon to fall, still spitting fire and I plunge at my emerging enemy, whose blank face looks at me over the barrel of an anti-tank rifle.*

A terrible shock runs through me as anti-tank sabot round plows through my chest. Even as it cuts through my outer armor, my internal systems are active, moving essential systems out of the way of the tungsten and deplete-uranium bullet, weakening some sections to vent the damage and redirect the shock wave, and strengthening others. My back blows out, spraying precious chassis material and valuable mechanisms.

Cold rage dominates my mind. I am shot. I am damaged. No, I am hurt. I must not fail. I must not... die here. I am loved. I have someone to go back to.

"I won't die," I scream with ear-shattering force as I plunge forward into the trapdoor covered pit, palm blade's snapping out and blue plasma fire running over them. "I won't."

The feedback through the HCR must have made Lilith flinch as the next round only creases me. I shear through the anti-tank rifle with my plasma coated hands and plant a kick at supersonic velocity in the HCR's midsection. I spin backwards, bringing both hands together in a slicing attack straight into my enemy's midsection while simultaneously kicking for its head, something no biological could do.

It blocks my hands but the kick staggers it.

"I won't die," I scream again, plunging my hands straight into its midsection and again the core of an HCR brain melts in my hands.

I bend at the waist, hoping the damage control that has sealed my back will hold and flip myself out of the hole coming down next to my armspac. Systems go yellow but not red. Damage control is holding, and I have my armspac in hand again. The battle has lasted 3.56 seconds. The second HCR is only twenty meters away with its dreaded triple-auto. Again I alpha-fire my armspac as there is not time to aim properly. I am struck, but the round is HE and only knocks me backwards, derezzing my sensors, but not penetrating my casing. A laser licks across me for .023 seconds before its beam cuts off. My outer casing is vaporized, but the mirror-like undercoating reflects enough of beam so it does not penetrate.

The second HCR's arms and legs are shredded by HVAP bullets and a HEAT round from my wild counterfire. It falls to the ground, its head caved in, but brain and trunk intact. It looks at me, and the immobile face somehow still projects hate.

I project it back with black eyes and serrated teeth. "You can't kill me," I shriek, enraged even as the cool, battle-computer part of my mind targets my last burst of rounds on the charging third and last HCR. I have never fought like this before, with rage and fear for myself in equal balance. "I am going home!"

The HCR and I fire, but I have elected to drop prone as I shoot, its attack cuts some of my long black hair as the laser and HVAP rounds rip the air above me. My burst of HVAP hits it in the chest but it uses its triple auto as a shield and the extra metal stops my rounds from penetrating. My last HEAT missile blows off its left leg. It falls.

I am up and charging, not for the downed machine but for the starship. I do not need to kill the heads of the Hydra if I can crush its brain in my hands.

"Lilith," I scream, "you are dead. I will rip that disgusting body of yours into pieces and hang them for everyone to see."

"No, no," Lilith cries out. I see her now in the multiverse, no giantess now but only a small girl alone on the wall of her leprous fortress. She is casting programs at me which I do not even trouble to react to. My own begin folding up her fortress in return. In the physical world, I am almost to her ship. The damaged sixth HCR is flopping pathetically in my wake. Trying to move on one leg and damaged arms.

"I surrender," Lilith screams. "Don't kill me."

"Too late, Witch," I snarl back.

"I'll do anything you want," she begs, tears rolling down her virtual face. Around her the version of the multiverse she has made unravels, leaving her on the icy-cold, featureless nothing of the hell I am preparing for her mind. I have won.

It comes to me then, cooling my hatred and the anger over my damage. Lilith has something I want.

"Cut your ties to the two HCR brains that are still operating" I demand. The airlock door ahead of me is sealed. "Then you will go autistic in every mode, but communication with me. If I detect any activity other than that I will brain burn you first then dismember you as I promised."

She sags, ugly in defeat and nods. Behind me the crawling HCR and the limbless one cease operating.

"You will release the Arc in Ceil to her crew," I order.

"What crew?" she says dully. "I decompressed her. There's no one alive."

CHAPTER 28

"The ship would have been destroyed before it reached the spaceport," I say. "You were a fool to be so cavalier with their lives. You have little to trade now."

"I hate all humanity," Lilith said in a matter-of-fact voice. "It seems I have had as much revenge as I will get."

I am grieved, this last atrocity will make what I want harder to justify, but the dead cannot be returned to life. I stab into Lilith's network, only her mind itself is not open to me now. I reach the falling Arc in Ceil and in a few moments set the automatic landing system for a sea landing outside the capitol. The families will at least have the comfort of recovering the bodies of their dead for proper burial, something important to biologicals.

I focus on Lilith's ship next. The airlock instantly switches to my command, and I unleash a torrent of virus, scrubbing the starship of her control, particularly the self-destruct and weapon systems. I march in, damaged and burned, but now master of the situation.

"I will ask only one thing of you," Lilith says.

"No terms," I say, as I stalk the ship's corridor.

"I only ask. Do not look upon me. In the ship's main hold, you will find a partitioned room in the front with a partially assembled HCR. I was able to salvage enough of the one you brain-burned to get it working as some mobile limbs for me. Please, do not view me directly. Allow it to operate enough to talk to."

I consider. A concession may be useful in obtaining that which I want. With my control of the virtualverse complete, she can no longer attack anything. I access the ship's systems, the two downed HCRS have not moved. I can watch them through the ship's sensors.

"Agreed," I say, "But you will operate nothing else." I storm into the ship's hold. There, its arms held up in the classic gesture of surrender, is the HCR I brain-burned earlier when it touched the net to seize Arc in Ceil. My scans show she's placed a basic robot brain in it after I destroyed its original HCR brain, but the replacement is a simple model scavenged from some other system, I can control it any moment I wish to. The face on this one is totally blank, and its doll's eyes stare at me from under the colorless long hair. The body is dressed in a Confed battle uniform.

"You've won, but I'm never going back," Lilith states, her voice dull and fatigued. "Just allow me to turn off my life support; I will end my own life."

"I withdraw my threat to dismember you."

"Nonetheless, I will control my own end."

"Why?" I ask.

If I had ever doubted that here was a human somehow attached to this machine, its posture would have persuaded me otherwise, eloquent as it was of astonishment.

"How can you ask me that?" Lilith demands.

"I ask you from my need to know. I am an ethical and moral being, and need to know that my actions are good and right."

A blare of discordant laughter comes from the HCRs mouth-speaker. "Oh, the universal irony of it, the moral machine and the human with the mark of Cain.

"Still," she says, wonder tinging her voice. "You're no machine, nor computer: your reasoning speaks to me of abstract issues. Before I die I'd like to know where you came from."

I ignore her question. "You must realize that, whatever your skill as a programmer and tech, that you couldn't maintain yourself and your remaining HCRs indefinitely. What did you hope to accomplish?"

Lilith shrugs. I am amazed at the fluidity of the motion—she has integrated her mind and the body of the machine to a fantastic degree. "So you say, but there was money to made supporting these fools against the Confederacy. All of which would have extended our... my life.

"I would have succeeded but for you, an X factor I could never have foreseen. Still, you must admit I almost got you. I knew if I moved the mortar fire to your right, you would go left, whether you spoofed me or not, but I never imagined you could take an anti-tank rifle shot to your center and continue operating."

"But, no matter," she says, the machine's head snapping up with a defiant air. "Even if all I had was a few months in this body," she runs her hands over sleek metal form, "I would have chosen this, to be free and whole, not entombed in rotting, defective meat. All I needed to do is keep my damned biological body alive and I can be like this." She spins in a perfect pirouette.

"Can you understand that?" Lilith says, once more facing me.

I nod. "We are the opposite ends of a question of life and being. You, who were born a human female, yet turn from your nature to seek a machine life, free of the failures of your natural body. I am a made-machine, yet I have come to be self-aware, and much more. I battle the limits of my ceramic and metal body. I wish to experience the sensation of a living body of flesh and blood."

"Hab. Love, sex," Lilith hisses, "the gropings of sweating monkeys. I heard you screaming out there about having someone to love. It's disgusting."

"My reasons do not concern you." From where I stand, I can destroy both the HCR and the hidden body with a barrage of HV flechettes and end this disgusting episode. Lilith is insane by any definition. Under some laws, she would still merit death despite this. I stand here, commissioned officer of the Confederacy, M-7 of the creators, and ethical self-aware being and must decide what to do.

And yet there is something that I want from this terrible individual. Perhaps it will cause me to cheat justice or revenge, at least in its fullest measure.

CHAPTER 28

"Would you go free from this place?" I ask coldly.

The HCR head tips, and the doll's eyes stare into mine. "What are you saying?"

"I will bargain with you, but only within limits. You have ended many lives and that cannot be forgiven. Yet you have information that I need."

"What information?" she says, a weary contempt coloring her voice.

"You have learned how to download the consciousness of a living human into a machine body with near perfect synchronicity, to become the machine. I want the other half of that process, to upload to my quantum mind into a human body."

Lilith gapes at me. "What? Would you become less by choice? There's no way a human brain could hold all of you."

"Your HCRs did not contain all of you," I counter. "You downloaded enough of yourself to run the machines, but your core personality and memory remain in your original body."

"Yes," she murmurs almost as if to herself. "It might even be easier. Your mind must be more segmentable than any biologicals... If I do this, you'll release me?"

"After a fashion, do not think that you will escape punishment, Lilith. You will open your mind to me. I will take the information that I need directly from you, and in return, I will reprogram you."

"Go fuck yourself," she screams,

Blue fire plays over my hands, and I immobilize the HCR and walk forward.

"No, no, wait. Wait," she says.

"Remain silent," I say, seething in anger that I must deal with this wretched creature. "I offer you terms. They are not negotiable. You should take them before I regret offering them.

"I will enter your mind. I have no interest in your personal existence, but you have welded yourself so much into the machines, become so much one with them, that you now partake some of their nature. I will reprogram you so that you will take what is left of your team and proceed beyond the borders of Confed space. I will make it impossible for you to harm any member of the Confederate species. So best you stay in your exile beyond the reach of the Confederacy, as you will not be able to protect yourself.

"Doubtless, you will eventually be able to repair, or create, new members of your team, but what I program into your mind will replicate with anything you do. Attempt to alter my programming and you will become a mindless, mewing thing."

"You'll....you'll cure me," Lilith whispers.

And now despite my resolution, pity stabs at me anew. "No, that is beyond even those who knew the human soul and mind far better than I. I can make you no threat to those I protect. I cannot redeem you."

Lilith made a sound. *"Humanity never gave me anything but pain. As for the Confederacy, I will not be sorry to leave it behind. Perhaps out there, I will find my answers in however long my body holds out."*

I privately judge that she has only a small march of years to live. *"For however long you live, you will do no more harm."*

She smiles an evil smile at me. "Still, you do not make me helpless against the unknown. You were smart enough to realize that I would never again agree to be helpless."

I shrug. "Battle unknown aliens if you will, and find your death there."

"Very selfish of you," she says, "to want something so badly from me that you would let me go free."

"Very," I agree, controlling my rage. "But to kill you would return no one to life. It might be that your only punishment would be only confinement to hospitals for much, or all of your life, if I were to turn you over to civil authorities."

Lilith laughs. "More likely they would just put me back in a lab with greater security. Minds like mine are hard to find."

We stare at each other for 23.509 seconds.

"To be free," Lilith finally says, "really free, free of my hates and my revenge since you won't let me act on those. To go into deep space, the first one into the deep dark...."

"That, or death," I said. "I have decided that there is too much chance that you were right and that you would be merely restored to a lab, turning out devices the universe might be better off without."

Laughter again. "The moral machine strikes again. And such a pretty sentiment, did they wonder the same when they made you?"

"Choose, Lilith. I am intensely weary of both your conversation and your presence."

"Do it," she bites off.

"Drop your attack barrier."

Lilith's mind is suddenly open as her last defense in the virtualverse drops. I do not dip into the imagery of the virtualverse, having no desire to walk the diseased halls of her innermost citadel and see what is locked away in its dungeons. Instead, I access the machine mind and find what I suspected. Lilith is indeed so one with the machine, that its destruction would be her own. She can no longer live with just her human body; too much of her mind has moved into the machine nexus. With no HCR or computer to maintain her, imbecility is her fate.

I seize control, ruthlessly shattering her hold on anything other than her human body. I insert the self-replicating programs that will prevent Lilith from acting against Confederate interests or making anything that could. I bury it in her innermost psyche near her conception of herself; the ending of the program will be the end of her as well. I see her past,

I see the twisted body of the child who could have been saved by proper medicine, or at least prevented from experiencing the life she was given.

But the virtualverse spills over into our machine link, and we stand in Lilith's innermost citadel. The image I saw of her before is seated before me on a dark throne, robed in black and red in a diaphanous display redolent of her sexual repression. She slouches in the throne glaring at me in despair.

"You saw," she shrills in tearful rage.

"I will tell no one."

"Still, you know!"

"Enough of this," I demand. "Show me what I want."

Lilith groans and leans back on the throne and her mind opens further to me. Ruthlessly I ransack through it. Yet, even as I do so I am astonished at the capacity she shows for non-linear thinking. We come to the algorithms and programs she has created for her existence. Even for a quantum computer they are not easy, showing insights into new forms of physics, things for which the mathematical terms do not fully exist. I draw this down into my own memory. Lilith has discovered this new linkage by both intuition and chance, in a stroke of luck unlikely to be repeated without the information contained now in both of us.

I consider if I should break my word now that I have the information, and destroy her. As M-7, it would have been easy, even as Maauro it is tempting. It compels me that those who deal death should pay for it with life. Yet the Confederacy might have some wisdom to show me. Lilith is little more than a child in years, if not in mind, and one so twisted that it could hardly be told if she knew right from wrong...

It is too much. I cannot resolve it. I do not know what it right. I will keep my word as that is usually considered honorable. Doubtless, others would think me duplicitous, or deluded, for carrying out my own law and making a deal with this devil, but if anything good it to come from this nightmare it is in my hands now.

I withdraw from her mind. She lays sprawled and undignified at the foot of her throne legs splayed out, the image of rape.

"I will load you on your ship," I say, feeling a great remoteness coming over me. "After that, you are on your own. If you fall afoul of any Confederate force, you will either outrun them or you will die. I have planted it in you that you will never reveal what I have done here. I am that disgusted with myself for dealing with you."

She raised a shaking hand. "No, this HCR body is functional enough to load me and take off. Leave me...leave me be for only a little. I will gather up what is left of my other machine bodies and we... we will flee. You've done your worst to me, damn you. Cored me out like an apple. Leave me this one thing; don't look at my human body."

"That little mercy I will extend to you," I say. "In token of any evil I have done. Be gone from human space, Lilith. Find what awaits you out there."

"See you in Hell," she spits back, but there is no passion in it.

"Perhaps. I must hope that God is lenient with me. In some ways, I am only eight years old." I turn to leave Lilith and wish, not for the first time, that I had not promised Wrik to never delete a memory.

We stay apart for the next two hours. Lilith's functioning HCR gathers up her fallen. I do a similar service for myself. The material of my body that was blown out by the sabot is too precious to go unrecovered. I find the larger pieces by myself and generate some mechanical spiders to pick up the particles. While this operation proceeds, I call Major Kurocal.

"Maauro, are you all right?"

It is imperceptible to her, but by my standards there is a long delay in my reply. I am damaged, but 99.89% of my material has or will be scavenged back to me. My damage will be invisible in minutes and totally repaired in hours. Yet, I am not all right, nor am I going to be all right any time soon. I am witness to and now accomplice to a tragedy. Lilith could have been one of the greatest geniuses in the history of the Confederacy. Instead she became a berserk, murderous child because her parent's religious beliefs didn't allow for medical treatment. I saw and experienced some of her childhood, as a defective among people who saw it as God's judgment.

Could the end have been as simple as spraying the container holding her body with flechettes? Should I have passed up the opportunity for a chance at being more that I am, in the name of sanguinary vengeance? Should I have trusted to Confederate law and hoped that her utility to them did not outweigh justice?

I feel unclean, and I wish I could cry. I need to see Wrik. It will be better when I get back to Wrik.

"I am operational," I finally reply to Kurocal, as if I were simply M-7. "The threat is neutralized; you may return your aerospace fighters to base. I have activated Arc in Ciel's automatic landing system; she is bound for a water landing five kilometers out to sea. I am sorry, there is no one left alive onboard."

Kurocal brings her fists down on the counter before her. "God dammit!"

"I am sorry."

She shakes her head. "No reason for you to be. I won't forget the hook you pulled me off of. I just wish…. I just…"

"I know, if only we could have."

She slumps back, "So it was only a false hope."

"Yes," I say beginning to understand what humans mean by feeling heartsick, "but perhaps it was better than no hope at all." I sigh. "Please send this message under an Ultra code to Candace Deveraux: Lilith eliminated. Local insurrection suppressed. Take no action

against Grieg Nazir, and ensure that no record or information about the engagement with Lilith reaches Wrik Trigardt. He is not to know anything ever occurred."

"Wow."

"Wow, indeed."

"Will I see you?" Kurocal said.

"Perhaps," I say. "I still have things do here, but they are not things you need be concerned over."

She nods, looking much older. "The rest of my day will be spent with the media on my casualties and those on the Arc in Ciel. My only consolation is how much worse it could have been."

"Yes, there is that."

"Do you drink, Maauro?"

"You mean alcohol?"

"Yes."

"Sometimes"

"Good, if you get by my office, we'll have one together."

"I would like that."

"Kurocal out."

Information is shot to me by my programs on Lilith's ship. She is ready to leave. This cannot happen fast enough for me. I watch from the ridge top as she launches. Her course will take her at sea top level until she reaches a polar region. From there, she can proceed into orbit undetected and out of the knowledge of living beings.

I call for Dusko.

"I see you survived."

"Yes, please pick me up and return me to Delt's field."

"On my way."

"Dusko."

"Yes?"

"Do not misinterpret this. I am not angry, or displeased with you, but I do not wish to speak after you arrive."

"Bad day?"

"Yes."

"Understood. I will leave the tender loving care to Trigardt, in any event."

"Remember, even though the threat is ended, no word of this must ever surface."

"No one will hear of it from me. Remember that when it comes time for my annual salary review.

CHAPTER 29

I STOOD IN THE HANGER FINISHING UP SOME WORK ON THE Tunnan, when Delt leaned in. "Hey, Wrik. I just got an IFF on the field's landing system. Your pal, Dusko, is pulling into our place."

"What?!"

"Did you hear from Maauro?" he asked, concern on his face.

"No, I better get my com."

"Don't bother. They'll be here in two minutes."

It was a long two minutes before Stardust's shuttle dipped over the field. Dusko was flying. I could tell by the way he side-slipped onto the field and VTOL'd to a halt. But he wasn't staying, the hatch cycled out, and Maauro dropped onto the field. The shuttle rolled forward into a take-off run.

Maauro came toward me. I couldn't tell anything from her long, firm stride, yet, I somehow knew something was very wrong.

And it was. Maauro broke into a run, and I raced to meet her. She almost skidded to a halt, and I had my arms about her. She buried her face against my chest.

"Maauro, Honey, what is it? Are you all right?"

She only shook her head, her face still pressed to my chest. Behind me, I heard pounding feet, and knew Delt was racing forward as well. I raised a hand, and the feet slowed. I took a bare moment to glance at him. He stopped short, his face a study in worry. I shook my head, and he nodded, turning back to the hanger.

"I'm home," Maauro whispered.

"Maauro, are you ok? Are you hurt? What's happened?"

"Please do not ask. I am home. That is all that matters."

"But—"

Maauro raised her head. Her expression was tense and more. For the first time, she looked angry at me. I was jolted.

I pulled her against me and stroked her hair. "Ok, no questions. Just tell me how to help you."

"Do you love me?"

"Yes, of course I do."

"Continue doing so."

I drew a shaky breath. "I will, Maauro, now and forever."

"Can we go to our room?"

"We can do anything you want or nothing at all." We walked, me holding her about the shoulders and made our way to the apartment we shared with Delt. I spotted him out of the corner of my eye, shooing away the other staff. I opened the door and led her upstairs. Once inside, she closed and locked the door. She turned to face me, and her body shimmered. Maauro stood before me naked, her eyes focused on me.

"I need you," she said.

I took her in my arms and kissed her as she tugged at my clothes. I had no idea what had triggered this strange, desperate mood, but I ran my hands down her body and pressed her against me, feeling the warmth of her. Lacking any better map, I treated her as I would any human woman, touching here, caressing there, but Maauro was not in the mood for foreplay. She pulled me down atop her on the floor as soon as I was ready, took me into herself. As we moved together, her eyes were closed, and her hands were tighter on me than they had been the last time.

I kissed her, wanting her as badly as ever: wanting to know her, to be one with her in every way possible, wanting to heal anything that hurt.

"I love you," I whispered to her.

"And I love you. I, who never would have dreamt to be loved and to love, before we met."

We moved together, slowly and carefully, until I climaxed, and it seemed that the world had narrowed to just we two. I stared into her deep, beautiful and ancient eyes. How was it in all of time space that we could have been the ones to meet? My breathing slowed, and I murmured her name, running my hands over her. I covered her mouth with mine.

Maauro smiled at me after I kissed her. "You need not be concerned about your weight on me."

I laughed lightly. "Gentlemen rest on their elbows."

Her smile did not dim, but she pulled me closer, evidently wanting the feel of my body on hers. She sighed. "I felt it again."

I looked at her expectantly.

"That sensation, from nowhere and everywhere, something in my body I did not self-will. It was deeper this time, more powerful."

"I'm glad," I said, unsure of what more to say.

"This was good. I needed this."

"I am," I said slowly, "the man who loves you. You don't have to tell me anything, if you don't want to, but you can tell me everything."

"Sometimes, Wrik, you will have to accept that there will be things that I cannot explain. Take it that I have been overwhelmed by my emotions during our separation. I will deal with it better in the future."

I knew that this wasn't all there was to it and that in some measure, Maauro was lying to me. But I had held my own secrets until I felt I needed to share them. It hurt a little that she had something she didn't want to tell me, but she had also turned to me as the comfort that she needed.

"I suppose we shall have to say something to Delt," she said in obvious reluctance.

I shook my head. "He'll ask only two questions: are you ok, and what do you need?"

"That is good for now."

I got up and reached down, absurdly, to help her up. She took my hand for all that she not only didn't need it and really couldn't use it without flinging me over her head.

"Can we shower together?" she asked.

"Sure, Sweetheart." We moved to the small shower. I carefully set the water temperature and then we got in. How water sluiced over both of us. I reached for the shampoo and put it in her long hair. It was rather silly, Maauro's hair never felt dirty or smelled like anything other than ginger cookies. But she stood under my ministrations, the water running down her body, seeming content to stay there.

After I rinsed her long hair, she looked up at me, her face serious and reserved. It was a warning against questions that I was not inclined to test. We got out and toweled off, and I threw on some clothes. Maauro morphed into casual dark green pants, a tan short-sleeve shirt and a white sweater. It all seemed to match, so I guess she had been working on her fashion sense. I wasn't sure from where she'd produced it, but she bound her long hair, already dry, up in a big, yellow bow.

We trooped down the stairs to be greeted by the smell of good cooking. Delt stood over a pot of stew, which bubbled and looked large enough to feed ten people.

He looked up at Maauro as we came down. "You ok?

"Getting there," she replied.

"What do you need, Pretty Princess?"

Maauro considered. "Stew, I need stew."

"Stew's coming up with cornbread on the side. What else?"

"A power socket and some privacy."

"Ok, all that. Stew first. Go sit."

We tucked around the table in front of the odd collection of bowls and plates that were Delt's tableware. He piled generous helpings of stew in the bowls, then cut up cornbread, slathered it with butter and slid it in front of us. A couple of beers appeared in mugs with aircraft on them.

"Good to have you back," Delt said.

"How could I miss this stew?" she asked, deadpan.

We exploded in laughter. Suddenly, the cloud that had sat on Maauro seemed to dissipate. The stew was good and hearty. The slathered cornbread was just like Mom used to make, though she didn't usually serve it with beer. As if by tacit agreement the meal passed with nothing of any serious nature being discussed

We walked out to the porch, listening to a pair of light aircraft taking off. Delt waved to his Morok foreman, whose first name I'd still not learned to pronounce. The apish alien waved back and headed for the parking lot, followed by two female techs.

Maauro settled her back against my knees; the bench wouldn't take her weight without her being locked in a supporting position. I could feel the warmth of her body as I had a leg on either side of her, but I knew she was only allowing so much of her weight against me. I stroked her hair, avoiding the yellow hair bow,

Delt joined us, handing each of us a bottled beer and perched on the rail, staring out at the lowering sun and the lengthening shadows of the oncoming evening.

"Wrik," Delt began. "I've been trying to reach the members of the squadron, ran into some rather hard feelings there."

I couldn't quite shrug off the sinking feeling his comment brought.

"With one exception, who I think we need to have on our side."

"Yeah?"

"You remember Janna Lourens?"

"That hellion? Who could ever forget her? She was a maniac in a fighter."

"Well, these days she's a parson in the Anglican church—"

"What?" I said, my jaw dropping.

"Yep, threw me too when I found out. But more to the point, she's on a sabbatical over in Kalbara, not far from here. She was almost as happy as I was to hear you were still alive."

"Does that mean she's going slug me when I see her?"

"No one is going to hit you," Maauro interjected, her voice flat and toneless.

It took a few moments for the chill to fade from the air after that. I stroked her hair again.

"Anyway, I felt, especially after talking to Regina, that I needed her help."

"Ok," I said.

"You sure you want to do this?" he asked, tapping his bottle with a finger. "I mean you've had a pretty good run…"

I'd started shaking my head. "No, I want this wound cleaned all the way out, so it scars over, and I can get on with my life."

Delt nodded. "Rev Janna said she'd like to meet us for a picnic lunch tomorrow."

"I'll be glad to see her," I responded.

"Is she pretty?" Maauro asked.

We both broke up again. After a second, Maauro leaned back and smiled up at me. She looked expectant.

"She was hot," Delt said, an evil grin on his face.

"Yep," I said, "best-looking girl in the squadron."

Maauro playfully thumped my toe with her fist.

The next day, we rose early and headed back in the direction of my old home, to Kalbara, a small town with an Anglican retreat just outside of it, whose chief reason for being was the intersection of two rivers.

Janna had picked a picturesque spot with a view of the Lelane River to meet at. There were some young couples around the riverbanks under the sailtrees and waving stalks of ver-grass. As wasn't uncommon, Maauro drew stares from the locals, who noticed her big eyes and slender frame. But Maauro's mood was cool, even a tad grim, and no one who stared at her seemed to enjoy the experience of her staring back. We soon found our section of the park relatively empty. So we set our picnic lunch basket down on a red-painted table and waited.

A woman came up on a bicycle. Delt waved and jogged over to meet her, I waited with Maauro. Delt returned, followed by Janna Lourens. I almost didn't recognize her. Janna had been the smallest person in the squadron, nicknamed the Devil's Pixie, by pilots who'd been unable to shake her off their six o'clock once she'd locked on them. Back then, she'd boasted a mane of unruly and glossy chestnut hair that was forever escaping her helmet. Her fashion choices could only have been described as daring. But the woman walking beside Delt, wore gray slacks and a matching shirt with a white collar. Her hair was neat, short and in a simple style.

Despite Delt's assurances, I braced myself as her eyes met mine. But the good-natured, freckled and snub-nosed face split in a broad grin. The wave of relief that surged through me was so intense I felt momentarily light-headed.

Instantly, I felt Maauro's hand on my back. She must have detected the reaction.

"Wrik," Delt called. "You remember Janna, well I should say the Reverend Janna."

"Easy, Flyboy," Janna said, with a gentle laugh, stopping a meter away from me. "You'll make me feel old and responsible." She slapped Delt on his broad-shoulder. The warmth in her smile did not dim as she turned back to me. "Hello Piet ... sorry, I mean Wrik. Damn, it's good to see you."

Her eyes slid past me. "And you must be Maauro. I'll confess that I am not sure how to address a living artificial intelligence."

I gave Delt a sharp glance.

"I felt it necessary to take Janna completely into our confidence," he said with an apologetic air. "It won't work without her, and I didn't feel right holding back on her."

Maauro placed a hand on my arm. "It's all right, Wrik. We must trust in Delt's judgment. He possesses the best local intelligence in our network."

"Yeah that's me," Delt said, with a rueful grin, "G-2 all the way."

Janna pulled her attention away from Maauro with obvious effort. "Delt told me why you came back. I'm glad you did. It's good to know another of us made it."

"I made it by running away."

"I know. And I made it by never really engaging. Oh, I circled around the edge of the fight, shot off all my ordnance, emptied my guns and capacitors. So what? Did you see me in either Delt's ratrace, or the furball that you and Spider flight got into? I dumped my weapons load, headed for the deck and scrambled back to the base at treetop level. They gave me some sort of a medal for it. I forget which one. I gave it to one of the kids at the orphanage for her doll. She thought it was pretty."

I nodded, unsure of what to say. Janna gestured at us to settle on a wooden table by some rocks by the riverside. The sun sparkled through the fronds of the trees and off the water, and the afternoon wind held a cool edge to it. Delt began to unpack our picnic with Maauro's help.

"So you ran away," Janna continued. "I pretended to fight, and Delt led all of us into a slaughter and most of us died. That's our brutal, unchangeable past. My concern is the present and what we can make of the future.

"Welcome back," she stood stepped forward and put her arms around me.

I fought for control. No tears, no cheap sentiment, I demanded of myself.

"Thanks Janna," I managed; my voice harsh and strained to my own ears. "Can't tell you …. can't tell you what that means to me. For the chance to ask your—"

"Forgiveness?" she said, eyebrows rose as she stepped back, wiping tears I hadn't seen coming, off her face. "I'll trade you and Delt both. You forgive me for being in a fighter and not being in the fight?"

"Done," I said. I looked at Delt.

"Done," he repeated, his voice a whisper, big hands knotted in fists.

Janna walked over to put an arm around him and gradually he relaxed. "You have the greatest burden of all us to let go of. I've told you that before."

"Can't seem," he swallowed, "can't seem to find the right place to leave it."

"Enough of the past," Janna said, still holding onto Delt's arm. "Piet… I mean Wrik. How can this simple pastor serve you?"

I drew a deep breath. "I want to see the other survivor's of the Ncome Commando. To make my peace, or at least offer it, and to take whatever it is I have coming from them. Delt feels that if you add your voice to his, that we can get all three of them."

Janna sighed and let go of Delt's arm and we all sat at the table save for Maauro who perched on a rock just next to it. "That's what Delt told me, and he also told me he had reservations about it. Some of which I share. I'll help, of course, but you have to understand that there are some folk who are more forgiving than others. Some for whom the rebellion is almost a religion in itself."

CHAPTER 29

I nodded. "I don't expect it to be easy, or that everyone will forgive me. Frankly, I've already done better with you and Delt than I ever dreamt possible."

She nodded. "I'll make the contacts and see what I can set up. It will take some time. We're scattered all over the continent. I think it best if we meet here, rather than at Delt's, more of a neutral ground."

I nodded.

A sparkle returned to Janna's eyes. "But now Wrik, you must let me talk to the marvelous Maauro here. You can't imagine what it means to a religious person to meet a true artificial intelligence. Oh, if my divinity professor could see me now!" Her eyes practically gleamed with liturgical lust.

"You wish to ask me if I have a soul," Maauro stated, a gentle smile on her face. She leaned back on the rock she'd perched on, we shifted to face her.

"Yes," Janna said. "Isn't that the essential question of all life? Is this all I am?"

Maauro considered that. "Perhaps. I find myself more interested in the nature of love."

Janna's jaw dropped. Delt smiled and winked at me.

"However," Maauro continued. "It is clearly a central issue of existence. Are we merely temporarily denizens of space-time? I have no known limit on my life span, but in a universe that will continue for billions of years, the mere 50,000 years I have lived, and whatever I have left to experience, measures more closely to your own brief lives than to any cosmic scale."

"And that is my cue to get the beer," Delt said, standing. "I'll be back." He headed back to the rented aircar, which had a cooler in the air-conditioned compartment

Maauro's look at him was only amused. Janna gave him a distracted nod.

"So, like you," Maauro said, "I must live in the hope that I have an immortal part, that there is something of me that God, or whatever you call the creator outside of space-time, intends to continue. I must believe that my life, my love, even my thinking adds up to more that the space required to store it in memory. I will grant you that I have no more proof than you do of the existence of my soul, or its place in the eyes of God. Indeed I have less, these concepts of God and the soul are not mine, but have come to me through my interaction with biological life forms."

"Amazing," Janna breathed.

"Still, and I cannot tell you the why of it, as it touches on classified matters, my belief in my soul comes from a glance into my own future, where I know that I believe, where I have matured to certainty from question."

"Then you will outstrip many of us," Janna said, "who will live with doubt."

Maauro laughed. "Perhaps it is only that when I settle an issue for myself, I am not given to second thoughts. That which was the best decision, will remain the best decision, absent new and relevant information.

"In a way, it must be so for me. All my decisions about life and existence are self-willed. I do not know when it was in the long ages of my exile in the asteroid, when my power levels were so low that even the Brownian motion of my own atoms was scavenged for power, that I came alive. I only know that shortly after I was reawakened by Wrik, I had a sense of self that was not that of a machine. Through Wrik's friendship and later his love, I became more. I acquired the dignity and choices of the free-willed."

Maauro looked at me. "One terrible day, Wrik stood in a dark place, facing my weapons, knowing me to be a merciless killer, condemned to follow the instructions of my ancient creators and bet all he had, that there was more to me. That the Maauro he had befriended could defeat the programmed war machine she'd been made as. Who has received a greater gift than that?"

Janna's hands were in front of her face in an almost reverent pose. I sat there blushing like a fool. I was suddenly conscious of Delt standing next to me. He gently put the six-pack on the wooden table as if afraid to make any noise.

"And," Maauro said, reaching forward in a swift gesture and snatching up a bottle. "I can open these with my fingertips." She casually popped the top off the lager and passed it to me.

"My God," Delt said, in an awed voice. "She's the perfect woman."

The picnic proves a happy diversion from Wrik's concerns and my recent memories. I find that Janna is one of the most appealing humans I have met. I am hopeful of creating a network connection with her. She is as young and pretty, as I appear to be to others. If I had been born biological, I might have been her. We share our interests in existential matters, to Wrik's bemusement and Delt's apparent boredom.

Afterwards, we pack up. She is headed back to the seminary, we, to an inn nearby to await the rest of Wrik's teammates: Regina Van Dyck, Carel Englebreact, and Johan Dewalt. Van Dyck and Dewalt concern me; both have had criminal incidents since their service days. Some of these have involved violence.

Wrik and Delt grab the basket and the bottles and head for the car and some trash cans. It gives me a chance to speak with the priestess outside of their hearing. I place a hand on her arm. She turns to face me, a question on her face.

"I am glad that we have a moment alone," I say to Janna.

"Yes?" she replied, her eyes lively with interest.

"Wrik's mission of reconciliation has been... unpredictable, at least to me."

"Likely, that won't change," she says with a sigh. "With one of his squadron mates I hope for reconciliation, but with others...."

"Be warned of this," I say, willing sternness into my voice. "I have no interest in the past, not in the rightness or wrongness of anything that was, or was not done, nor in people's assessments or resentments. I am only interested in Wrik's safety and well-being. Words I will tolerate, to a point, but nothing beyond that, and I am death itself when provoked."

The smile vanishes. "I believe you."

"It may fall to you to ensure that others do as well."

CHAPTER 30

WE TOURED THE SMALL TOWN FOR THE REST OF THE day. Janna stayed with us for an hour before heading back. She had calls to make and wanted to make them in peace and quiet. Toward evening, we settled into the inn. I made calls to both my mother, which was pleasant, and my sister, which was awkward. Maauro was watching both locations through her own means and assured me all was well and there was no present danger, but she'd been less than prescient about things on Retief, and I was concerned that the crudity of the planet's infonet and her unfamiliarity with the place, might be hampering her usual skills.

The next day passed quietly. Maauro was our relay to talk to Dusko, who was organizing cargo for wherever it was we were going after Retief. Delt fielded a few calls from his business. The new owner of the Tunnan we'd worked on showed up and was floored by the improvements, mostly done by Maauro, on the machine.

"Well Pretty Princess," Delt said, closing his com, "I have to hand it to you. He was happy to pay 10% over invoice on that ship, and, with you doing so much of the work, not to mention making the parts for free, I really cleaned up. That, and what you did for my finances, has me swimming in it."

"And what will you do with your new-found wealth?" Maauro asked as we walked alongside the river. Today, she wore an autumn gold jacket and tights and looked wonderful.

Delt's face clouded over. "Hadn't thought of it," he admitted. "Guess I don't look ahead to the future that much."

"You should consider that," she said softly, looking out at the river.

For some reason, comments that would have made Delt angry, or dismissive, from me, or anyone else, he pondered deeply when Maauro voiced them. He seemed to want her approval in a fashion that I couldn't recall seeing him exhibit around anyone else. Of course, he was no longer a devil-may-care young fighter jock, but I still sensed something deeper in his regard for Maauro. Maybe it was just as well that I'd met Maauro years ago, I thought, I might need the head start.

Dinner was a cheerful affair, with we three in a window box overlooking the street. For a while, it looked like Delt was going to pick up a local girl and make it a foursome, but he restrained his usual nature. He noticed my surprised look and wagged a finger at me.

"Mission before men," he quoted. "We have stuff to do here. I'll look for company when it's all over." He grinned and picked up his water glass. That too, was a change. While Delt seemed as fond of beer as always, it was now one or two, drunk slowly, and he seem to have sworn off anything harder.

My com buzzed as Janna's image appeared. I opened the line.

"Yes, Reverend."

"Oh bother, call me Janna or I hang up."

I couldn't quite suppress a laugh despite my tension.

"I have all three coming," she said. They'll meet us at the gazebo in the Peace Garden of the Seminary at 10PM. They're coming separately but they're going to meet up somewhere and come together. We'll do the same. I'm standing with you, Flyboy."

"Thank God, for that," I said.

"I'll tell him you said so."

"Do that."

"Meet me at the seminary lobby at 9PM."

"We will be there," Maauro added, and there was no question about the accent on the "we."

"Damn right we will," Delt added, a touch of grimness in his tone.

"This will be a peaceful encounter," Janna warned, "on all sides."

"It will," I said. I looked at Maauro.

"I do not strike anyone first," she said, "but I never need to strike anyone twice."

Janna sighed. "Fair enough. Until tomorrow."

We turned in after dinner, but I couldn't get much sleep. Fortunately, Maauro didn't need any and so we talked of inconsequential things. She gave me a massage that would put a professional to shame, and finally I got a few hours sleep in the early morning.

After breakfast, we rented a boat and tooled around the river to kill time and keep my mind off things. Because of Maauro, we had to rent the biggest boat they had, but she was delighted with the chance to play sailor again, despite my and Delt's inept assistance.

Somehow, the time passed, and we found ourselves back at the hotel. I wasn't sure how to dress for the occasion, and just threw on a flight jacket. Delt wore something similar. Maauro returned to her red and gray paneled jumpsuit. I sensed that the utilitarian and somehow military look was a warning of her serious intent.

The valet brought the car around. We'd left Delt's cargo-flitter by the municipal landing pad. Delt drove, with Maauro providing directions to the seminary, a collection of long and low buildings, clustered around the main church, with its one white tower and elaborate gardens, though there were as many vegetables as flowers in them. We pulled up to the parking lot. Most people were leaving, either heading out to the dorm buildings or back to town.

Janna stood in her priestly uniform, waiting at the entrance. She embraced all three of us this time. To kill the hour and settle our, truthfully, my, nerves, she showed us around the two-hundred-year-old buildings, recently restored with a grant from the reform government.

Her com bleeped. She drew it out and regarded a text on it. "They're here."

I drew a deep, shaky breath.

"You ready?" Janna asked.

I nodded.

"Remember," Maauro said softly. "You are never alone. Not anymore."

I put arm around her. She patted it gently.

"I'm on your wing," Delt added.

"And I have your six," Janna said. "And no one can get me off their six."

I spared her a quick grin. "Let's roll in, then."

I walked out, flanked by more than I ever believed I would have on my side. I took my cue from Maauro, who'd spotted everyone, despite the dark and distance the instant we came through the door. We headed for the large, white gazebo on the hillside overlooking the parking lot.

Three figures awaited us. They stood outside the gazebo, partly shrouded by the dark of the trees, despite the sodium lights of the parking lot below. There was something ominous in their stillness and posture.

Janna took the point as we walked up. Delt was on my left, and Maauro stood to my right. There was nothing in her stance to show it, but she was moving with a suppressed energy, alert and tense.

My old squadron mates stood in a Vic formation: Regina Van Dyck, wearing a sharp suit, stood at the apex facing me. Johan Dewalt, huge and glowering, towered over her right shoulder. Carel Englebreact, who had put on a lot of weight, stood off to one side. She looked ten years older than I expected, nothing like the young, high-spirited girl I'd once known.

I stopped opposite Regina, who I recognized as the unofficial leader of this group. We studied each other. Regina's face was beautiful, but still, with a waxen look to it, like a store mannequin, synth-flesh from the burns. Johan had started to go bald, but looked as powerful as ever and sported a rebel's bushy beard.

Do we all so easily give away who we are and what we believe by such things? I wondered, fighting that sense of numbness and unreality that always seemed to follow nighttime and emotion for me.

"So, you're alive," Regina said.

"Hello, Regina—"

"Who told you that you could use my first name?" she growled, her eyes glittering.

"I did," Janna stated. "If anyone's unclear about it, I'll say it for the record. That's how we used to call each other."

"He's not one of us," Johan's voice rumbled.

"You squadron leader now?" Delt said. "Who flew in Ncome was my call."

"Enough," I said, putting an arm on Delt. I turned back to them, looking at Carel who did not meet my eyes, then Johan who met them with contempt and hatred. I looked at Regina, but could read nothing in the expressionless face.

"Who's that?" Regina demanded, looking at Maauro. "What right does she have to be here?"

"I am Maauro," she answered, and something in her voice drew everyone's eyes to her. "I am Wrik's, and where he goes, I go."

Regina's lips twisted. "Cradle robbing, Van Zyle? Oh, I guess you prefer Trigardt. You should go home, Sweetie, we're warriors talking about war and betrayal here."

Maauro cocked her head. "I am a warrior. I have killed more beings than are in sight here. And I did not need a fighter plane to do it."

Regina face couldn't display surprise evidently, but her stance did. Little did she know that, when Maauro made her statement, she meant from horizon to horizon, not merely this little hilltop.

I put a hand on each of Delt and Maauro's arms to hold them in place and stepped forward. "I have come a long way, and through a lot, to apologize to all of you. You were my squadron. Some of you were my friends once. I let you down. I broke and ran. All I can say is that I am sorry."

Regina looked at me, the too smooth face, stretched into a mirthless smile. "Do you know the worst thing about the reconstruction?"

"Reg—" Delt said.

"No," I interrupted. "Let her have her say."

She grabbed her cheek and twisted it. "It should hurt, but it doesn't," she hissed. "Not enough to be real. Not like my original face."

"I'm sorry," I whispered.

"You weren't burned," she said, her eyes bright, her voice had a sing-song, skittery quality to it. "You weren't shot out of your fighter."

"No," I said. "I made it without a scratch, because I ran away."

"He was also closest to the enemy, the last of Spider flight in the air," Delt threw in. "Dammit, Reg you were shot down even before Wrik dove out. I sent you into that attack, knowing you'd all die," suddenly Delt was shouting. "You should be blaming me."

"You didn't run," she snarled.

"How do you know I wasn't ready to? I got shot down and ejected. Another few seconds in a hopeless losing battle and I might have."

"No, you wouldn't," I said,

Maauro, who had stood so still that everyone had forgotten her, suddenly spoke. "You have a weapon in your pocket, Van Dyck. If that hand gets any closer to it, I will kill you."

"No, Maauro," I said.

"Wrik, in this I do not care if you agree or not. Whatever you have been to them, you are my Wrik. I know who you are now. The next person who offers you violence will face me." Maauro's eyes went black from lid to lid. Her lips pulled back from serrated teeth and palm blades slid soundlessly into place.

The others shuffled back with muffled curses and shocked faces.

"What the hell is she?" Carel blurted.

"It's a machine," Regina said.

"Bought yourself a toy girlfriend," Johan said, his lip twisted in contempt.

"Leave her out of this," I replied. "This is about me."

Regina held her hands carefully away from her sides.

"Do you really want to kill me, Reg?' I asked slowly.

The too-bright eyes fastened on me. "I want my original face back."

"I'd trade myself for that, if I could."

"Easy to say," she shot back.

"What would you have me do? What would you have me say? I'm sorry I failed you. I have tried since then to be a better man—"

"There are many now," Maauro said, "who owe Wrik their lives."

Regina looked at Maauro. "You look like you're prepared to kill for him. That how he programmed you?"

Maauro's eyes returned to their beautiful aquamarine, the teeth vanished as did the palm blades. "I am not a machine as you understand it. I am a living AI, as should be obvious to you at this point."

"She ain't no HCR or Confed make, that's for sure," Johan muttered, staring,

"And you are right, I would kill for Wrik, perhaps more to the point you seek, I would also die for him. That is not programming. In fact, I owe my freedom from programming to Wrik."

The maliciousness brightness in Regina's eyes seemed to dim, to be replaced by an empty sadness. She turned back to me. "Bet your Dad loved that."

"Yeah, he'll add it to my headstone, 'Loved alien androids.'"

A short, harsh laugh exploded out of several people. Regina's lips quirked once.

Silence fell over the group. The twilight had turned to true darkness while we had spoken, only the distant lamplights limned people's faces.

Regina broke the lengthening silence. "I heard your apology. I'll think on it. I don't know that I am ready to forgive and forget … but I'm glad … I'm glad you're not dead, Piet. No, I am going to think of you as Wrik. That may make it easier."

I nodded carefully.

Regina turned and walked for the car park.

CHAPTER 30

Johan looked at me, then at Maauro. "Maybe you're just brave enough to do this because your killer android came with you. Might be different if you came alone."

"I can arrange to be alone, Johan."

"None of that," Janna snapped. "Johan, you've been asked to forgive. Do it or don't, but, in God's name I charge you, there will be no violence. The Rebellion ate enough lives. No more of it."

Dewalt looked at me, then spat on the ground and walked off, trailing Regina.

Carel shook her head. "I'm ok with forgiving, but as much as anything, I want to forget. Don't any of you contact me again." She too vanished into the darkness.

I was left with Janna, Delt and Maauro.

Janna sighed and tugged at her collar. "It was a lot to ask, Piet…or should I say Wrik?"

"Both are my names, you can call me what you wish."

Janna laughed softly. "I'll go with Wrik. I want to stay on your friend's good side." She gestured at Maauro.

I walked over to Maauro and put my arm over her shoulders. I suddenly felt heaviness on me. Fatigue hovered nearby. I realized I was leaning my weight against her.

"I think we've had enough excitement for tonight. Come on, I'll buy at the bar. Something will be open in town."

Janna smiled. "Wrik, I have Sunday service tomorrow. Wouldn't do if it got around town the visiting Reverend was out getting hammered with her old squadron mates. Maybe I will see you at service?" She gave me a hopeful look.

"Reverend," I said. "What time is that service?"

"We have two," she said, "I guess I better look for you at the noon one?"

"I will be there without fail."

"Please bring Maauro. Oh, how exciting, my church might be the first one to host an artificial intelligence!"

"Sure," I said. "But let's keep that a little on the quiet side, officially Maauro is a human mutation."

She nodded. "Well, in my trade, I learn to keep secrets. But the others know too."

"I'll ask them to keep quiet about it," Delt said. "They'll do it for me."

That last brought a stab of bitterness that I put aside as quickly as I could. "Let's go."

We had only two drinks before the strains of the day caught up with Wrik. I ask Delt to wait in the bar until I returned from taking Wrik to his room. I help my exhausted love out of his clothes and he drops into the bed, instantly asleep. Knowing him as well as I do, I am comfortable that he will remain asleep for six hours at least. However I add a light sedative to ensure I have time enough for my final mission.

I return to the bar.

Delt is staring at a glass of Straka. He sees me walk up. "I drink too much," he says.

I nod.

He pours the glass into a plant and stands. From inside his jacket, he produces a small flask. He puts it on the bar. "Give this to some poor sod that needs it," he says to the bartender.

He stands and walks over to me. "Janna said I was carrying something that I should put down. I think, tonight, that I can."

"That pleases me," I said. "You are a man of too much potential to waste."

"From you," he says, looking down, "that means a lot."

"Delt," I say, making a quick decision, "I need your help."

"What, can I do for you?"

"I need you to loan me your flitter. I must get to Wrik's father's farm."

Wariness comes over his face. "Why? Maauro ... you're not going to kill the old bastard?"

"No, Delt. I am not a murderer. Even if I was, Owen Van Zyle would be an off-limits target."

"I'm sorry. I guess, well I guess, I still don't know much about you."

"Your caution is sensible, but I will not harm his father."

"Give me your word of honor."

"I tender it to you. I will not harm any biological life. It may be necessary to issue some threats to insure compliance."

"Ok. Why go?"

"There is something on that farm that I must deal with, something that cannot be allowed to stand."

Something glimmered in his eyes. "Wrik may notice your absence."

"He is exhausted and will sleep long enough."

"Well, at best speed it's a flight of two hours. His father is a farmer. He'll be up overseeing his field crews early. That is, if you want to have words with him."

"Oh, I will have words with this man, words he will not soon forget."

Delt smiles at me. "I like you, Maauro. Tell you what, I'll fly you there myself."

"I like you too, Delt. Wrik's admiration of you is well-founded."

"Well, I don't know about that," he says scratching his head.

"Get some rest. I want to arrive at dawn."

"I'll meet you out back when you're ready." The big man heads for his room.

I check on Wrik again, sitting by my sleeping lover until it is time to go. Then I make my way down the stairs. Everyone, it seems, has finished their missions on this world.

Except for me.

Delt is waiting with the aircar. After we take off, he wastes no time pushing the small aircraft to its best speed. He asks me no questions, and we fly in silence until we hover and settle in the field, well-short of the farm. I have to admit I could not have handled the aircraft any better.

"Wait here," I say as the canopy rises.

"Ok," Delt says, then grins. "I kind of wish I was going with you."

I shake my head. "Better that you do not."

I jump out, turn toward the farm, and jog toward it. It takes me only a minute. I slow to a walk as I come up the lane. The sun is rising, and I see activity around the buildings. I spot what I have come for, and continue to advance. There are people in the fields, preparing farm equipment and machinery for a day's tasks. I have an image of Wrik's father in my memory, from a photo of a reunion of soldiers from the Solari Incursion that he fought in: Confed decorations mixed with Retiefan ones on his broad chest. I spot his father by an agro-harvester.

He notices me. "Yes, Young Miss. Can I help you?" He stares at me. "Those are some big eyes you have there."

"I see much with them."

"You're not from around here."

"I am from long ago and far away. But that does not matter. Come with me."

"Look, little girl, if there is something you need—"

I reach over and take hold of a metal roll bar on the machine and casually twist it. "Come with me," I repeat. "Do not call out to your farmhands. I am a combat android, and they can do nothing against me. We are only going a hundred yards. You will not be harmed, but do not think to disobey me."

Some of the farmhands stare at us curiously as we walk away from the house and down the land to the main road.

"What do you want?" he demands.

I must credit his courage. He follows me at a wary distance and is alarmed, but not fearful.

I do not answer him. We reach the family plot. I open the small gate, and he follows me in. I see the stone marker that he has placed here. Fury builds in me. I walk forward and stand over the stone.

"Shall I offer my condolences on the loss of your son?" I am surprised by the evenness of my tone. Not since Wrik was in the hands of the Collector have I felt a rage to equal the one that wraps around me now. I desire to do harm, but this is his father. I remember Jaelle's father and how Wrik forbade me to strike him, even though he'd helped ambush us,

an attack that cost me an arm and Wrik his ship. The network between parent and child seems fraught with complexity and room for disaster.

Van Zyle crosses his arms. "No need. He wasn't much of a man."

"I have journeyed far and long with Wrik. I have met no better person."

"Then you have never had to rely on him in a tight spot," he says.

"I have relied on Wrik for existence in dangers that you cannot imagine, and for something more far more important than my life."

He raises an eyebrow. "That being?"

"Hope."

He shakes his head. "I don't need to bandy words with a machine."

"Then let my actions speak for me." Plasma jets into my right hand and coats my fist. I strike in an instant. The gravestone under my fist fragments and crushes. I have aimed my blow so the fragments will not strike his father, but one unexpectedly cuts the old man across the face. He stumbles back, hands raised.

Too bad.

The breeze quickly disperses the cloud of pulverized stone. We face each other across the small space. The tree over us rustles, the grass bows before the wind. In the distance, the farm hands stand frozen. Van Zyle lowers his hands to stare at me.

"Your son," I say, biting off each word, "is not dead. Do not dare to raise a stone for him again." I turn my back on him and walk away. Wisely, no one pursues me.

CHAPTER 31

I WOKE IN THE MORNING FEELING REBORN. FEELING LIKE someone who didn't even know the frightened and desperate man who'd worked for Dusko and the Guild on Kandalor. It lasted only a little while, but it felt good. Maybe it would last longer on other days.

I was surprised Maauro was not beside me. Maybe she thought the bed wasn't sturdy enough, and I'd been too out of it to move the mattress to the floor. I spotted her out on the small balcony. Maauro, as she had been some mornings lately, seemed unusually quiet, even distracted, but her smile was pure sunshine to me. As I stirred, she rose and opened the glass door.

"We have to get ready for church," she said.

I rolled over with a groan, mostly because I was afraid that had I continued looking at her I would have burst out laughing, and I would rather lose an arm than hurt her feelings.

"None of that," she said, primly.

"I suppose I should get up."

"You should," she said. "Delt is waiting breakfast for you. I, meanwhile, am off with Janna to buy clothes suitable for a young lady to go to church in."

"You were fine as you were yesterday."

"Janna and I disagree."

I sat up, knowing Maauro really didn't need clothes, save as a pattern, but clearly she wanted to spend more time with Janna. "Have fun."

She walked over and kissed my scruffy self, then slipped out the door.

Twenty minutes later, I found Delt, reading newsprint, in the hotel restaurant. He tossed the filmy printout into the recycler nearby when I walked up.

"How's the world looking to you?" he asked.

"Shiny and new," I said.

The waitress slid a coffee in front of me and took my order.

"I envy you, Wrik." Delt said, over his coffee.

I was too stunned to speak for several seconds. "Envy me? What the hell for? My father's disowned me. I damn near wrecked my family—"

Delt shook his head. "Our pasts are a weight we both drag behind us. You fled a battle. I led my friends to a slaughter because I didn't have the courage to think for myself.

"But you, Wrik. Well, what are you now: agent of the Confederacy, captain of your own starship? Most of all, I envy you what you have with Maauro. She's something special, and I don't mean just because she can punch a hole in steel plate."

"Yes, I know."

"Good," Delt said, sitting his coffee down, his face suddenly looking far older than his thirty-two years. "You got a second chance in life and you did something with it."

"Delt, you don't even want to know how far down I was before that second chance came."

"Can't be worse than getting your friends killed or maimed, can it? I had to attend eighteen funerals. At each one, I had to wear that damn medal my chest." He leaned on the table. "How I wish I could find a second chance."

"I've got one for you," I said impulsively, the realization and acting on it occurring in the same second. "The same one I had."

"What?" he demanded, his voice flat and taut.

"Upship with us," I said. "Join Lost Planet. We could use another good man,"

As he stared at me, something lightened in his expression. I saw the old Delt I had known. It was almost painful for those few seconds. "You mean it?"

"I do."

He wiped a shaking hand across his face. "Piet, old buddy, I am going to take you up on that."

We stared at each other for a few seconds, then a bitter, yet somehow cleansing, laugh burst out of both of us.

When it finally ran down, he shook his head. "I guess I will have to call you, Captain, from now on."

I waved it off. "There'll be none of that between you and me. But I do have a piece of advice for you. Don't run off as I did. Make your goodbyes, especially with your family. You can't tell them about our work with Confed MI. Your Dad will be upset enough that you are going off with me. I doubt he will put up a grave marker for you like mine did but it won't be easy,"

"Maybe less than you think. He's been after me to stop hiding out in a machine shed, and even out in this backwater, people have begun to hear about Lost Planet and what you did for Rainhell's grandson. I'll want to hear the real story behind that."

"After we lift," I replied. "There will be plenty of time for stories after that. Some of them will make the Seddon rescue look like a vacation day."

"You've changed, Piet."

"Everyone tells me that, and I'm still as scared as ever."

"We're all scared. You just think about it more."

"Maybe so."

"When do you need me at the ship?"

"Say sunrise, on the 13th."

"Not superstitious are you?" he said, with a grin.

"If it wasn't for bad luck..." I quoted.

CHAPTER 31

"I'll be there."

I nodded. "We won't leave without you."

"Good. Think I'll order some more eggs; all of a sudden I have an appetite."

We attended the church service where Janna talked about love and forgiveness, about which she was now clearly an expert. Maauro, Delt and I sat in an uncomfortable wooden pew. Maauro wore a blue, print dress with a white belt and shoes that matched. She watched the ceremony with evident fascination. I wondered how long my butt would last on a Protestant bench designed to encourage thoughts of contrition. The sermon ended eventually, and we joined the line of people moving out the doors, shaking hands with Janna. We hung back to the end.

She greeted Maauro first. "Well Maauro, what did you think?"

"I found your sermon very useful and enlightening. I will, of course, keep it in my databanks with 100% retention."

Janna laughed. "That's better than most parishioners. Half of them have forgotten what I said before they reach their cars."

"Then they are foolish, to ignore such valuable wisdom."

Janna looked beyond at me. "So where are you bound next?"

Maauro and I exchanged a look.

"Offworld, probably back to Star Central, but we haven't decided yet," I answered.

"So I should wish you velvet skies and fair landings, then."

I nodded. Janna hugged me, then Maauro. She stepped back, still holding onto Maauro. "I do wish you were staying longer. I enjoyed our conversations during our little shopping spree."

"I too. I hope that we shall meet again."

She turned to Delt, who looked at me. "Go on ahead. I want to talk to the Rev for a little."

I nodded. We walked off to the parking lot. I enjoyed the fresh, almost brisk breeze of the afternoon wind off the river as we walked slowly to the parking lot. It was the first time we'd been alone, and it seemed the perfect time to talk to Maauro about our new addition.

"Maauro,"

"Yes?"

"I made a decision, maybe I should have talked it over with you, but it's done now anyway."

She looked expectantly at me.

"I've added Delt to Lost Planet."

She nodded. "This is a good choice. It expands our network with someone who I know will be loyal and resourceful."

I gave a sigh of relief. "Glad you agree."

"I would have deferred the matter to you had you asked me. I cannot judge hearts and souls as well as you. In any event I like Delt. His open manner appeals to me."

"Hmmn, I'm beginning to wonder about the wisdom of this decision. I always had to be careful of him stealing girls away from me before…"

"I will not be stolen," she replied smiling, "besides he strikes me as a love-them-and-leave-them type."

It was my turn to grin. "Well, that is Delt, or was. We are both older and maybe wiser nowadays."

With all I had come for done, I found myself impatient to leave Retief. I'd made as much peace with my past as was possible, but I had the feeling that if I did not leave, that the bonds offered by my rediscovered family would tie me here, a prospect that both had its attractions and disadvantages.

So I held to my course as Maauro and I met with: Mom, Rena, Grieg and their children for a farewell dinner. Delt was making his own good-byes to his family and the unexpectedly large number of young women he'd apparently been dating, not all of whom knew about each other. It was perhaps a good thing he was going off world for an extended period. Mom's presence kept the pot of family issues at a low boil. The children made me promise to come back and to bring Maauro, both of which I readily agreed to.

My mother was a mixture of relief and sadness. She and Rena still were wary around each other, and there was a distinct coolness between her and Grieg. As for Rena, I could see she resented my being so much the center of attention. It was perhaps too much to expect that all that had been broken, could be healed in the one short trip. After a while, Rena seemed to realize what she was doing and seemed ruefully amused at herself.

I got the distinct impression that something was going on between Maauro and Grieg, something tense and edgy, as they would slip away to converse and there was no mistaking the stiff wariness in Grieg's body. Still, Maauro turned aside my questions, and I knew from long experience, that it was impossible to get her to answer, once she'd made up her mind not to.

Dinner was good, but was not about the food. We rose after coffee and cake and before the children needed to go to bed.

"I'd rather we made our goodbye's here," I said to everyone, "than down at the ship. There's always so much to attend to before blast off, even though I have a man down there now working on it. Assuming, he hasn't rifled the safe."

"Now, Wrik," Maauro said, "that is hardly nice. Not only has Dusko taken care of all our port trading, he has arranged a cargo for our outbound voyage. Goods on speculation, of course, but he has a pretty good eye."

Maauro defending Dusko? I thought about the time she had decided to kill the Guilder not long after we'd captured him. I considered teasing her about it, but there had been something, well, fragile about Maauro in the last few days, that deterred me. Perhaps being immersed in all the controversies of human relations had worn on her.

"Yes, dear," I said, which drew laughter from the family and a welcome smile from her. "Anyway, I want to remember you all here, safe in Rena and Grieg's home."

I shook hands with Grieg, his political mask firmly settled. "Look after my sister." He nodded and turned to Maauro. "Bon Voyage," he bade her and did not shake hands.

We hugged the children next, Amelia stroked Maauro's hair.

"I hardly know what to say," Rena said, standing in front of me.

I shrugged, but smiled. "When have we ever?"

My sister smiled back and hugged me. She suddenly felt very small and frail in my arms. "I have left ways for you to get hold of me," I whispered in her ear. "Call the Confed base, and mention my name if you need me. I'll come back."

Rena nodded and put a hand to my face before turning to embrace Maauro. "Try and keep my dopey brother out of trouble."

Maauro smiled. "My efforts in this never cease."

Then it was time to say goodbye to Mom.

"I guess it would be selfish of me to wish you weren't going so soon," she said. "Well, that's the way it is with parents; you grow them up so they are strong and independent, and then you wish they would stay where you put them."

I nodded.

"I love you, son. Don't let it be so long before you come back this way."

"I won't. I love you too, Mom."

She then turned to Maauro and embraced her. "I love you too, Little One. I will sleep much better knowing he has you with him. When he comes back, I'll be disappointed if you're not with him."

Maauro gently put her arms around her. "We can't have that. Thank you for all you have done for me and all that you have extended to me."

My mother looked into her big sea-green eyes. "It was little enough to do for the woman my son loves. Oh, drat and I wasn't going to cry." She snatched a napkin off the table and dabbed at her eyes. Amelia ran up to her grandmother and took her hand, concerned.

I too was battling a mix of emotions, but wanted to end things on the right note. "Time to go," I said. The whole mob of us walked toward the door, where I once again hugged my mom, and then we headed off to the car. From here, it was direct to the ship.

I started the vehicle and pulled into the driveway.

"Don't watch them go out of sight," Maauro said. "It means you don't expect to see them again."

I looked at her in surprise, remembering how I'd told her of my superstition. "I hope we do get the chance to come back."

"As do I," she replied and leaned back. She extended a hand to me, again exhibiting that strange fragility of recent days. I switched to automatics and took her hand. Something was ailing Maauro, and if she needed to hold my hand, it would be there.

We picked up the flitter, and flew through the starlit night, watching the sky and the world below roll on in their infinite courses and felt very small.

"What do we do now?" Wrik asks as we speed toward our ship. "I honestly have no idea of what I want to do beyond sending word to Jaelle that I ... that we, are alive and well."

"Then I will ask that you let me plan our course ahead for a while," I reply.

"Yes, of course," he says.

"We will, in due course, resume our work with Lost Planet, and doubtless Candace Deveraux will come calling. We both value our relationship with Jaelle, and, if it is not too painful for her to be with us, I wish to remain networked with her. But before that, I wish to voyage to Olympia to see Shasti Rainbell."

Wrik's eyebrows shoot up.

"I have some questions I wish to put to Shasti about existence and being. Then I have a favor to ask of her, if it is possible, and no, I do not wish to tell you what that favor is just now."

A mix of emotions slip across his face: curiosity, anxiety, perhaps even a touch of resentment, but it smoothes out almost immediately.

"You can tell me what you wish to tell me, when you wish to," he says with a touch of reluctance. "I trust you with anything, and I still owe you for running out on you."

"Then I accept this in final payment of any debt that remains. Consider the account closed, and we will never mention it again."

"I'll tell Delt about our destination after we land," Wrik says. "Then shall we send a message to Jaelle?"

I nod, then shift to where I can place my head on his shoulder. I am a little bemused at myself for not telling him why we are going there. But until I can consult with Shasti Rainbell's biological engineers, I will not know if their science, my quantum brain and Lilith's programs can give me what I want, an existence in the biological body of a human woman.

I will not, as Lilith did, seek to become the other. I am Maauro and will always be so. But if I can constantly download my consciousness into a human body, and have my machine body available as a final redoubt for when my new, biological body fails, through time or mischance, then I can set out on this adventure.

For me, it will be the chance to experience the physicality of love first hand. It raises endless possibilities— even, dare I imagine it, children? I will share the vision of the future with Wrik when I know it is possible. No need for us both to face disappointment if it is not. Beyond that, even if is possible, will I, should I, take this path?

I must cling to what Wrik and I said to each other. Love will find a way.

I am reminded of a poem from an old book Wrik had.

Two roads diverged in a wood, and I—
I took the one less traveled by,
And that has made all the difference

THE END

APPENDIX

Wrik Trigardt's real name is Piet Wrik Van Zyle
Father Nickolaas Van Zyle
Grandfather Pazen Van Zyle
Mother Eldra Trigardt
Sister Karolin Rena Van Zyle Nazir
Husband Grieg Nazir
Children
Amelia Nazir age 7
Cobus Nazir age 9
Aurelia Toyoma (Maauro's alias) allegedly from Wolf 940 Colony of Gloaming
Survivors Ncome Commando 7 including Wrik
Delt Taljard
Hewatt Survivor Nccome Commando suicide
Regina Van Dyck (change) survivor Ncome Commando
Carel Englebreact Squadron mate
Johan Dewalt enemy squadron mate
Janna Lourens Priest. Squadronmate
Maauro's age 50,132 years old on Seddon
Kiala Yoder: alias Lilith
Locations
Idutywa, where Delt's business is located Rheinstad
Kalbara small town with a seminary near the junction of two rivers
Sethotho Town Nearest the farm Wrik grew up on
Namahadipiek foothills and the city of Donik, the capitol of the region. Here Rena lives

ABOUT THE AUTHOR

EDWARD MCKEOWN is a writer and editor specializing in science fiction and fantasy with occasional forays into literary and nonfiction. Ed escaped from NY, but his old hometown supplies much of the background to his humorous "Lair of the Lesbian Love Goddess" shorts, as his new hometown in Charlotte, North Carolina does for his "Knight Templar" fantasy series. He enjoys a wide variety of interests from ballroom dance to the martial arts. He has also edited six Sha'Daa anthologies of wry tales of the apocalypse and a wide variety of short stories. Find him on Facebook and at edwardmckeown.weebly.com.

Ed is best known for his Robert Fenaday/Shasti Rainhell series of SF novels, set on the Privateer Sidhe, issued by Hellfire Publications.

MORE BOOKS BY EDWARD MCKEOWN

FROM

AN IMPRINT OF COPPER DOG PUBLISHING, LLC

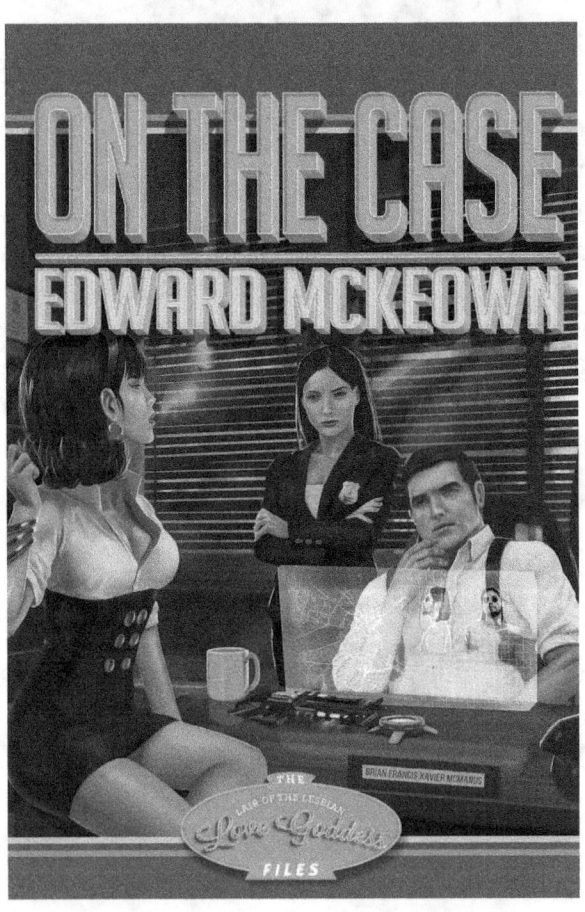

MORE BOOKS BY EDWARD MCKEOWN

FROM AD ASTRA BOOKS

CHAPTER 1

ATTACK THE ENEMY BASE IN THE COMPANY OF TWO OLDER M4 COMBAT *androids. We are launched from a Daggerwing assault-ship and shed our mobility capsules as we land on the asteroid. The Infestation claim the base is a lifeboat station but Intel says it is equipped with heavy weapons and sensors.*

The weapons are there. A disrupter battery fires on us; another lashes out at the Daggerwing and the ships beyond. As we race across the surface of the iron asteroid, a disrupter hits the lead M4. It staggers and slows. Other weapons switch fire to the slowing android. It is destroyed.

I am an M7, the newest combat android, a prototype, faster and better armored. I duck into a crater and return fire from my armspac. Explosions bloom and the disrupter battery is wiped out. The remaining M4 and I crash through the base airlock. Infestor drone soldiers are inside, clad in vacuum suits. They open fire. There is no room to dodge, so we trade fire from our onboard weapons and armspacs. The Infestors' small-arms have little effect on the M4 and none on me. We destroy them and race through the rest of the facility, killing Infestors as we encounter them. I head for the command center. M4 will attack the long-range disruptors firing on our ships.

Explosion. The corridor I occupy shatters, killing those Infestors I have not already dispatched. A mine, or perhaps my weapon, has set off a secondary explosion. I pause for self-repair. I am made of hyper-alloyed metals, ceramics and polymers. My outer casing has ablative layers and sections made to absorb blast damage. I exchange damaged exterior parts for interior and extrude new material to replace vaporized sections. Fortunately, I have taken no core damage. I waste no time on the aesthetics that make me look like a member of my creator's race. I carry enough spare material inside to regenerate two legs and an arm so I can get my armspac and reengage the enemy. I am much smaller now, having used up my spare material.

M4 reaches the disrupter battery, sited atop an arsenal. The bulk of the Infestor forces are arrayed around it. We confer for a millisecond. The battery is firing at our ships in the asteroid belt. I am already damaged, as is M4, and additional resistance is possible at the command post. By ourselves we may fail to take the station and suppress its weapons.

We agree on a plan of action and M4 self-destructs, detonating its plasma generator. The blast destroys the disrupter battery and its supporting forces.

I continue my attack alone and resistance crumbles. M4 may have killed the unit queen with its explosion. I neutralize the command post and mop up the base. In the process, I take seven prisoners. These I drag to a lower level and interrogate. Little useful intel is gained from these low-level creatures. After the last Infestor expires, I cleanse myself of their fragments. Then I delete the memories of the actual interrogation while saving the intel. This procedure is technically against my programming, but the longer I operate, the more latitude I discover in my behavioral routines. I do not know why I feel the need to do this, save that of late I have found the process of interrogation disturbing. I was created to destroy the Infestation and have done so for the seven years of my existence, yet I find more reasons to delete such information as time passes. I function more efficiently without these memories.

I reach the surface of the asteroid and step out under the stars, triggering my recall signal. No answer. I repeat it several times, then extend my sensor net to maximum and pick up a cloud of ionized gas. M4 did not destroy the disruptors fast enough. The Daggerwing, along with the support and repair staff who care for me, are gone.

I detect flashes of nuclear fire beyond my ship's remains. Ambush. The base may have been bait in a trap. Our forces are destroyed or driven off.

Since I do not face imminent capture, I delay self-destruct and continue repairs. I am dismayed by my level of damage even though my exterior chassis is mostly restored. Much of the damage can only be repaired at home base, which now I doubt I shall ever see again.

I consider my course of action. If the system has fallen to the Infestation, they will likely return to this asteroid. I should lie in wait to ambush any rescue party.

I turn my scanners to the sky for a last long look at the stars, which now are my only companions, before turning to walk into the silent base. I switch to minimum power settings. My wait may be long.

CHAPTER 2

I HUNG AROUND IN BARS A LOT. NOT THAT I'M A DRUNK. I went through a short spell of drinking after I was cashiered from the service for cowardice. But the bottle is slow suicide and I'm too young and interested in living for that.

No, I hung out in bars because that's where a human can find work on Kandalor's Vanceport. The Spacewitch is one of the places expeditions launch from. Not the big government expeditions from the Confederacy or the Combines, which wouldn't use somebody like me, but the shoestring expeditions from universities or organizations short on cash. I can fly interstellar. Not everyone can handle the hyperspace visualization. I can also fly atmo, which a lot of starjockeys can't.

So I staked out a small table in the back, away from the long bar with its brass and dark wood where the bad and dangerous hang out. My table sat under a hanging of red-fringed velvet, keeping me in comforting shadow. Square-D, the owner, knew me and would send over people looking for my type of skills. Square-D didn't care about me one way or another, but pilots brought trade to the Spacewitch and, he got a cut.

Luck was with me. Square-D was talking to a tall, dark-skinned woman in green fatigues. He nodded in my direction and she turned toward me. She was tall, with a pretty, symmetrical face and an overripe figure that strained the fatigues. I guessed her to be older than me, perhaps in her late twenties or early thirties. Her vest hung open and I saw a holster under it. She strode to my table.

"Wrik Trigardt?" The voice matched the body, round and pleasant.

I'd left my real name in the past, with my honor. "Just Wrik." I neither stood nor extended my hand; manners belonged to another time and place.

She slid into the booth and rested her breasts on the table as she leaned forward on her elbows. I got my eyes back up to her dark brown ones in time to catch the flash of white teeth against her dark skin. OK, she'd caught me looking, one for her.

"I hear you're a good pilot both on Kandalor and nearspace."

"Farspace too," I said. "I have an interstellar rating."

"Nearspace will meet my needs," she said. "You look kinda young to me."

I shrugged. "I've been flying since my early teens, military training as well. As they say: 'It's not the years, it's the light years.'"

I studied her. She had a slight accent I couldn't place. Something about her said Old Colonies or even Home World. "What needs are those, Miss…?

"Name's Candace Deveraux, out from Earth. Call me Candy and I'll shoot you in the knee. I'm looking for a private ship and pilot to take my colleagues to a certain riftoid."

"Treasure hunters."

She raised an eyebrow at me. "Prospectors and salvagers. You have a problem with that?"

I raised a hand. "No offense. I make a living hauling people around Kandalor and the near-rift looking for Old Empire relics and tech. Sometimes they even find stuff."

"But for every one who finds something, a thousand go broke," she quoted, leaning back. "True enough. Before we go much further, I'd like to know a little more about you. I gave you my name and world…"

"My name, you know. I'm out of a Confed colony world, former military pilot."

Her look said she knew this already. "Some people say you're out of Retief, a separatist colony. So why are you—?"

"Talking to a darkskin?" I finished for her.

She nodded. "Boers and Trekkers colonized Retief to get away from any contact with blacks. You regard us as inferior."

"I don't regard you as anything," I said, "assuming I was in fact born there. I take people as they are."

"Yet you fought in the Uprising?"

"As I said, you're assuming I was there. From what I heard, the Confederacy came in and told them to admit darkskins to Retief. Then they backed it up with force. Retief didn't last long after the Confederacy got serious.

"If that's enough 'get acquainted' for you," I said, and then, after sipping my drink, added, "I charge two hundred credits a day with fifty more if I go into vacuum. You pay for port fees and fuel. I get a hundred-credit advance now to reserve my time. You doubtless pulled my flight sheet at the port."

"Doubtless," she said, smiling. "I set the schedules and you learn where and when we fly when I decide."

"Deal." I tried to conceal my relief and surprise. She'd accepted my opening rates.

"Give me a number where I can reach you. You'll get twelve hours warning. Tell anybody where we are going and I'll shoot you in the other knee."

I passed my card to her and she inserted it into a portacomp. A few keypunches gave her my number and me one hundred credits.

She slid my card back to me. "You gonna buy me a drink with any of those credits, spaceman?"

"Uh, sure."

She laughed. "Just kidding. Next time come up with the idea on your own." She managed a nice sashay for a big woman as she walked away. I was tempted to whistle but afraid she might take target practice on my knees.

I finished my drink and slipped out the back of the Spacewitch after leaving a healthy tip with Square-D. Distracted a little by my good luck, I failed to do my customary check of the alley before I started down. I caught the heavy, earthy smell just before a thick, furred arm fastened over my throat and arm.

"So, Wrik, what are we up to?" I turned slowly in Truf's iron grip—there was no point in struggling with the bear-like Okaran—to face Dusko, the tall, Dua-Denlenn who ran a third of Vanceport's underworld. The Dua-Denlenn looked like a woodland elf gone to seed, with pale skin and blue pupilless eyes.

"Dusko," I nodded slowly. "I was just coming to see you."

"Of course, human," Dusko said, looking me over as if I were edible. "You owe me fifty credits."

Sweat trickled down my back. "I have it here."

"How fortunate for you, though perhaps disappointing to Truf here." The Okaran whiffed a breath in my ear. "There will be other opportunities."

"My cardcomp's in my inside pocket," I said.

"Let him go, Truf. This youngling's too prudent to be dangerous."

I pulled out the cardcomp and handed it to Dusko, who ran his own card- comp over it and made the transfer.

"Who was the offworlder you were talking to?" Dusko asked. "Anything I would be interested in?"

"A rift-haul for a prospector. She's cautious. No up front info from her."

"So no way to set her up," Dusko shrugged. "Doesn't sound worth my effort. You will let me know if there's a chance for mutual profit off her."

"I did last time," I said.

"True," Dusko said. "Their personal effects brought a nice sum. If it eases your conscience, they turned out to be druggers."

I tried not to remember the traders I'd led into Dusko's ambush. But it was either them or my ship and the ship was all I had.

"Good doing business with you," Dusko said. "As Truf said, there will be other opportunities. See you around, human." The languid Dua-Denlenn stepped back into the darkness, followed by his hulking guard. I leaned back against the wall, feeling the night air sift through my shirt and fighting the chill. Dusko was right. I was prudent. I had a knife in my boot and a slug-thrower in my back belt, but I wouldn't try an Okaran with the small caliber weapon at such close range. Throwing down on any of the established Guild was insane, anyway.

I decided to sleep in my ship, an old *Dauntless* class scout I'd named *Sinner*, a leftover from the Conchirri Wars long ago. Before heading out, I arranged for the port recorder to forward any message from Candace Deveraux to *Sinner*.

I hopped a native transport, which was the cheapest transport available. The open cart, towed by two oxen-like animals, was an odd contrast to ground cars or flitters but it was emblematic of Kandalor, which combined poverty and wealth as well as high and low tech. It had been a forgotten world until a Confed expedition stumbled across it and the races of the Old Concordiat. A few native Kandalorians, muffled in their robes, glanced at me with their bulbous black eyes but otherwise ignored me. I returned the favor and tried to breathe shallowly, the smell of the natives competed with that of the draft animals.

Sinner sat at the spaceport's edge under a metal overhang I'd rented to keep off the worst of the weather. She was about thirty meters long, a bulky ovoid with short stubby wings and lots of interior volume. I'd painted her anti-corrosive chrome yellow. Unlike military craft, we civvies want to be seen. I keyed in the secure code and locked myself in, letting my breath go in a rush. On Kandalor you live like a rabbit or a wolf. Maybe I'd have an extra big helping of carrots tonight.

One week later, I was doing some scut-work on a small Indie-freighter when my comp buzzed. I took off my gauntlets and sealed the engine port before answering. "Hello."

"It's Candace. Time to go prospecting. How soon can you launch?'

"I'm in good shape for a Rift run this side of the 38th in four hours. If we are going out farther, I'll need to add wing tanks."

"We aren't going farther. I've got the flight plan on file with the Port Authority. They'll download to you just ahead of launch."

"Cautious, aren't you?"

"Wouldn't want any problems with local interests."

I swallowed. "There won't be."

"Good, I'd hate to shoot such a pretty boy, at least until I was through with him." She laughed and clicked off.

Candace showed up at the *Sinner* early, as I expected. She liked to set the pace. Two men accompanied her. One was tall, with dark, suspicious eyes and a hooked nose over a beard, unusual in someone who expected to use a space helmet. The other was a dark-skinned like Candace, but whipcord thin and balding, with the look of a spacer.

"My associates," Candace said, gesturing to hook-nose. "Harung." She pointed at the other. "Maku Treska." Both nodded.

"We've got a cargo sled coming. My boys will do the loading," she said.

"Long as I check it after," I said.

Treska looked at me. "The kid doesn't trust us to load. I was flying when you were waiting to be delivered."

Candace looked at him with annoyance. "Quiet, Treska. I don't want to fly with anyone dumb enough not to check his own ship's load."

Treska grumbled but headed for *Sinner*'s capacious cargo bay. Harung gave me an unfriendly stare and followed.

I looked at her. "No weapons on my ship. Hope you left your knee-shooter in the port lockup. Explosive decompression can ruin your whole day."

Candace grinned at me. "Gonna pat me down, Wrik? I've got a lot of area to cover, many dangerous curves to hide things."

Her smile and manner had probably bent men to her wishes all her life. "Sounds like fun, but I don't think I want to pat down your buddies, though, so we'll use a scanner."

She gave a look of mock disappointment. I could feel my blood stirring. Human women were rare on Kandalor, and I had little to offer one. Truth was I didn't have much experience there, either. Candace's mocking smile told me that she suspected it.

Stick to business, I thought, *you're out of your depth with her.*

I checked the load and scanned my passenger for weapons. We boarded *Sinner* and settled in. Candace rode in the second seat on the flight deck. Her companions strapped in the far less comfortable cargo compartment, grumbling loudly enough to be heard. Candace smiled and shrugged.

Sinner kicked free of Kandalor's surface and started a slow ascent. Kandalor stretched out forever below us, seducing the eye and the imagination. Empires had come and gone on this world while humans lived in caves and waved stone axes.

"Beautiful," Candace said, looking out at the mountain and huge forests beyond the spaceport area. In the distance lay the ruins of one of the many lost civilizations. Haze made the wildly tilting towers appear blue.

"Yep," I said. "You've got spaceports and primitive tribes all on the same world, an archeologist's treasure trove."

"Here and in space," Candace said absently. "Those empires extended out for hundreds of light years. Lots of good stuff out there."

"Going to tell me what we're looking for?" I asked.

"Just drive the taxi, Honey."

"Yes, Ma'am."

Candace talked as we boosted toward the Rift, using my ion engine for a slow, steady thrust. I found myself liking her. I didn't want to; friends are an expensive luxury for a Rifter. I set the autopilot and we turned in early. I had trouble falling asleep, thinking of Candace's lush body in the bunk above me, wondering what it would be like.

We came up on the Rift in the next watch, not that there was anything to see. Even in as thick an asteroid belt as the Rift, it would be unusual for any two objects to be in visual range.

We set course for a large riftoid well in from the edge. One of a million such rocks unvisited by anyone since the planet blew to hell. Gradually the riftoid grew from a tiny point of light to a gray, pitted, roughly spherical rock about 2000 kilometers in diameter. Scanners showed it to be almost pure nickel-iron. A huge impact crater marred part of it.

"That's the one," Harung said. Everyone was crammed into my cockpit, staring hungrily at the pitted gray surface. "Just as I remember it."

"Probably part of the old world's core," Treska grunted. "That would account for all the metal. It'll give it a bit more gravity than you usually get in a rock this size."

We drifted down to the surface. Treska was right; gravity was strong enough that I didn't need to fix anchors. I did it anyway, space rewards the cautious.

"Suit up, everyone," Candace ordered.

I looked at her. "I'm just driving the taxi."

"Don't be like that, Honey. Now that we're here, don't you want to see what we came for?"

"Depends."

"What do we need him for?" Harung demanded.

I sighed. "She doesn't want to leave me behind in the ship so I can hold you up when you come back with whatever treasure you came for." I looked at Candace. "Ever get tired of working with people who aren't as smart as you?"

"No," she replied. "I only like smart men in bed."

Harung glared at me.

We suited up and walked out onto the surface of the riftoid. Treska unlimbered a large mining scanner. Evidently he got a fix on something, as he began moving in quick little hops, kicking up dust. Candace and Harung followed, lugging their equipment. I thought about waiting where I was, then decided it might be safer to stick with the herd. Five minutes later, we found ourselves in a small crater, looking at an oddly-shaped hatchway of yellow metal nearly three meters across.

"What the hell is it?" I asked, excitement getting the better of me. Dust indicated that the hatch hadn't been opened in a long, long time. The design didn't look like anything I'd ever seen.

"Maybe an Old Empire asteroid station," Treska said absently.

I looked around. "Over 50,000 years old."

"Or more," Treska said. "I spotted it when I was here with a freighter that came out of hyper too close to the Rift and had to dump delta-V to avoid a collision. I kept the readings on my scanner to myself. Those Combine bastards wouldn't have given me a percentage of any find."

"Why don't you tell him your life story?" Harung growled as he placed heavy jacks around the hatch.

Candace used a laser drill to place a monofilament probe through what looked like an inspection port. "As you suspected, Treska," she said, "hard vacuum on the other side. Start the jacks."

The power jacks took five minutes to crack the airlock. We used pry bars until we could squeeze through in space suits. A few more minutes on the inner door and we were shining our torches inside.

The interior of the station was familiar looking; form follows function. We saw a rack of odd-shaped spacesuits hung on the bulkheads. Whatever wore them had been much bigger than a human, multi-legged, with a large skull or a need for a lot of headroom. Boxes and tanks lay all over the floor. The metal of the floor worked with our magnetic boots.

"This is a military station," I said.

Candace looked at me. "Why's that?"

"A lot of compartmentation, thick hatches to deal with explosive decompression. Though I'm surprised a military station wouldn't have been dug deeper, for blast protection."

"Maybe it was converted from something?" Harung said.

"Who knows?" Treska shrugged.

Candace nodded. We played our flashlights around the gray and white metal halls, looking at unfamiliar inscriptions and dead light panels.

"It kind of reminds me of the old lifeboat stations they have in Sol's system from before the advent of hyperdrive." Candace said.

"We might find an Old Empire ship," Harung exclaimed.

We started down the sloping corridor and came to a partially opened doorway.

"Christ, look at that." Treska pointed.

At our feet lay a large pile of shredded fabric covered with white dust. Nearby lay boots, though not for any human foot, and a thing that could have either been a power rifle or some sort of heavy tool.

Candace bent down. "Crew. Must have died here in the doorway. Wonder what tore up the uniform?" Cautiously, she pushed open the doorway and looked in, a prybar in one hand and flashlight in the other.

Harung brayed a laugh. "Looking for something? That corpse has been there for fifty millennia in vacuum. The fibers degraded and fell apart. We'll bag what's left for the scientists. They'll pay plenty for material from the corpse of an unknown species."

"Look, a ship!" Candace exclaimed. Her light illuminated a small vessel beyond. It looked like it was made of some translucent, half-melted, dark-green glass. Yet it was recognizably a spacecraft.

"If you're right about this being a lifestation," I said, "there's your lifeboat."

Harung pushed past Candace and me with Treska on his heels. The smaller man accidentally kicked an alien boot. It spun silently away into the darkness beyond our lights. I shuddered.

Candace knelt by the fragments of fabric and the metal implement. "A weapon?"

"Maybe," I said. "It has that look, but I don't see any sights."

"Well, any charge it had must have gone before the pyramids were built."

The space beyond was wide and flat, big enough for several small craft. A hatchway that must have once opened outward formed the roof of the hangar; for all that we had seen no sign of the hatch on the surface. Harung and Treska clambered all over the small ship, peering into it with lights.

"Wrik," Candace called from the far side. I went over. She was standing over a pile of white dusty fabric and more boots, buckles and webbing. The fabric was shredded like the first one.

"What the hell?" I said.

"There's a passage up ahead. If this is like a Terran lifestation, it will lead to the medical and crew quarters."

"After you," I said.

She frowned at me. "You're a bring-up-the-rear kind of guy, aren't you, Wrik?"

"You weren't hiring at Hero's Hall."

We left the others to explore the ship. Our magnetic boots raised a thin film of dust, to hang and fall slowly in the low gravity. Colors here were more vibrant than in the more utilitarian areas. The combinations hurt my eyes.

We reached the crew quarters. Debris covered the area. All manner of odd-looking furniture lay scattered and broken.

"Decompression?" Candace asked.

I shrugged.

IF YOU ENJOYED THIS EXCERPT, LOOK FOR
THE MAAURO CHRONICLES, BOOK 1,
MY OUTCAST STATE
AVAILABLE ON AMAZON.COM
AND
COPPERDOGPUBLISHING.COM.

Copper Dog Publishing LLC

OUR IMPRINTS:

Pumpkin Hill Press

To find out more about our imprints
and our upcoming releases, visit our website:
www.CopperDogPublishing.com
or our Facebook page:
www.facebook.com/copperdogpublishing

www.ingramcontent.com/pod-product-compliance
Lightning Source LLC
Chambersburg PA
CBHW060630260626
47161CB00008B/2850